# My Life in Sports

ALSO BY DAVID OLLIER WEBER

FICTION

Vanity
Baja
Family Fun
Catch/Release

NON-FICTION

Oakland: Hub of the West
Accustomed to Hope: The Episcopal Church on the Mendocino Coast

# My Life in Sports

## A Novel in Four Quarters

David Ollier Weber

Kila Springs

Kila Springs Press is an imprint of the Kila Springs Group, Placerville, CA.
E-mail: press@kilasprings.net

*This is a work of fiction. Names, characters, places and incidents are products of the author's imagination or are used fictitiously and are not to be construed as real. Any resemblance to actual events, locales, organizations or persons, living or dead, is entirely coincidental.*

First Edition, First Printing

ISBN-13: 978-0-9716481-4-2
Library of Congress Control Number: 2010909825

*For Eleanor and George, for Steve and Nancy, and for all the persons living or dead whose resemblance to characters in this work of fiction are entirely coincidental*

# Contents

*The First Quarter*

Suicide Squeeze

# 1

**"Just be loose in there, Ricky!" my father called.**

He clapped loudly. "Ricky!" he repeated. "Loose! Just stay loose!"

There was something odd, some subtle insistence in the cadence of his words. He was straining to penetrate my oblivion but at the same time maintain a pretense that this was simply routine chatter. Secrecy, after all, was the point. And belatedly the message registered. At least, I recognized there was a message.

As the pitcher finished glowering toward Daddy and Brian MacIntosh, who was taunting him with a bold lead off the bag—bobbing spraddle-legged down the line, a nervous flicker at the margin of my vision—I uncrouched and raised my palm.

"Time," I said.

The pitcher rocked into his windup. He was a stocky kid, a tow-head taller than anyone else on the field, the meat on his big-boned frame in brief, sinewy transition between baby fat and adult flab. He disdained the stretch with only a runner at third.

I'd backpedaled out of the box. "Time!" the umpire barked.

The fastball steamed into the catcher's poised mitt with a dusty, contemptuous *fwap*. A perfect strike, all right. The kind of pitch that looked as if it could grapple the bat right out of your fists—if you ever got around on it.

Not that many of us had. We were hitless since the fourth inning. I'd had the last one, in fact, a sharp off-field single down the first-base line that drove in Timmy O'Connell for our second run—blindly uncorking my swing at the instant the pitcher's arm spaghettied up over his cap-button, then locking in, goggle-eyed with adrenaline, on the tiny blur enlarging toward me. Some miraculous neural calculus finely adjusted the plane of my wrists so that wood actually intercepted ball. Sliced it cleanly, mostly on its own reversed momentum, into the sunburned crabgrass behind the first baseman's feebly waggled mitt. Even then I'd swung late. And next time up all I could manage was a pop-foul into the cage before going down on a curve that left me gaping.

Except for walks in the seventh and eighth and a long fly to center by Danny Messingschlager, our catcher, strikeouts had been the rule. The big kid strutted cockily around his rubber, stooped to spatter himself with clumsy dollops of white resin from a bag at the lee of the mound— more commanding with every inning. Until Brian, our lead-off man and shortstop, dribbled a grounder that took a bad hop. It skittered off the second-baseman's shoulder into right. Then while I nervously crowded the plate from deep in the batter's box the way Daddy had shown me, refusing to offer, sweating out the umpire's corroborating judgment, Brian scampered to second and third on successive balls. He was quick of foot, never hesitant to launch the abrasive slide. And their catcher's pegs were hard but wild. So now the count was two and oh. One down, bottom of the ninth, score tied two and two.

I bent, tugged at the tongue of my left spike, folded it flat over the laces and scraped up a handful of granular khaki dirt.

"Hey, that was a good pitch, ump," somebody squawked—an adult from the opposing dugout. "He stepped

14

out too late!"

"No pitch," the umpire rumbled. He was a peremptory, florid-faced stranger who might just have emerged from a swim in the Ohio. Despite the August heat and humidity he affected the full regalia: sodden black serge coat, its lumpy pockets weighted by scuffed, nicotine-colored "Official Knothole League" baseballs; frayed black tie wrung into an ancient knot under a dingy white collar; short-billed black chauffeur's cap and a floppy orange air-mattress of a chest protector. It and the shin-guards under his black pants conferred an Olympian beefiness he didn't necessarily possess in everyday life. But whether or not he was really some meek, scrawny milkman or billing clerk flush with the weekend power to regulate the recreational scurryings of thirteen-year-olds, from my foreshortened perspective he embodied adult authority. His was the aloof, indifferent and final justice meted out by the social institutions whose jurisdiction I was inexorably now growing up into... would soon have to cope with on my own, unshielded by parents or the excuse of childhood. Maybe it was the austere costume. Ursuline nuns had educated me through eight grades. In a month I would timorously present myself to the cassocked Jesuits of St. Xavier High School. Scholastics, most of them, true, not technically ordained yet, but still cloaked in the same harsh uncolors. God's uniform. Shared by this imperious playing-field arbiter bowed ponderously before the plate—scrubbing at it with his whiskbroom, the slender green bible of rules by whose chapter and verse he sanctioned our triumphs and exacted penance for our transgressions jutting dog-eared from his rump-pocket.

I glanced at Daddy. Furtively, feigning preoccupation with the grit I was sifting through my fingers. I didn't want it to appear obvious to the other team that I was taking a sign. Or to Daddy that I'd failed to notice the first time around. At this level, he'd decided, we were old enough to remember

15

a few. And remember to look for them.

He stood at the front of the coach's box with his arms folded. Bare ropy forearms reddened by the Midwestern sun but pale above the sharp demarcation at the biceps where his short sleeves normally belled. There was a poignancy about that private whiteness, a peek at something tender and perhaps a bit effete. Daddy was a lawyer. His days were spent behind desks or before the bench, poring over wills, scribbling briefs, making motions. Oh, he was an athlete—or had once been, at least. I was proud of that. So was he. A six-footer, he'd played center for the University of Cincinnati back in a more diminutive and patient era, when there was a center jump after every basket. And he'd been a star spiker in YMCA volleyball. A tennis player good enough to have been matched against Tilden in the Western Open (though as it happened Daddy lost in a different flight). A two-thirty-average league bowler for the Cincinnati Club. A golfer whose antique woods and rust-scabbed irons now rested in the old coal bin in the basement, doilied by cobwebs—he'd abandoned that pastime in frustration, he admitted, after one too many defeats by MiMi, my maternal grandmother, the plink-plinkingly consistent onetime Woman City Champion of Birmingham, Alabama. In fact, our cellar was a musty trove of sprung rackets in warped presses, moldering canvas shoes, limp balls shedding their husks like withered fruit... the generations of equipment Daddy had cast aside as age diminished his ability to perform a sport to his own exacting level of satisfaction.

Naturally he'd played baseball—semipro, even, a catcher, oddly, despite his willowy build. His teeth, a recurrent source of pain and medieval surgical ordeals, were mostly false now, wired to lengthening bridges ever since a defective face-mask had caved in to a foul-tip. Several of his otherwise graceful fingers were gnarled at the knuckle and segmented at unusual angles. Nevertheless, baseball had always been his first love. He mourned and jubilated with the fortunes of the Reds (once mighty under the likes of Lombardi and VanderMeer, but lately declined to the perennial mire of seventh place). I must have been no more than four or five when he'd resurrected his mitt from the limbo of serially discarded athletic gear. Some of my earliest memories were of him hunkered before me, murmuring gentle approbations as I joyfully heaved a rubber ball at that round, plump, pungently Neet's-foot-oiled leather target.

Crossed arms meant a steal was on. Daddy had been standing that way, folding and unfolding his arms with ostentatious languor for the last two pitches. So much I'd been aware of—the reason I'd edged deeper in the box to crowd the catcher, my duty. Now Daddy leaned toward me and stared hard from under the bill of the red-and-white team cap he'd consented to wear during games. Abruptly he untwined his arms, doffed the cap and wiped his palm across the wispy brown hair raked flat against his pallid scalp. A distinctive scar pulsed high on his forehead, just above the left temple—a divot in the skullbone acquired as a teenager when somebody had carelessly flung away a bat. It fascinated me, that crater, as if beneath the flimsy sheath of flesh it was his brain I could see churning—engorged with fatherly knowledge but dangerously vulnerable, at risk moment to moment through this chink, my intellectual Daddy's Achilles brow.

He screwed the cap over his temples again. His sunken eyes were masked by shadow. The stripe was indented by the bridge of his nose, an emphatic Indianhead-nickel beak whose inheritance I wouldn't reveal for another year or so. The aquiline prominence was accentuated by the gauntness of his cheeks. Corrugated bone showed at the vee of his pastel blue sport shirt, and his knees protruded like doorknobs against the baggy, pleated gray slacks bundled precariously around his hips. Daddy had lost a lot of weight in the past six months.

Sure of my attention, he enacted a flurry of additional false gestures. Then, firmly crossing his arms, he urged, "Loose, Ricky! Just be loose in there."

I touched my cap in acknowledgment. Gave it an extra wiggle to settle the bulky plastic insert tucked for safety against beaning under the band. Tiptoed my right foot into the combat zone, the faintly chalked batter's box, and worked my spikes until they seemed to grip some underlayment in the dusty hole dug by generations of bucketfoot-planters before me. I bounced my bat-tip off the outside edge of the rubber plate, appraising my distance, jawed the tasteless patty of bubblegum I'd plied to the consistency of an old eraser. I filled my lungs for courage... and waded in all the way.

From the covert of his crotch, the catcher, squatting behind me, began to flick fingers at the pitcher. I could almost feel the radar emanations of their conspiracy. I flexed my knees and took a couple of quick, jittery practice cuts. The big kid peered intently from his promontory. It made him seem immense, even separated by sixty feet six inches. Finally he nodded. His squint seemed to tighten, an anticipatory snicker. I chopped my bat at him once more—defiant, jamming the spell, like signing the cross to neutralize Dracula.

"You can do it, Ricky. Get a little bingle. Drive 'im in. Make 'im work. Look it over, baby."

My teammates on the bench behind the chain-link backstop shrilled a ragged chorus of exhortation. The constant undertone of hoots, claps, whistles and clichés was a tradition Daddy insisted on as evidence of involvement and unity. And somehow there was encouragement in it, a subliminal distraction from the drumming of my heart. I slowly coiled and went motionless—weight back, wrists high, bat full-cocked for homerun carry.

It was sham. And I trembled secretly under my sudden, inescapable burden of responsibility. No matter where the ball was, I had to manage to poke my bat in front of it. Lay down the bunt Daddy's code phrase had demanded. Brian would already be sprinting toward home from third—dependent on my intervention to prevent his being tagged out by the catcher, who'd otherwise be waiting smugly with the pitched ball. The suicide squeeze. Daddy had explained it in practice a couple of times. But we'd never before tried it in a game.

"Okay, baby, baby," droned the catcher. "Zip it in here, baby, baby." He pounded the pocket of his mitt. "This one's no hitter."

The taunt didn't bite. All sensation was attenuated. I was alive only through my eyes. Riveted to my looming antagonist as he glanced toward third, bowed and pumped. Now my focus narrowed to the glove in which he cupped the ball. He reared, kicked. His throwing arm lashed out from behind the screen of his swiveling blue socks and flapping Yankee-striped uniform.

"Go!" Daddy shouted to Brian.

At the same instant I'd whirled to face the mound. I jerked my right hand up along the barrel of the bat and cradled it loosely at the oval label—"Hillerich & Bradsby, Louisville Slugger"—scorched into the grain.

The pitch sailed high, inside, shrieking up into my face. Instinct snatched me backwards. I flung the bat up as I cringed. Punched out awkwardly, desperately at the ball. I saw the contact, forefelt in my wrist-bones the limp *tlock*, the soft carom....

No. No.

I stumbled, falling. Found my feet.

"Watch it! Get him!"

The catcher bustled across the box.

"Block the plate!"

"Slide!"

Still astonished by my self-betrayal, I watched Brian gallop in, doomed. He dipped his shoulder in a final, plucky feint and hurled himself full out, one leg extended, the other folding under as Daddy had taught us. He arched his spine, rolled his hips—trying at the last moment to hook around the genuflecting catcher's barrier mitt and armored shins. The catcher pounced. Brian shrieked. Dust exploded.

"Aa-roo!" the umpire bellowed. His rigid thumb slashed through the acrid swirl.

The catcher hopped upright. His teammates chortled and danced. He fired the ball triumphantly to third base and began to pummel himself clean.

Brian still lay on the ground. Inert, I thought, in disappointment. Bleak fury welling too—at me, at my failure, the agency of his humiliation. Brian was a fanatical competitor. It was only recently that he'd stopped weeping after every loss, as if each were a bitter, personal repudiation. But then I saw his self-absorbed grimace. He struggled up on one elbow, moaning. Tears started to dribble down his cheeks. He writhed. I lurched forward, helpful, hesitant, apologetic, awed....

Daddy and the umpire quickly bustled me aside. With the other coach and several adults who'd come out of the bleachers they clustered over Brian for a long time. Waved back, we players scuffed our spikes at the fringes of their ministry—sympathy and curiosity gradually dwindling into boredom. We gossiped in hushed knots, began to toss balls, cast occasional glances at our counterpart twitching prostrate between their legs. I stood by myself most of the time. Timmy and Danny, my friends, shouldered up to me, nonchalant. I was glum, laconic. The privacy of my own guilt was what I sought and deserved. Though no one else seemed to appreciate my accountability.

"He shouldn't have tried that," Danny mused. "That

guy's pretty quick today, huh?"

"The squeeze was on!" I muttered. "Weren't you watching? The sign from my Dad? I was supposed to bunt it! It was my fault."

"Yeah? Well. Huh. You're still up, anyway. You can get him. Hang in there. You want to go swimming at Coney this afternoon?"

Finally they hoisted Brian out of the dust and trundled him solicitously to the parking lot. He'd composed his streaky face into a brave, uncertain half-smile. His left leg jutted stiff inside a makeshift splint of two bats lashed together by a belt and a sweatshirt. Mr. Messingschlager drove him to the hospital. Daddy gathered us before we resumed play.

"Okay," he announced. "It does look as if Brian's got a broken bone. He caught a spike. I don't think it'll be too serious, though."

"Will he have to wear a cast?" piped Eddie Leinsdorf.

"Yes," Daddy nodded, "I imagine he will, for a while, anyway. But he'll be okay. The thing I want you guys to do now is to just go out there and forget it. Can you do that? Just play the game. We can still win this thing. All you've got to do is keep your eye on the ball, settle down, stay loose at the plate and make their pitcher come to you. He's fast but he's not overwhelming. We're hitting him. We did it early on, and we can do it again. Right? *You* did it!"

We blustered dubious assurances.

"Okay, let's go."

We all clapped and Daddy ambled back to the coach's box. I struck out on two swings. They scored three runs in the tenth and we lost, five to two.

**I crawled into the front seat of the Packard and wadded myself against the door.**

My throat was clogged as if by a bone I couldn't dislodge. My eyes were swollen with congealed tears.

"Take off your spikes, Ricky," Daddy said. "Or else sit still. You're not supposed to have them on in the car anyway. You'll wreck up the floor rugs the way you're squirming."

The Packard was a year old. I guess Daddy still thought of it as new. Worthy of kid-gloves occupancy. I did. Even with the windows down you could still sniff the faint aroma of the factory in its upholstery. Sometimes a whiff would remind me of the afternoon he'd led us all outside for the presentation. Clutching Mother by the hand. It was the first new car in our life—well, mine, at least—an emblem of the breakthrough of his private practice after five threadbare years. Before that he'd worked for the government. Why he'd chosen this humpbacked, whitewalled, metallic green boat—already in the twilight of its consumer popularity—to replace the doughty gray Pontiac that had served us since my birth I'm not sure. Maybe he'd been offered a good deal by a client or some Cincinnati Club cohort. Maybe it was an uncharacteristic indulgence in a bit of professional rodomontade—less brazen, more sedate than a pushface Cadillac or tinselly Lincoln. Nobody in those days had ever heard of a Mercedes.

My only previous associations with Packards derived from the immense black limousine model that used to pull up in front of our little stucco house at the end of an invincibly middle-class Hyde Park cul-de-sac whenever my grandmother was visiting from Tuscaloosa. A colored chauffeur in umpire livery would emerge to usher a lady identified to me as Mrs. Farquhar out of its crepuscular rear depths. She was tall and white-haired, a widow of suitably patrician bearing and dress, who'd acknowledge me in a soft accent like my mother's before heading up the walk to fetch Jamieson—her name for my grandmother—to tea at the Cincinnati Country Club.

There, in some rambling colonial suite of almost unimaginable social rarefaction, Mrs. Farquhar actually lived. Before the two women emerged from the house, the chauffeur would settle against one of the Packard's bulbous fenders and smile at me as I continued to bounce tennis ball pop-ups off the curb under the sweetgum tree. Despite the fact that MiMi—the name I'd unaccountably lisped as a baby and which thereafter adhered—was eking out her own genteel widowhood as a fraternity housemother at the University of Alabama, the Kirkpatricks had once been the Farquhars' peers. Mother's Daddy, Edwin Kirkpatrick, had been an industrialist—scion of an Alabama first-family, his deceased elder brother a revered long-term U.S. Senator. Then the Depression had shriveled the business: "frogs and switches," some kind of wonderfully suggestive but obscure steel railroad accessories forged under the statue of Vulcan on Birmingham's red-clay heights. Driven into Northern exile, the grandfather I'd never known had died within a couple of years. Nobody said as much, but I gathered he'd been worn down by the tumble from grace and the subsequent grubbing to salvage a vestigial subsidiary that supplied Cincinnati's machine-tool manufacturers. Foremost among whom was Mrs. Farquhar's late husband. Anyway, I wonder if Daddy's choice in cars hadn't somehow been related to that other grand exemplar of wealth and power that had shuttled through the margins of his marriage—an offering to my mother and her mother, a scaled-down but nonetheless equally swan-prowed and snob-valued token of the success whose threshold he'd finally managed to scrabble across.

"Quit squirming, Ricky. Daddy said."

"Shut up," I growled at Paul. He clung like Kilroy to the rim of the seat above my shoulder. The humid presence

23

and eager vigilance of a little brother were hardly palliative.

"Leave him alone, Paul," Daddy snapped. "But I don't want to hear you saying 'shut up,' either."

"Brat," I muttered.

"Richard...," Daddy rumbled. His knuckles on the steering wheel mottled. Sometimes for grave offenses—flagrant defiance, exceptionally sadistic sibling-baiting—he spanked us. I hadn't received that punishment for several years now, though.

I heaved myself forward. A sob of self-pity was almost loosed by the exertion. I untied my spikes and shucked them off.

"Pee-yew!" Paul observed.

Daddy decelerated. The road ran along the river, the flood plain broad and flat here on an inside bend. Boat-launching ramps led off through the stands of willows and elms to the brown water. Lumps of excrement were said to swirl in its brisk currents. The Kentucky bank was green and pastoral, but seedy drive-in restaurants and ancient box-houses with second-story watermarks from the famous nineteen-thirty-eight flood lined this side.

"Paul, I'm not going to tell you again. Sit back and be quiet," Daddy said.

Paul wormed away momentarily. He too was costumed in miniature baseball flannels, freshly soiled and grass-stained. His eight-and-unders game had been played earlier in the morning. One of his teammates' mothers had dropped him off at our field, where he'd amused himself in the litter beneath the bleachers until Daddy and I were through.

We turned up Eastern Avenue. A hot wind soughed through the car windows, sluggish and oppressive, muffling the impulse to talk. The scar on Daddy's forehead pulsed. Here we were, the three male Schuberts, together but isolated in our individual reveries.

"Dad...," I finally croaked. "I'm... sorry." It proved harder than I'd expected to squeeze the words out of my constricted throat. "I'm sorry I messed up."

"Don't worry about it," he said.

"But if I'd...."

"You didn't mess up," he added quickly.

"Yes I did."

"He sure did," Paul chirped. "Timmy *told* me."

"He did not! You didn't, Richard. And you shut up, Paul. You missed a bunt," Daddy said. "It was a tough pitch. It would have been hard for anybody to handle."

"But I'm a *lousy* bunter! A *lousy* bunter!" I wailed, accusatory. Why had my father put me in this position? Talking made it more difficult to throttle the urge to cry. But I was a teenager, after all. Almost a man now, and men have to be brave. About their failures, their incompetencies, their losses. Daddy was brave.

"You're as good a bunter as anybody else on the team," he assured me.

"No I'm not. Brian could've done it. Danny could have done it. If I hadn't missed, Brian wouldn't have... broken his leg." Actually saying it, using that phrase, made the injury sound enormous. Crippling.

"He'll have to go around in one of those wheelchairs now, huh, Daddy?" proposed Paul.

"No he won't, stupid!" I snarled. "Will he, Daddy?"

"No!" my father exclaimed. "No, he'll probably walk around on crutches for a couple of weeks, with a big cast up to his knee that everybody'll autograph. He'll get a lot of attention and be a baseball hero. Just keep out of it, Paul."

"Anyway," I mourned, "it *was* my fault. We'd have won...."

"Look, Richard," Daddy said. "That was my decision. All you can do is do your best. Which you did. You always do. And the reason Brian hurt himself was that he caught a spike and got his leg twisted in a strange way. It's not your fault. You drove in one of our runs, you were solid in the outfield. You made a great catch on that fly ball in the fifth, remember? That could've been the game right there if that had gotten through...."

The reminder triggered a fleeting, pleasurable kinetic rush. The imprinted sequence looped back through brain and synapses like some natural precursor of the instant replay TV had yet to introduce: distant crack of bat... my startled hop as the ball streaked skyward and I picked up its climb, whirled and canted backwards, legs churning, feet pounding flat on prickly spikes across the treacherous turf... even ducked my head for speed for a moment, daringly chanced taking my eyes off the ball to gain efficiency the way I'd seen Joe Dimaggio do it in the newsreels.... Then the anguished squint back over my shoulder, desperate scan of vacant blue until I found the white speck again... yes! trajectory matched to mine now, steady, dropping.... "I got it!" I howled. And then the stumbling outstretched upward stab of left arm, the stinging whap as the ball plummeted leaden into the unpadded pocket of my Grady Hatton official autograph model Rawlings—the trusty glove resting on my lap....

I worked my fingers under the strap and jabbed my balled right hand into it reminiscently.

...Mild astonishment, sudden elation, braking prance, whoops and applause crackling as I brandished my trophy. Quickly rifled it, on only one bounce, into the infield. Arm was my main weakness—a scatter-shooter. Coupled with a tendency to shy from hard grounders. But nobody could out-judge me on a fly. And I was fast. Which was why Daddy had put me in center.

A smile was fighting its way through my dejection.

"All in all you played a fine game," he said. "The whole team did. Their pitcher was just too good for you guys today.

That's okay. Nobody has anything to be ashamed of."

"We almost pulled it out," I agreed, "didn't we?"

The modifier was a crack through which fantasy could seep. I imagined *us* leaping, screeching, punching our fists at the sky. There was consolation in the very possibility. Even if *I* was the hinge on which our potential exultance had flipflopped—straggling off the bench to offer grudging handshakes, heads hung, eyes down, "good game" mumbled, "good game" echoing back hollowly off their superior nods and barely mastered smirks.

Sometimes it didn't bother me at all to lose. To have lost, rather. Jaunty and nonchalant through the ritual hypocrisy. So long as I'd played well. But today I'd wanted to hurl myself into the dirt, grovel, wail, smash my fist into that bully of a pitcher's face, shatter a bat against a backstop post....

## At home Daddy uncapped a bottle of Hudepohl.

He went into the sunporch and turned on the radio. Waite Hoyt was doing the Reds play-by-play. Originally a long Midwestern verandah, the porch had been enclosed the summer before. Louvered storm windows filled the voids between the rough stucco corner posts. At the ceiling, against the inside wall, you could still see the outlines of the long, knobby tubes that used to decant sluggish wasps whenever I'd daringly thump them with a broomstick. Otherwise the wasps kept to themselves.

This had been my favorite place to shelter on rainy summer afternoons—the sky dark, the air suddenly chill, a fine spray ricocheting off the rails and the lip of the concrete stairway that led down into our overgrown side yard. The pulpy pages of the comic book in my lap would slowly swell in the damp. Mother would be inside somewhere, vacuuming maybe, although she didn't do a lot of housecleaning. Paul at my feet would be busily scrubbing crayons through drifts of cheap letter paper. And I'd be languishing ecstatic, in and out of body—combating the wily Joker with Batman and Robin in Gotham, riding down bad guys with the Lone Ranger and Tonto or Red Rider and Little Beaver or—my favorite serial sequence—combing the fogbound Andes with Donald Duck seeking Inca hens that laid square eggs.

Now, though, the mildewed glider with its ripped cushions and protruding springs had given way to a hide-a-bed couch and a pair of overstuffed chairs. Chintz curtains were tied back from the aluminum-screened storm windows. Tucked into the lee of the chimney for the living room fireplace was a compact gas heater to cozy the den in winter. And dominating the far wall, the focus of the arrangement, was a walnut-grained TV console. It too had been acquired—like the Packard, the dishwasher, the mangle in the ironing nook by the kitchen and the enameled washer and dryer in the cellar—during the past eighteen months. Compensation for the previous years of stinting.

With what bemusement, I wonder now, had Mother greeted this cornucopia of appliances? She was a pampered debutante who had never got the hang of folding a hospital corner, and whose culinary repertoire was pretty much exhausted by fried chicken, spaghetti (the sauce from a can) and sauerkraut with boiled spareribs. Those last two she'd learned to cook from Daddy's mother, whereupon she'd served them every Thursday night—catering dutifully to her concept of his Cincinnati German palate. Just as Daddy dutifully picked at them. He never ate a whole lot. And only years later did he allow—in casual response to my wife's direct question—that in fact he'd never cared all that much for sauerkraut and spareribs.

The Phillies were at Crosley Field today. The Whiz Kids. They'd become my favorite team. You had to have an alternative to the hapless Reds. I'd trailed Daddy through the living room. I was still slightly dazed in the aftermath of our game's high key.

"Don't sit down here in that uniform," Daddy said. He'd become more tidiness-conscious since GaGa, his mother, had moved in with us. "Go change. Tell Paul to too."

"He's out playing. I want to listen to the game."

"That's all right, just change first. Your socks and pants are filthy. Anyway, you won't miss anything. I've got to turn this off for a few minutes while I call Brian's parents."

I'd sunk into the flowered chair. Now I was curious to eavesdrop on that conversation.

Daddy poured beer into a tumbler and sipped through the bonnet of foam. It left a tiny white mustache. He licked his lips and blotted them with a finger. Richie Ashburn drilled a single over Virgil Stallcup. That brought Seminick home from third. Daddy growled and switched off the radio. "Richard," he said pointedly. "Did you hear what I just told you?"

"Okay," I nodded. Not moving, temporizing. A new subject had suddenly crossed my mind. A subject that had been troubling me for several weeks. Each time I responded to or addressed my father it kindled and flickered, a subtext to whatever conversational business was at hand. I'd been gathering my nerve to root it out into the open. Brooding over my arguments, rehearsing the exchange—anticipating his displeasure and hurt, my embarrassment and contrition. But that was only the negative possibility. My father had always been accessible. Empathetic, accommodating. My resolve abruptly crystallized. I went rigid in my chair, gathered myself physically for the emotional declenching. My skin tingled and I could hear my pulse rising in my ears.

"Dad... Dad... Daddy," I stammered. "I'm, you know,

almost... fourteen now. Can I...? I want to ask you something. Can I now?"

My father slid back slowly against the couch. He assumed a more formal posture—forehead wrinkled slightly, shoulders stiffening to accord me a dignity that would invite and reassure. His eyes searched mine with a concern so intense I had to blink into my lap.

"Sure. Certainly you can, Richard," he replied softly, responding to my seriousness with my full name. "Anytime. What is it?"

"I... well... sometimes... it makes me feel funny when I'm with my friends and I still say 'Daddy.' You know? Like I was a little kid? I mean... what I'm wondering... would you...? Would it be okay... would you mind... if I... well, called you 'Dad?' Started to call you 'Dad' now, instead, from now on? I mean... it wouldn't mean I didn't love you anymore or anything!"

The two deep furrows that curved down from the flanges of his nose spread. He expelled breath through his nostrils—a speculative sound, directed inward rather than at me. But he'd begun to smile. He dug into his shirt pocket and fished out a packet of Kents.

At Mother's urging he'd switched to filter-tips when they'd come on the market. Upstairs in his top dresser drawer—in among the keys, the cufflinks, the gold pocket watch incised with his father's florid initials, the Phi Beta Kappa key and chain he'd earned at UC, the loose pennies and dimes and half-empty cylinders of Wint-O-Green Lifesavers that always distended his pants pockets—way back in there I'd found a couple of stubby cigarette holders. I guess that's what he'd used before. There was also a scattering of little cartridges filled with crystals, which I'd eventually figured out or been told were the filters you inserted inside the holders.

Because I was allowed to go up and fetch things from

that drawer for him sometimes, I considered it permissible by extension to inventory the contents at admiring, clandestine leisure. Back under the balled black socks, for example, I'd found a medal with a brilliant silk ribbon. It was in a cardboard box along with a certificate of commendation for Daddy's contribution to the Allied victory as area rent control director for the Office of Price Administration. I loved the aroma in that drawer—Daddy's distinctive scent of tobacco laced with wintergreen. Occasionally I'd filch a lint-flecked Lifesaver. Or test my image as an adult, smirking back at myself from the frame of the mirror with a cigarette holder jutting from my bared, clenched teeth like President Roosevelt.

Harry Truman, of course, was the President now, ever since the sunny afternoon when I'd come inside from my scooter to find Mother's eyes red-rimmed, and the somber voice of Arthur Godfrey on the radio. Daddy had always detested Roosevelt. Oh, he'd grudgingly acknowledged a certain efficacy in the New Deal and some of its agencies; venal landlords had been his nemesis while he was with the O.P.A. But ideologically Daddy was a staunch Taft Republican. Mother, on the other hand, was a daughter of the Solid South. Each election day they cheerfully conceded that their votes had just canceled each other. Only MiMi, because she visited rarely, still argued politics with him over the dinner table. Now she too was in the hospital, though. Far away in Birmingham.

Daddy tapped out a cigarette and lit it. "Dad, huh?" he grinned. "Sure you wouldn't rather just make it 'Tom?' Kind of a man-to-man basis?"

The suggestion was appalling. I was ashamed of myself, even as I recognized that he was only teasing. Polite deference to adults had been so ingrained in me that years later I would still find it difficult to address someone older by a given name, no matter how close our relationship. "Tom"

31

was how he was hailed by people who crowded the living room during my parents' infrequent parties, the ruddy men with paunches and shrill wives to whom I was introduced in pajamas before being shooed up the staircase. "Tom," the downtown sandwich-munchers and beer-sippers would nod as we threaded the tables of The Wheel, the cafeteria across from his office in the Atlas National Bank Building. I'd ride the open-caged elevator up to the seventh floor when I came from the dentist's, banter for a moment with Miss Ross, the wise-cracking nasal spinster secretary who sat in a front cubicle with Dictaphone earpieces over her perm, and then descend with Daddy—"I *figgered* 'at was your son, Mr. Schubert. Good-lookin' boy you got there," the brass-buttoned operator would fawn in a Covington twang—for a wedge of apple pie and a slice of orange cheese. But close friends and family always called him Thomas. Oh, once or twice I'd heard Mother purr "Tommy" through her teeth. They'd be romping on the couch, and at that Daddy would wrestle her across his knees and deliver a couple of stagy whacks on the buttocks.

"Sometimes," he'd pant at me, winking, "when they're really bad, women need to be spanked too."

Actually, Daddy's name was, for him, a sore point. Thomas J. Schubert, Jr. "J." for Jefferson. I suppose the presidential christening had been a sort of pledge of allegiance by my shoemaker great-grandfather, whose own shoemaker father had packed him off to America from a Schwartzwald village during the upheavals of 1848. And my grandfather, who'd died before I was born, had apparently not felt the same discomfort about the immigrant moniker as would his sophisticated only-child, to whom he'd passed it in proud turn. For business purposes the middle initial was preserved—along with the Jr.—to distinguish Daddy from the four other unrelated Thomases, including a second Thomas J. (not a Junior) on the page of Schuberts in the

Cincinnati telephone directory. Its significance, though, was a secret guarded zealously from all but a few intimates.

"Oh, no!" I exclaimed earnestly. "Gee, I...."

"Ricky," he interrupted, "'Dad' is fine, if that's what you want."

"It is?"

"Yes, it really is." He shrugged. "Might take me a little getting used to. But I'll manage."

"You won't be mad at me?"

"Of course not."

"Well, there's another thing," I said.

**His face had relaxed into pleasant expectancy.**

"What's that?" he asked

I let the silence lengthen.

"Go ahead. Shoot," he prompted.

"Well, Well, you know how we always kiss goodnight?"

I tried to look him in the eye. Bravely confront that grayish jaw whose nap rasped my own tender lips and cheek when I bent and nuzzled into his ripe evening smell: the sour-sweet bourbon pungence. We were cheek-kissers, our family. Anglo-Saxon propriety and hygiene, I suppose. "Maybe... maybe we ought to just shake hands?"

Daddy's lips twisted open. The incisors and canines beneath were yellowed but perfectly, artificially, proportional. "Ricky," he said, his voice rippling through his grin. "Who's around to see you kiss me goodnight? I mean to make you feel embarrassed about it?"

"Well... nobody."

"Uh-huh. So you think you're too big now for us to go on kissing, just on general principle. A man shouldn't kiss another man, even if they're father and son, is that it?"

"Well... I don't know."

"Look, I tell you what. I understand what you're feeling. But I still reserve the right to give you a kiss—for all that I recognize your increasing maturity and self-consciousness. My strapping young teenager now, huh? How tall are you? Five...?"

"Five-two," I acknowledged fiercely. That was my mother's height, which I was now day-by-day proudly, microscopically surging beyond. *En route* to the next milepost level, Daddy's magical eminence. I'd get there, I was certain. Or tried to remain. Despite the fact that suddenly I was tilting my neck to take in my friends' brittle baritones, their bulbous noses and fiery stipplings of nodes and pustules, their downy mustaches and darkening sideburns. Most, I'd found out in the locker-room of the tennis club or the Coney Island pool, boasted intimidating tufts of hair. It sprouted under their arms and haloed their penises. Fatter than mine. You could gauge that unmistakably even by eye. All I had—so recent I was only beginning to be frightened—were puffy nipples. Spongy and tender. Was some grotesque hormonal error on the verge of manifesting itself? I hadn't yet mentioned that humiliating, horrifying symptom to Daddy. How could I?

His grin relaxed. He might devil us, twit our pretensions, but he was careful never to mock or ridicule. And I must somehow have telegraphed the drift of my concerns. "So... are you beginning to develop?" he asked.

"De... develop?"

"Do you know what I mean?"

"I... yes, I think so," I nodded. "Um. I guess... not yet, really."

"Well, you will soon enough."

"I... these...." I cupped my hand over my flat breasts. My fingertips rested on bone—the gaunt ribs into which years of glutinous raw-egg milkshakes had been sluiced and cod liver oil spooned in the hopes of promoting padding. I'd always been skinny. Like Daddy—a frugal bundle of fast-twitch muscle-fiber. "My, um, nip... nipples?"

The awkward anatomical names of sex-parts always resisted pronunciation.

"...Are kind of... swollen a little bit. And they kind of hurt. A little bit." I winced. "Is that wrong, do you think? Do you think," I blurted, "that... Daddy, could I be getting...?" But I gagged. The word was just too much.

"No, no, Ricky, no," he hastily assured me. "I'm sure that's perfectly normal. Just a sign of all those potent juices that are starting to slosh around inside your body. Pretty soon your voice is going to crack and get deeper. Hair'll start to grow... well, you know. Don't you? Do the nuns, or a priest, or somebody... has anybody else except us ever talked to you about these things?"

"Well, yeah."

"And what did they say?"

"Oh," I shrugged, "you know." I squirmed in my chair and hooked my leg over the arm. I began to jiggle my dangling calf. "About how we get older and get... certain desires and all. And, you know: impure thoughts. And what you said. Our... bodies change. Stuff like that. Like Mother always explained."

I thought of my mother, lolling in the bathtub, the brown swatch of fur undulating in her lap under the soapy puddle. I'd called it "fur." She'd laughed, corrected me: "That's hair. Animals have fur. People, grownups, have hair down here. You will too, someday, like Daddy."

Her breasts were compact. The nipples stood out like pink jelly candies. She'd nursed me, and Paul—a surprising, slightly eccentric naturalism for an urban matron of that sterile era, I believe. And our bathroom door was never locked. I'd watch Daddy hosing pee into the bowl out of a knurled tube of lavender flesh that looked immense to me. But we had not, I realized, blundered into each other's toilets for a long time.

"Are you starting to have those impure thoughts?" he asked.

My voice caught. I cleared my throat, kept my eyes averted. "Some... sometimes, I guess," I quacked.

"And do you have wet dreams? 'Nocturnal emissions?'" He grimaced slightly. "Do you know what I'm talking about?"

"Well, no, yes. I... mean I've heard. Mother... and Father McKenna... said. But I, um, don't think so."

Daddy nodded. He understood my jibber. "You will," he told me. "And they're nothing to worry about. Or feel guilty about."

"I know," I agreed sagely.

"How about... do you ever play with yourself? Touch...?" He shook his head at his own evasion. "Masturbate. Have you...?"

"Oh, no!" I exclaimed. But suddenly I regretted the urgency of my denial. I'd cut off whatever elaboration Daddy might have been about to offer. Masturbation was a mortal sin. On that Father McKenna had left us in no doctrinal uncertainty. However, I remained totally ignorant of its tantalizing mechanics.

"Self-abuse... spilling your seed." Those were the phrases Father McKenna used. Little kernels, I pictured, with squiggly tails. When Father McKenna wrote SPERM on the blackboard, he drew commas. The heads must be the shells—kind of like the poppy specks on ryebread crust, I guessed. Only they were densely suspended in some kind of solution. Still, abrasive, it would seem to me, when they squirted through the tender orifice of your penis. The idea made me itch. I supposed the fluid base was what kept it tolerable. "Semen." That was another word. The wet stuff that

36

would leak out to define the lurid dreams Father McKenna magnanimously promised and permitted us. No need, he emphasized, to include those in our confessional catalogues. To do so would be "scrupulous." Mornings, I would often burrow under my blankets to inspect the sheets: scientific curiosity, spiced with hope of discovery. The evidence at last, tangible and damp, of my impending maturation. I hadn't found it yet.

"Oh, I'd never do that!" I declared. "That's a mortal sin!"

"Well...." My father compressed his lips. Until Mother had converted, he'd seldom accompanied us to church. Baptized a Catholic but a public school student in the days before Cincinnati's parochial system flourished (he'd been learning classroom German along with English when Wilson led America into war against the Hun, and all remnants of Teutonic culture were patriotically expunged), Daddy was the product of a relaxed European tradition of male religiosity. You were baptized in the Church, confirmed in the Church, given First Communion in the Church, married in the Church and buried in the Church. Except for those occasions you mostly stayed out of church, and took all Rome's dogmas and devotions—if they impinged on your consciousness at all—*cum grano salis*. Rosaries, miracles at Fatima, papal pronouncements on faith and morals (Mother, I later learned, had used a diaphragm) were the esoteric preoccupations of widows and clergy. And maybe Irish or Italian Catholics.

GaGa was churchgoing. Hardly zealous, though. Her forebears were from Alsace. German-speaking but with a French surname: Tisserand—my middle name. She'd married my grandfather, a musician and friend of her foster father, when he was forty-one and she twenty. Five years later he'd retired to live off his minority share in a popular Over-the-Rhine District saloon owned and run by his brother,

John A. (for Adams, naturally).

Thomas Sr., my grandfather, had suffered polio as a child. He wore a club-soled shoe and walked, I was told, with a labored gait. Tootling the flute in a marching band for a decade hadn't ameliorated the handicap, either. During most of my father's childhood, his father sat at home amiably reading newspapers, playing parlor quartets with friends and sipping the dandelion wine he vinted in his Clifton basement. Daddy was in high school when Prohibition shuttered Schubert's. He had not expected to be able to go to college. But by then GaGa's two brothers had carved out improbable successes—one as proprietor of Chicago's largest job-printing plant, the other as president of Hudson Motors' European Division. (And both, because GaGa's parents had died during a typhoid outbreak when she was an infant, had been orphanage wards who'd set out into the world at fourteen—not much older than I—clutching all they owned in a carpetbag. More fortunate, little Antoinette, her real name, had been taken in by cousins.)

Uncle Robert, the printer, sent his sister stock certificates for her birthdays. Out of nostalgia for Cincinnati, he mostly bought Procter & Gamble. The dividends kept the mortgage paid and food on the table. Uncle Richard, the auto executive and perhaps my namesake, quarried archives for a noble coat of arms to emblazon on his china plate. And he decided his nephew ought to study business at the local university. When Daddy was a senior, his father died. ("Antoinette, would you please pour me a glass of wine?" he reportedly requested from his bed, where he was nursing a bad chest cold. When she turned to hand it to him, he lay unbreathing. I've always hoped my own last words might be so admirably debonair. Having undergone a number of close scrapes with skidding automobiles, jibing boat booms and ungrounded electrical tools, however, I'm afraid that what posterity will record as my final utterance, if there's anyone around to record it at all, will pretty certainly be the standard: "Oh, shit!")

Uncle Richard proposed to put Daddy through law school, too. He recommended Harvard. Daddy shrugged and went off to join Alger Hiss on the Law Review. After graduation, drawn by a sense of duty to his widowed mother, Daddy returned to Cincinnati. Soon he met a perky Sweet Briar grad with a degree in art history, a dimpled chin, bobbed hair and an "r"-less Alabama lilt. Because she was an Episcopalian they were married on the verandah of Mrs. Farquhar's Grandin Road estate instead of at the foot of an altar. But Mother had agreed to raise any children in Daddy's nominal faith, so a priest was persuaded to perform the ceremony.

When it came time to school me, I'd revealed myself as asthmatic, prone to colds and accompanying bouts of stentorious wheezing. Mother and Daddy gave away the cat, to which I was allergic, and enrolled me in an affordable private school that shuttled its pupils to and from home in weatherproof buses. It was a Catholic school. While I ingested every jot and tittle of the catechism, lay ill abed wondering why I couldn't match the saintly demeanor of the little leukemia victims and childhood martyrs celebrated in *Manna*, a magazine we were handed each month in school, Mother and Daddy provided a counterbalancing indifference. That both troubled and consoled me. They weren't pious like the nuns, or like my friends' parents, dutifully ranked in familial clusters in the pews of St. Mary's Sunday in and Sunday out. It was GaGa who took me, usually. Daddy or Mother would drive us, and sometimes Mother even came inside. But then, just two years before, as Paul was being groomed for his First Communion, Mother startled us with the announcement that she had taken instruction and was going to join him. Afterwards, Daddy found fewer excuses to absent himself from Mass. Vestments and candles, incense and organ music helped make it palatable to him, so we usually went to High Mass. I don't think Daddy cared much for Confession, though. He never got up to join the files shuffling toward the Communion rail. Mother exhibited all the convert's enthusiasm, but she wasn't preachy. Somehow they both seemed to feel that you could be a Catholic and still maintain a certain theoretical and practical autonomy. The nuns had never led me to any such supposition. Nevertheless, Daddy was always circumspect about contradicting the presumably orthodox tenets I reported my teachers as having imparted. Now he pinched his lower lip and squinted.

"I wouldn't," he shrugged, "be so sure about that. Admittedly I'm no authority on mortal sin. But I have a hard time believing that... masturbation... belongs in that category. It's something almost everybody does. Sometime. And when you, when you're... well, you will too, I'm sure. So don't feel too bad about it. Is all."

He hunched forward, stubbed out his cigarette and drew a breath.

"And as far as 'impure thoughts' go... those are really perfectly natural too, Ricky. Something every man, every woman, has, sometimes. It's wonderful, I agree, if you can... can save yourself, be 'pure' as it were, until... for your wife, for the woman you love, that you marry. It makes it... special. A special sharing. Like your mother and me, we did. We did." He nodded. "Had."

He closed his eyes and rubbed them. Daddy often had to lie down with the shades drawn and a damp washrag folded across his brow.

"But looking at girls, their bodies," he continued, "thinking about them, imagining... well. And getting aroused from time to time. That's normal, natural. It's nothing to be ashamed of. It's just your being human."

"But Daddy...?"

"I thought it was going to be 'Dad' from now on."

"Oh. I mean... Dad?" The word suddenly sounded curt to me. Flip and distancing, at a moment when the last thing I wanted was distance. But I had made the proposal. Manhood meant carrying through. "Um. Uh. Never mind," I muttered.

"What? What is it, Ricky? Or should I start calling you Richard now? As part of our new adult relationship?"

"No, I don't care," I said.

"What do you want to say to me? Go ahead," he coaxed. "This is the time. We're talking, I'm listening."

But in fact, I no longer knew what I'd wanted to ask. Sort of... nothing in particular because everything: When was that hair going to start popping out on my slick body? How exactly do you masturbate? How do people make love? I mean, I sort of knew, technically and all. But what does it feel like? The idea was somehow simultaneously provocative and revolting. And how were Mother and Daddy entwined when I'd started to barge into their bedroom at the top of the stairs one afternoon—and abruptly thunked up short against the door, a barring chairback propped under the knob inside?

"We want to be by ourselves for a little while, sweetie," I'd heard Mother pipe. Her inflection had been sharp but her voice muffled. "Go out and play. We'll be down in a few minutes."

Too much, all these uncertainties. Discomfiting and taboo. "I... I forget," I muttered. "Really."

"Well, if you do remember... if you ever have any questions at all, about anything, Richard... you can come to me. You know that, don't you? Not that I have all the answers. But at least I'll be honest with you. I hope you won't be too afraid or ashamed."

"I won't."

"I hope not."

41

I lolled in the flowered chair, splayed across its arms, mulling the disturbing and exhilarating conversation.

"Now, son," Daddy said. The word, not to mention his tone, was a clear shift back to business. "Go on upstairs and get out of that uniform. I'm glad we had this man-to-man talk, but now I have to get a few things done. All right?"

"Okay, Daddy," I agreed.

"'Dad,' I believe," he corrected me. "And how about a big kiss before you go?"

I was untangling my legs to rise. He lunged off the couch. I saw him reaching and gyrated in panic, flopped to my knees on the throw rug and scrambled desperately to escape.

I got under him, past his legs, but he managed to snag the back of my belt. I started laughing, crawling futilely, gasping, "No! No!" He bent and pinioned me. I tucked into a ball, hands on the back of my neck, arms tight against my ears. "No kissing!" I shrieked. He tried to hoist me upside down, grunted and dropped me. Then he humped across my back, heavy and rough, tousling my crewcut, his sharp nose burrowing at my turtled nape and ticklish ribs. I writhed in convulsions of adamant joy.

Suddenly the dank atmosphere of nicotine and hops evaporated. I ventured a peep and saw him on his haunches, panting, grinning at me.

"You may be right," he said. "You're getting to be far too damn much trouble to kiss anymore anyway."

# 2

**Danny called.**

His sister was being allowed to use the car to drive to the Coney pool, and would suffer us as passengers. She was seventeen, tall, black-haired and bony. Her breasts stood out under her sweaters with the conical precision of teaching aids for a class in solid geometry.

Pools were just becoming sexual places to me that summer. For the first time I'd begun to notice the curly stragglers at the elastic margins of girls' bathing suit crotches. I'd make it a point to splutter to the surface squarely in front of them as they sat spraddle-thighed, dandling their shins from the tiled pool-lip. My friends would be hooting at some giggly knot of eighth graders bound for St. Mary's or Walnut Hills in the fall—a parochial and a public school respectively, which conferred on those girls a virtually undifferentiated mystique of worldliness and potential wantonness—and I'd find myself furtively eyeing the swell of flesh above their stiff Wonder Woman bras. Or studying the glistening, faintly stippled mounds of their shaved armpits.

I, on the other hand, had become increasingly reluctant to reveal myself in the changing room or shower. Not that anyone teased me—it was my own sense of inferiority. At the tennis club, which Daddy—Dad—had joined so I could take lessons, I could forego that ordeal. Simply dress at home and return, sweaty, to the privacy of the bathroom. So I declined Danny's invitation on the grounds that I needed to practice.

It was stifling in the upstairs front bedroom I now shared with Paul. I could hear him and his playmates outside snapping cap-pistols and cartwheeling from yard to yard. All the windows were open, but there was almost no breeze. At least the sun had arched behind the roof-ridge. You could smell the vegetable essence simmering out of the leaves of the shade trees along our walk. As a twelfth birthday present Mother had allowed me to move by myself into the guest room next door. Only when MiMi visited—detraining from the "Hummingbird" at Union Terminal, an awesome place with its soaring ceiling ringed by huge pastel WPA murals and the concourse abustle with redcaps and holiday travelers—had I been dislocated temporarily back to this childhood twin bed. But then GaGa had settled in with us. The guest room was the only place she could stay.

A new *LIFE* had come in the mail. I'd brought it upstairs with me. I stripped off my mucky baseball outfit, stepped over the pile and stretched out on my quilted bedspread. I devoured all the magazines we subscribed to— the *Saturday Evening Post* with its enthrallingly illustrated Seventh Cavalry and Hornblower stories (in an access of narcissistic pathos, I'd once taken off my shirt, bound my wrists with my bathrobe sash and strung myself from the coat-peg on the door of my closet in imitation of a flogging scene); the *National Geographic,* full of wooly-headed aborigines hunkered bare-breasted before the camera (anatomically instructive but never, to me, particularly arousing); the *Reader's Digest,* which I combed for risqué anecdotes— they did stir the imagination; *Boy's Life,* now lapsed along with my interest in Scouting. *LIFE* was actually the most titillating. Its photos of starlets and models, embedded in a redeeming matrix of news squibs, essays, four-color reproductions of masterpiece art and riveting depictions of violence, combat and death, were the principal feedstock for my burgeoning fascination with the architecture of the female body. Or rather, its fleshly embellishments, its secret coves and prominences. Whose presence and structure I had to infer from protracted contemplation of these lounging, stretching, moueing, naked-limbed but otherwise demurely clad exemplars of hale mid-century beauty.

Not that I'd ever burrowed down with the express intent of indulging such impurity of thought. Nor did I now. First I read the letters to the editors. Then I thumbed past "Speaking of Pictures"—where I often found the cheesecake, but not this time. I skipped an analysis of the expected confrontation between Taft and Eisenhower for the presidential nomination. I lingered at a profile of U.S. Open hopefuls including our own local stars, veteran Bill Talbert and the up-and-coming Tony Trabert. As I read the captions I scratched absently at the chigger bites that welted me each summer. They burned in my armpits, around my ankles and along my groins. My navel had a swollen red corolla. Bites thickened the pink prune-flesh of my scrotum. The invisible scarlet mites lurked in the grass, and tunneled into human skin wherever it was snugly banded by clothing.

I flipped the page, glanced at a picture of a French soldier crouched in a rice paddy cradling a machinegun. The place, "Indo-China," sounded exotic. I often daydreamed of visiting far-off corners of the world. I tried to turn the page, but the slick paper resisted. GaGa licked her thumb as she leafed through magazines. Mother told me it was unhygienic, a quaint lower-class habit. I fumbled and got a grip on the paper.

Linda Darnell, grinning wet-lipped, slowly exhibited her body.

The article was about five of Hollywood's most promising new contract leading ladies. In fact, their poses were chaste enough. But Darnell reclined among stuffed lions and tigers in a clinging silver-lame gown that lacked one shoulder strap. The bodice was unconstructed. Her breasts slumped apart naturally beneath its molding. I could almost conjure her nipples. My fingertips rested inside the pouch of my underpants. My penis stirred against my palm.

Erections were an odd but not unfamiliar phenomenon. I'd had one when I was hanging masochistically from that closet hook. At the age of about ten I'd taken a snapshot of my up-rammed weenie with my Brownie camera. That Christmas Mother and Daddy had outfitted me with my own little darkroom in a niche in the cellar. I'd learned to develop and print the Brownie's broad spools of film. One afternoon Mother had casually shuffled through a stack of contacts I'd left on my dresser-top and come across the unusual self-portrait. She'd consulted Daddy, and then quietly told me, "Ricky, I found this by accident the other day. It took me a while to figure out what it was." I'd blushed. Snapping the shutter had been the orgasm. The artifact was only an embarrassment. "I really don't think you ought to take any more pictures like this," she'd counseled. "Not that there's anything terrible about it. It's… just not in good taste, honey."

Now as blood infused my stiffening penis, I rolled my underpants down to free it. And to look at it. I'd been circumcised. The mushroom head had a kind of cowl. Its flared edge was slightly puckered and rosy, like lip-skin. The central slit loured at me like a cat's eye. I dilated it experimentally with my fingers. A concave bead of moisture gave off a viscid glint inside. I was almost dizzied by the intensity of the sensation. My hips jerked awkwardly, my abdomen quivered. I'd grasped this cartilaginous nub before. But now it ached with a strange, pulsating exigence. The image of the supine actress sucked at my attention. It mesmerized me, lubricious out of all proportion to its general-audience sensuality—as if the very printer's ink had been tinctured with pheromones....

Slam. Clump, clump, clump.

I gasped and almost catapulted off the bed in recognition of Paul's footsteps, pounding up the stairs at his customary run. Light-headed with fright, I snatched my underpants up over my waist and flopped prone, burying the rigid protuberance under me.

Paul banged through the door and began rooting inside his dresser drawer. "We're gonna go over to Henke's and play capture-the-flag," he announced breathlessly.

"So what?" I snarled—testy big brother, dampening by reflex any enthusiasm my sibling might be unwary enough to volunteer. Anger and resentment had immediately replaced my initial panic as I'd assured myself he'd noticed nothing, suspected nothing. Paul had the little brother's uncanny knack of intruding on my privacy at its most vulnerable instants. "Who do you think gives a darn, you little creep?"

He ignored me. The exchange was pretty routine. He flung off his baseball knickers and hopped into shorts.

"Make it quick," I commanded. "A person can't even get left alone for five damn minutes around here without you barging in."

"You said 'damn.' I'm gonna tell."

"Be my guest, blabbermouth. Dad says it too."

"Dad? Anyway, that doesn't mean you can."

I reached under my stomach, lifted myself slightly and covertly adjusted the bony digit flattened against my lower belly. Within about 10 degrees of deviation from the polar navel, my erect penis was comfortable bent back. Tugged further off true by underwear or wrinkled bedclothes, it hurt. On its own it sidled clockwise up my groin from its cozy nest between the testicles—coming to elongated halt somewhere around McBurney's point. (Two inches from the belly button and two inches down on the right, Mother had taught me. That was where she routinely prodded me when I complained of stomach aches. It was the apex of her own pink appendicitis scar.)

"What are you reading?" Paul wondered.

I flinched and slapped the magazine shut. I'd neglected to hide the incriminating focus of my arousal. I was as ashamed as if if I'd been caught poring over the dog-eared European pulp-porn photo collection Billy Gerlach— who went to Withrow, of course—had nauseated me with in his bedroom one afternoon. Fattish women wearing awful leers displayed toothbrushy pubic swatches and melon breasts. They all had hair under their arms and long braids or coils atop their heads. That made me sure they weren't nice Americans. From some combination of pride and rectitude, I'd refused them more than one quick glance apiece. I'd always wanted to be the gallant kid extolled in Father McKenna's lectures who strode away from the group—conscience uncompromised, earning grudging admiration—whenever some lout began to tell a dirty joke. Actually, the first two smutty stories I remember hearing I repeated to my mother. I accepted the snickers of my pals as evidence of the humor in them, but I was puzzled by it. Mother laughed at the first. The second was merely an excuse to speak forbidden words, she suggested.

"Just because a joke is about sex, that doesn't automatically make it funny," she declared. "And the same thing is even more true about going to the bathroom. Bodily functions. That's not to say there aren't some very funny jokes you could call 'dirty.' If you don't know which is which, try them on me." And from then on I always had.

"LIFE," I answered Paul defensively before remembering the more characteristic reply. "It's none of your business anyway, though, nosy."

For all our squabbling, I think Paul and I basically got along well. He was sufficiently charitable or distracted to let this pass too. "Why'n't you come?" he suggested. "Glenn and Trey are gonna play, I think."

"Nah. I'm gonna go to the club," I said. Paul wanted me to join his capture-the-flag expedition. He was trying to entice me by citing a couple of neighborhood kids closer to my own age bracket. There were less than two-dozen houses lining our S-curved "No Outlet" street. Among them they probably disgorged close to forty children. And that was despite the sprinkling of aged and reclusive residents—the "crabs" and "grouches" whose yards you penetrated with anxious stealth to retrieve lost balls, who yelled and cursed at you from behind lace-curtained windows or turned their garden-hoses on you when you zigged into their driveways during bicycle chases.

Most of our recreations were democratic, but there were definite age-clusters. Paul and I usually amused ourselves in separate cliques. Still, I might have accompanied him, especially knowing that Glenn was playing. There were definite pleasures to be found in the exercise of one's status as a haughty, seasoned elder. Henke's Woods was a vast private estate with a great stone mansion-house surrounded by meadows, dense stands of hardwood and rocky creekbeds you could swing across on ropes tied to tree-limbs, like Tarzan. Only the house was guarded, and that by a seldom-seen caretaker. We clattered down Henke's steeps on our sleds when snow accumulated in winter. In summertime we stalked one another across its wild acres on rambling capture-the-flag campaigns that sometimes continued for days at a stretch.

Crawling through brambles on patrol in enemy territory during those combats had filled me with no less terror and exhilaration than I'd have experienced in real war, I'm certain. And along with the accounts in *LIFE* and *Time* of ground-battle in Korea—GIs cowering in icy foxholes as waves of fanatical, bugle-driven Chinese infantry pounded

49

at them with fixed bayonets—those stealthy flag-stealing forays, those sickeningly dawning suspicions of impending ambush, those agonies of camouflaged motionlessness (never, you learned, telegraph your presence by looking directly at a sentry or someone searching for you), those horripilating whoops when they discovered you and you broke from cover—flailing heedless through thorns and poison ivy toward the distant safety of your own home ground (we played tough: you could only be taken prisoner if you were caught on the wrong side of the rusty barbed-wire fence that served as boundary between the two territories, but you had to be physically subdued)... all that convinced me—had already made me certain at twelve or thirteen—that when it came time to be drafted I'd fight for my country in the Navy. No way was I going to be a foot-soldier.

"Don't make your headquarters down by the creek, if that's your territory," I advised. "They always look there first."

"I know," he agreed. "I'm gonna take the other side, up in the big fields."

I had to admire his daring. Hinckel's back acres were more open and elevated, and I'd explored them less thoroughly. Somehow that had always been the enemy's enclave. I'd gained a certain confidence about penetrating its borders after years of tactical probes—indeed, one of the most triumphal memories of my lifetime remains the day I noted freshly trodden grass up there and tiptoed along its narrow course toward a copse of gnarled apple trees. Sure enough, there I spied Billy Gerlach's team flag fluttering above a canvas lean-to around which he and his troops sat eating sandwiches.

Timmy and I had ventured across the fence to take advantage of just such a possibility, that our adversaries' vigilance would lapse at lunchtime. I froze and gestured urgently at Timmy to backtrack. We scrambled behind a grassy promontory on the other side of the main trail, where we hid, suppressing chortles of nervous glee, until we heard the enemy finally roistering off. Then, just in case a guard had been left, Timmy lobbed clumps of dirt into a distant stand of bushes as a distraction while I worked my way close enough to make sure the camp was vacant. It was. I dashed in, snatched Billy's red bandanna and kicked down the lean-to as a celebratory fillip. Still, I'd guess his team had more often been the victor. The shadowy groves around the lowland creekbanks had been Timmy's and my habitual choice of turf—probably easier to sneak through tree-to-tree than the sun-splashed, thinly-wooded heights. So Paul's selection did have cunning if not family custom behind it.

"There's a bunch of old apple trees off to the right of the main trail that'd be real neat for your flag-camp," I suggested. "The only thing is, you've got to be careful not to leave a path showing in the tall grass when you and your guys walk to it, you know?" The grizzled campaigner, bestowing his hard-won wisdom on a new generation, was also extending a token of affection and palliation for his initial surliness.

"Hey, yeah, I think I know what you mean," Paul nodded.

"I might even come over later," I allowed. "Probably not, but...."

"Okay," Paul said cheerily. "'Bye."

## My penis had begun to soften.

When I heard the screendoor clack downstairs, I wriggled to the windowsill and lifted myself on my elbows. I glimpsed Paul's back zipping out of sight beneath the trees. Okay, coast clear. I rolled over, furled my underpants around my thighs again— itself an erotic act—and, dry-mouthed, opened the magazine.

But my lust had ebbed too far. This garish, slightly out-of-register Linda Darnell now lay baleful on the page, as flat and insipid as the dregs of a day-old soda. After a couple of minutes I tossed the *LIFE* aside and hobbled up.

I stirred the floor of my closet and found a pair of passably clean seersucker shorts. I struggled into a fresh white tee-shirt from the neat pile GaGa had arranged in the top drawer of the little *Chinoiserie* chest at the foot of my bed. That reminded me. I gathered up my soiled baseball stuff and wadded it down the clothes-chute in the hall outside my door. With a sneer I picked up Paul's too—what a good boy, I congratulated myself, am I. But I was ruefully aware that I was not a good boy at all. I put on clean white socks and my pink tennis shoes—canvas stained by a summer's clay and sweat.

As I'd dressed, my fingers had felt thick, all my joints oddly hinged. Nothing dramatic—just a mild, distracting hollowness. The excitement that had galvanized my body had never quite properly discharged. I was struggling against shame, too. Daddy had seemed to sanction whatever I'd just done. *Nothing*, after all. Yet part of me knew Father McKenna would consider it something—and condemn it as impure and sinful. I didn't feel quite clean.

But I had to be resolute in suppressing that impulse to self-accusation. If I didn't acknowledge a thought, word or deed as wrong, it wouldn't *be* wrong, would it?

Except... that would mean God's judgment is always in suspense. Dependent on my ratification. And that couldn't be right. Would murder be okay so long as you simply held fast to the proposition that there's nothing wrong with killing somebody? You *would* have to firmly believe it, not just fake it. I understood that from catechism. But still—would pure denial of a sin make the sin all right? Who knows, after all, what God considers wrong?

Well, there's the Ten Commandments. Which certainly do cover murder. If you believe them. A pretty startling idea, that—questioning something so basic as the Ten Commandments. Sometimes I disquieted even myself by the blasphemies that oozed into my head. Of *course* God would condemn murder. Hadn't He made man in his own image and likeness? But what about more piddling stuff, the private stuff... like... masturbation? Did Father McKenna really know more about how God regarded that than Daddy? He was a priest, sure... but I hadn't seen any evidence to lead me to regard priests as a supernal breed. They were just men in black suits, glorified umpires. Who murmured Mass and prayed a lot, presumably—they were always walking around reading to themselves from little books. They never got married, either. That made them special, I'd admit, but still I'd pit Daddy's access to the mind of God against any priest's. Honor thy father and mother, He'd ordered. So ha!

But would I have wanted Mother to find me lying there with my thing poking at the sky? Maybe taste *was* the crux... at issue here as much as morality.

I went into the bathroom and wee-weed. That was the family's baby-word. We seemed to find the preservation of a lot of them comfortable. Urinated. Oh, I knew the technical terms too. Mother had taught me. All the Latinates.

But the harsh Anglo-Saxonisms—*piss, shit*—were heard only on the streets. In our household we regarded them as vulgar, *déclassé*. And in Mother's lexicon, *vulgar* carried a lot of emotive freight. It was even worse than *tacky*. The previous autumn, I'd encountered the word *fuck* for the first time. It was scrawled on a wall, and it took me a couple of readings to realize what was meant. Then I'd snorted in derision at the ignorance displayed by whoever had chalked it there. Some vulgar illiterate, I'd sneered, taxed even by this tacky single syllable. As an avid reader and a good second-year Latin student, I knew the word—so powerful it never saw print and was only spoken on our street in a fearful hush—had to be spelled with a *ph*. And probably a *qu*. Eventually I decided to share my amusement with Mother. She astonished me by authenticating those coarse consonants. The word seemed even more disgusting.

The upstairs hallway was lined with bookcases. In them were the Harvard classics, some of my parents' old school texts and a sprinkling of murder mysteries and popular novels in tattered jackets. There was a political biography commissioned for one of his campaigns by my great-uncle, the Alabama senator. And a curious memoir titled *The Adventures of Two Alabama Boys*, detailing the odyssey of MiMi's grandfather and his brother after their company of Confederate soldiers found itself marooned in Northern Virginia by Lee's surrender. There were also a couple of dictionaries and an encyclopedia.

It had occurred to me as I swiped at the soapdish and passed my hands under the faucet that simple research might yield the information I wanted.

I tipped the M-volume of the encyclopedia out of its tight rank on the shelf. I carried it to the cedar chest that served as a stair-head bench. Despite its heft, the book's cigarette-paper pages didn't seem to have an entry covering my interest. I was pretty sure of the spelling, but given previous misconceptions I checked all the alphabetical permutations I could think of. No luck.

I tried the newest of the dictionaries. My heart leaped in triumph as I spotted what I was looking for immediately below *mastoiditis*. *Mas.tur.bate...* "to practice masturbation." And next, in bold-face, was the noun, its definition: "sexual self-gratification; onanism (def. 2)."

I scrutinized both entries again in case I might have missed some encrypted message. Then, blood heating my face as if I were nosing through pornography, I fumbled hopefully to the os: *onager, onagraceous... onanism!*

"1. *Psychiatry, Physiol.* withdrawal before occurrence of orgasm. 2. masturbation [from *Onan,* son of Judah: see Gen. 38:9....]."

We didn't have, as far as I knew, an Old Testament. What a disappointment, anyway. Just the usual circuitous opacities. But at least the concept was endorsed to the extent that it merited mention. I found nothing at all between *fuchsin* and *fucoid,* between *pisolite* and *Pissarro...* not that I'd expected to. For thoroughness' sake, I looked up *gratification.* And *orgasm:* "A complex series of responses of the genital organs and skin at the culmination of a sexual act." Pfff! I checked *culmination* and then set the book aside.

There was a second dictionary. Taller, its spine broken so that it shed pages in messy clusters. My detective impulses had just about been bored out of me. But persistence sometimes pays, I knew, and sure enough, here to my surprise I encountered all kinds of provocative leads.

"Self-induced orgasm through manipulation of the foreskin," I read. Which prompted a bit of mulling. Foreskin? I was led to *prepuce:* "the fold of skin which covers the head of the penis or clitoris...." Another new word. And exactly what fold of skin did they mean? It would still be several years before I'd recognize that circumcision is not the universal and normal condition of the male organ. (A nudge of the elbow at Timmy as we stuffed our clothes into Coney lockers: "Hey, did y' see that guy's dick? It looks like a pencil. What d'you think's wrong with him?") Then the trail forked via *vulva* to *labium.*

Daddy shuffled across the hallway below. Obviously he had not yet become Dad in my inner ear. Fortunately, he didn't look up, because the fly of my shorts was distended by a lump again. Though I couldn't really visualize them, all those references to women's nether pleats had inflamed my imagination.

But now I needed a respite, air. And I didn't want to tempt discovery. I straightened the books in their shelves like a cat carefully burying its... well, I still thought of that as "go-toity."

## Daddy sat at the dining room table pushing a ballpoint pen across a yellow legal pad, a couple of leather-bound law books and his briefcase at his elbow.

Mother had finally given up trying to protect the elegant Duncan Phyfe-style table, a wedding present. Its once glossy surface was a palimpsest in which could be descried the shallow residue of our years of between-meals enterprise at this family desk.

Daddy often worked here late into the night. I'd stumble to the bathroom for a drink of water, see a light downstairs and find him hunched in the glow from a floor lamp he'd trundled across the hall from the living room. He'd be drafting a brief or scripting a cross-examination. He hated trial work, he complained. But, he added, he had to take what he could get. And for all the insomnia it caused him, the nervous pacings and obsessive midnight studies over butt-heaped ashtrays and half-finished cups of instant coffee, he was apparently good at it.

A major contributor to the affluence that had triggered his recent buying spree had been an insurance case in which he'd won what was then the largest personal injury verdict in Hamilton County history. His client had been a young railroad switchman, father of three, whose legs had been severed at mid-thigh by a backing train. I can remember overhearing Daddy describe to Mother the man's anguish as he lay across the tracks, his ankle vised in a misthrown switch, desperately waving his lantern and screaming at the oblivious engineer. Daddy's opponent, the insurance-company lawyer from Cincinnati's most prestigious firm, had been Potter Stewart. Years later, when he was a Supreme Court justice, we were introduced. When I identified myself through reference to my father, Stewart announced to me and those around us, "Thomas Schubert gave the most moving closing argument I've ever heard in a courtroom in my life."

Daddy looked at me over the horn-rimmed dime-store magnifiers he wore to read.

"'Bye, Dad,'" I said. I'd rehearsed. It still sounded odd.

"Where're you going?" he asked.

"Over to the club. See if I can find somebody to volley with. Maybe get in a game or two."

"Fine. Just be sure you're back by dinnertime. Where's Paul?"

"He went out. Didn't you see him? He's playing capture-the-flag over at Hinckel's."

"Doggone it," Daddy exclaimed. "He didn't say anything to me and he knows he's not supposed to cross Linwood without asking. Oh well. I'll deal with Paul later. You be back by six, huh?"

"Six!"

He nodded.

My tone of voice had signaled protest, but I let it drop. Under Mother's regime we'd always eaten at 7:30 or eight. Mostly that was because Daddy chose to stay at the office late. He seldom left home in the morning before nine. And when he got home they liked to sit together in the living room chatting over a highball or two. Mother would either dart into the kitchen every so often to tend the simmering meal or she'd assemble it from cans in one last-minute flurry. My playmates would have eaten hours before our little foursome even sat down in the dining room's lyre-backed Phyfe chairs. In summer they'd loiter outside the open windows, watching us through the screens and wheedling, "Can Ricky and Pauly come out now, Mrs. Schubert?" Finally she'd order them away. Paul and I were never excused before everyone else at the table had finished. So gobbling only meant an excruciating ordeal... watching other people dawdle, chew unnecessarily, fiddle with their knives and forks and talk about boring stuff while the light outside turned purple and the lightning bugs began to pulse. Now that GaGa was the cook, though, suppers were being served at a more nearly normal Ohio hour.

I pedaled my bike out Erie Avenue past stately houses set deep on grassy lawns. By the time I arrived at the club my tee-shirt was transparent. My legs and arms tingled under a glistening film of sweat. Actually, by Mother's genteel preference, Schuberts "perspired."

Despite the bludgeoning sun and the humidity, all the courts were ascurry with people in white. Adults had priority over children on weekends, so I practiced my serve against a green plywood backboard for a while. Then I moved in close for some hoppety-hop, bang-bang reflex stuff until I was adequately winded. I wandered over to the shade of the terrace and scraped a white metal chair up to the glass-topped table around which lolled four of my fellow weekday lesson-takers. Shrouded in summertime ennui as thick as the air itself, they eyed me with all the enthusiasm of a pack of basset hounds.

Daddy had played instructive catch with me, had taken me and my neighborhood pals down to Lunken Airport's playfield diamond to catch his fungoes on Saturday afternoons. He'd even allowed himself this year—with Mrs. Knoop in her last months of pregnancy—to be cajoled into taking over her Knothole baseball team. It was a distraction. But after a few frustrating bouts of painstaking mime followed by an hour of unresponsive flailing on my part, he'd relinquished my tennis education to a pro.

He'd signed me up for my first lessons here the summer I was ten. For the last couple of years he'd paid my youth membership in the club as well. Its facilities were limited to six clay courts and a utilitarian clubhouse, no frills like a pool. So the membership was unexclusive. Having lost all interest in tennis as soon as he could no longer even fantasize a center-court appearance at Forest Hills, Daddy of course didn't join. Mother had never gone beyond recreational play. For the first time, Paul too had taken six weeks of morning lessons this summer. His instincts for the game were superior to mine—even I had to grudgingly recognize that. But strangely, for all my inability to respond to Daddy's instruction, I'd proved an eager, conscientious and absorbent instrument under my teacher, the club pro.

His name was Elmer Ingram. He was in his late twenties, I guess—slender and of middling height but with lumps of hard muscle in his brown arms and slightly bowed legs. He possessed the polite affability requisite to his line of work, along with the capacity to suffer fools easily. The bucolic surname was, naturally, a source of some jest, but he chuckled and bore it with dignity. And that joshing was made permissible by his counter-stereotypical looks—clean and dark, with a broad white smile. Women flirted with, mothered and adored him. He was a farmboy from Indiana. It had been a big farm, though, which meant a childhood of some privilege. He'd gone to school at Culver Academy, where he'd captained the tennis team, and then to Purdue for a year. In nineteen forty-two he'd volunteered for the paratroops. He'd survived the Battle of the Bulge unscathed, but somewhere along the banks of the Rhine had been wounded by a grenade. His back and buttocks, I saw in the shower one day, were welted by ugly, angular purple scars. If you found him in the right mood he'd tell stories from the war—riveting anecdotes of snafus and unspectacular combat spoken in a soft matter-of-fact voice that could somehow lull me into a state of saucer-eyed near-hypnosis. I used to beg for those stories.

Elmer returned from the occupation with a battlefield commission and resumed his schooling under the GI Bill. He played Big Ten tennis and graduated with a degree in business administration, which earned him a job offer from Procter & Gamble. Office work very quickly palled, though, and within a year he'd applied and been hired as tennis pro at the newly opened club. He was my first and only teacher. Though there were others of us who dated from that inaugural class, I was his star pupil. My neatly bristling flattop was cropped in careful imitation of his military haircut. His fingernails were always clean—nervously bitten to the quick, as it happened. I'd tried but not enjoyed nibbling my own. Nevertheless, I scrubbed them assiduously, and religiously clipped away the least emergence of a white. Elmer was my idol. The mechanics of my game were his in miniature. I fawned on him—though from behind a veneer of wise-cracking indifference; I was aware enough to try to protect the relationship. I'd never have acknowledged the phrase—but I loved Elmer.

I'd just settled into my chair and leaned forward to announce, "Hey, guess what!" when Elmer sauntered by. He cradled a pair of rackets in the crook of his arm. With his free hand he ruffled the top of my head.

"How's it goin', champ?" he winked.

"Hey, Elmer!" I said. I ducked, but at the same time reached out to encircle his calf. "This guy, this friend of mine, on my team? He broke his leg this morning! At the baseball game!"

"Yeah? I told you to watch out for that so-called sport, didn't I?"

"He was sliding? And it just twisted under him? Went

snap or something? He was crying and all. My Dad and some men made this kind of... what d' you call it. A splint. Out of some bats. It was pretty neat. They took him to the hospital. My Dad said it was the... tibula."

"Fibula," Elmer corrected me. "If it was the leg. Speaking of which, how 'bout letting go of mine? I got a lesson to go to."

He turned and glanced at a woman who was standing a little to his rear. She wore a primly scoop-necked tennis dress over ruffled panties. Her tanned legs were lithe and youthful. The sun had etched wrinkles around her eyes, though, and turned the skin below her collarbone pebbly. Still, men her age would probably have considered her a knockout. To me it came across as a kind of pleasantness.

"Hi, Richard," she said, taking a step forward. "You probably don't remember me."

"Mrs. Pflueger," Elmer interjected helpfully.

"Goodness, you've grown! I'd hardly have recognized you. My!" She flared her tilde eyebrows in a conspiratorial aside to Elmer. "He's stunning!"

"The Pfluegers just moved back from Pittsburgh," Elmer said.

"Oh yeah," I acknowledged, angling to my feet politely. "You used to live up on Grace."

"That's right. My son, Lodge...."

"Yeah, where's Lodge?"

"Well, our new house is in Mariemont. He didn't come to the club with me today, but he will. It'll be nice for you boys to get back together again."

"Yeah," I nodded.

"And how are your mother and father? And your brother, didn't you have a brother? Paul?"

"Oh." I glanced at Elmer. His face had abruptly turned dour. He looked at me uncertainly. "Paul's fine," I said. "And my Dad's okay. My Mother died last February, though."

# 3

**It didn't bother me to say it.**

In fact, I'd come to derive a kind of perverse enjoyment from the bald announcement of my mother's death. There was defiance in it. Though of what I'm not certain. Of sorrow itself, perhaps—since it couldn't change anything. Of the comfortable assumptions of other people. I liked, in a clinical way, observing their reactions.

Not that I wasn't disconcerted by the maladroit expressions of sympathy I provoked. I'd look down and shuffle my feet and nod dismissively. Suffering through condolence was a penance I had to bear for maintaining fidelity to my mother by proclaiming her death. That was my duty to her now. Terse candor was the armor I wore in performance of duty.

"Oh, my goodness," Mrs. Pflueger said. "Oh! I'm so sorry to hear that."

"She got leukemia," I said. The explanation was part of the ritual.

"Dear." Her high, rounded forehead knitted in formulaic distress. I don't think she knew my parents very well. And like most sensitive people—those who didn't gush out of proportion to the circumstance—she was at a loss for what to say to me. I just stood there. Silent, meeting her eyes the way Mother and Daddy had taught me to deal with people. Straightforward.

"Well...give your father my... and Paul... my... deepest

regards and sympathy. It must have been very hard on you all. If there's anything I can do...."

"Thanks. My grandmother's staying with us now, taking care of us."

"Well. That's good. I hope it's all going all right. You'll have to come over some time. Lodge'd love to see you. He'll be here at the club now, too."

"I take lessons every morning. During the week."

"Rick's kind of our up-and-coming Trabert," Elmer said. "He's won every tournament we've coaxed him into so far. He'll do okay if he doesn't break a leg sliding, or get his brains conked out by a beanball. Right, champ?"

I shrugged. "I guess."

"Mrs. Pflueger tells me Lodge has been comin' along pretty strong himself, though. Maybe got yourself a little new competition there, fella. Have to watch it. There's a couple of these guys already nippin' at your heels, huh? Figure you're about ripe. Right, guys?"

My slouching comrades stirred and grunted. I was glad Elmer had directed some of the embarrassing attention away from me.

"Hey, come on," he said. He grasped Mrs. Pflueger's elbow. "We're gonna lose our court if we don't get out there. And I've got two more lessons after you."

I'd become accustomed to a certain separateness. Though I didn't feel it as resentment, I recognized my compeers' mingled feelings of respect and annoyance at my consistent ability to beat them. In fact, while there were others in my age range at the club who could force me to play to my limits, none of the four here at the table were serious challengers. Occasionally when I was really drubbing somebody I'd ease up, blow a point or two on purpose, miscall a close line in my opponent's favor. I felt bad watching their grim ineptness. I didn't want to be the agent of anybody's humiliation. If Elmer saw me at it he'd beckon me aside and mutter firm counsel: "Always play to your ability, Rick. How'd you feel if you thought somebody was givin' *you* points? Besides, you'll mess yourself up."

I still wasn't altogether comfortable about winning. My delight and relief were diluted by awareness of the other's misery. Not that every loser appeared to be miserable. It was my own projection: losing made *me* feel that way. So I was always playing against two contrasting impulses. The first was not to compete at all, simply avoid the instance of victory (the joy of which I always felt mildly apologetic about) or defeat (which somehow seemed more just, more true a condition to life in general, but nevertheless a distinct unpleasantness in the particular). The second was to compete but only superficially, calloused against the pain of possible loss by supposed indifference to it... which in fact meant concession from the outset.

And somehow the latter approach never quite worked. In the heat of battle care rekindled. Once, playing a kid who was clearly my inferior, ahead four-love after a six-love first set, I purposely double-faulted. Then I hit a couple of balls wide to give him a game. On his serve I decided to experiment with unlikely shots, blithe and sloppy. A mile-high lob, a drop-volley service return. He plugged away and suddenly we were four-all. It seemed time to turn earnest again—finish him off, but with the satisfaction I'd generously accorded of having done well against me. Only now my timing had utterly degenerated. And he'd gained some kind of psychic upper hand. Everything I did went awry; everything he did was crisp and effective. Helpless, fury mounting, I watched myself fall relentlessly behind. And this guy, my opponent, was a mediocrity I ought by every right to have been mopping up the court with. Talk about humiliation. But it was a watershed lesson. Now I hardly ever yielded to the seductions of empathy. And I was growing much blander, much less ambivalent, about conquest.

My mother's death—the fact that she had died, an enormity no one else I knew had experienced despite occasional half-competitive, half-consolatory evocations of the decease of a cousin, an uncle or a grandparent—also tended to set me apart. If I stood ready to inform people who hadn't yet heard, I was considerably less keen on reminding those who had. Nevertheless, there were sufficient occasions like this one to maintain my peculiar status as a mourner.

Actually, it was hard to figure how one ought to mourn—publicly, at any rate—in the cultural milieu I inhabited. Somehow from my father, I suppose, but through osmosis rather than any explicit instruction, I'd acquired the ideal of the stiff upper lip. Its primary wellspring seemed to be a kind of preferential concern for others—the premise being that excessive emotional effusions only upset those who have to witness them. Don't frighten the horses. And since whimpering doesn't ease pain, grumbling doesn't correct annoyances and blubbering won't cure disease or bring back the dead, all the less grounds to indulge them. The Indian brave keeps his jaws clamped and his face impassive through the torture session. To display affect would give satisfaction to his enemies. And helpfully map vulnerabilities for them. Whatever the rationale—certainly there was a mishmosh—composure was our etiquette.

So no open bawling, no keening took place at the funeral home where my mother's waxy effigy reposed in its ebony container. Mr. Flaherty, who owned the place—it looked like Monticello—was a friend of my father's from the Cincinnati Club. He herded us through the paneled rooms with hushed efficiency. The air was so syrupy from the perfume of the banked flowers and the heat shimmering off the radiators that you could hardly snuff it through your nostrils. My armpits, under my clammy tee-shirt, dress shirt and blue flannel suit, squished when I moved.

At first, people I hardly knew—friends of my parents

and grandmothers, cousins of various ages and removes—arrived to shake hands, to hug and utter commiserations. But after the initial *de rigueur* somberness, they turned almost jolly. Anyway, sociable. There was a buoyancy to the atmosphere. Daddy wore a haggard smile. Groups chatted, renewing acquaintance. Paul and I were presented to extend our hands and agree to previous meetings we didn't remember. We were told how handsome we were, and how astonishingly we'd grown. Why, the last time they'd seen us we were just teeny little things!

After a while Mr. Flaherty somehow willed everyone into the chapel. Its ghostly inhabitance I'd been pretty much trying to ignore. And pretty well succeeding. Now Daddy and Paul and I, flanked by GaGa and MiMi, drew obediently together against the wall opposite the coffin. I could just barely see the familiar profile peeping horizontal: round forehead, round nib of nose, dimpled chin. The flesh was bright with cosmetics. But there was a hard luster to it that didn't for an instant lull me into forgetting it was dead.

Mother had wasted in the two months since I'd overheard Daddy on the telephone—I was lurking on the staircase, drawn by the ring and then immobilized by the strange, constricted voice rising with the light through the vee between the kitchen doortop and jamb.

It was late. And I didn't usually eavesdrop. But somehow I'd immediately recognized that the call was about Mother... was the doctor reporting... and was fraught with some immense, chilling portent.

She'd been feeling "peak-ed" for several months. That was how she described it—nothing dramatic, just a general malaise. Finally she was persuaded to see Dr. Kaufman. He prescribed iron. It didn't seem to do much. So after a while there was another visit, and a tentative diagnosis of paratyphoid. Whatever that meant. Mother, creaky and wan, didn't really know either, she told us. She was gathering a few things to pack into her overnight bag. Periodically she'd sag on the edge of the bed. It was a wintry Tuesday afternoon, drizzling. Paul and I had just clattered in from the schoolbus. Our blue sweaters, white shirtcollars and salt-and-pepper corduroy pants—the school uniform, its initials sewn on the sweater-breast—were soggy. Bundling into our jackets had seemed too much trouble for a half-block scamper on such a muggy day. Mother kissed us and said she'd be back in just a few days. We nodded—uncertain but excited by the curious prospect of a stretch without her in the household.

"Now y'all be helpful to Daddy, hear?" she instructed. "He's certainly"—she added wryly—"going to need it."

We agreed and dashed downstairs to burn ourselves cocoa and smear peanut butter and jelly on the counters. Daddy snuggled Mother into the Packard for the drive to Good Samaritan Hospital.

She was supposed to get a good rest, have some further tests and be home for the weekend. She would never cross the threshold again. Never pat powder on her nose before the round dresser mirror, never fumble with the new appliances, never finish the pink-clay bust of an Indian—the nose unmistakably Daddy's—that had been drying under a veil of petrified terrycloth in the basement for as long as I could remember. I think I knew she wouldn't be back even as I craned into the gloom to listen to Daddy's halting end of that Thursday night telephone conversation. I gathered it less from the words—though the most technical and terrifying I actually recognized from those old *Manna*s—than from his stammer, his ghastly quavers and pauses of incredulity.

"You're absolutely certain? There's no question? My God. Oh, my God."

After he hung up there was a dense silence. Then I heard a match scritch. Several times. Then the familiar exhalation—only it was repeated, over and over. Suddenly I realized he was sobbing.

I'd never heard my father cry. The sound was dry, breathy and arrhythmic. Once, twice it ended in a kind of moan, a deep, anguished lowing. I sank back behind the parapet and scuttled up the stairs. Even in my terror and consternation I remained stealthy—keeping to the cushiony edges of the runners, placing my weight carefully on the treads whose squeaks I'd memorized. I twisted the guest room doorknob softly so the latch wouldn't click and sidled between the sheets. I lay on my back in the darkness motionless, staring open-eyed at the tumult in my brain.

After a while I began to pray.

"Dear God, don't let my Mother die. Please, God."

Daddy came upstairs a few minutes later. I heard him pause on the landing outside my door. Suddenly an ell of light raked across my wall and ceiling.

"Richard?" he said. He came in, leaving the door ajar. I could feel his bulk looming over me. I'd closed my eyes reflexively, slowed and steadied my breathing. I read a lot at night. So I'd refined my ability to react to patrol checks on an instant's notice—douse the flashlight propped under the humid tent of blankets while rolling prone atop the book. The idea was to go limp and present one's back. Because the flickering eyelids always gave you away. (No one knew to plead REM sleep in those days.) But this time I'd been surprised face-up. The possum reaction was a fright-response, more habit than intention.

"You were listening to me on the telephone just now, weren't you?" Daddy murmured.

I opened my eyes and acknowledged with a twitch of my head against the pillow.

"Could you understand anything of what was being said?"

His face looked strange, lumpy. "I... it's Mother, isn't it?" I said.

He nodded. "Ricky... I'm afraid... she's very, very...

sick, very sick."

"Is she going to die?" I blurted.

He stared at me. "Yes," he said.

He took a long breath. "But we're all going to die. All of us, someday. It's important to remember that. Your Mother's... very young. For it. But... she has a disease, a terrible disease, they just found out, called leukemia...."

"I know," I said solemnly. "I read about it, I think. There was this little girl, in a story."

I racked my memory for details. All that lingered was an image of ethereality: languor, whiteness, the attenuated glow of holiness.

"She died," I offered lamely. Went to Heaven, to be with God.

"Well," my father said, "the doctors think your Mother... might too. Very...." His voice broke. "...Soon."

He bowed his head, shook it. "I don't want to scare you, Ricky. But I think you're old enough to know. Understand what's happening. We're all going to have to try to be brave. And you'll have to help me, with Paul. I don't want to say anything to him quite yet. Can you help me with that? Keep it to yourself for a little while longer?"

"Yes, Daddy," I said.

My chest pounded with anxiety to share the news. Rush into the other room, pounce on the bed and jolt Paul awake with my astonishing, apocalyptic knowledge. I often vented and defined my own emotions through observations of his. He was my alter ego—the primal child, less confused and conditioned in his reactions than I, with four more years of maturity. But that maturity would enable me to check the urge, if Daddy demanded it.

"And of course," he said, "we can never know for sure. There could have been... some, some kind of... I don't know. Horrible mistake. They're doing more tests. Or... she could just get better. People do. Do that, sometimes. Or the doctors might suddenly discover a cure. All we can do is keep on hoping. Hoping. And praying. Just pray. We all have to be strong, Ricky."

We went to early Mass next morning. He took us nearly every day during the five weeks she wasted in the hospital. At night I prayed myself to sleep—straining for an earnestness, a fervor that the all-powerful, all-knowing, all-loving eternal Listener, the Father of fathers, up there somewhere, couldn't deny. I made promises, gradually hiked the ante—doubled and redoubled my burden of *quid pro quos*. I was always scrupulous, though, not to surpass my capacity to fulfill the bargains if they were met. Honest appraisal of my character and capabilities seemed essential if I was to convince God to respond to my entreaties. I couldn't pledge *never* to tease my brother again. But I could undertake to *try* with all my fiber to restrain myself. I couldn't offer to become a priest—though I soberly weighed the possibility of venturing such a stupendous chip. I was pretty certain a true vocation had to be built on something more solid than pure sacrifice. At least its value oughtn't to derive completely from the repugnance overcome, the degree to which one belied one's own nature. And somehow I couldn't picture myself a happy priest. But I could promise to drag myself with adequate good will to Mass every day for the rest of my life. Make novenas, take Communion with pious frequency (two times a week... no, three—*that* ought to impress a reasonable God. Make it five). I could say a careful Rosary every day. For two years! Five years! Ten!

Perhaps even so I was too circumspect. Too selfishly protective of my own future. Mother got no better. We went to visit her at Good Sam. That's what Daddy always called the vast red-brick eminence sprawled across a Clifton ridge—his way, no doubt, of whistling against the darkness. Paul and I would fidget on and around the hard couches grouped in an open lobby while Daddy and MiMi disappeared behind swinging doors we children weren't allowed to penetrate until summoned.

Our moments at Mother's bedside were brief and almost formal. Filing at last down the long, sterile corridors, our footfalls and abashed voices echoing off the brittle surfaces, we were reminded that she tired easily. We had to behave ourselves. Sit still, talk in a calm pitch, be cheerful. We entered and kissed her—me first, then Paul on tiptoe. We retreated to perch on straight-backed metal chairs pulled close to the high, white bed. The room was stark. The place, beyond the swinging doors, was laced with an acrid, anesthetic pungency. I got nervous the minute it hit my nostrils—I'd had my tonsils out, long ago, but the distinctive atmosphere still set off reverberations of that ordeal: isolation, ether, unconsciousness yielding to febrile, fiery-throated recuperation....

Mother would greet us with a soft smile. Until the last days she wore a satiny gray peignoir Daddy had brought her as a present that first Friday morning. There'd be a vase of flowers in the room, a rumpled newspaper or book open face-down on the stilt-legged Formica table that rolled away from the bed... and sometimes the fascinating remnants of a meal: melting ice cream in a fluted glass with a stem, a slice of layer cake, a heel of grey meat. Paul and I would be allowed to polish off these leavings as a treat. Meanwhile, we'd recount incidents at school, in the neighborhood, or boast of the chores we'd done to supplement Lillie Mae's four-hour stints.

Lillie Mae was our "cleaning lady"—another component of affluence. Originally a once-a-week easing of Mother's burden, she now straightened and scrubbed and left us casseroles on Mondays, Wednesdays and Fridays.

Lillie Mae was from Alabama too. A tall, stringy, bird-legged woman with ash-gray shins and elbows—she was colored, needless to say. That was the polite term of

71

reference, Mother taught us. It had a softening reticence that accorded them dignity. Not like "nigruh," which slurred dangerously close to the despicable epithet of low-caste, red-dirt prejudice. "Nee-grow" was an ugly and unnatural pronunciation no Southerner, certainly, could manage without a sneer, and anyway it was too clinically racial a term—suitable for sociology texts, perhaps, or news accounts derived from police blotters, but hardly for everyday discourse. And as to "black," if anything it was a snide archaism then, something you might encounter in an eighteenth century novel but wouldn't dare paint anyone in contemporary Avondale, where they were beginning to edge out the Jews. (Among them Daddy's three law partners, Stu Weinstein, Marv Jacobs and Larry Ehrens. When they'd decided to go into partnership together, they'd drawn straws to determine the order of names. Later, Daddy laughed, someone had pointed out that chance could have given the firm the appropriately lawyerly acronym JEWS. As it happened, he pulled the longest straw. They became, he liked to say, a variant of sewage.)

Mother gradually weakened. How soon she knew she was dying I'm not sure. The doctor and Daddy and the adults had all agreed, after a lot of deliberation, not to tell her she had leukemia. It was too hopeless, too final a sentence. The withholding troubled Daddy. Me too, but I was just a kid. Might the world—my family—conspire to dupe me as well in some equally climactic passage? I supposed so. But I didn't really dwell on it. The motive, after all, was love—and I, who understood less, shared that motive.

So I'd scrutinize Mother's face for signs of deterioration even as I exclaimed, and tried to believe, that she was looking better. On a day to day basis it was true—the fading, the dwindling of life force behind her blue eyes was almost imperceptible. But after a week had passed there was no mistaking her decline. She slumped lower in the bed, her head lay deeper in the pillows. To speak was an effort, though she licked her lips and gamely indulged us with acknowledgments that, yes, she was feeling a little stronger today, or perhaps would tomorrow. I think Daddy thought—that is, he allowed once, in a kind of mitigation of our subterfuge—that she was dissembling in her turn. And out of the same protective instinct—for us.

She may not have known it was leukemia that was killing her. But she was not deluded. There'd be no turn to this ebb.


**At first, shock and desperation clubbed us into a state of fatigue that blurred the days.**

My days, anyway. Up before dawn, to kneel in the dank, echoing gloom of St. Mary's bowed before a side altar's guttering votive candles. Droning hours in the classroom. Tedious bus-rides through leaden winter streets. Homework, morose meals, the evening trip to the hospital. Then the bleak interval before sleep—voicelessly hissing prayers, finally shuddering into bewildered tears that gave no relief from the facts as they stood: I was going to be without my Mother soon. She was about to be subtracted from our family. From life.

Poor Mother.

Poor us.

Before very long, though, the emergency routine lost its emergency. Routine settled into just that. I fell asleep without the semisensate blubbering, woke, ate, went out to play. The fatigue I would later identify as the substrate of life's milestone events—a rawing of nerves that gives them all a similar and characteristic emotional flavor, whether tragic or celebratory: deaths, births, weddings, infidelities, important voyages all attended by wearing vigils, labors, preparations, arguments, broodings, complicated arrangements, and all sharing a tendency to occur at inconvenient hours—that weariness dissipated. Mother's dying became ordinary.

They rammed tubes up her nose. Hooked needles into her forearms. An IV bottle emptied into her as she dozed. I kept glancing at it as I might an hourglass. Seeing her like that was scary. Paul and I were taken to visit less frequently. Daddy's nightly departures after supper were hardly remarked, just a part of the new schedule. Our questions about Mother became sporadic. Daddy would shrug, and devise some laconic reply that fostered neither hope nor despair.

MiMi had come to stay in the guest room. I was allowed to overhear their dour conversations. They'd sit ill at ease, son-in-law and mother-in-law, politely anesthetizing themselves with bourbon in the intervals of domesticity that couldn't be avoided.

MiMi was a jowly woman, broad-bosomed and waistless but with Mother's pretty features in matronly caricature. Her fair complexion showed emotion as a flush, and her cheeks now seemed permanently rouged. Her eyes and eyelids were pink with engorging tears, yet she never broke down in front of us. She gave Paul and me our snacks when we came home from school, settled on the couch between us to fill a watercolor pad with odd, idiosyncratic automobiles and airplanes and horses and stick-figurish humans—subjects Paul and I eagerly proposed in order to admire the quirky, painstaking path of her pencil point. Like listening to Elmer tell war stories, watching MiMi draw had an effect on me as powerful and sedative as the hypnotist's proverbial swinging watch. After supper—which she cooked (even more rudimentarily than Mother) on days Lillie Mae hadn't preassembled a meal for reheating—she'd oversee our homework and dispatch us to bed in Daddy's absence. She'd have taken the bus to the hospital earlier, during the midday visiting hours.

MiMi had rushed North on semester break, and there was a question now as to how long she could remain away from the Sigma Alpha Epsilon house she was being paid to manage and chaperone. (It was SAE's purple-and-yellow pledge beanie that I would opt to don in college, though the grandmotherly legacy had long since been forgotten. When Dad reminded me, I realized with astonishment that the chapter she'd tended was the very seat of the fraternity's founding—revered "Mother Mu" herself. There, at the antebellum University of Alabama, a coterie of romantic dandies led by one magnificently if improbably named Noble Devotie had organized the adolescent secret society. An ill-advised mention of my claim to distinction earned me an extra fifty pushups during Hell Week. It was a petty harrassment I acceded to good-naturedly enough. But when one of my "brothers" flourished a paddle at me, I balked. There ensued an earnest two-hour discussion about my "attitude" in the chapter president's room. In the end, it seems, my tennis and my grades were sufficiently desirable that they overlooked my refusal to grovel. I lived in the fraternity house for three years—but somehow, from that moment, was always less than a noble devotee.)

Mother was "holding her own," Daddy could report—but the prognosis still had no immediate term. The breakthroughs in chemotherapy and associated treatments that have since dramatically prolonged the survival of adult acute lymphocytic leukemia patients were still decades away. We prayed for a telescoping of that span, whatever it might be—for some improbable but not unprecedented medical coup like Fleming's penicillin or Salk's vaccine, which a few years later would free children and parents from the annual summer scourge of polio cripplings. We prayed for a remission, one of those random, inexplicable wanings of the disease that, temporary or not, would reprieve us all and allow medical science more time to elaborate its practical miracles....

But God chose not to respond. One afternoon I was summoned from my classroom to the principal's office. I found Daddy waiting for me, with Paul. We were told to get our coats from our lockers. He drove us to Good Sam. GaGa was there. Daddy turned us over to her, to sit in the lobby. After a while MiMi shuffled through the swinging doors. Then Daddy returned and beckoned to Paul and me. We traversed the maze of corridors, the route by now familiar—past the cafeteria and lounge byways, the gurneys and wheeled tables clustered here and there against the walls like railcars on sidings. I didn't recognize Mother's room at first. There was a portable screen in front of the doorway. A few yards down the hall, another screen hid several metal-and-plastic chairs. Daddy told us to sit in them until he called us.

Nobody had spoken much, either on the ride over or in the hospital lobby. Even Paul seemed daunted by the gravity in the air. The adults' distracted faces, subtly discolored and misshapen, had silenced us too. Rigid as our chairs, sweating under our woolen school pullovers in the shaft of amber sun that slanted through the mulleted lens at the end of the corridor, we hardly glanced at each other.

Daddy came back after a few minutes. He stood over us and then slowly lowered himself into a squat. He put his right hand on my knee. He grasped Paul's shoulder with the other.

"Your Mother's sleeping," he said into Paul's eyes. "Doctors call it a coma. She maybe... sounds as if she's in pain, as if something's hurting her, but it isn't. Nothing's hurting her now. Nothing's going to any more. So don't be frightened. Don't worry. She can't see you or hear you, or talk to you. But I think she knows you're in there, somehow.

Her soul or... anyway, I don't know. But I just wanted... I felt you, Paul... Richard... even though you're still just children, I realize. And maybe I shouldn't... but she's.... This...."

His voice seemed to curdle in his throat. He pushed himself upright. His knees cracked. The pressure of his wobbly weight tipped me forward. The rear legs of my chair seesawed up and clattered down against the floor as I hopped to my feet to keep from falling.

Daddy didn't notice. He squeezed my arm. His viscous eyes and creased gray jaw and pulsing concave scar looked as stratospherically distant as the face of an angel peering out of the clouds at me, and almost as unfamiliar.

"Just quickly," he murmured, herding us before him. "Just quickly."

We edged past the screen and through the doorway into Mother's room. Still another rectangle of opaque fabric was stretched on a tubular frame within, perpendicular to the wall so as to curtain off the view of the bed from the corridor. Waiting down the hall, senses bristling, I'd been aware of some mysterious guttural rhythm underlying the hushed rumblings of hospital business. Now as I shuffled forward, Daddy's hand in the small of my back, I realized that the sound had been growing louder. That it came from inside this room, that it came....

I stepped past the last curtain. My breath—which had gone sharp and shallow as if I were in the throes of an asthma attack—seized. Paul trod on the back of my shoe. I stumbled ahead, allowing him to squeeze alongside me.

Death should be... what? Dramatic. Solemn. Noble. Or else terrible. Cataclysmic. Bone and tissue rent, blood spurting. Fulfillment of my movie fantasies.

This was neither. Just banal. Mother might as well have been drunk. She lay with her jaw slack, her hair unkempt, a few oily strands clinging damply to the margins of her sallow face. Tubes distended her nostrils. Her flesh was so colorless the pores stood out – as if her cheeks and nose were stippled with blackheads. The crescent of her upper teeth glinted rodent-like beneath her lip. The fine hairs at its corners seemed to have darkened into a mustache. Worst of all, she was snoring.

That was the sound. And now I heard the death in it. No longer was this torpid body the temple of a human presence. It was pure animal organism. The stricken, adenoidal croaks were simple reflex, crude cellular pertinacity about on a level with the last frenetic laps of a decapitated chicken. And even the reflex had lost its essential regularity. A child would have been arrested by, could have diagnosed, the mortal extremity in Mother's faltering stridor. I did. I presume Paul did too. I, we, ought to have erupted in shrieks of anguish. Howled out our grief and terror. Vomited, collapsed, fled a sight that would burn in our marrows forever—haunt, wrack, pervert our every effort to lead a normal future life....

But, of course, we didn't. We simply stood there. Looking. Feeling too much to feel much of anything. Already busily secreting whatever psychic nacre coats these irritants and renders them abidable—good vague stuff to dredge up later for psychiatrists or parody on the printed page. The determinants of all and the explanations of nothing....

After a few seconds Daddy turned us by the shoulders and steered us wordlessly into the hall again. A half-hour later we left. The bill had been squared, the arrangements completed. We plodded to the parking lot. Daddy drove. His hat brim was tugged low over eyes that smoldered in a face the color of his cigarette's ash. I devoted myself to a study of my manicure. I'd clipped the oblong nails so close they were almost perfect circles, like Elmer's. Paul sat in the back, cowering between MiMi and GaGa, who took turns acceding to stifled sobs.

Daddy poured them all drinks when we got home.

They sat in the living room trying to mumble comforts. Danny rang the doorbell and asked if I could come out. I told him my mother had just died. I felt apologetic, but at the same time slightly boastful. Danny looked unsure, and impressed.

"Yeah? Gee," he said.

I didn't feel like crying. The event was overwhelming. Besides, I'd already paid my quota of tears in anticipation. I was empty. And at loose ends. I went into the living room and told Daddy that Danny wanted me to go shoot baskets. Should I? I needed advice on propriety. Daddy said some people would be coming over soon. They'd be bringing food, supper. I should expect to be called in then; meanwhile I was free—in fact, he encouraged me, ought— to go amuse myself normally. Paul too.

"We gotta take Paul," I told Danny.

We dribbled and heaved the ball at the hoop in his rear driveway as dusk thickened and the light from his dining room window grew bright on the pavement. It gave us haloes—the vapor of our breaths, the steam rising off our bodies in the deepening chill. My fingers began to lose sensation. I started to wheeze. Danny's mother appeared in silhouette at the kitchen door and summoned him to dinner. Paul and I went home. The house was full of grave, solicitous people we sort of knew. They fed us, sent us upstairs to bathe. We got to skip homework. In the dark I heard the soft catches for air that meant Paul was crying.

"Paul?" I murmured. "It'll be okay." My own chest was tight. I hadn't the vaguest idea what the platitude I'd just voiced might signify.

"I don't want Mother to be dead!" Paul squeaked. "I want her to come back!"

"Yeah. Well, she isn't going to!" I snarled. The naiveté enraged me. It needed brutal stanching. "That's what dead means!"

His breath slushed through his nose. "I... know," he agreed.

I lay listening to the sounds of the house. People moving about softly downstairs, voices, the creak of Paul's bed. After a moment I rolled out from under my covers and darted across the rug.

"Move over," I hissed. I sidled in beside him.

## That was pretty much the extent of the solace we had to give each other, though.

It was a function of Newton's third law: a simple physical reassurance in the other's mass. Still there, providing its familiar gravitational push-pull. We were minor planetary clots, earth and moon numbly obeying the forces that whirled us through a system wrenched into chaos by the abrupt extinction of a central body.

Before whose cold crust we were marshaled to pray two days later at the funeral home. I couldn't have told you what emotions wrung Paul in the performance of that excruciating rite, though we edged together elbow to elbow in the arc of our elders. They stood behind us, heads bowed, hands limply folded, eyes trained sorrowfully on the freshly clipped napes of our necks and the scrubbed hollows behind our ears.

Paul's voice seemed to pipe up firm and on cue with Daddy's and GaGa's: "...Blessed art thou among women, and blessed is the fruit of thy womb...."

Episcopalian MiMi mumbled along out of ecumenical good grace. She was always a few telling, deliberate beats late, though. The prayers and a *pro forma* eulogy were intoned by Monsignor Carroll, the broad-minded cleric Daddy had found to wed him to his Protestant bride in the first place. Monsignor Carroll was a tall, elegant man with immaculately brushed white hair, a golfer's tan and a mellifluous voice in which the unavoidable bromides of religion, if never quite transubstantiated, at least came out in phrases that suggested they might afford some sort of intellectual purchase. He possessed all the social graces, a dry wit and a genuine ease with heathens that was unusual in a priest of that era and place. Daddy said it was this suspect quality that had probably stalled his career in mid-rise after a meteoric youthful ascent toward a bishopric, maybe even a cardinalship, someday. Perhaps it was just as well. He always looked great in his tailored cassock with its monsignor's scarlet piping and scarlet-pompomed berretta.

I suppose I chimed in audibly on the choruses too. I usually did what was expected of me. But my passive face masked an inner scowl—I could feel the muscle tension between my eyebrows. I had to force my voice up through my larynx. For some reason I didn't want to be saying these prayers.

In a few minutes we'd all file out to the cortege of elongated Cadillacs and Packards that would take us to St. Mary's for the requiem Mass. The men in dark suits Daddy had asked to be pallbearers would awkwardly muscle the closed casket out of the hearse like an oversized piece of luggage. They'd heft it to their shoulders, clutching its brass rails, and hump it down the center aisle. Knees quavering, they'd lower it to a skirt of flowers square with the red-and-blue rose window over the main altar. There'd be organ noodlings and crescendos, and Monsignor Carroll again in brocade vestments chanting Latin in that special off-key head register priests must learn in the seminary, or perhaps come to affect as a badge of their authority (the divine connection placing them above the demands of music just as the Hippocratic oath dispenses doctors from the mundane requirement that penmanship be legible).

Afterwards we'd resume the procession to Spring Grove cemetery. There'd be more somber trudging, more flowers, more prayers over the casket. Which would be balanced slightly out of plumb on the fresh brown dirt mounded alongside the neat pit carved among the gravestones under the Schubert family monument.

The latter was a limestone replica of Cleopatra's needle. German script was chiseled into panels at the base of each facet. The incising had weathered badly, but you could still make out a few patriarchal names and dates: "Georg Schubert, geboren nach Stuttgart 16 juli 1827, tot nach Cincinnati 4 oktober 1891.... Christian Schubert.... Thomas Jefferson Schubert...."

I knew the terrain well. Every month or so of my life we had come here after Sunday Mass to spike canisters of off-season flowers bought from a roadside greenhouse into the ivy beds below my grandfathers' headstones. The Kirkpatrick family plot was in a nearby annex, a less sylvan and less exclusive section of the huge, park-like burial ground. In that, at least, Daddy's family could boast social precedence. MiMi would eventually lie beside her husband. But their only child would nestle among her acquired relatives, these generations of German-growling, hasenpfeffer-gobbling, Republican-voting mid-American *petits bourgeois*.

When Monsignor Carroll had evoked the final pre-Mass "amen," Mr. Flaherty strode forward and reasserted his role as master of ceremonies.

"Would you boys," he commanded in a sonorous murmur, "like to come up now and give your mother a last kiss?"

No one had prepared me. Did Daddy have foreknowledge? Did he nudge me now? Or was I propelled forward by the engine of a lifetime's compliance with adult wishes? My repugnance was so instantaneous and overwhelming I almost fainted. Girls were the ones who fainted—suddenly slumped on pre-Communion empty stomachs into the space between the pews. A muffled thud, a hushed flurry of concern from those around them.... Boys knelt firm, no matter how awful they felt. I had to hold firm. Refusal was unthinkable. I was trapped, a prisoner of the sad good will oozing over me from this gantlet of onlookers. Somehow I found myself shuffling toward the casket in Paul's wake—a cynosure in this tiny, maudlin bit of funerary showbiz guaranteed to wring a sigh if not a tear from the most hardened observer.

But God, I didn't want to put my lips on that rubber doll! Even if Mr. Flaherty did insist it was my mother. It wasn't, it wasn't. It was empty, soulless—the most elementary tenet of the faith. Couldn't these people appreciate that? They were nibbling their lipstick and dabbing their mascara over an effigy. A tenuously preserved piece of statuary. Mother wasn't dead! She was just airy, insubstantial now—floating around in and out of us all, a vivacious memory, a vaguely mischievous mid-20th-century handmaiden of Mary up in some gauzy paradisiac Heaven. Formlessly lolling with the formless *basso profundo* Father and His benign, bearded Son and the inexplicable, ghostly pigeon that completed the Trinity. The images, of course, were nebulous. All I knew was that to kiss the corpse would be to deny them. To acknowledge in some hideous way that this carcass was still Mother—about to be consigned to the stifling dirt, to bloat and suppurate and churn with maggots.

Not that such macabre images took shape in my head either. They couldn't be allowed to. I believed in the ineffable. That required all the protective will I could muster against the subtle, shameful power of the carnal, the material....

I watched Paul rise on tiptoe and bend over the casket. No particular dread or dismay seemed to convulse him. He straightened and returned toward Daddy.

I stepped forward. Mother's rigid shell lay waiting

my homage. The eyelids were tucked shut over the immobile lumps of cornea. The frozen, pasteled lips were molded up at the corners in an expression of vague complacence. I remembered her sitting behind the wheel of the Pontiac one afternoon as we drove home with our groceries from Kroger's. She was quizzing Paul, who was then in kindergarten, on the distinction between animate and inanimate. We liked to play these educational games.

"Rock," she proposed.

"No, a rock's not alive," Paul declared.

"Cow."

"Yeah, a cow's alive," he nodded.

"An ant?"

"Alive, of course!" he chortled, smug in his five-year-old acuity.

"How about a car?" I chimed in.

"Not alive," he snapped.

"What," Mother prompted, "makes us think of something as alive or not alive?"

"Well, if it moves," Paul suggested.

"A car moves," I pointed out—the sophist inserting the logical catch.

"Yeah. But... it has to move all by itself, sort of, huh?"

"A car's got an engine," I muttered.

"What about a tree?" Mother smiled. "Is a tree alive?"

Paul frowned and chuckled, engaged by the proliferating complications of the world....

I swallowed for courage and leaned into the white maw of the open coffin. I prickled with jeopardy, as if the top might clamshell shut to swallow me. I pecked at the cold vinyl cheek. The sensation sizzled from my lips down my spine. Like a bolt of electricity, it scalded me of the last trace of emotion.

Mr. Flaherty's limousine driver had a crewcut I admired. And his stubby, gnawed fingernails fascinated me.

As people gathered for the post-funeral brunch, I went into the bathroom and clipped mine again. So close they bled. Then, wincing, I scrubbed them with a brush. Afterwards I wandered into the backyard and idly hauled myself up the wooden rungs nailed to the trunk of the weeping willow. In its fork Danny and Paul and I had built a treehouse. It was just a snaggle of weathered planks held in place by a few bent nails and idiosyncratically knotted ropes. I scrambled out onto it and sat hugging my knees. I stared through the scrim of branches at the brown Henke's hills. They were covered with skeletal winter trees. The boughs of the willow drooping around me were brittle and leafless too. But here and there an embryonic sliver of green peeped from a bud.

Dead but alive. Spring would bring resurrection to the trees.

# 4

## It was past 4:30 before a court came open, so I didn't get in much tennis.

Daddy had cleared away his papers and Paul was setting the table by the time I banged in. GaGa had made sauerbraten. We polished it off with dispatch.

Mother and Daddy used to linger at the table sipping coffee after we'd finished the packaged pudding or Jell-O that was our weekday dessert, if any. Every so often I'd even stay there with them, listening unobtrusively. By tacit agreement, cocktail hour was Mother's to recount the neighborhood gossip she'd picked up that day, to evoke sympathy for the stresses our squabbling and negligence and crabapple-pitching had provoked, and to confer Daddy's share of pride in his sons' moments of achievement. The postprandial lull was Daddy's forum, in turn, to recite tribulations: the motion denied by a judge too partisan or senile to recognize its manifest logic, the convolutions and follies that were begetting draft after draft of some testy or penurious client's will....

Tribulations certainly seemed to be the depressive order of his everyday day. But now and then there were leavenings. Like the whiplash case.

"Can't hike m'arm up no higher 'n this since th' accident," the plaintiff whined. Daddy was representing the insurance company at the deposition.

"How high could you raise it before?" Daddy inquired.

"Oh, before," gushed the hillbilly litigant with a nimble gesture, "I could lift it this high!"

Years later, startled to encounter a variant of the same tale from a different source, I realized it must be some hoary bit of law school apocrypha. But in my first hearing the sly triumph was Daddy's own, and whether he claimed it or not, my pride in his cleverness has never been so shaken as to fully discount the possibility. Perhaps he was indeed the protagonist in a real-life Cincinnati enactment — although more probably it was simply I who suffered a childhood confusion.

Since Mother's death our evening meals had become perfunctory. Daddy's appetite, modest at best, had dwindled to near nonexistence. Bourbon and lunch at the Cincinnati Club or Wheel must have furnished most of his calories. GaGa was a quick and nervous eater, a compulsive progressor from *tsk* to task, who had grown accustomed to the efficient feedings of those who live alone. Paul and I, of course, were usually itchy to inhale our sustenance, earn whatever sugars constituted dessert and flee to play. So these exercises in altered familiality tended to be shallow and pretty brief.

It was still only a quarter to seven when Paul and I had cleared the plates and distributed the evidence of our mess in greasy whorls across the table surface.

"It's all done, GaGa," we assured her as we tossed the filthy washrag into the soapsuds and nested the last cups at her elbow. Daddy had installed a dishwasher, needless to say. But GaGa was a traditionalist. She preferred to douse and scour everything first before entrusting it to dubious technology.

"I'm gonna go down to the Mt. Lookout with Danny," I informed her.

"Talk to your father," she advised me.

"Can I sleep over at Trey's house?" piped Paul. "He invited me."

"It's up to your father," GaGa repeated with a shrug of her old lady's humped shoulders. Only in his absence did she assume authority. Because of this reluctance, I begrudged her the power to permit me my designs. I always stated my intentions, never tendered them to her with a question mark. Not that I wouldn't acquiesce to her provisional judgment when appeal to Daddy wasn't feasible. And while she had plenty of opinions about how we should behave and be reared to behave — I'd overheard sharp conversations on the subject between peevish mother and morosely defensive son — she seldom forgot herself enough to rule when divisive challenge was a possibility.

Daddy said I could go to the movie. It was *Cyrano de Bergerac*. I'd seen it once before already, in first run at the palatial Keith's in Fountain Square. I'm not sure which had exhilarated me more, the film's bravura swordplay or its florid wordplay. It was the first time in my life I'd sensed with such immediacy the presence and power of literature.

I'd gone with Billy Gerlach — he was a year older, already then a high school freshman, and the one who'd insisted on the choice despite my lack of enthusiasm. Perhaps it was his unabashed delight in the Rostand bombast, sugar-coated by Jose Ferrer's swagger and extravagant rubber nose, that primed my own receptivity. Billy's mature endorsement permitted me to enjoy poetic dialogue too. (A little later the re-release of Olivier's Henry V — flights of arrows over Agincourt, knights in armor so ponderous they had to be winched aboard their horses, a pretty French princess whose English anatomy lesson expanded my repertoire of *Alouette* verses — would open my eyes and ears to still another literary weight class.)

I'd told Danny how great the movie was, emphasizing the duels and cannonades. When I'd declined his pool invitation earlier, I'd suggested that he and Glenn come with me to see it tonight, if my Dad would let me. Danny's relationship to Glenn was like mine to Billy—we were Four Musketeers, but abreast, not in a circle, Danny and I united in the middle. Billy had left the week before to be an apprentice counselor at a camp in Michigan.

I'd dialed Danny's number hastily after getting the okay, but his mother had told me he and Glenn were already gone. That annoyed me. They hadn't even bothered to call first to see whether I'd be able to join them. Cracks were beginning to open in the tight palship Danny and I had enjoyed since the day five years earlier when he and Billy had appeared at our door to introduce themselves to Mother and ask if I could come out to play. The moving van was still disgorging our furniture.

"Ricky! There are a couple of boys here who'd like to play with you," Mother had called. I was cowering in a corner of the menacingly bare, strange-smelling, alien space I'd just been told was to be my new room. She harried me outside into their intimidating company against all my sulky instincts. The cell at least offered safety; who knew what wantonness the local cons and the yard might harbor? And of course I'd been wrong.

Except about Glenn. He was considerably smaller, a bantam by any standard, and the short-changing seemed to rankle. Maybe he was jealous at my materialization in the neighborhood. I'd never up to then encountered such bristling aggression. He shoved me to the ground the first time we met, and chased me home every day for a week after. Finally Mother observed what was going on.

"Why do you run from Glenn?" she asked.

I sat panting on my bed, rubber-lipped, struggling to regain nonchalance.

"He says he's going to fight me. He says he's going to punch me," I muttered.

"But you're bigger than he is," she pointed out.

"He doesn't care. He'll hit me anyway."

"Well, then maybe you'll have to hit him back."

"But I don't *want* to fight him!" I complained.

"I know that, honey," she nodded. "I'm glad you don't want to fight. But sometimes people have to. Or at least they have to be willing to fight, to stand up for their rights. Do you like it when he makes you scamper inside and hide from him? On a nice afternoon like this?"

"Of course not," I sniveled. At least, I thought proudly, I could use adult expressions.

"Then next time don't," she suggested.

"But then he'll punch me!" I protested.

"All right then. What'll you do if he does? You're bigger than Glenn, aren't you? Stronger? For goodness sake! Show me a muscle."

"Mmm...," I conceded—self-conscious, pleased, temporizing.

"Come on, show me a muscle," she insisted.

Reluctantly I crooked my arm and clenched my fist.

Daddy's biceps always hopped up oblong and lumpy as a darning egg inside a sock. Elmer's right arm bulged like Popeye's. Mother squeezed my hopeful imitation through my school uniform blue sweater. Her grasp tickled. I wriggled loose with a snicker.

"That's a *good* muscle," she declared.

"If I fight him," I mumbled, resenting the grin she'd almost relaxed me into, "I'll get my clothes dirty."

"Well. If you tell me that's how they got dirty," she countered, "I won't scold you. That does seem to be a rather newfound concern, though, sweetie. And in fact if you do resist the urge to turn tail the first time he looks cross-eyed at you, he may very well think twice about wanting to take you on."

"Huh?"

"Cowards... I mean, people who're afraid to stick up for themselves, people who always run away... well, they may think that's the way to avoid a fight and keep safe, but it's usually just the opposite. That kind of behavior tends to bring out the bully in others. I think now that Glenn knows he's got you buffaloed, he's going to test his power over you every chance he gets. The only way you're going to be able to break the cycle is to stand up to him. And when you do, Ricky, I think maybe you and he will be friends.

"He's a dummy," I snorted. "I hate him."

"Right now you do," she agreed. "Because he's making you ashamed of yourself. But there's absolutely no reason for you to be afraid of anybody. Anybody even halfway close to your own size. Which is about all Glenn is, you know." She smiled.

I pictured Glenn. She was right. Scrawny, red-haired, freckled... the classic Our Gang runt.

"I'm not!" I objected. "It's not *him* I'm scared of."

"Well then, what is it? Why do you run away?"

I examined the scuffs on my box-toed leather

bluchers. I shrugged.

"Hm. Darn it, anyway," she said. "Your Daddy's probably the one who ought to be talking to y'all about this stuff. But...." She sighed. "Here. Let's see you make a fist. Come on, make a fist."

I tucked my thumb under the fingers of my left hand. It was a protective convention that something as daunting and formal as an acknowledged "fight" demanded, I imagined.

"No, no," Mother frowned. She pried my thumb loose and recast the fist more naturally. "You'll hurt yourself that way. You'll hurt your thumb or your fingers. And you can't hit hard that way. This...." She caressed the top ridge of knuckles. "...This is what you want to use. See?"

She placed her own cool fist against my cheek in demonstration. I leaned away and slouched glumly, head canted.

She considered me. "Now is that really how you'd stand if Glenn or somebody told you they were about to punch you?"

"Mmm-mm."

"Excuse me?"

"I 'n know."

"No," she said. "You wouldn't. You'd stand like this."

She knelt in front of me and tugged my legs apart. She gave me a second's appraisal.

"Okay, no," she decided, "the other way. 'Cuz you're right-handed."

She grasped my ankles and rearranged my stance, left foot forward, right planted slightly behind—straddling my center of gravity. "Okay? But not so stiff," she counseled. "Feel yourself balanced. Loose."

I remained rigid, arms dangling.

She flicked the brown hair that had fallen over her forehead and made a wry face. "Anyway.... Now put up your dukes."

"Huh?"

"Look, wait a minute here," she said. Her finger shot out and poked my breastbone.

I stumbled backwards.

"You call that ready? Now get yourself ready. Here."

Once again she molded me into something resembling a fighting pose. This time she cocked my arms up, elbows out, fists in front of my face.

"That's better. See? Now you can protect yourself. That's the way boxers do it, right? Haven't you seen pictures of them, in the newspaper? Joe Louis? That's so if somebody tries to punch you, you can block it. Like this...."

She manipulated my forearm with one hand to ward off a slow-motion poke with her other. "See? Or if they're aiming down here...." She reached toward my stomach but deflected the probe by steering my elbow in tight against my ribs. "See? That's the idea. Now, what are you going to do back?"

"What do you mean?"

"Are you just going to stand there? If somebody's trying to hit you?"

"I don't know," I mumbled. I did know the right answer probably wasn't the one I'd immediately thought of.

"Sure you do."

"I guess... like this," I said. I rocked onto my rear leg and hiked my toe tentatively into the space between us. Instinct suggested a sharp kick was the least vulnerable way to keep an assailant out of range of my face.

"No!" she snapped. "No. Don't do that. That's dirty. Dirty fighting. Men don't kick. At least... well, gentlemen don't. Not in a fair fight. An even match. Or close to even. It's okay to punch or wrestle, but not to kick. Or for that matter to scratch or bite. Or pull hair."

Those seemed like useful suggestions for defending

oneself, but I'd been cautioned against employing them since kindergarten.

"That's the way girls fight," I observed snidely.

"Well, I suppose sometimes," Mother allowed. "If they don't know any better."

"What if a girl...?"

"Not," Mother interrupted, "that girls who are ladies *ever* fight. And gentlemen never hit ladies, do they? Especially at your age," she added, "when the girls may be bigger." She grinned at me. "There *are* occasions when discretion is the better part of valor."

"Please?"

"Never mind. We're getting off the track here. Our immediate problem is Glenn, isn't it? And what you're going to do the next time he says he's going to hit you. What *are* you going to do? Run home again?"

"No, Mother."

"Are you going to let him chase you over hill and dale?"

"No, Mother."

"Why?"

"Why? Because... I don't know. What do you mean?"

"Because you're a big, strong boy. A capable young man. Because you're not afraid to defend yourself. Because you know *how* to... more or less," she added in an undertone. "Isn't that right?"

"Mm-hm."

I raised my fists and tucked my nose against my thumb, hoping to please her. I wasn't happy.

"You don't look so sure."

I peered over my knuckles at the curtained window off to the side, at the little Chinoiserie chest of drawers beneath it, at the rumpled white anchor embroidered in the center of my blue bedspread. I tried not to imagine Glenn's blows thumping in through these feeble buffers.

"Okay. Let's just see how hard you can punch," Mother said. "Show me."


## Punch!

Through infancy in GaGa's dimly remembered Clifton duplex, where Mother and Daddy and I had lived until Paul was born... through age five and six, riding wagons and swinging with neighborhood playmates in the weedy backyard of the bungalow Daddy had rented until just after V-J Day... through kindergarten and first and second grade recesses under the sentinel nurture of the Ursuline nuns... never in all those years could I remember having punctuated a squabble, no matter how loud and bitter, with the sharp, closed-hand gesture described by that word.

A punch.

Why not? I guess I was on balance pacific. Introverted. And so assured of my pet status among family and teachers that regal aplomb had become my normal mien. Timidity and self-sufficiency fed each other, so that withdrawal from the odd playground flare-up of hostility or jealousy didn't even feel like cowardice. Just good sense. Daddy even used to recite, in grinny singsong doggerel: "He who fights and runs away, lives to fight another day." And of course, I was fortunate enough to be surrounded by a lot of nice, polite little homogenized facsimiles. If there were any schoolyard Glenns, their impulses had been restrained by the watchful ubiquity of the black-and-whites.

I flapped my arm out lamely.

"Come on," Mother chided. "That's not a punch."

"I don't know how to," I whined.

And indeed, there was the essence: I'd never felt the motion. Never felt the result. I was terribly worried about the blinding, disorienting anger I imagined I'd have to indulge to trigger such a violent act. And at the same time I was apprehensive that I couldn't do it violently enough—that my own tentative, uncoordinated spasms would only produce feeble pats, useless at warding off an assailant's swarming, seasoned determination to hurt me.

"Well, *I* think you do," she said quietly. "It's not particularly difficult. Is it really? Maybe all you need is a little practice. What do they call it? Sparring? You need sparring practice. Here, you get yourself ready again. Make a fist, a good hard fist. Both hands. And now arms up. Right? Head tucked down a little bit, into your shoulders. Like so. That's good. And now bounce up and down. On your toes. Just kind of relaxed and easy. See? That's great!"

I tried to do as she bade me. I felt clumsy and heavy-footed, like some unwieldy, lumpish marionette.

"Great," she nevertheless approved. "Now. Let's see you sock me. Right here."

She tilted her dimpled chin up and jutted it forward. She tapped the central indentation with her finger. She was on her knees, eyes level with mine.

"Punch me right in the jaw," she commanded.

"Oh, Mother...." I wailed.

"No, really. Right here."

"But...."

"I want to see what kind of muscle you've got in that punch of yours. Give me a good sock."

"As hard as I can?"

"Sure," she said. She knitted her eyebrows resolutely, clamped her teeth and beckoned with more taps on the target.

I gathered my eight-year-old main obediently. But I was still hesitant. "Won't it hurt?" I worried.

"I don't know," she replied archly. "Will it? That's what we want to find out. Don't we?"

"It... probably might," I nodded.

"Yes, as a matter of fact I don't have a doubt in the world it will," she agreed. "See? You know perfectly well you have a good hard punch. Now all you've got to do is persuade yourself to use it. When you have to. And only when you have to. I tell you what, Ricky. You just try hitting me about half as hard as you think you'd have to hit Glenn if he still insists on fighting with you. Okay? Right here."

Uncertain, I drew my arm back. "Really?"

"Well, um.... *Half* as hard, though," she reminded me.

I searched her eyes for final approval. It seemed to be there. So with an abrupt, numb, dutiful release of constraint, I let fly.

Mother was gritty. She didn't dodge or flinch. The clack of bone on bone merged with her gasp. Her head snapped back.

"Owww!" she gasped, eyes wide. She clamped her hand to her mouth. "My goodness! Oh, ouch!"

Then she began to laugh. Although there was a quality in it of the whimper transformed.

"Hey, buddy," she said. "Didn't I tell you to take it easy?"

"I *did!*" I yelped. *"Really!"*

"Boy, that's some roll of dimes you've got hidden in there. I'd hate to feel what it's like if you were swinging full out."

"I don't have any dimes...."

"I know," she nodded, rubbing her chin.

"Oh, gee, oh, gee," I keened, grimacing at mother's distress and the residual sensation in my knuckles—pain that was not really a pain. I kneaded my hand.

"I'm sorry. Did I really hurt you, Mother? I *knew* it! I *knew* I would. I didn't *mean* to!"

"Let's just say I can sure feel it," she grinned. She

massaged the crest of her jawbone. "But I'll be okay, Ricky. Don't worry. Hey, I mean it. Don't worry. And see? Didn't I tell you you've got plenty of muscle? What in the world, what in the *world* are you doing letting a little pipsqueak like Glenn Colnett send you high-tailin' home every afternoon? Huh? Now can you tell me that?"

Not anymore, I couldn't. Flush with new assurance, I lavished manly succor on the mother, the adult, the inspiriter and victim of my unsuspected strength. When she asked me to kiss the bruise, I indulged her jaunty enough to get pleasure myself from the joking reversal of our baby-medicine.

Mother's chin and temples ached for a week, she complained.

"Serves you right," Daddy laughed at her. "You must be a masochist."

"Just a good mother," she huffed.

"I guess there's not that much difference, is there?" he nodded.

She'd doped out Glenn accurately, too. Next afternoon he darted at me from his yard, as usual. Instead of taking to my heels, I squared around. He skidded to a halt.

"Better get out of here, sissy," he snarled. "I'm gonna beat you up."

"I can walk wherever I want to," I replied. "It's a free country."

The words came out in a squeaky quaver. I was scared, no question, but resolute in my defiance. I was confident now of the secret force I could draw on if necessary. My fists, clenched at my hips, felt swollen to the size of Ezzard Charles'. What's more, I had the law behind me.

"This is a public sidewalk," I informed Glenn righteously.

"It is not!" he squawked. "That's stupid. It's *my* sidewalk. It's in front of *my* house."

"Well, for your information, if you're so smart," I corrected him, "that still doesn't mean it's yours. It belongs to the city. And I'm part of the city too. My Daddy told me, and he's a *lawyer*. *All* sidewalks," I declared with a superior inflection, "are perfectly public."

Glenn scowled uncertainly. He eyed me for a moment, pondering. "Maybe so," he finally muttered. "But you're not allowed to step on our *grass* here. That's for sure." He toed the boundary edge of his worn and patchy front lawn.

"Who wants to anyway?" I sniffed.

"You just better not," he warned.

"I could if I wanted to, and you couldn't stop me," I maintained. "'Cuz I'm bigger than you. But I don't want to, so you don't have to worry."

Glenn retreated a couple of steps into the square of crabgrass that was his acknowledged domain. He picked up a football.

"I could call the police on you if you did," he said. "And they'd arrest you. They'd put you in the workhouse. The only way you can come into *my* yard is if I invite you."

He spun the football tentatively. "But you could stand out there and play catch with me. If you want to. Wanna?"

I'd just been sent home from my new friend Brian's house. It was time for him to do his homework. The November light was fading. A single amber stripe low on the western sky gave a temporary vibrance to the dull brown leaf-scraps still fringing the trees. I'd be called in soon, and so would Glenn, probably. I shrugged. "Okay," I agreed.

He flung a tight spiral at me, harder than I'd expected from so close. A test shot. With a deft hop and twist I cradled it into my skinny chest.

It was a preview of our future roles. Though I'd never play more than intramural flag-football, I would always be an end or defensive back—the sure-handed workhorse receiver and interceptor for the Interfraternity Cup runners-up two years in a row, no less. And as to Glenn, his belligerence and slingshot arm would shape him into a good, feisty little quarterback. A star quarterback, actually.

There's an irony here, too. Somehow I think I always had more fundamental self-confidence than Glenn ever enjoyed. At least as a child. His bravado was a veneer—an arrogant face shown to the world out of resentment, and to forestall the dangers the world poses to the smaller and the weaker. Compensation. Yet he was able to draw on it, reinforce it. He would become the starting quarterback on his high school team as a sophomore (his family had moved away the year before, back to Huntington) and go on to a solid performance at the University of West Virginia (where the limelight was usurped by a phenomon in a different sport, Jerry West). Too short at five-nine to be considered seriously by the NFL, he tried out in Canada and spent three seasons as a backup and occasional starter with Winnipeg. Hardly superstardom. But it's a level of achievement only a handful of North America's aspiring jocks can ever boast. And it certainly contrasts with my own irresolute athletic path, beginning from a privileged base of supposedly superior psychological and physical gifts.

I found my friends, after a tour up and down the Mt. Lookout Theater's canted aisles, in a middle row. There was an empty seat beside Danny. They'd expected me after all. I squirmed between the banks of heaving knees and recoiling shoulders and plopped down just as the flickering gloom brightened into color.

"Hey, where you been?" Danny hissed.

"How come you didn't call me?" I complained.

"I thought it was set."

"Anyway," I said, "I got here in time for the Selected Short Subjects. Huh, Glenn?"

He took his eyes off the screen. "'Say, Rick," he

nodded.

I leaned across Danny and extended the open box of *Good N' Plenties* I'd just bought. "I was telling Danny I always try to get here for the Selected Short Subjects," I told him, "'cause I figure one of these days you're gonna be the subject they select."

"Har-har. That's really pathetic, Schubert," he replied with a mocking grin. He snatched the candy box out of my hand. "If I had your sense of humor I'd commit Harry Carey."

"Shh!" someone grumbled imperiously from the row behind.

Danny ripped off a loud, defiant fart in response.

"Oough! Yaaach!" Glenn and I groaned. We pinched our nostrils and writhed away from him in gleeful disgust.

## Danny lived at the top of our "No Outlet" nub of a street, whimsically dubbed by its developer Nirvana Court.

His house was actually around the corner on Grace Avenue. (In a few years I'd find it amusing that Nirvana could only be reached by Grace.)

We walked home together after the movie and waved goodbye at his porch. Then I trudged half a block further up the ridge, snuck between two houses and ducked through a backyard hedge into the long vacant lot I called "the shortcut."

A trek through its brambles would bring me out at the dead-end of Nirvana. During the two or three storms a year that were cold enough for snow to stick to the ground (Cincinnati winters were mild throughout my childhood), this was the launching ramp for a sled-run that leveled out a few hundred feet below, in front of our house.

An irascible elderly neighbor had cultivated a patch of the vacant strip as an extension of her vegetable garden. She was a kind of living scarecrow whose straw-hatted apparitions from behind her cornstalks, screeching witch's invective, had frightened us out of playing there much. So the place had associations with trespass and risk. Beyond that, there was something disturbing in its dereliction: jewels of bottle-glass in the dust, a jagged can-top here, a shred of old newspaper there—so stiff and yellow you figured it had to have been peed on by the stray dogs that trampled aimless paths among the clumps of brittle ragweed.

Henke's, rising on the other side of Linden below us, was noble wilderness. Even the most neglected of our yards bespoke order and possession. But in the lot, at night—hardly a glimmer of backwindow-light visible from the bordering houses sheltered behind tall fences and black silhouetted trees—one felt intimations of abandonment, rejection, ill-fate. It wasn't until about a year earlier that I'd mustered the nerve to negotiate this eerie no-man's land in the dark. And still it was something of a test of courage. Especially after any kind of scary movie, when the bogies from the screen had had time to filter out into the world and secret themselves in the shadows I had to ford. In fact, I believe my graduation into the fellowship of pure reason probably occurred the night I forced myself across that lot after seeing *The Thing*.

As a matter of fact, Cyrano had been jumped by would-be assassins in the night. But somehow this evening I harbored no dread of similar ambuscade by rapier-wielding louts in knickers and plumed hats. Fortunately, my post-cinema phobias tended to the literal. (Malevolent vegetables from Outer Space could never be discounted entirely.)

Even at ten o'clock the air was oleaginous with heat. The humidity was its routine ninety-eight percent, no doubt. But not a cloud obscured the sky. The broad avenue overhead, framed by the rustling black crowns of the trees, was pellucid, a smear of stars. There was no wind. The leaves seemed to be breathing, though—still exhaling sticky vapor. Crickets and katydids chirruped raucously. Was it a seventh year? Actually, they seemed to come more frequently than that, those late-summer mornings when we'd find the crisp locust-husks, backs split open but otherwise uncannily perfect insect vestiges, crouched vacant around the trunk of the weeping willow.

Whatever, the night was a commotion. Ragged snowflakes of phosphorescence swirled above the weeds. I made out a tiny, hovering presence within reach and snatched at it. The hollow of my fist glowed dial-green for an instant. I peeked at the tickle of insect inside. Its antennae wigwagged busily and its abdomen lit desultorily. It seemed stolid, nevertheless, totally unfazed by this abrupt landfall. I flattened my palm like the deck of an aircraft carrier. The lightning bug refused to taxi. After a second I blew. It spread its carapace—black rimmed in gold, Navy nightfighter colors indeed—and buzzed aloft, struggling for altitude with the ponderous grace of a blimp, or an autigiro.

A linear motion suddenly registered somewhere high and peripheral. The stars were fixed, the lightning bugs in random molecular dance. I glanced up hastily, but as usual too late to really say I'd seen the evanescent, slanting trail. It was always Mother who'd gasp and try to nudge my attention into the right quadrant. "Look, a shooting star," she'd whisper. But I almost never saw them. I guess I wasn't patient enough.

Mother had taught me to identify the elementary constellations: Orion of the three-jeweled belt and dangling sword; Casseopoeia's sagging M (or toppled W) of a couch (the queen must be overweight, we giggled); the angular Dipper with its bent handle. The mythological references and the pure joy of taxonomy were what engaged Mother.

She did, however—anticipating the Boy Scouts—show me how to track from the two ladle-front lodestars to Polaris.

From then on I'd had the habit, more or less automatic, of orienting myself whenever I stared up at a clear expanse of night. Now, neck craned far back, mouth agape, I pirouetted and groped across the celestial map until my index finger locked on the North Star.

I flung my left arm behind me. South. I lined up my shoulders, a human compass. Head straight, I was gazing west. West... through the stand of buckeyes and Indian cigar trees at the far axis of the lot, through the invisible bulk of the colonial brick house facing Sexton, the next street over... across Hyde Park and the seven, so they said, hills of Cincinnati—the spires of Mt. Adams, the tracts of Price Hill (where everybody talked with a funny nasality, swallowed syllables and distorted their vowels: "bi'ness," "crick")... across the serpentine loops of the Ohio, under William Henry Harrison's bluff-top tomb... to the limestone hollers of Indiana.

This, come to think of it, was the first summer in five that Daddy hadn't taken us there. Half a day of boredom squirming in the back seat of the Pontiac on winding roads through hamlets with bullet-riddled sign-names that Mother and Daddy always called our attention to, chortling: Bean Blossom, Gnaw Bone, Stony Lonesome. Then a week of Hoosier lodge meals at Brown County or McCormick's Creek state parks, birdwalks, community sings, evening square dances whose jolly familiality was what seemed to attract my parents in principle, but which they almost always avoided in practice. Paul and I did eventually enjoy ourselves, though. Once we'd overcome our first four or five days of shyness.

Past central Indiana it was all *terra incognita*. Years of Red Ryder comics and Saturday matinees in Republic Technicolor, patchwork Mercator projections tacked above blackboards and the lyrics of one patriotic song had nevertheless painted a vivid geography in my imagination. My face tingled to it, as if my puny flesh were actually subject to the gravitational force exerted by that romantic Western immmensity out there. I could picture it—horizon upon horizon of waving amber grain, the Rockies' purple majesty jutting snow-capped above the orchards of the fruited plains. From there it was cowboys and Injuns, heaving broncos, scarlet mesas, Arizona cactus and the citrus-bearing palm trees of Los Angeles. Someday, someday I was going to see it all for myself.

There were no streetlamps on Nirvana. Downtown was far away and, except for the Carew Tower, modestly low-rise. Linden Road, the closest urban light source, threaded a ravine. The night was moonless. The only sound was the incessant cheep of the crickets—and now and then a tinny, attenuated gabble that hinted of a radio or television set playing behind some distant window-screen. Maybe that was what touched off the sudden pang of isolation. I was alone in the middle of an unkempt field, in the middle of a somnolent, indifferent neighborhood, in the remote middle of a yawning enormity of continent, islanded by the vast seas of this...

...Of this infinitesimal planet. The scale abruptly telescoped. As dizzy as if I were physically enveloped in some cosmic cinematic reverse zoom, I felt myself contracting. My mind's camera slewed up and out, rocketed into space— deeper and deeper into the limitless reaches of the glistening firmament overhead.

A few seconds ago I'd been a colossus carelessly commanding the fate of the lightning bug. Now I'd shriveled. We were both mere motes, rudimentary pricks of consciousness closer to equal than not—quasi-invisibilities marooned on a fleck of planetary lint spinning adrift in the unencompassable universe.

No. Amend that. The mind of God encompassed it. God the Creator, source and sustenance of everything. So huge He was huger than infinity—a word I loved to bandy, but a concept I couldn't toy with long before a perplexed chuckle snapped its spell. Infinity. God was necessarily infinite Himself, too. Spirit beyond all spirit, insubstantial yet the author and embodiment of all this starry substance. I had to blot out the dumb Michaelangelesque image that kindled on the heavenly screen. Even at thirteen, in the presence of such celestial extravagance, I was uneasy about the old simple anthropomorphism. Baby stuff. The God responsible for this array, these solar systems unto solar systems, couldn't even *have* a face, I understood. No body, no beard, no robes, no form.... Besides, He—She, It too, then, whoo!—was supposed to be a trinity. You had to believe that or you weren't a Catholic! Three in one: Father, Son, Holy Ghost—immanent natures, distinct yet indistinct. And not really what the names signified, either. Just looking up, you knew you weren't dealing with some old guy, a bearded carpenter and a bird. Still, Jesus was part of it. At the same time man like me, human, *and* God. However you were expected to fit all that together. The paradoxes of the faith resisted the grip of my feeble brain.

The stars burned with an incandescence and a profligacy that made the patterns of the constellations difficult to distinguish. I wasn't able to find Orion, even. (Not that I should have. The hunter trots the rim of the northern hemisphere in summer.) But that made it all the easier to lose myself in the awesome anonymity of the Milky Way.

**I remembered one night walking hand in hand with Mother across the damp meadow between the Abe Martin Lodge and our own little cabin at Brown County.**

We'd been staring up, hoping to catch a streak of falling meteorite.

"Gee, Mother," I'd finally said. "How many stars do you think there are, anyway?"

"Well, I suppose you could try counting them," she'd replied.

So for ten minutes or so I'd lingered there, methodically poking at the sky and rattling off numbers. I'd appreciated almost at once, of course, the futility of the task. But I was taunting her with my stubborn literalness. And taking pleasure in sequence itself.

"...Ninety-eight, ninety-nine, one hundred. A hundred and one...." I wanted to hear what it was like—and show off—if I forged correctly through the nine-hundred-nineties to one thousand. I even entertained the fantasy of chanting to a million. Needless to say, Mother's patience expired well before my ambition.

"Good luck, honey," she'd finally announced after I'd ignored two or three gentle urgings to yield. "I'll be back in the morning to see how you came out."

She'd blown me a kiss, spun on her heel. I still had a clear image of what she'd been wearing that night: brown-and-white saddle shoes, white cotton socks rolled at the ankles, a plaid skirt and white blouse, a cardigan draped over her shoulders against the chill that percolated out of the turf and the pines.

I could still picture her dwindling into the darkness as I stood my increasingly nervous ground—tenaciously lipping the cadence and stabbing my finger at the sky, though of course I'd hopelessly lost any approximation of place. A moment later some hiss of ogres in the surrounding woods sent me panting off in her dew-tracks. I could remember the whole little episode.

What resisted recall, I suddenly realized, was her face.

Mother's face! Why couldn't I see it? If I concentrated, her clothing presented itself in almost mocking detail. Fuzzballs dotting the sleeve of her tan sweater. ESK monogrammed in fine parallel pastel stitches on her blouse. Strings of tiny holes punched around the margins of the brown leather saddles on her shoes. Even the shape of the hand that enfolded mine gave me no trouble: nails clean and trim, filed with an emeryboard into gentle points. The third finger oddly longer than the first, just as her second toe projected further than the big one. Both were signs of nobility, she wryly informed us. Especially the latter, a characteristic she and I shared, she showed me, with classic Greek statuary. But for all that, I couldn't triangulate to her facial features.

Oh, I had a vague sense of them, of their presence  a snub nose, mouth, eyes, cheeks, forehead, chin. Yes indeed. The full human complement. I could even, based on the traditional conversations by which children and parents compare and observe the operations of genetics, assign specific attributes to certain of them: "pug" (mine was beaky and bridgeless, like Discobulos and Daddy); "blue" (mine were his too, hazel); "dimpled" (my smooth childish flesh, on the contrary, was now beginning to sprout its first angry, pustular adolescent convexities).

When I strained to see her, I had a general impression of radiated benevolence. Maternal femininity, love.... But the harder I worked, the more resolutely my mother's face refused to solidify as an image.

For a desperate instant I tried to remember how she'd

looked pillowed in the coffin. That picture did threaten to come in.

I blanked to Polaris.

North.

South. I turned slowly, like a wind-vane suddenly confounded in the eye of a hurricane.

West.

East.

What lay in this direction? Coney Island was the furthest east I'd ever been. But I knew about... Pittsburgh. "The confluence of the Allegheny and Monongahela Rivers." Daddy had drummed that description of the source of the Ohio into our heads almost as soon as we could talk. He thought our grave baby-recitation of the word "confluence" was amusing.

...And Harvard. And Lexington and Concord, where colonial farmers had fired the "shot heard 'round the world." Spatter of musketry from behind a low stone fence, distant line of redcoats faltering. I had that scene on the mental reels too, thanks to Daddy's dramatic bedside descriptions.

...Old North Church, Paul Revere. Cambridge had confirmed Daddy as an American history buff. In turn, he had made Nathan Hale and Patrick Henry, Benjamin Franklin and George Washington (whose namesake fort-site, commemorated by loops of heavy chains dangling from piles of patinaed cannonballs, we passed on the way to Daddy's office when we turned left off the downtown ramp of Columbia Parkway) as vital a bunch of American characters as Babe Ruth or Ty Cobb.

Out there too was New York. Empire State Building, King Kong clinging to its upper floors, swatting at biplanes. And the Statue of Liberty. Regal defier of European rank and prejudice. Every cobbler the Kaiser's equal. "Give me your tired, your poor, your huddled masses yearning to breathe free...." Daddy carried a lot of verse in his repertoire. And we acquired it in turn through repetition. Starting with "*Arma virumque cano...*," to which, two years later, I'd contribute "*Anthropo ennepe, mousa....*" He loved it when I taught him that one, out of homage. Beamed as he traced the sounds of the Greek letters I scribbled for him in fluid lower case on a sheet of lined paper from the Homer section of my St. X notebook. You'd think I was giving him some expensive Christmas gift.

I rotated south. Now I faced the defining river. Every summer afternoon we'd catch the faint oompahpah of the *Island Queen's* steam calliope. Stern-wheel beating white lather out of the khaki stream, enroute from the Front Street landing to Coney Island. The melody echoed across the heights of Alms Park, reverberated off the bluffs of Newport, Covington and Fort Thomas. I never did know which was which. Daddy said the Mafia ran gambling joints over there. Sometimes he'd take me with him to pick up cartons of cigarettes and cases of bourbon from his Kentucky "bootlegger." It was a way of avoiding the taxes Ohio collected through its antiseptic state-run liquor stores. We'd "smuggle" his booty back in the car trunk, nervously traversing the Suspension Bridge (capitalized in print and vocal inflection as if ours were the only one in the world), despite the fact that I never saw any border police.

Certainly police were scarce in Kentucky, where hillbilly women with garish faces teetered on high-heels on the sidewalks, inviting men, I gathered, to put their penises inside them for money. (Neither Daddy nor Mother could resist defining a good polysyllable like "prostitute" when I kept them at it.) Just beyond the ticky-tacky towns stretched the pride of the state, the horse-farms. Miles of undulant white fences, tiny cast-iron jockeys in blackface at the gates, rolling fields of bluegrass that remained, no matter how hard you strained to dye it so in your perception, a disappointingly prosaic green....

109

There again my personal experience guttered out. I felt a blood-claim on the deeper South, on the magnolias and plantations, the Spanish moss and far, far Suwanee of Stephen Foster. Certainly like all good little Yankees I admired the wart-faced Emancipator who smiled on me out of postage stamps (even at thirteen, I'd seldom seen a five-dollar bill). How could one not be horrified by the perverse institution he'd abolished? Or applaud the defiant morality of Harriet Beecher Stowe—whose dour grey boxhouse, hung with anachronistic metal fire escapes, I saw from my schoolbus window daily. It was open to tourists, who could descend into its dank basement to imagine black fugitives cowering there, safe over the Mason-Dixon Line but still in jeopardy until the Underground Railway finally shunted them across Lake Erie into Canada.

Cincinnati had a strong abolitionist tradition. Nevertheless, I also felt an allegiance to the Stars and Bars. "Johnny Reb" had a plucky cachet. And my Alabama ancestors had "loved their slaves," MiMi assured me, had always been kind and decent to them, and had been loved in return. What's more, she said, my Uncle Francis had finally been defeated in his ultimate senatorial bid because he'd staunchly spurned Ku Klux Klan support.

Mother's last visit to her birthplace was on her honeymoon. Daddy's major reminiscence from that trip was of astonishing his new relatives by pouring milk and sugar on his grits. That was a mistake I'd never make. Mother served us buttered grits for breakfast regularly. And what she called "Duke's mixture," a bowl of soft-boiled eggs, shredded toast and crumbled bacon. Southern fried chicken was among her accomplishments. We ate it with black-eyed peas and turnip greens. Or stewed okra. Sometimes she baked cornbread. Or deep-sizzled our favorite, the little balls of cornmeal and chopped onions called hush-puppies. Those dietary supplements endowed me with proprietary pride in a region as strictly mythological to me, really, as Nero's Rome.

Not, as a matter of fact, that I didn't have a pretty strong sense of connection to DeMillean, *Quo Vadis* Rome as well. It had been scared into me by the nuns' tales of early Christian persecution. There *I'd* have been the refugee in the catacombs... skulking in fear of my life, liable to capture and martyrdom as a crucified human torch or sporting fodder for the Coliseum's lions.

Would I have had the courage to remain steadfast as the slathering beasts crunched my bones? I wasn't at all sure. It was only recently that I'd outgrown a lingering fear that one day I would be set on by a band of rowdy Protestants from public school. Those words, "public school," filled me with dread. The toughs would encircle me and demand that I "renounce my faith." Exactly which of its tenets might bother them never took explicit shape in my apprehension. After all, I hadn't the faintest notion what Protestants actually believed. Except not in the Pope. And to tell the truth, I wasn't all that keen to risk injury or death quibbling over prune-faced old Pius XII, myself. But then, one did have to be staunch in whatever one professed. So in my fantasy I'd refuse, and they'd stone me.

Cincinnati was one of the most Catholic cities in the United States. We were something like a seventy-five-percent majority, according to an astonishing census statistic I later encountered. Yet—tribute to the Ursulines' indoctrinatory skill or evidence of my own tremulous nature—I went through childhood actually believing that I was in imminent jeopardy of martyrdom for being one.

So it was no wonder that my romantic, impeccable Alabama heritage was a consolation. Mother had been rich there. Niece of a U.S. senator. Her maiden name (Paul's middle name) was chiseled over a major state office building. An old blotter-paper scrapbook that shed tiny black triangles and curling sepia snapshots every time you turned a page showed her at the wheel of the Stutz Bearcat she'd been given for her sixteenth birthday... in a vestal white tunic dancing among a chain of classmates across the spring lawn of the Mary Baldwin Seminary for Young Ladies... grinning in a raccoon coat beside Johnny Mack Brown, the Alabamian cowboy movie star she'd gone out on a date with once (so nervous at his celebrity, she admitted, that she'd let out a humiliating "ppprrrrp" of flatulence in the middle of the dance-floor).

Oddly, I realized, those snapshots had popped to mind in crisp facsimile. It was Mother younger, the features plumper and more embryonic, the hair bobbed or crammed under a flapper cloche. But it was Mother. Maybe the only way to mentally "see" a face was to pull it from the files in reproduction. Recapture it while artificially stilled. Maybe I'd been worried unnecessarily, demanding something impossible. Maybe a *living* face, no matter how ostensibly in repose, is really in too constant a play of physical and emotional processes to ever be captured, fixed, on the unstable emulsion of the brain.

I tested the hypothesis. Squeezed my eyes shut and tried to summon a sharp vision of Daddy. Of Paul. Of GaGa.

And I could. They appeared almost as distinctly in abstract—images ordered and composed from smeary fragments of recent memory—as in the photographic concrete that abruptly intruded to compromise the comparison.

We'd had a family portrait taken two Christmases earlier. The best of the proofs had been printed and framed, to decorate the living room mantel. Daddy was smiling in some stilted way that made him look simultaneously jowly and hollow-cheeked. He'd been at odds with his latest set of porcelain molars. GaGa goggled as if the photographer's pole-lights had lobotomized her. MiMi and Paul and I, at least, had managed to synchronize a twinkling photogenicity that didn't look too false. And Mother? I could place her in the group, trace her outline like one of those caption-keys you find in magazines. But I couldn't fill it in.

Oh God, what was happening?

Dead since March, that's all. Five months. And already I'd lost even this vestige.

I opened my eyes and stumbled into a panicky trot. My inner ears creaked and bubbles of light exploded across my vision. I was like a diver suffering an attack of the bends—too abruptly emerged from my rapture of the heights.

A snaggle of root caught at my shoe. I sprawled into the dust.

I'd hurt my lip, I discovered. The uneven path had deceived me in the darkness, caught my chin sooner than my out-thrust hands. A tooth had gouged the tender inner skin. I spat grit. My tongue tasted salt, but I couldn't tell how badly I was bleeding. I cupped my mouth.

There was no one to see me. The pressure behind my eyes had been building. Would have erupted had I not fallen.

I pulled myself to my knees, head hanging. "God damn it," I whimpered.

The insult to coordination, the injury had made tears too easy. And, paradoxically, suddenly easier to resist.

I patted my shirt-front, spat again and limped home.


**The porch light was burning under a plasma cloud of frenzied beetles and fraying moths.**

The screen door was unlocked, but the downstairs was dark. That confused me.

GaGa often went up to her room early to snore over a book—she was always jerking upright in whatever

113

easy chair she'd occupied, announcing to whoever might be in earshot that she'd only been resting her eyes. She claimed to get almost no sleep at night. And to have been disturbed for good by the birds or the anticipation of dawn at a symbolically premature—because unvarying winter or summer—five a.m. Then she'd lain in bed for another hour, she'd report, cataloguing her worries. Indeed, Paul and I, no matter how early we chirped awake, always seemed to find her in the kitchen in her bathrobe, boiling coffee water and grimacing over her two-finger good-morning jolt of bourbon neat.

Daddy, on the other hand, seldom went to bed until long after I had—even on those nights, like tonight, when I'd been allowed a dissipation. True, that didn't exactly mean greeting the garbagemen. But no matter how late for me I might sidle through the screendoor or drone over some unwonted accumulation of homework, Daddy could be depended on to be at the dining room table, still scowling over his yellow legal pad, or slumped on the sunporch glowering at the TV screen.

He almost never went out. The car had been parked as usual at the top of the driveway. An evening stroll or a visit with neighbors would be utterly uncharacteristic. So I supposed I should go ahead and close the front door and throw the deadbolt. It was not a customary responsibility.

I flipped the switches that doused the porch globe and lit the ceiling fixture in the front hall. We always left that on as a safety feature—though by what reasoning this invariable and unimaginative precaution was expected to deter burglars I can't say. (As a matter of fact, I once heard a veteran burglar tell an interviewer the only house he would *never* enter is one in which no lights were burning at all.)

The French doors to the dining room had been pulled together. Those across the narrow hall into the living room were ajar. The barely perceptible draft that had eddied through them, between the screendoor and the open louvers on the sunporch, suddenly revealed itself by its extinction. Minuscule beads of sweat instantaneously dotted the hairs of my forearms. That was Cincinnati—to enter any demi-confined space in summer was to submit to a steambath. It was a natural phenomenon, a discomfort I registered, but—knowing nothing else—somehow never remarked. The previous July, Daddy had been able to afford the luxurious state-of-the-art countermeasure. He'd had a big electric window fan installed in his and Mother's room. This summer he'd gotten one for GaGa too. It would be another decade at least, though, before the house on Nirvana would encapsulate the eerie chill of air conditioning.

"That you, Ricky?"

I flinched violently.

It was Daddy's voice, not very distant but distanced by the darkness, and its unexpectedness. There was an odd hoarseness in it, too.

"Oh!" I gasped. "Daddy? Dad! You're up! Where are you?"

He wasn't, I could see, lurking in any visible part of the living room. Nor could I spy him in the gloom beyond the sunporch door. But he was out there somewhere, I realized.

"Yeah, still up, sure. G' night. Don't hafta come kiss me." He chuckled. I didn't hear a lot of humor in it. In fact, it took me a beat to understand the joke.

I wandered closer, through the darkened living room. I was curious now. I almost always bade him goodnight face-to-face anyway.

I heard him stir at my footsteps and clear his throat. "So, uh, how was the movie?" he asked.

"Great! Cyrano's really neat, Dad! You should see how he fought off these three guys all at once, with his sword. And he's always saying these really neat poems, while he's doing

115

it even? About his nose? They're really funny, see, because he has this super-long nose, you know? That people are always teasing him about... or anyway he thinks they are? Noticing and making fun of... except they're all really scared to mention it, because he gets so mad. And he's such a great swordfighter. But there's this lady he falls in love with... see, he has this friend-like...."

"I know the story, Paul."

"Gee, why...?"

"I mean Richard."

"...Are you sitting out here without any lights on?"

"Had, um... little headache."

"Anyway, can I tell you about the movie?"

"Actually, I'd sort of rather you wouldn't. Not tonight. Maybe in the morning, 'kay?"

"But I just wanted to tell you this one really neat part. See, where Cyrano...?"

"Richard. Not now, huh?"

I acquiesced with a glum shrug. I was hurt that he'd refused my gift of enthusiasm.

"Okay. G' night, then," I muttered. I spun without looking at him and scuffed off.

"Sorry," he called after me. "I'm just not feeling all that well right this minute."

My tongue-tip nestled exploratorily against the ragged contour of my inner lip. I had an injury to report too. Tough. Now he'd never know. I noticed the *LIFE* magazine I'd been reading earlier lying open on the hide-a-bed couch. I snatched it up absent-mindedly as I passed.

"Can you allow me that?"

"Mm-hm," I grunted. I exited into the living room.

"Richard, come back here," Daddy said. Then he tried to mollify the order. "Please?" He sighed. "You can tell me whatever it was you wanted to, I guess, if you can only make it short. That possible?"

"Nah, it's okay," I said.

"C'mere for a second," he repeated.

I hesitated in the half-light from the hall. Abruptly I felt the eyes of the miniature silhouettes of our former family personae raking me dimly from the mantelpiece. I strode closer and leaned forward to squint at Mother.

How could I have been so deluded as to think I'd forgotten this indelible image? Which of these features and their particular set had seemed to evade recall? It must have been some aberration, a temporary amnesia.

I examined my own face at right, sitting next to Mother in the lower threesome of the pose. Paul crowded against her other arm and Daddy stood in back, his hands cupping her shoulders gently, a gesture of attachment rather than possession. Stout GaGa and MiMi peeped over us from Daddy's flanks.

So that's what I'd looked like to the world then. Almost two years younger, callower, flush with childish candor and bonhomie—or so it appeared. Not that I hadn't studied the photograph often enough since, always with the same curiosity and mild discomfort. To tell the truth, I spent plenty of long minutes each day staring into mirrors. Tilting my head this way, cocking it that—eyes rammed into their socket-stops as I sought profiles, dabbed at my forelock, fluffed and patted the bristly definitions of my crewcut. Straining to catch a glimpse of my own mysterious essence.

At the same time, of course, I was busy trying to shape, to an uncertain and never more than fleeting satisfaction, what superficial manifestations of Richard Tisserand Schubert (real mouthful, huh?) I could control. And analyze, come to terms with, those I couldn't.

Like my chin. Was it strong enough for the nose and forehead? My ears. Did they wag out too far, like Dopey's or Dumbo's? The little raised black mole with the three long, coarse hairs curling out of it, just beneath my right sideburn. Was that a freak's adornment? Mother had called it my "beauty spot...."

I'd forgotten Daddy's summons. And as I stood there on the tile hearth with my toes under the dusty gas-log—absorbed in this memento of a world less than two years behind me, but now as coldly historical as Victoria's England or the Russia of the Romanovs—the emotion I thought I'd long since walked off seemed to coalesce again. It was a vague, mostly physical sensation, a kind of constriction of the sinuses....

"Richard," Daddy insisted. "I said for you to get back in here." There was no mistaking the peremptory crispness now.

"I'm coming!" I protested. I was resentful, as if his impatience were unreasonable. But in fact I was grateful to be roused. Still, I trailed my fingers reluctantly along the edge of the mantel as I shambled in obedience's direction. I skirted the spindly rocking chair and sidled into the sunporch murk.

"What!" I demanded sullenly.

"I don't want you stalking out on me like that, is what. You come in here, jabbering away like a magpie, and then when I tell you to calm down you act as if you've been insulted. I also don't like the tone of voice you're using right this minute. It's not polite. I'm your father, remember."

"Yes, sir," I muttered. I rarely used that term, so the irony was patent.

"Look. I just don't need this, any of it, right now."

"Yes, sir."

"Please. Please!"

He almost whined the words. The repetition had a ripple of anguish. The abrupt shift in temper and its apparent lack of proportion disquieted me. I patted under the shade of the big table lamp by the hide-a-bed, found the switch and gave it a tweak.

"Ooough!" Daddy cried. He thrashed in his chair and

slapped his hand up over his grimace as if the light were a sudden splash of sulphuric acid. "Turn that off!"

"Oh, my gosh!" I blurted. "I'm sorry!" I fumbled in panic to undo the harm I'd done. My own pupils had been better adjusted to darkness, or at least semidarkness, than to this garish detonation of candlepower. I exhaled with relief too when I'd stanched it. "I didn't mean...."

"Thank you. I told you... I have a *splitting* headache! Anyway...sit down for a second."

I lowered myself onto the edge of the couch.

"I wasn't going to tell you tonight, but now I will. This just came a little bit ago." I heard a crinkle of paper. He was fingering a crisp sheet of it tented over the chair-arm. My eyes had begun to accommodate to the reflected light from the front hall and the filtered beams from the streetlamp outside, behind the maples and sweetgum. "It's a telegram," he said. "From Birmingham. Your grandmother MiMi died this morning."

"She... died?"

"She was sick, you know."

"Yeah, but.... Really?"

"Mm-hm. I'm afraid so, Ricky."

"Oh, my gosh." My stomach knitted hard. But somehow it was more a formulaic response—death is bad, be astonished on hearing the bad proclaimed—than a reaction to any true emotion.

I considered the concept. MiMi is dead. Like Mother. What did that mean? No more MiMi around. She hadn't been around—Cincinnati-around—for a long time. But she could have been. If she'd chosen to be. Now she couldn't. Well....

"What was wrong with her?" I wondered.

"Not sure yet, exactly," Daddy said. "What the actual cause was. Pneumonia, s'pose. What she went into the hospital with, anyway, according to your cousin Roscoe. Some kind of complications. She hadn't been in good health, though, since... you know. Your mother. Didn't have that much to live for, I guess was how she basically felt. Any more. Never expected. Her own daughter. Go, die. Before she did. Me either. Think, for an instant, that I'd outlive...."

His hand floated to a tumbler resting on the narrow table beside his chair. There were three chairs in the room, but only one could be swiveled away from the TV set. That's where he slumped now, heels kicked up on the footstool he'd snagged from the facing chair, his usual roost. He'd sluffed his shoes. There was a hole in one sock. A dime-size circle of bare skin shone at the ball of his foot. Top foot, ankles crossed. A corn had probably rubbed through. Daddy's feet were exceptionally long and narrow, difficult to fit. They'd suffered as a consequence. Size 12 triple-E. If GaGa had seen, she'd have stripped the worn sock off with a remonstrance and huffed away to her sewing basket. Mother had given up darning socks. We all refused to wear them—her lumpy mends, we claimed, caused blisters. Such ineptitude and neglect would have scandalized GaGa. If she'd found out.

Daddy raised the glass to his lips. I didn't hear any ice clink. He must have been nursing it for a while.

"Gee," I said. "Gee."

I was still straining to bring my mind to bear on the fact that my grandmother was suddenly a lack in my life. I felt shaky. Death, news of it, made me nervous.

"Got the grippe right after she went back, after the funeral," Daddy mused. "Never could seem to throw it off. Just in her early sixties still. Too young...."

It was a surprising adjective to hear applied to MiMi. She'd always been a symbol of age to me. And yet at the same time ageless, a personification of the extremity of adulthood, let's say. From my earliest memory she and GaGa had been elders, widows, stout, grey, dowdy eminences. Not that MiMi wouldn't have been insulted at that description. She'd always been vigorous, a trig if conservative dresser. She carried white gloves, wore seersucker suits and open-toed high heels in summer, and perky little hats swathed in vestigial veils, pinned at a fashionable rake. But she was no longer svelte. And as the mother of my mother, her fate was to be lumped into the generational category defined by GaGa, who lived at hand and was a good ten years older.

But neither had ever entered my consciousness as images of senility—old in the mortal sense, imminent candidates for death. Sure, I'd known MiMi was in the hospital. Daddy had been so informed several weeks ago by her brother-in-law, Cousin Roscoe—an attorney too, a Princeton graduate who lived in Anniston, the Kirkpatrick family seat. But this extinction had been visited as unexpectedly as Mother's as far as I was concerned. More so. I hadn't had time to turn sad.

"She wanted to come up here and live, but I didn't think she should," Daddy went on. "Maybe I was wrong. Would have helped or something, I don't know. Be closer to you boys. She doted on you, you know. You and Paul."

"Mm," I acknowledged.

"But her job was there. Her friends. I don't know. I was pretty discouraging about it. Probably saw it as a rejection. I wasn't too enthusiastic, it's true. Would've been strained. With Mother... your GaGa.... Still. Kind of selfish on my part, I suppose. She was sick already.... I wonder."

My vision had adjusted completely now. Daddy slouched low in the upholstered swivel chair. His face in this twilight was spectral, cadaverous. The vestigial flesh was shrunk taut around bulbous bone and sharp cartilage. His eyebrows were thin, so pale as to be almost nonexistent. That, and his receding hairline, accentuated the skeletal evocations. Hooded deep under the forehead ridge, his eyelids fluttered shut as he spoke. It was a mannerism that was both familiar and curious—of recent onset, I suppose. The impression conveyed was that thought required extreme inward concentration, and speech was immensely wearisome. His finger absently, obsessively traced the outline of the concave scar at the crest of his brow.

"So," I said, "what? Is there a funeral? Gonna be or something?"

In voicing the prospect, I triggered a sudden foreboding. I remembered myself bending into the coffin, lips poised.... My mind, as usual, slewed away from the image. I shuddered. Was that a feature of all obsequies? Was I going to have to go through the same ordeal all over again with MiMi's taxidermied remains?

"Yes, sure. Don't know what the arrangements'll be for it yet, though. Probably... have to work that out with Roscoe. Have it in Birmingham, I guess. Is best. Or maybe Anniston. Don't know. Down there somewhere, anyway, probably. Which'd mean we'll have to take a trip. Maybe you and Paul too. She'll be buried up here, in Spring Grove, though."

A headstone. I could picture its location exactly. Gray slab of polished rock, next to the matching one that read "Edwin Beale Kilpatrick." Chiseled letters, numbers beneath—ancient, forgotten dates. That's all I'd ever known of him. For some reason, Mother's Daddy was far more nebulous a progenitor than Daddy's father. The lame, gentle sybarite whose blood I felt in my veins and whose dark features I was told were emerging on my own face. Not that I could see that precise a resemblance in his few photographs. Both my grandfathers must have been camera-shy. I'd had to manufacture a sense of my maternal grandfather incarnate from one dour portrait in which he stared smileless and immobile through a pince-nez, *a la* Warren G. Harding or Calvin Coolidge. He wore a round-point celluloid collar of the era, and a rep tie wrung into the minutest of knots—exostructural girdings of such ponderous rectitude it was hard to distinguish the human contents, which one suspected might simply go "poof" if unconfined. So he was a true ghost—the Spirit of Business or something—whose emanations percolated vaguely up out of the ivy once or twice a year, when we went to pay homage to his boxed bones.

Now MiMi's too would be sequestered down there. Mother's... a whole stratum of skeletal Cincinnatians latticed with the earthworms in the rich black loam beneath the root-canopy. Compost, bodily garbage. That's all it was, really. Their souls were at peace in Heaven. Or still sweating off their venial misdeeds in Purgatory. Or burning, writhing in the perpetual fiery agony of Hell.

## Hell.

It seemed a remote possibility in MiMi's case. Still, she was a Protestant. You couldn't discount it completely.

Suffering beyond all suffering the living could imagine, according to Father McKenna. Worse than the cruelest tortures of the Gestapo, or the Apaches. Who buried their captives up to the chin beside anthills, I'd read, and then smeared their faces with honey. Millions of tiny mandibles nibbling at your eyeballs, swarming, chewing their way up your nostrils... uugh! But Hell was worse.

Yes, worse than having your chest caved in by a steering wheel. Worse than watching your bowels ooze across the front seat of a crumpled station-wagon. Worse than being hashed into bloody fragments by a Chinese hand grenade, or tipping a kettleful of scalding water over your arms, chest, penis. Worse than roasting in a pile of bodies jammed against the locked door of a blazing nightclub.... Oh, I had a ready supply of phobic comparisons, thanks to my constant foraging in print.

123

But those torments, no matter how intense, were all temporary. If nothing else, surcease came when you died.

After which, if you had the misfortune to be blemished by a mortal sin—malign black blotch fouling the pristine *pneuma* God had generously conferred on you at Baptism (Adam and Eve passed it along stained, but the holy water in the fount worked on Original Sin like Clorox)—the anguish resumed. In spades. And *for all eternity!*

That's because God is just. Oh, merciful, sure. But we stumble through this life with our eyes open. Especially if we're Catholic (which, given missionaries and parochial schools, almost everybody in the world has a chance to be. Except for a few lucky qualifiers as 'Invincibly Ignorant.' I wasn't sure what the criteria were for that exemption, but I was sure I'd lost *my* eligibility). Man gets what he merits. A willful disregard of any of His Commandments is an abomination to the Lord. Fail to repent, to Confess and mutter a sincere, if rote, Act of Contrition (that's God's mercy there, forgiveness on demand and a second chance)... well, then you can kiss your Eternal Bliss goodbye.

Since human fortune has a certain observable randomness to it, though—God knows you, loves you and watches over you, Father McKenna assured us, but He has set the world in motion according to His laws, given you Free Will to operate within them and then, as it were, taken a bemused pace back—I was somewhat uncomfortable about the deal. It had at least one yawning, potentially catastrophic loophole.

Suppose, for example, I've led an exemplary life. But one day I do happen to commit a mortal sin. Decide, say, what the Hell (ah, precisely), I'll go ahead and satisfy my craving for a White Castle. Or a four-way chili. And it's a Friday. And before I have a chance to feel sorry, repent— maybe just as I'm chewing that first bite of wafer-thin meat-and-oatmeal, or dabbing the red sauce off my chin at the

Empress—a car careens through the plate-glass window and smushes me.

I'll go directly to Hell, right?

Right. Mortal sins are mortal, no gradations, we had learned. So I'll sizzle and bleat—or the supernatural equivalent—alongside Joseph Stalin, Adolf Hitler and Henry Wallace until the end of time. Doesn't seem fair, I'd carped.

Father McKenna warranted it was. God is an absolutist. His mercy is limitless, but it's only granted through the sliding black cheesecloth screen of the confessional booth. ("Say three Our Fathers, three Hail Marys and a Glory Be, and now make a sincere Act of Contrition," the priestly silhouette would instruct me after I'd reeled off my pitiful catalog of childish strayings from perfection—"I teased my brother three times, and I didn't make my bed twice, and I disobeyed my mother"—both of us pretending to a solemn, ritual anonymity). Or *in extremis* by a simple heartfelt regret.

But absent either, God's allegiance is to justice. And the souls in Heaven, chortling to His presence—their only, but sufficient, reward—share the priority. Pops and little Bobby and Grandma and Grandpa are down there frying. Too bad, always will be, forever and ever. But they brought it on themselves. Only right, after all: missed Mass, stole a hubcap, got remarried after Gramps ran off with his secretary. Now they're exiled perpetually from our family company. Wracked by the ceaseless anguish of separation from the Holy of Holies. No matter. It's justice—on a level of such theoretical rarefaction only incorporeal spirits can appreciate it.

The moral, of course, is not to sin. Or, barring that impossibility, not to be caught dead with a Big One on your soul.

Now, for a kid, I figured, that was probably within the realm of achievability. But I suspected it got a good deal harder as you grew older. So don't go too long between Confessions, is the idea. And squirrel up a trove of Indulgences. They'll be useless, of course, if Hell is your destination. But they can commute a lot of hard time in Purgatory. Which is itself no picnic, apparently.

Sort of a mini-Hell, Father McKenna suggested. Really awful, scary, but tolerable because you know it's determinate. A sentence, let's face it, every one of us except a rare martyred few could look forward to having to serve. Kind of like being funneled through the disinfectant foot-bath before you're allowed to cannonball into the cool blue Coney pool.

Purgatory's where MiMi must be right this moment, I mused. My nice elderly grandmother, naked down to her soul, twitching in Heaven's torture-chamber anteroom. Being singed and tweaked and abased at God's orders in penance for her pettinesses, her omissions, her shortcomings. She wouldn't have had Last Rites, for example, Extreme Unction. (For years I'd thought the obscure Sacrament must have something to do with additional prayers by friars gathered around the deathbed, since it was called Extra Monktion.) No priest would have been at her Protestant bedside signing the cross and murmuring "*ego te absolvo*." Solemn in satin stole, like Monsignor Carroll when he'd ducked through the curtain from Mother's hospital room. The knell of hope. But at least that had assured that my Mother's soul would waft quickly to God's side. Daddy and Paul and I were still at risk. I most of all. I knew just how frail was my faculty for virtue.

"I guess MiMi's in Purgatory, huh?" I proposed.

"What?"

"I don't know. I was just thinking," I shrugged.

Daddy grunted. He reached for the tumbler and swallowed off some more bourbon. He shook his head.

"Heaven," I said, "'ld be where Mother is by now, I guess. Don't you think?"

"Oh, Ricky!" Daddy groaned. He shifted in the

chair and swelled his ribs with a long intake of air. The tails of his shirt were out. It was bunched messily around his slumping torso—all bone and sinew except for the graceful male pectorals I hoped I'd soon develop. Daddy's physique reminded me of Jesus's. And vice versa, whenever I considered the slender seminude asquirm on his crucifix in the gloom above an altar. With two such ideals I was unmoved by the appeals of Charles Atlas—mesomorphic chest swelled blurrily on the backs of comic books. As it happened, I weighed exactly ninety-eight pounds that summer. But I didn't identify with the descriptive "weakling." And I couldn't imagine anyone daring to kick sand in my Daddy's face. Who had once, he liked slyly to recount, sent a rival basketball center into the third row of chairs at courtside with a deft flick of elbow and hip after the guy had insisted on guarding him by holding onto his waistband. Anyway, Jesus had certainly been tough, for that. He'd *let* the Pharisees abase him. Let the soldiers hammer spikes through his ankles and palms. That took guts.

Daddy sighed. "Your mother was a good person. Good in the finest human sense. So, yes...." he nodded. "Only... you know, Ricky... sometimes it's... hard. I'm sorry. I shouldn't probably say this to you. But I'm not sure I believe in any of that stuff. Really."

Daddy's fingertip was relentlessly circling the hollow in his forehead. My own brow puckered. My heart accelerated and my mouth suddenly had a tinny taste.

"I mean, explain to me!" he groaned. "I sit here, and I try to see what purpose...! What could possibly be the... good served? Someone like your mother.... Just in the prime of her life. Two children. Who needed her. *Need* her! A husband... *I* needed her! And with everything to live for. Full of love, kindness... faith. She was the one who believed! A new convert. And for the first time... things were just starting to go...."

He stopped and rubbed his hand across his mouth. His whiskers scritched in the stillness.

"I haven't been a success, Ricky. The way I'd hoped." He shook his head. "I should've made a lot more money by now. Harvard...." He snorted. "Law review... none of it meant a God damn thing when I came back here. New York, yes. Boston... but not Cincinnati. I doubt there's anybody out of my whole class that hasn't done a whole lot better. But at least finally...! And it wasn't that your mother ever complained. Not a word. Sounds trite, but it's true. She was always the one who was bucking me up when I got blue. She just wasn't the worrying kind. Sort of that easy-going Southern way of hers, I guess... take what comes. Cheerful...."

He covered his eyes and pinched them together between his thumb and forefinger. Then he began kneading his eyebrows. Slowly he worked his way up, massaging the wrinkles out of his forehead, smoothing back the high wispy remnant of the widow's peak he'd lost to "yellow jaundice" in his arduous second year of law school. Again his finger found the pulsing crater near his temple.

"You remember when I was in the hospital? Couple of years ago?"

I nodded at once. I was eager to accord him that solace, my complete attention. The memory was extremely vague, though: an absence, a reappearance, some atmosphere of anxiety permeating the house. It must have been soon after we'd moved in.

"Thrombophlebitis."

"Oh yeah," I agreed. In fact, I did recognize that improbable train of syllables. But Daddy wasn't looking for a response.

"People die of it. Not uncommon at all. Why didn't I?"

"What's, um? I forget what it is," I admitted.

"Oh. It's... a blood clot. In a vein. Leg it was, in my

case." He arched his knee and patted the inside of his calf. "Here. Phshew! And very painful! And the dangerous thing is, they can break off... sort of a little lump of sludge that gets jammed inside the blood vessel. And if part comes loose, it can travel...." He traced the saphenous vein to his groin, then scuffed the finger across his chest. "...Right up into the heart. Block it off, like a dam, choke off the blood supply. So the muscle starves. Goodbye quick if that happens. Heart attack."

He paused, thoughtful. "I was damn sick. I couldn't walk, couldn't work. Finally they had to cut me open. And all this time I was watching the bills pile up. Marv and I had just started the practice. We'd just bought this place, your mother and I. I used to lie in bed at night thinking I'd be better off dead. You all would. Because the one thing I did have was life insurance. You and your mother would've been a whole lot better off, I figured."

He groped for his highball glass.

"I shouldn't be saying any of this. Sorry."

He tilted the glass to his lips before recognizing it was empty. He set it aside. Suddenly he expelled air through his nostrils.

"Seven years older!" he groaned. "*I should've died first!* Naturally I expected that. Always... I mean I didn't *want* to live longer than she did. All I hoped was that I could leave her and you boys a nice estate!"

"Oh Daddy," I objected. Seeing him like this filled me with anguish. I wanted to comfort him. Only I didn't know the words. Words were the way, I assumed. If only I could find them.

"She would've taken care of you right," he said. "I'm not."

"Yes you are!"

"Mother... your grandmother... sure, she's been a lifesaver. But how long can she go on like this? I can't expect...

she's just too old. She'll get worn out eventually. Then what?"

"It'll be okay," I whimpered. "I'm sure."

"And now Jamieson. Your MiMi...."

"We can help more. Paul and I," I offered. "We're getting bigger."

"What's the sense? Where's the moral here, the lesson? Isn't that what we're supposed to be finding somehow out of all of this? *You're* the one who's on the receiving end of all this great religious training. *You* tell me!"

"Well, it's... God's plan," I squeaked.

"Plan!"

"We don't understand."

"Is that," he lowed acidly, "so?"

"But it's for the best! It is! It must be!"

"How can you say that? This is best, for you? For your Mother? For Jamieson? I wish I could believe it! I know that's what I'm supposed to believe. But it just *isn't* for the best. No. No. That's patently...."

"Mother's in Heaven!" I bawled. "With God! He must have wanted her! And... and it's supposed to make us stronger, I guess."

"Mm. Just the way it worked with your grandmother. MiMi."

"Or like a penance. Because...."

"What did you boys do to deserve a penance?"

"Well, we... you know, teased. And, like, I guess we didn't...."

"No! No, you've done nothing, Ricky. Nothing that isn't perfectly natural and normal. No sins. No real sins. You and Paul have nothing to feel guilty about. And certainly not in your mother's.... No. No, for God's sake, don't for a minute let...."

"Well... but like death's a reward! Father McKenna...."

"Okay," he acknowledged. "Maybe you could.... Only you think she wanted it? You think your mother wanted to be separated from you boys? And have Paul crying himself to sleep night after night? And you... whatever. I mean, there was a time when I *did* want to die. Not that I didn't hate the idea of missing you all. But because it would be for the best.... And as much as she tried to accept, as much as she loved her... religion... God... it scared her. Not so much for herself. For *you!* For *me!* Where's *your* reward in this? Innocent kids! Where's mine? My punishment, maybe. After she had me going to church again. Every Sunday, communion, confession, the whole.... Even studying Aquinas together! My reward...!"

His mouth suddenly wrenched apart at its corners. Through the contorted lips burst a series of unvoiced, sibilant barks. The first may have been an acid laugh. Or else that's what he'd strained to transform it into. He clapped his hand over his eyes. Silent, unbreathing, he held himself in check. But below his cupped fingers I could see his lips still warped in that awful grimace. And when he did finally take in air again, it bubbled—a shuddering sigh like those Paul and I always drew involuntarily in the aftermath of tears.

Daddy's eyes were still shielded by his palm. But I recognized those sounds—I'd heard them once before, as I fled up the stairs into the arctic asylum of my room. There was no escape now, though. It was too late. And I couldn't abandon him anyway. I sat transfixed. By pity, impotence, dread....

"Christ," Daddy croaked. "I'm sorry, Ricky. I didn't mean to put you through this." His voice sounded diminished, clogged, as if he were speaking to me underwater. "I'm just in bad shape tonight. Don't pay attention to anything I said."

It almost hurt me to watch him rubbing at his face. His teeth were bared, and he plied the surrounding flesh as if it were a sponge he could squeeze the grief out of if he were simply brutal enough. There was no disguising his sobs now. They came in triplets. I found myself counting. I often did that—chewed numbers like mental gum as I paced black-and-white linoleum checks to the chapel, mounted stairs, bridged cracks in the sidewalk. Often I'd find myself at my destination dazed, the purpose of the errand subsumed by the autonomous chant—just as now I regarded Daddy as vacantly as one of those seven-year locusts. Pith replaced by ciphers: four-five-six... seven-eight-nine.... I was at twenty-one when he tamped the heels of his palms hard into his eyepits and wriggled erect in the chair.

"All right," he sighed. "That's enough. Forgive me, Ricky." He dug around at his hip pocket and extracted a wad of handkerchief. He scrubbed briefly at his face and honked his nose. "Listen," he said, shoving the handkerchief back where he'd found it. "You have a gift. Faith. Your mother had it too. Don't let anything of what I'm saying undermine it. This is just... garbage. The oldest, tritest bunch of questions in the book. There aren't any easy answers. I should know better. And you're right. We're going to be okay."

"Mother'll watch over us," I murmured. "MiMi too, now."

"Mm," Daddy nodded. "Anyway it's late now. You better get on up to bed."

"I locked the door," I said.

"I know. I'll be up myself in a minute."

"Dad... don't be sad any more. Okay?"

"Well, of course I can't *not* be sad. I'll always be sad in some way. I'll always... miss your mother."

"Yeah, but I mean tonight...."

"Tonight," he shrugged, "I'm sad about Jamieson as well. Certainly you are too."

"Oh, yeah," I confirmed.

"Sometimes you have to be sad. And let it out."

"I know."

He fixed me with lusterless eyes, as dun as his skin. The lids seemed chafed. A smudge of damp clung to the hollow below his near cheekbone. "Do you?"

"Mm-hm," I nodded. I examined the nubbly seersucker of my shorts. I tucked my tongue over my lower teeth and probed the raw slit inside my lip. It prickled—as I'd known it would. Stupid to test what you already know is going to hurt.

"I hope so," he said. He fished a tattered, flattened Kent pack from his shirt pocket, slit it open with his finger, looked for a cigarette and, finding none, wadded the wrapper and discarded it in the ashtray next to his empty highball glass. An open carton rested on a stack of books on the windowsill. The books were from the Hyde Park branch of the library: Nero Wolfes and Perry Masons, long overdue. I'd read them. Daddy, who'd checked them out, probably still hadn't. He reached for the carton, tilted a fresh pack into his palm and unzipped its cellophane.

"It's all right," he told me softly. "I won't cry any more, if that's what you mean."

"Yeah," I acknowledged. I meant to say more, but my throat felt plaited, like rope.

Daddy struck a match. In its flare I could see how blotched his face was. He shook out the match and exhaled smoke.

I ducked into the fragrant haze and pecked him on the cheek. My lips tingled to whiskers and salt.

"G'night, Dad," I coughed. I darted for the door.

"'G'night, Ricky," I heard him say after me. "I... really appreciate that."

# 5

**I opened the door quietly, expecting to confront the lump of Paul splayed and trussed in its customary welter of sheeting.**

He slept as if the victim of a series of brutal nocturnal muggings. But his bed was still made and unoccupied, like mine. I remembered he was spending the night with Trey. I had the room to myself again, at least for these few mostly unconscious hours.

I snapped on the overhead light—the first exercise of solitary freedom. Then I went to the mirrored dresser I shared with Paul and turned on the radio.

Daddy had let us have this old family table model, the size of a toaster and the semicircular shape of Union Terminal, when he'd finally replaced our ancient Victrola with a combination radio-phonograph set. The catalyst was the appearance of miniature records with doughnut holes that wouldn't fit the Victrola's spindle. There was also a wafer-thin new species that could be played without adapter, but which produced weirdly accelerated music and chipmunk voices at seventy-eight.

Now I could lie in bed sick and listen to *The Breakfast Club*, *Our Gal Sunday*, *Sky King* and *Sgt. Preston of the Yukon*. On rainy Saturdays we tuned in to *Let's Pretend* ("Cream of Wheat is so good to eat that we have it every day..."), *The Buster Brown Show* ("That's my dog Tige, he lives in a shoe...") and *Grand Central Station*. The first two I professed to have outgrown. The last was invariably boring. But its breathless, engine-chuffing, whistle-hooting account of the rail approach to New York City was the most thrilling intro on the air, I thought—and may just have been the genesis of my determination to one day experience the romance of the wide world.

I kept the volume low. GaGa would be snoring on the other side of our common wall. I rotated the knob until I found music—Rosemary Clooney, singing "Come On-a My House." To tell the truth, I didn't much care yet for the Hit Parade. In fact, when I'd gone to buy my first records for the new turntable, I'd come home with D'Oyly Carte renditions of *The Mikado* and *HMS Pinafore*, and a complete cast album of *Showboat*. Daddy used to plumb the depths of his shower-baritone on "Old Man River." But pure chance led me to sample these particular selections in the store's listening booth. I was immediately taken by the rich choruses and orchestration, the half-familiar melodies, the excitement of the stage and especially the cheeky English patter of Gilbert & Sullivan. Soon I'd learned the lyrics of all three by heart. Still, I recognized that mine was an aberration in musical taste to be kept pretty much to myself while I cultivated a more commonplace adolescent ear. Popular songs, after all, had uncommon usefulness.

They were an excuse to touch girls.

To Nat King Cole's mournful invocations of "Mona Lisa," you could steer their stiff, fragrant weight around gym floors, test the sensual charge in a crinolined thigh or a cashmered chest. Two pubescent buds softly returning the brief collision. Not that you could feel much. But imagination was enough to stiffen your own bud. Edging with each movement up out of its snug cotton pouch, obstinately aflame—and relentlessly uncomfortable (until at last you limped to the men's room and freed it from the elastic binding in which it invariably got itself stuck). Most of all, embarrassing. Far too intimate, of course, to let any partner bump against. To reveal my own male arousal would have been unthinkable—a violation of the girl's moral privacy. Tantamount to rape. Only years later would it occur to me that she might be just as curious to sense my body's secrets as I hers. That a subtly disclosed hard-on, to put it bluntly, might serve as a come-on. But, of course, that would constitute a cosmic leap of intent. All I sought at this stage was a little education, a modicum of titillation.

I'd learned the waltz and the foxtrot at Madame Federova's the winter before. But it had become obvious that the really interesting possibilities lay in the more contemporary steps. Not the jitterbug or mambo, which required skill and coordination, but the slower, unstructured stuff—the plain unvarnished shuffling and swaying you could get away with toward the end of the evening, when the crepe paper festoons hung in shreds and the rheostats had been successfully dimmed and the chaperones were too busy policing cigarette smokers on the front steps to indulge in pecksniffian dance-floor intervention.

I'd gone on my first "date" the month before: a Cincinnati Club-sponsored hayride for teens. Our parents had arranged for me to accompany Joan Greenfeld, the daughter of a friend of my father. We'd gone to school together at Ursuline Academy up to the sixth grade—I think her mother was Catholic or something. Now she was where you'd expect her to be with that name: Walnut Hills. A nice, skinny, dark-haired girl with a pointy nose and lively eyes. We got along fairly comfortably that evening. Considering that both of us were scared zomboid to be out in public as a formal pair.

I'd greased the pompadour fronting my brushcut with Daddy's pungent J.C. Pineaud Hair Tonic. I wore stiff new jeans from Shillito's—real, expensive Levis no less, with authenticating copper rivets, a leather label under the belt and blue inner seams that showed when you rolled the cuffs. I had on argyll socks and polished oxblood bluchers which, always at the forefront of fashion, I'd decked out with coral-pink flourescent laces.

Joannie, for her part, dressed to suit the hayride theme in a checked gingham pinafore, frilly white blouse with bobby-socks to match and flat-heeled black Mary Janes. She'd gone to Mme. Federova's too—one of the few girls there, in fact, I could grasp and face more or less eye to eye. Usually I was staring at the moist vee of their collarbones.

So, after the preliminary barbecue and backroad jounce on a straw-strewn flatbed trailer to some lantern-strung Kenwood barn, I acceded to duty. Four rounds of Cokes drained and conversation attenuated to sporadic mutters, I finally grimaced, "Wanna dance?"

She shrugged, nodded. The three-piece hillbilly combo was on break. The dance floor, therefore, had filled. A recording of "The Tennessee Waltz" was playing over the PA. I figured this might be my best shot. We got up from our folding chairs, edged nervously among the hay bales, found an opening and squared off. With a wince of bravura—elbows out, my thumb locked in her sweaty palm, the fingertips of my left hand hovering a wary inch off the rigid small of her back—we sallied forth.

Left foot forward, right foot forward, slide left to right. Right foot back, left foot back, slide right to left.... Silently counting out the sequence, we measured our Viennese boxes as sedulously as if tracing some pattern painted in the dusty floorboards. But when the music stilled, we grinned at each other in triumph. I'd led, she'd followed, and I hadn't trodden on her toes once, not once. Grazed maybe, but nothing serious enough to wring a gasp. I'd carved a reasonable course through the jostling couples around us... vindication at last of those necktied, white-gloved Friday night ordeals under the tutelage of the "Madame" with the stage-Russian accent and the hennaed hair. We were so encouraged we persevered through "My Foolish Heart" and "Because of You."

I remembered that night now as Clooney's full voice on the radio—she was from Cincinnati, the *Enquirer* proudly reported, had gone to Mercy High—was replaced by a whiny plea for teenage marriage. We'd danced to it, Joannie and I: "Too Young," the last song before "Goodnight Ladies" and the awkward moonlight ride back to the spot where our parents were to pick us up.

Some of the older kids had lain entwined in the straw. Even kissed. Joannie and I nested at a suitable thirteen-year-old distance and distracted ourselves from the dalliances at hand by dredging our last stores of banter. (It would be some six years, no less, before I'd find the courage to place my own lips on a date's lips—perhaps, for all the ridiculously freighted expectation, the most anticlimactic experience of my life.) Fortunately, the constellations came to mind as a topic. Protracted silences for contemplation punctuated by terse moos of awe were appropriate. But the fact that we still had even shreds of dialogue left in us by then was a testimonial to how well matched Joannie and I actually were. I liked her. Though she was a girl, she had the attributes to be a friend. And during "Too Young," relaxed at last into each other's clutches, our spindly flanks glancing rhythmically, her female aura had indeed made my penis rise. It was my introduction to the pleasures to be found in the simple immediacy of girl-flesh.

**I'd had a full day.**

I should have been tired. But exertion and

eventfulness are stimuli that linger in the nervous system like caffeine when you're young. My mind churned with thoughts and images, each demanding its moment of attention but too besieged by the clamor of the others to be sustained. Every time I'd remind myself of what I ought to thinking about—MiMi's death, for example—I'd be distracted by some trivial interloper. I couldn't seem to give that grave circumstance anything like its somber, uninterrupted due. Maybe such events are boulders for the brain, too ponderous to be hefted in a neat clean-and-jerk. Rather, you have to sidle up to them obliquely and chip away at the facets over time, dandle the shards, absently stow them in this or that pocket until one day you discover that the whole has subtly been accommodated.

I lay down. I hiked my shoes onto the bedspread— not without a twinge of guilt and a precautionary glance at the edges of the soles in case some clot of dried mud or dog-doo adhered. One thing about the absorption of an ethic, whether the code of Catholic virtue or the rules of civilized domesticity, you never lack for opportunities to experience the *frisson* of defiance.

I crossed my ankles and clawed briefly at a fresh chigger bite behind my left knee. I folded my hands under my head. There seemed to be a special poignancy in the music— muted out of deference to a sleeping household—filtering across the Midwestern night to me from the lonely studio of some darkened, all-but-deserted radio station. Too bad Danny always warbled: "They tried to sell us egg fu-yung." I could no longer listen to the plaintive lyrics with anything like sustained solemnity.

Anyway, my attention was almost immediately diverted by the watermark on my ceiling. Searching out the images in its familiar contours and shadings was an involuntary bedtime ritual that nevertheless required conscious mental effort, like inverting an optical illusion.

Every so often, too, I could discern a new one. That stain was like a Rorschach blot—its elephant, its winking face (reminiscent of Procter & Gamble's man in the moon), its two snakes twining around each other, its breast and nipple... the plaster over my bed mapped my psychic development.

Lying flat with my elbows crooked high and my ribcage hoisted I became aware of my stomach. Of its deflation. I wished I'd stopped by the refrigerator before coming upstairs. Nice cold glass of milk. Maybe a nibble off a cold, gray sparerib. Slice of peanut-buttered Wonder bread. Clumping downstairs now, though, would be too much commotion—what with Daddy still on mournful vigil. The last thing I wanted was to penetrate his sorrow again. Come to think of it, tomorrow was Sunday. Keeping my fast would allow me to go to Communion.

I thought of the papery wafer on my tongue. It always glued itself there instantaneously, like dry ice. The clammy cling of Jesus' skin. I hadn't been to Confession for a long time, though. Not since school let out. Summer was slack time for the Sacraments. I'd accumulated sins on my soul, obviously. Selfishness, uncharity to Paul, foul words, impure thoughts.... Nah, I wasn't clean enough to feel comfortable about Communion. We'd probably go to 11:30 Mass anyway. Daddy hadn't even come inside the last time. Just driven us, the way he used to. It would be hard to pass up food through that much of the morning.

Eating might be painful, though. I hadn't thought about that. Cut lip, salt. Which reminded me, I hadn't brushed my teeth. I cranked myself off the bed and went into the bathroom.

I folded down my lip before the mirror and studied the purplish welt in the glistening underskin. The indentation was shallow. But I winced at the sugary astringence of the toothpaste. Maybe that's what called Brian to mind. Lying in his bed right now with his leg awkwardly immobilized in plaster. Throbbing with each heartbeat where the bone had snapped. Hurting a lot worse than this, for sure. An injury I'd caused him.

Because no matter what Daddy said... no matter what Dad said... everything would have been different if I'd bunted the ball the way I'd been supposed to. Brian had had the lucky role. The easy one. All he'd had to do was run. Let himself go, just surrender to the command of the coach and take off. No longer his to worry whether it was the right moment or not. Didn't matter what the count was, where the fielders were playing, whether the pitch was high or low, inside or outside, muffed by the catcher or blooped on the fly toward a waiting glove. All he had to do was cast off. Hurl himself into the void.

Suicide.

But I, in the batter's box, I'd had all the burden of his fate humped on my shoulders. As if mine alone weren't enough. Up against that hulking fireballer I could get my ribs stove in or my skull fractured if I didn't stay on the alert. Couldn't afford even an eyeblink's lapse of vigilance. Poised to bail out if the missile homed on me    as it seemed to almost every other pitch—fling myself into the dust for salvation. Each turn at the plate was an excruciating series of those snap life-or-death judgments. Which was why we were striking out so much. We were scared. Every swing was the follow-through to a flinch. Only suddenly I wasn't allowed that luxury any more. I had to sacrifice myself in more than just the metaphoric baseball sense—which after all would be the triumph. Presumably my trickling bunt would be scooped up by a fielder, too late for anything but to throw me out at first. Allowing Brian to slide across the plate and score in the meantime. Everybody'd be screaming jubilantly as I veered into foul territory.... pat on the numbers from Daddy, cordial plaudits from my teammates... as I trotted back, a heroic casualty, to dugout Heaven.

Before that could occur, though, what was required of me by the squeeze play was a sacrifice even more fundamental. I had to relinquish the option of knee-jerk self-defense. No longer could I simply jump back because I felt like it, because I was intimidated. Shake my head in wry acknowledgement of situational cowardice and resume my stance for another routine turn at redemption. He who ducks and spins away lives to duck another day. But I had to forswear that elementary caution—even worse, *broaden* the target. Square around full-face, in the classic bunt pose. And somehow, on top of that, manage to insert my bat in front of the ball. So my role was equally if not *more* suicidal.

Only Brian's I saw as freeing. Mine was just one more deadening acquiescence to the yoke of responsibility.

And, as usual, I'd failed.

Why had my father done that to me? My own father! He of all people should have empathized. Spared me. Let Danny try it if I didn't get on base. I might have had a run batted in if I'd been allowed to swing away. No consolation at all Daddy's *pro forma* assurances that I was capable, worthy of the test. I'd shown everybody on the field and in the stands just how true that was. A bumbling goof. Practically falling on my face. And to add to the humiliation, setting up my teammate to break his leg.

I hunched over the basin and let the chlorine-laced river water from the faucet sluice into my mouth. I swished and spat. I was too dejected, too self-contemptuous to confront my face in the mirror again as I slotted the toothbrush in its holder. I left the bathroom light on—another prescribed signal of house-occupancy while we slept—and shuffled back to my room.

Ricky Schubert, Number Twenty-One, center fielder, batting second: goat! Walking disaster. Just looking for the right opportunity to flop.

"This one's no hitter," the catcher had taunted. Dumb-ass creep. Wish I'd foul-tipped a couple back into his mask. Bounced one up under his cup. Smushed his nuts. Then drilled a home-run into Clermont County.

Only I hadn't. And he'd known I wouldn't.

That's what was so galling. Just like my coach Elmer—who'd told me to forget baseball. Well... had almost said as much, anyway. He recognized that I wasn't any good. He'd just been hedging to be kind. The way everybody was. Probably I wouldn't even be playing if I weren't the coach's son. Brian had stung me with that suggestion once after I'd grounded feebly into a double play that snuffed a ninth-inning rally. Stranding Brian at second. The tying run. Brian's fervor did make him act like kind of a dick sometimes. We'd both sobbed on the bench after that game. Brian at the loss and I as much at the revelatory insult as at my ineptitude. Daddy had growled comforts then, too. Which only reinforced the contention. Any other manager would have confirmed it, the obvious: I stank. Even Elmer used the word from time to time. "You're stinking up the court, Schubert. Follow through!" And tennis was supposed to be my game.

I shut the bedroom door behind me and threw myself on the mattress. The despondent dead-body flop reverberated through the floorboards and walls. I'd get in trouble if I weren't quiet. So what? I deserved it—thoughtless, useless. Loser! Pretty soon that's what I'd be in everything. Elmer'd warned me. How many games had I blown that afternoon? Sloppy strokes, clumsy footwork, lack of anticipation....

I rolled on my hip, kicked my legs off the side of the bed and lurched up into a sitting position. Slumping, more like it. I stared morosely at my shoelaces. After a moment I roused myself to reach down and grasp a frayed end.

The loops evanesced at my jerk. I crooked my finger wearily under the half-hitch, flipped it apart, wormed the

143

fingertip under the top X of laces to loosen the tongue, wriggled the sneaker off and bowled it in the general direction of my closet.

The sock was still a dingy yellow-white below the ankle knobs. Two distinct crescents of sweat-impregnated clay traced the curve of the shoe-top. A cheesy reek struck my nostrils. Sneering daintily, I peeled the sock inside out and floated it after the shoe. I flexed my toes. The pallid skin across my instep was oddly textured by the imprint of the wool.

I shifted on my butt and tugged at the lace trailing from my left shoe. One loop had long ago worked open. (The knot Mother had taught me was a granny, I would realize only twenty years later, when I took up sailing.) The remaining noose tightened on itself—and abruptly snagged. I yanked harder. The mess only fused itself more solidly.

Shit.

The word didn't escape, but it filled my mouth—the first time in my life my brain had triggered that particular expletive. I expelled it as a generalized sibilance.

My face crumpled. I sagged forward, bowed low over my thighs until the hollow of my left eye rested on my knee. Whimpering, I picked half-heartedly at the intricate snarl my carelessness had created—one more just reward for my stupidity.

And true to form, I found myself inadequate to the diagnosis. Without fingernails, I couldn't even get a purchase to try out the various possible undoings anyway. I pawed futilely at the kinks until despair overwhelmed me.

Which took about fifteen seconds.

I cocked my knee and began grappling with my foot—a ridiculous posture. I couldn't even wrestle the shoe off! I'd snubbed the laces too efficiently.

"Shit!" I hissed.

I went motionless. Then the rage imploded.

"Fuck!" I gurgled. I slammed my heel on the floor. The interior detonation flung me backwards, asprawl on the bed.

I bounced upright, flailing to my feet, and began an aimless, manic zigzag of the room. One shoe on, one shoe off, bare sole now cushioned by rug, now slapping hardwood, I limped from bed to bed, closet to dresser—moaning, panting and spewing all the foul words I could think of....

"Piss! Cockshit! Dick! Turd! Asshole! God damn! God damn son of a bitch! Fucking Jesus Christ! Mary... fucking... mother... asshole...son of a God damn...," I keened. "Screw tit Jesus...."

The spasmic sounds rasped my palate. I was still aware and self-protective enough, though, to restrain myself from poisoning the brooding somnolence beyond my door and walls. So what came out were more like dry heaves than speech.

Still, I was conscious to accord each muffled blasphemy, each scatology and obscenity its full phonetic due. Jeer of teeth on lip, pop of tongue... throttled but shaped, *my* words, afloat now irretrievably on the ether. Contained by the door, I hoped, but rippling outward from my lighted window to the planets and stars, to the ends of the Universe.

I could hear them.

God could hear them.

It was a new sensation. No whiny self-justifications this time. Just sin upon sin. Pure violation of conscience— willful release of all the evil essence that churned in the sump of my soul. Anger, lust... sloth, envy... the Seven Deadly ingredients... flesh made words. All down there festering, all right, seething under the shoddy crust of good intention.

And even that wasn't good. Just benign. Its mortar wasn't virtue. Only cowardice.

I stalked the room on lightning paths of discharging fury. And between each grounding spatter of profanity I began to hear a faint, terrifying subliminal monologue:

See me, God, it whispered. Hear this? You're the *Prick!* You're the *Fucker*... the *Murderer!* There now, will that do it? Will that bring down the retribution? Will that make You prove You exist? Go ahead, I dare You. *Fuck* You! Vaporize me with the lightning bolt. Celestial Turd. Sacred Fart. *Send* me to Hell! I'll risk it. I'll burn for Your lost, reviled love for all eternity.

Because at least that way I'll know Mother's in Heaven....

But my vocabulary range in this unfamiliar band was pitifully narrow. And repetition, I was learning, immediately drained those drab monosyllables of their meager charge. The frustration was giddying. My curses disintegrated into pure slobber, inchoate grunts of anguish, desperation... anger unrelieved and unrelievable. My eyes burned. I lurched...

And drove my sneakered toe through the lowest drawer of the little flowered chest under the sill at the foot of my bed.

## It was made of pressed cardboard.

I hadn't realized that. The front ruptured with a sodden crunch.

Such pitiful naiveté. A piece of cheap furniture. But once across this threshold, things would quickly escalate. Tennis rackets splintered and eviscerated against net-poles... plates hurled against walls... dresser-tops cleared in reeking explosions of toiletries. My expensive high school graduation watch, an engraved gift from my father—dashed to smithereens against a sidewalk after I lost a ping-pong game. The front door of the house I rented when I left the Navy—chopped to kindling with an ax. Life has its provocations. And that's as bad as it got—no assaults on living beings. (Except myself: a broken knuckle and two fractured metacarpals from punching walls. And, okay, I'm excluding a slap in the face endured by my first wife. And my kids. To my eternal shame. I guess I can't claim *any* high ground.)

Never, though, would I achieve quite this same first-time catharsis.

Its life-span was the synaptic arc of utter disinhibition. (Well, pretty utter; for all the apparent mindlessness and spontaneity, it wasn't the bare foot I'd ventured, was it?) But its power—and intense, perverse pleasure—was derived from the instantaneous aftermath.

I gaped at the damage I'd done. Wincing, I withdrew my foot from the ragged hole. I was appalled. And panicked.

What, holy moley, was I going to do about *this?*

The blood ramming through my temples effervesced with fear. But it felt... wonderful! All that turbid bile that had clogged my veins had miraculously clarified. I'd made a pivotal discovery. I *could* flush the sludge of anger and frustration. All I had to do was let go—release myself into the awesome *terra incognita* of destruction.

In the years before he died, one of my father's favorite pastimes would become the visit to the discount store. He'd spend hours prowling the aisles of those cavernous suburban cathedrals to consumerism, heaping his cart with marked-down bottles of aspirin, tubes of toothpaste, ballpoint pens, rolls of toilet paper, assortments of screws and neoprene washers, pot-metal socket-wrench sets, flasks of detergent, pocket flashlights, plastic raincoats.... Chirping over the economies he'd realized, he'd stow these bargain treasures in the cellar—whose cabinets were already stuffed floor to ceiling with unused gewgaws and enough backup supplies to run the household for six months.

So maybe there *was* some ambient reverence for

material objects I'd absorbed—and maybe it wasn't all that latent or incipient. The Packard, the new appliances, after all, had been the manifestations of Daddy's love for Mother. Objects did seem to possess for me a special... anima. A "thingness," a "thereness" that entitled them to respect. And routine exemption from harm. Perhaps I'd simply osmosed the American ethos: "goods" are $s made tangible. At any rate, breaking taboo with my voice—snarling forbidden words, blasphemy—was one kind of sin; desecrating a cardboard chest of drawers elevated me to a whole new plateau of wickedness.

Funny, too, isn't it, that I'd been willing to take on God and Eternal Damnation. But the prospect that Daddy would discover a curious crater in one of my room's furnishings instantly reduced me to a funk. ("How did that happen?" he'd frown. Not that I could remember the last time I'd seen him inside this door. Let alone inspecting what it enclosed. But Paul would report—if nothing else, I could depend on that: "Gee, you should see how Ricky's little chest got messed up, Daddy. Ooh, it's *all* bashed in! You oughtta come look." Ultimately, I was going to be forced into a despicable—and no doubt fishy—lie. Or some kind of mumbled quasi-explanation: "Well, like, I was trying to get my shoe off, see, and, uh, I kind of stumbled...." Already I could anticipate the abject confession. In either alternative there was shame. And virtual assurance of punishment. At base, though, what I was really afraid of was only Daddy's disapproval. His disappointment in me. Against those, the ineluctable wrath of God was a pallid threat.)

I hunkered and fingered the dangling fragments of punctured cardboard. The whole front of the drawer was concave now. I tugged it open with difficulty—the drawer was twisted in the frame and the pull was loose. I sorted despairingly through the crumbs strewn across the folds of my wadded pajamas inside. Maybe I could fit the bigger shards back together. I tried to squeeze the dent out of the panel from behind so I could realign the buckled fringes.

A noise startled me. A creak. Was it Daddy on the stairs? Coming up to find out what the ruckus had been? Retribution en route. I'd defiled a precious artifact. Wantonly vented my petty vexation on this treasure suffused with the memories of my mother and grandmother.

Why had I done that? How could I be such a pervert?

I listened trembling—the clamor of my heart all but deafening me. There was no repetition. Just the gradually intrusive background doggerel of "Shrimp Boats" pumping imbecilic cheer at me out of the radio. Must have been the house settling. I bent with renewed urgency to the puzzle.

It was obviously beyond solution. The damage I'd inflicted defied reconstructive surgery. Nevertheless, I embraced, reveled in, the distraction. All the better that the task was hopeless. That I'd created a consuming predicament. The apprehension and remorse it provoked, the anxiety, regret and shame were as excruciatingly refreshing as an ice-cold needle shower.

After a minute or so, though, the little purgatory lost its edge. I had to resign myself to the inevitable, anticlimactic come-uppance. I untensed with a sigh and shook the debris out of the pajamas I'd stuffed into the drawer that morning. I set them aside on the floor and shook the same flecks out of a second, clean, folded pair. Now the incriminating evidence dusted the pillowcases stacked beneath.

I managed to work the drawer almost shut. Then I tucked a corner of the worn pajama top into the gap and draped it so it spilled out in a slovenly fan. I stepped back to contemplate the effect.

I was satisfied. The studied untidiness certainly ought to fall within the bounds of my established capacity. It would only be a matter of time, of course, before GaGa would bustle in to right the mess, or to deposit an armload of fresh laundry. But there wasn't anything I could do to forestall that now. Maybe a better inspiration would occur to me after a night's rest.

Which meant, I abruptly recalled, dealing with my shoe problem.

Ah yes, the peculiar, petty inconvenience that had detonated this whole outburst. I pinched my lip and considered the intransigent knot. Slowly I began to understand, if not fully enjoy, the humor in the situation. Glimpse something other than humiliation in the hapless figure I presented. To which, as further solace, I was, after all, the only audience.

"CINCINNATI TEENAGER TRAPPED IN SHOE," I composed the headline. "AMPUTATION SEEN AS ONLY REMEDY."

Every so often I'd tested my own name as a substitute in newspaper boldface... cultivated the usual childhood fantasies of future sports-page acclaim: "SCHUBERT LEADS U.S. TO DAVIS CUP SWEEP"... "REDS CLINCH SERIES ON SCHUBERT SLAM." This variation, though, startled me for its sophistication. I had a sense that it might even be funny, actually, in an adult way.

Mother would have laughed. I was sure of that. Crinkles at the eyes, cheeks dimpling in triad with her chin. If only she were here to appreciate me. Share my maturing wit, approve the palliative self-mockery. The joke was exactly the kind she would have made. It echoed already, in fact, in Mother's voice.

Stupid, futile! A waste of emotion, missing people who were dead. Mother was dead. So was MiMi. And before long GaGa would be too. And Daddy. And me. But while I was here, they'd all still exist. In the bits of my personality they'd shaped.

Of course, I realized, that was just another way of whistling in the dark.

I paddled to the dresser, rummaged through drawers until I found my official Boy Scout clasp knife and sawed the knotted lace apart with the small blade. It was sharper than the big one, dulled by too much mumbly-peg. I took off my clothes and got into the clean pajamas. I turned out the overhead light and squirmed under my sheet.

I heard Daddy—no, it's Dad now, I had to admonish myself—plodding up the stairs. I reached out and clicked off the radio. I doused the goose-necked bed-lamp and lay blind, unmoving, in a dark that would soon relent to the glow of the streetlamp silhouetting the sweetgum leaves at my window.

Bugs slapped the screen. I heard the long, muffled splatter as Dad drained off his evening's bourbon.

When his bedroom door had shut and the house was silent, I kicked my feet out from under the cloying sheet. My hand crept beneath the waistband of my pajamas. I thought of Joannie's musk. The galvanic touch of her nervous body. I pictured the moist, knowing smirk of Linda Darnell. I recalled the dictionary entries, and the process I could infer. I summoned memories of the only breasts I'd seen naked, the only patch of pubic down....

Fist clenched, I brazened Hell.

*The Second Quarter*

# Love in Rangoon

# 1

**We steamed up the broad yellow river and moored at a concrete quay on the outskirts of the city.**

Showing the flag, it was called, and ours was the first American naval vessel to have carried the colors into this backwater in over a decade. What recondite political purposes we were serving we never knew. But once lines were doubled, our boatswains dressed ship—festoons of light to blaze aloft, perhaps even visible when the Irawaddy's swells lifted our radar mast above the rococo brick warehouse that screened us from the populace. In the afternoon our bemused crew lost at volleyball to a team of polite, giggling little seamen from the host Burmese Navy. In the evening there was a dance. That was where I met Victoria.

In a vast, dreary hall, an insufficiency of "nice" girls—daughters of Anglo-Burmese families—had been marshalled to sway in the awkward clutches of our scrubbed and grumbling men. The humidity was stifling. A few puckered balloons and strands of crepe paper hung limply from the peeling walls. The punch was non-alcoholic. Fortunately, it was supplemented sometime later by tubs of tepid bottled beer. By midnight, a few of the more determined among the enlisted men had become successfully disheveled and bellicose.

Under the banyan trees at the naval base, as officer in charge of the volleyball party, I'd exchanged cigarettes with the slender, dark-skinned Burmese sublieutenant who came forward to greet me when I entered the dance. I extended my hand. To my growing consternation, he failed to relinquish it. We stood that way for about five minutes—he chatting brightly, grinning, clutching my sweaty palm as I nodded and replied in distracted "mm"s through a grittily courteous smile. Then he led me hand-in-hand across the floor to the long table where the captain and my fellow officers, melting into high-collared tropical dress whites, eyed our approach over glasses of iceless pink punch.

I could only presume, given its openness, that hand-holding among friendly males was an innocent custom of the land. As an ambassador of the *pax Americana*, the last thing I wanted was to offer offense. Which I feared might result if I were to attempt to forcibly disengage my fingers. So about all I could do was flare my eyebrows furtively as I settled into a seat beside my newfound admirer.

More explicit mugging was ruled out by the gazes of the Burmese officers and their wives who also surveyed me from across the table. Captain Rogers—his nickname "Buck," needless to say—sat among them, heeled at an angle that would capsize a destroyer. He was deep in conversation with the svelte Eurasian woman seated to his left. She was Mrs. Tommy Burgess, I would learn from the ensuing roll call. Wardroom intelligence had it that the skipper actually managed to go to bed with her that night. To her left was the cuckold-to-be, if that was true: Commander Tommy Burgess of the Burmese Navy. He was an impressive figure, six feet tall, blue-eyed, with chiseled, burnt-sienna features, obviously more Anglo than Burmese... a man who spoke with impeccable good grace in a clipped U accent that might have been acquired on the playing fields of Eton. I had the impression, however, that he was slightly... well, can't say drunk, but that he'd fortified himself with plentiful charges of gin-and-bitters.

The remainder of the names spoken to me that evening were forgettably alien and monosyllabic. Except for one. And because my ears and brain always refuse for some reason to cooperate during introductions, I failed to retain all but the convoying "Mrs." as I bobbed my head and smiled dutifully from face to face the first time around.

My glance kept returning to its owner, though, while my attentive young Burmese comrade shyly plied me with questions about America. She was very blonde, her face and broad shoulders deeply tanned. A woman in her late twenties or early thirties, I guessed—more from her air of mature self-possession than from any hints of age in her regular, lightly made-up features. She sat erect and aloof—cropped hair, straight nose, strong chin, granite eyes seeming to glint with mockery when a smile was called for... a handsome, bored woman whose fair Western looks clearly fascinated my fellow officers as much as they did me.

She was insulated from all of us at first by the stolid Buddha-like Burmese flag officers seated on either side of her. No Mr. Whatever was in evidence. That alone was a pretty engaging attribute. Our wives or girlfriends were far away, in Yokosuka. We were two months out of that homeport. Those of us who were unmarried could scarcely remember the last time we'd encountered an even remotely available "round-eye." So as soon as circulation could be established, my wardroom mates began eagerly to jockey closer.

It was the Executive Officer, though, who swooped into the adjoining chair the instant it was vacated. And infiltration of his beachhead, I was pretty sure, would be accomplished only at the intruder's peril when we lined up for Officers' Call next morning. As for me, I was scared to budge anyway, lest my companion—Sublieutenant An was his name—grab my hand for another cozy public promenade.

Eventually he did excuse himself. I leaped to the chance to unbend my legs safely. I fled in search of moving air outside the muggy hall. Carmichael and Denison, our Communications Officer and First Lieutenant respectively, stood smoking on the front steps. I joined them, to endure their anticipated speculations on the risks in bunking near me, now that my true sexual proclivities had revealed themselves.

"I gotta admit, he is pretty cute," Denison allowed. We groused about the dim prospects for the days ahead, on the evidence of this dance.

"Well, I guess you're taken care of, anyway," Carmichael grinned. "Here comes your date."

Sure enough, An was working his way toward us through the crowd. I'd noticed tall French doors opening onto a balcony or terrace at the rear of the building. I excused myself and sidled into the shadows—not exactly invisible in my sodden white tunic.

The brassy, off-the-beat music of the band pulsed through the open windows above me as I fled down the narrow walk beside the hall. I surprised one of our ET's kissing a skinny, black-haired girl in crinolines. She started like a sprinter when she heard my footfalls. The sailor restrained her with a nonchalant armlock. He grinned at me. "Evenin', Mr. Schubert."

I nodded. "Evening, Krebs. Don't do anything I wouldn't do."

"No, sir," he agreed happily.

At the rear of the hall there was indeed a terrace where a number of people lounged. I trudged up the cracked concrete stairway and perched at the corner of the parapet. A knot of sullen, unattractive girls hissed gossip in the doorway. They were as disgruntled, no doubt, as most of our men. I'd lapsed into vague musings on cultural anthropology when I was startled to see the woman whose name I couldn't remember zigzag through them and drift toward my corner.

The XO was nowhere in sight. She strolled to the balustrade, fished in her purse and extracted a cigarette. Almost without calculation, I found myself on my feet, leaning forward to proffer my Zippo.

"Oh, hullo, then," she said, slightly taken aback.

I lit her cigarette. I tapped one from my own red pack of Pall Malls. She eyed me quizzically.

"I'm sorry," I smiled. "My name's Schubert. Richard Schubert. I'm afraid there were so many introductions going on back in there I've forgotten...."

"Yes. You're the one with the charming little mate, I believe. I'm Victoria Cashman."

I laughed, embarrassed. "He does seem to be kind of fond of me, doesn't he? I suppose... I mean, I guess that's more common or something, in this culture, huh? Holding hands? Men...?"

"Can't say that I've noticed. In these circles, at any rate."

"Yeah? My gosh. Hm! You think...? You live here, too, don't you?"

"Indeed." Her voice was husky. I'd heard enough to place the accent as Australian. "But don't worry. I'm something less than an authority on Burmese ways, I'm afraid."

"Well," I chuckled, "Contrary to appearances, I want to assure you that I don't love him." I winced. "Phew. Wonder what kind of reputation I'm carrying around now...?"

She laughed. Perhaps she really had mistrusted my orientation at first. But as we finished our cigarettes, she seemed to relax into a less studied cordiality. I was able to draw out a little more information about her. She was the wife of the Australian naval attaché. He was up in the Shan territory "for a fortnight"... gathering intelligence or advising someone on counterinsurgency or something. She was vague—less from discretion, it appeared, than from simple lack of interest. She'd been here eighteen months, she said. Her flat tone indicated she was not exactly thrilled by the assignment.

"Do you have to come to a lot of these functions?" I sympathized.

"Not a lot," she replied. There was a glint of humor in her eyes. She seemed to be subduing a temptation to add a sardonic qualifier, like "fortunately"—and allowing me to appreciate the restraint. I was flattered.

"So what does one do for amusement here?" I wondered.

"Very little, actually. You can visit pagodas until that pales. Then there's gardening, bridge, swimming... clobber of that sort. With the other diplomatic people. Tennis. Bloody boring, most of it, I'm afraid."

"Well, it sounds as if we're in for a ball."

"Oh, you won't find it so bad, I expect. Actually, does anyone on your ship play a decent game of tennis?"

I shrugged. "I've been known to hold a racket, as a matter of fact."

She nodded. She stubbed out her cigarette on the parapet. The light filtering from inside highlighted golden strands of her close-clipped hair.

"Maybe you'd like to play some time," I offered. It seemed a promising possibility. One I shouldn't let drop, no matter that my initial reaction had been reluctance. I don't much care for pitty-patting with hackers. Still, she was tall and looked reasonably coordinated. Besides, the game itself was hardly the point here. "Is there a place we could do it? I mean...."

"Yes, actually," she said. "We've got quite an adequate court on the grounds of our embassy."

"Well then, why don't we give it a try? Oh, but... excuse me. I don't mean to be too pushy. It's your court, after all."

She gave me a sidewise appraisal. Thanks to a seven-inch growth spurt during my senior year of high school, I stand almost six-foot-three in my socks. Still, she met me almost eye to eye in her high heels.

"Not my court, sorry to say. The ambassador's," she corrected. "You play a Sunday game? Or...?"

"As it happens," I said, "I lettered in tennis in college."

She looked blank. I realized the wording was perhaps infelicitous. "That means I played... intercollegiate tennis," I explained. "Competed with some pretty good players, in fact. Barry MacKay? Olmedo?"

"You played them?"

"Well... we didn't actually schedule Michigan or Southern Cal," I admitted. "Could've, though. We beat Wisconsin and Indiana. And I only lost four matches my senior year. But don't worry. I haven't had much chance to keep my game up the last couple of years."

"That's too bad," she said. "Perhaps we can try to help you work back into form. Duty clear. Have you free time during the day?"

"Here, we do, yes. Our mission is to be the perfect guests. I believe we submit to all offers of hospitality."

We both looked around simultaneously—at the wooden Burmese senior officers and their prim wives, the anxiously circulating subalterns, the civilian dignitaries in their soggy suits, the American j.g.'s unenthusiastically guzzling punch, the few sailors and girls grittily dancing while the majority huddled in gloomy segregation against the walls and the band tootled its unrecognizable music at them.

"Q.E.D.," I grinned.

We both laughed.

"I don't suppose you'd like to dance," I said.

Before she could respond to that hopeless invitation,

the XO hove between us. He thrust a glass of punch at her and glared at me. I wreathed my face in neutral geniality and backed off half a pace. He shouldered into the relinquished territory. Even as I drew breath to offer some bland comment that would guard my place in the conversation, I felt a gentle plucking at my sleeve. I looked down to find Sublieutenant An beaming in triumph beside me like a puppy who'd recognized its lost master.

Mrs. Cashman and I traded glances but, though I repeatedly tried to maneuver my way into an appropriate situation, no further words that evening. I dragged back to the ship with the rest of the wardroom party at eleven p.m.— wrung out from the prolonged, unremitting effort to be pleasant, jaw aching after four hours fixed in a goony smile, relieved to be out from under An's crushing camaraderie at last... but disappointed at what I was sure was an irretrievably fumbled, now totally dissipated, opportunity.

**I was bowed over the chart table on the bridge plotting latitude and longitude coordinates for the MovRep we'd have to file before departure when the captain summoned me to his cabin after breakfast next morning.**

I had just been invited to participate in a tennis match at the Australian Embassy, he informed me. He had, of course, accepted on my behalf. An embassy car would be calling at noon.

Southern Crosses flapping from its front fenders, the Cadillac limousine purred into a driveway that curved toward a gray stone mansion set in a vast expanse of manicured grounds. Every border was resplendent with tropical flowers. A long, awning-shaded verandah flanked the residence—English country-seat architecture replicated in colonial Burma. At the foot of the pristinely clipped lawn, surrounded by banks of blooming shrubs, a cluster of white wrought-iron garden furniture nestled under a parti-colored umbrella. There sat Mrs. Cashman in tennis whites, tanned legs crossed, sipping what looked like lemonade with a slightly older woman dressed in a bright, obviously expensive summer frock. It was a perfect Kipling scene. The Burmese chauffeur deposited me near them. Mrs. Cashman greeted me with a correct smile and introduced me to the ambassador's wife, who extended her hand.

"I understand you once played tennis for your university, Lef'tenant," the woman drawled. That broad, faintly Cockney diphthongization of every vowel contrasted with the practiced formality of her intonation. (Mrs. Cashman's accent too, I must admit, sounded slightly coarse to my Masterpiece Theatre-trained ear.)

"I know it can be quite difficult to find suitable facilities
when one is overseas. That's why we're happy to make this court available to you and your fellow officers while you are here. It really doesn't get as much use as it should do. Mrs. Cashman and her husband are our most regular, how shall I term it? Contestants? Commander Cashman is up-country at the moment, however."

I nodded.

"And Victoria is looking forward to testing your mettle, I daresay. She was one of our ranking juniors a few years back."

"Oh?"

"Too many to count," Mrs. Cashman interjected.

"I do hope you will enjoy yourself, Lef'tenant. There's lemon squash here, and you may change in the house. The boy will show you where. I'm afraid I have to be off now." She

165

sighed. "Sinmalaik Ladies' Garden Society. We also serve...."

"Who only lose our strokes," I quipped.

Suddenly I was embarrassed. Had I overstepped the bounds? But Mrs. Cashman smiled.

"Indeed," the ambassador's wife acknowledged, showing teeth. She offered her hand again—a sleek, brisk woman who radiated diplomatic confidence. "Have a pleasant afternoon."

And that we certainly did. After I'd exchanged my slacks and loafers for shorts and tennis shoes—the former creased and yellow from having rested untouched so long in my cabin locker—Mrs. Cashman led me to the court. It was an impeccably rolled and chalk-lined plot of red clay inside a chain-link fence thickly grown with fragrant climbers. Immense blossoms of scarlet, pink and amber exploded at every hand. It was winter in Yokosuka, bleak and rainy. At least four months had passed since I'd even taken a racket out of its cover.

The first return I attempted sailed a good two feet beyond the baseline. Mrs. Cashman had looked a bit skeptical as we'd strolled across the lawn from the house. For an ex-Number Two singles at Cincinnati, my appearance was admittedly pretty ratty. The uppers of my tennis shoes were beginning to crack, and I'd been plagued by my usual trouble with laces—one had broken as I'd pulled it tight, and I'd had to make an emergency repair that created two frayed, unsightly knots. I've always believed in the psychological efficacy of dressing and equipping oneself below one's class. I'd affected a shirt with an enlarging rip at the armpit throughout the Missouri Valley Conference championships. Notwithstanding, I'd been named All-Tournament Second Team. But this wasn't an occasion for gamesmanship; the impression I wanted to make was debonair. That little bombshell about Mrs. Cashman's national ranking—an Australian yet—had tightened me up even further. So it took several rallies before I gained anything like a normal rhythm.

Adding to my difficulties was the fact that she possessed a murderous topspin, aided by her height and the hundred-and-thirty-or-so pounds she could pivot behind it. She had the good woman's steadiness, plus excellent anticipation and a coach's dream of technique. Before long we were rocketing the ball from corner to corner, exulting in the sheer muscle of it, grinning and streaming sweat, skidding and grunting—utterly absorbed in the simple mechanics of propelling a fuzzy sphere with as much force as we could corkscrew back on and release. Of course, I had more power. But absent strategy, I couldn't blow by her. Except for my serve, I'd never been that much of a banger anyway. After a while we played a set. Shifting to touch and rusty, I actually lost. Six-two, no less. We toweled off, sucked down some lemonade and giddily congratulated ourselves on finding each other.

"What the hell are you doing tucked away here in... for God's sake... *Rangoon*?" I goggled. "You ought to be at *Wimbledon* or something!"

"Sometimes I bloody well think so too," she laughed. "But it's a bit late now, isn't it?"

We played another set. I opted for conservatism. At twelve-all, with the light beginning to thicken, we called it quits. My sealegs were turning rubbery.

"I'll get you next time," I promised. "Now you've made me mad. I'm gonna destroy you. A good man can always beat a good woman, no matter how tough she is."

"Taunt, taunt. You bloody Yanks are all mouth."

I said I'd better be getting back to the ship. Supper would be served in the wardroom soon. I wondered about how to summon the limousine. She said she could drive me. Great, I exclaimed. I'd have to get my clothes first, though. She inquired if I didn't want to take a shower. I said I could do it on the ship. She said I could do it here—or at her house, for that matter. She could make me a drink meantime if I'd like.

Needless to say, I accepted. We showered serially and sipped our Scotches. She'd put on a halter top, tailored shorts and sandals. Her damp hair was combed back mannishly. There was nothing else mannish about her.

"You'd be the Queen of Wimbledon, that's for sure," I bravely ventured.

She was at least five years older than I. Married. Very worldly in my eyes. Although the Navy was beginning to make me worldly, I was very nervous. I lit cigarette after cigarette.

"That's why you were huffing and puffing out there today," she chided me. She was smoking too.

I swallowed my Chivas and struggled to think of properly diffident things to say. I didn't want to make an ass of myself by assuming an attraction that didn't exist. Nor did I want to queer the possibility for more of this afternoon's uncomplicated enjoyment. I asked if she had children.

"No. I... did have. A son. Robin was his name. He... drowned."

"Oh, gee...."

"Five years old. It was a long time ago, though." She inhaled deeply on her cigarette and ground it in the ashtray.

The large room, its rattan blinds down, was growing dusky. A hot, red twilight guttered beyond the narrow slats. I rose to go. She fetched her keys and purse and followed me to the door. I held it for her. She brushed against me. Impulsively, muscle-weary and liquored, I touched her shoulder.

She sagged against me, tilted her face up and parted her lips.

**At 10:30 we wolfed hastily grilled steaks, and then she drove me back to the waterfront.**

She let me out on a shadowy corner. It was ten minutes to midnight when I floated across the quarterdeck. The somnolent watchstanders eyed my tennis racket quizzically.

On a ship as intimate as a destroyer it's pretty hard to go about independent business unremarked. So my daily absorption in tennis at the Australian embassy naturally became a topic for wardroom conjecture. When Denison slyly wondered at the coincidental nationality of that knockout we'd met at the dance the other night, I squirmed and shoved bacon into my mouth and cast a weather eye at the XO. Who, it must be said, seemed to have shrugged off Victoria's subsequent unavailability without animosity toward me. If I were even associated.

My tennis had always placed me in a unique category. From the outset, I'd good naturedly accommodated each of my fellow officers who'd suggested a game. But the sessions always seemed to devolve into lessons, and the chasm between levels would eventually prove daunting. It was a source of vicarious ship's pride when I won the Long Beach and Yokosuka championships—hardly, I might add, earth-shaking achievements. Nevertheless, all that meant that the arrival of a diplomatic limousine each morning to whisk me off in solitary, racket-laden splendor (now that I knew Victoria's ability, I could arm myself fully without fear of unnerving her) nicely accorded with my protective mystique.

Besides, it was just another exotic element in a daily

smorgasbord of them. Our nebulous mission to this out-of-the-way port allowed for holiday routine, with liberty call at noon. By breakfast the next morning the wardroom table would be a babble of excited reminiscences about the ormolu glories of the Sule Pagoda, the decayed gentility of the Strand Hotel, the bazaars thronged with saffron-swathed monks and cheroot-puffing crones—all duly memorialized on dozens of trayfuls of Kodachrome slides and thousands of feet of eight-millimeter film. Hong Kong had provided us with plenty of bargain gadgetry.

Except to me and the captain, possibly—he also munched a quiet, introverted breakfast—the entertainments offered by Socialist Burma seemed to be pretty chaste. I listened, smiled, nodded with polite interest and encouraged accounts of others' activities... all the while inwardly humming to an electric satisfaction, my body loose and limber, assuaged by the unctuous calisthenics of the bed (when my fingers strayed near my face I could surreptitiously invoke Victoria's most intimate scent), exulting in the secret, incredible fortune of experiencing my first affair with an older woman. A married woman. And one, for that, of my own race.

Avoiding scandal was essential, of course. So we had to fit our private dalliance around lots of innocuous public tennis. Not that either of us, I think, considered that a hardship. Nor was it very public—I saw the ambassador's wife on only one other occasion. She gave us a fleeting, friendly wave from the verandah.

On the second day of our visit I got the captain's okay to take off at midmorning. A quarterdeck phone call to Victoria—husky Australian voice conjuring voltaic images of her pressed naked against me the night before—brought the limousine. We played on the freshly groomed court until nearly one. Then, eyes stinging with sweat, crowns sizzling and feet blistered by the sun-seared clay, we broke for lunch.

Inside her house, in the cool shade, we flung off our saturated whites and instantly meshed pungent bodies in voracious celebration of the agility and suppleness we'd admired across the net throughout the morning.

I'd never been particularly turned on by women athletes. But this was a jock relationship at its essence, for sure. We stroked, explored, memorized each other's sleek contours with the earnest fidelity of cartographers preparing relief maps. After a prolonged diet of plump, short-shanked Japanese bar hostesses, I traced with wonder, insides quivering, her minimal breasts with their conical nipples, her wide shoulders, her compact hips and buttocks, her long, smoothly defined thigh and calf muscles, her flat, navel-punctuated abdomen underlain by its wispy tuft of light brown—almost blonde!—hair. And in turn, she lulled me with leisurely appreciations of my own angularities, and my unflagging twenty-five-year-old's erection. I think, except for the hours on the court and in uniform, I spent that entire week with a hard-on.

After showers and sandwiches, served by a fat Burmese woman who materialized and dematerialized through some ectoplasmic magic of Victoria's, we returned to the embassy court. By now it had been miraculously watered, dragged and rechalked. We played at a much more relaxed pace until five, when by pre-arrangement the limousine returned and we shook hands goodbye as the chauffeur bowed me into the rear seat.

I ate aboard that evening with the duty section. A couple of the less adventurous officers were also present: Barlow—a callow new ensign from Georgia Tech with a sunburned neck and retrograde opinions that accorded with its hue, expressed in a whiny accent you could use to etch glass—and Ungerer the Gunnerer. He was (as one might figure from the sobriquet) our Gunnery Officer, a mustang (a former enlisted man), a devout Mormon in his 30s whose wife had refused to quit Provo for Yokosuka but had nevertheless presented him with two of their five children in the past eighteen months.

After dark, as Ungerer was setting up the nightly movie in the wardroom (*North to Alaska*, with John Wayne—I'd seen it when we'd shown it the first time, two days out of Singapore) I shucked my khakis and went forward to the quarterdeck. Carmichael was OOD.

"I'm gonna go have a drink with that Burmese guy," I said. "You know, the one who was holding my hand the other night?" I grimaced.

He leered.

"At their O Club. Guess I oughtta be safe there, anyway."

It occurred to me that I was lying. Through the teeth. But I'd had to provide some acceptable excuse for departing the ship alone, since we'd been instructed to travel in pairs at all times. Burma, like Kowloon—on the mainland bordering the People's Republic of China—was considered too hazardous for safe soloing by kidnap-bait like us top-secret-laden American naval personnel.

Once around the corner of the warehouse and out of Carmichael's view, I hopped into a battered taxi—they sat there in hopeful queue 24 hours a day—and directed the driver to a suburban intersection near Victoria's house. She'd told me the names to say. I paid the driver his fare, peeled off a few more *kyat* and gave him half with the promise of the rest if he'd wait. I adjusted the hands of my Hong Kong Rolex to read eleven-thirty and showed it to him in the glow of the dashboard. He nodded. Then I strolled away into a residential darkness thick with the exudations of tropical plants, the hum of insects and the chirp of frogs.

Victoria lived in a compound of diplomatic residences surrounding a small lake. I turned down a tree-shaded drive between tall hedges and found my way across a sloping lawn—walking gingerly, musing on kraits—to her doorstep. She was waiting for my surreptitious rap. We drank brandy, chatted distractedly for a few minutes for form and ended up very soon in the rumpled double bed.

With minor variations, that was our routine for the next three days. Having given up serious tennis in graduate school and even further diluted my skills through two years of Navy destroyer duty—in college it had become clear that I'd never rise above a certain journeyman, early-rounds level in major tournament play—this kind of intense daily concentration on the game was both unaccustomed, an evocation of the past, and exhilarating. Victoria had been playing more regularly than I, but her game too seemed to gain in sting and finesse as she honed mine. Interspersed with sets, we worked on individual strokes. She'd offer commentary on my form and I'd volunteer pointers on hers—something we'd both been coached enough to welcome and benefit from.

Once my serve and volley began to lock into the groove again, I had the edge on her. Not all that much, but enough to be confident I could take the set when I wanted it. Interestingly, that marked a change in the character of our love-making, too. It was never conscious; maybe tennis wasn't even connected. But where at first I'd been tentative, slightly passive, dependent on her to set the pace and focus of our pleasure, as a winner I slowly became more inventive and insouciant... the initiator.

## Not that I was all that skilled as a lover, to put it mildly.

I was twenty-one before I'd slept with a woman. Felt that lubricious hilting....

173

She was a hostess at a Manila nightclub. I was working my way to Europe for the summer the long way around, as a deckhand on a Norwegian freighter. A fellow graduate student had suggested the possibility of finding such a job through a place called the Scandinavian Shipping Office in San Francisco. So, one drizzly April Thursday, dispirited by another post-lunch wallow in "The Pastoral Tradition in English Poetry," I'd let curiosity walk me across Sproul Plaza and onto a transbay bus. And indeed, there was a freighter at Pier Twenty-Nine in immediate need of a *dekksgutt*, a tow-headed clerk informed me. No experience required. Just a valid passport—which I had in a drawer in my room in International House. The listed ports of call read like an index to the works of Somerset Maugham. The ship sailed Monday... and I was aboard, queasily watching the bluffs of the Golden Gate dip beneath the spumy Pacific. I was unhandily tapping a hammer at scabs of rust on the poopdeck rail. My master's degree could await a matriculation in life.

The lower bunk of the cabin to which I was assigned had been claimed by a burly onetime hod-carrier from Newcastle (upon-Tyne). He called himself a "navvy." Deaf to idiom, the Norwegian first mate assumed we shared a language. What we had more precisely in common were age, a given name and a bemused fascination with the nuances of our vast national and social distance.

So after polishing off our *aftens* of fishballs, cabbage and boiled potatoes, Richard Blackwell and I darted down the gangplank to explore in company the iniquitous nightlife of our first Oriental landfall. Six or eight San Miguels later, though, I found myself alone in a cab with the shortest—and I thought the prettiest—of the two plump young women who'd sidled in to flank us at the last raucous hole-in-the-wall.

I'd readily accommodated her requests for a couple

of Scotch and waters (in reality, she later admitted, they were only iced tea marked up to a whisky price, on which she was given a sliver of the house profit). And I'd taken my modest pleasure in the insistent pressure of her plush breasts and thighs, busily trying to squeeze an erection out of me as we shuffled in the crowd around the blaring jukebox. But only when my cabin mate led his companion off with a lewd wink did I realize that I too was free to indulge the experience that had been my unacknowledged errand from the moment I'd inhaled the first faint land-fragrance of Luzon.

It was the foreignness of the setting and the mitigating constraints of the occupation now defining me—I was a seaman, a wanderer of the world's oceans who only occasionally alit for what brief restorative interludes might be snatched on alien strands—that allowed me to pay for my sexual initiation. I could never have permitted myself such a lapse from *noblesse oblige* in my own culture, such a compromise of self-esteem. Still, for all the sweaty hours I'd put in slouched under steering wheels exploring tongue with tongue, for all the vertiginous triumphs as I'd insinuated my hand under a bra to cup the bare swelling flesh beneath, to find and finger its palpitant nub... somehow I'd never succeeded in coaxing a girl to wriggle out of her panties. I had not known the strategy or been willing to feign the commitment that might have overcome their final reluctance. Of course, those were the days before the pill.

Like a lot of long anticipated events, my deflowering proved a lot less momentous in reality than in fantasy. She lived in a tiny second-floor room in a board-and-batten hovel in a warren of peeling Spanish Colonial tenements. Her walls were adorned with garish portraits of Jesus and Mary scissored from magazines. The crate on which were arrayed her toiletries doubled as a shrine or altar. A rosary was draped in a careful loop between two stubby candles. She lit them before peeling her flowered sheath dress over her head and raking a comb through her dense blue-black mane. She gestured at me to undress. Then she popped out of her bra, shucked her cotton briefs and hopped nimbly into the narrow bed, allowing me in the process a peep at the pubescent pink dimple between the globes of her cocoa-butter buttocks.

The sheets looked clean enough. But I'm not sure what revelation of filth or intimation of disease might have been enough at that pass to indispose me—the fatalistic glutton for experience. I had a rubber in my wallet, cleverly disguised inside a sugar packet—in case I were ever hit by a car. I wasn't about to scrabble for it now, though. I glanced breathless at her compliant, lambent, utter nakedness. Clumsily I crawled alongside her. I kissed her—I couldn't imagine any other prelude—and groped her spongy breasts. She squirmed and brought me atop her, thighs splayed. With practiced fingers she guided me into her tight, moist vaginal clasp. I shuddered and came in about five strokes.

So that was it. I mounted her with awe three times that night. For which I left the specified gratuity on the dresser-altar as I stumbled out, sore and blearily hung over, into the dawn. However many *pesos* it was, I regarded the transaction as an incredible bargain. It was neat, too. Fulfillment of a market demand without any of the complex subtextual expectations—the promises or guilt over their withholding that you paid with on the homefront, where engagement or rape seemed the only alternatives to celibacy.

What's more, the impassive witness of Jesus and the Blessed Virgin had paradoxically assuaged me. In the Philippines the flesh and the spirit, I concluded, could be independent domains. The Catholic faith of my childhood had shattered in large measure because sex and sin were its weld—the very structural seam of doctrine.

Although I penetrated other girls in other ports on that voyage—the clinical verb is accurate—I learned

176

almost nothing about how to satisfy a woman. I liked the coy pidgin conversations over sticky tabletops cross-hatched with match games. I enjoyed the brief moments of postcoital domesticity from which I could begin to descry an individual personality. I treated the women with the grave respect the offer of their bodies deserved—I was an earnest newcomer to a realm in which they were seasoned, though in fact most were younger than I. It wasn't so much different from blind dating, really. Only the outcome was assured. In which I did hope for the validation of their pleasure. But I didn't spend a lot of time analyzing the gasps and yips they accorded me as I ejaculated. Which, to be honest, was my preoccupation.

In Japan, on my return three years later as a Navy ensign, I'd begun to transcend that self-absorption.

"You make love to many girls?" smiled the first one I went home with, the morning after.

"A few," I shrugged. It was acknowledgment and boast—modesty and exaggeration. She was maybe the sixth. And none had been unbought. Or American.

She giggled.

"Why?" I demanded, suddenly wondering if there was an innuendo... some hint of dissatisfaction with my technique—which in fact was nonexistent.

She didn't reply. She gave me a motherly pat. She was a matron of about twenty-eight. "Butterfly," she winked.

From then on I tried to be more tentative, more sensitive. On the Yokosuka (pronounced "Yo-kooska") bar scene, promiscuity was deprecated. The epithet "butterfly" was a reproof. Regular relationships (of a few weeks' or months' duration) between American Navymen and hostesses (whom we did not consider prostitutes but a sort of subspecies of geisha) were encouraged. In bars that catered to officers, at least, you seldom if ever heard price quotations for a "short time" or "all night." That would be offensively blunt. Instead, gifts of cash—in sufficient amounts—were expected:

favors for favors. And prolonged allegiances deepened and broadened the sexual menu.

There was Chieko, who called herself "Rinda"—each hostess affected a Western alias, often of the most jarring incongruity and maladaptation to the Japanese tongue. They clung stubbornly to these fanciful alter egos too. Only with great reluctance did Linda finally reveal—but glumly refuse to acknowledge my attempts to substitute—the far more attractive (to me, anyway) name with which she'd been born. She was my girlfriend for the first several months. It was her implied or suspected criticism that stung me—as well it should have. Only later did I figure out that she'd been resentfully giving me no help at all as I'd drunkenly burrowed and thrust at her. I'd thought there was some odd anatomical incompatibility. But when I showed up the next night to buy her more drinks, and when I'd been sobered and cleansed in the scalding depths of her wood-fired *ofuro*, she opened up, so to speak.

From Linda—Chieko—I learned the male-under alternative, and the shuddering credentials of a true female orgasm, deftly self-induced astride my willing auger. She was saving money for an operation to have her eyelids Westernized. I thought it was an appalling idea. But she maintained that it would add longevity and give a competitive boost to the career whose twilight she was now definitely entering. In fact, she was frugal, and hoped eventually to buy her own little bar. When my visits gradually became less frequent, she had her lawyer telephone me on the ship to remind me that the account was not yet closed. It was unnerving, and a reminder of the thoroughly commercial grounding of our liaison. (But then, how different is that from a lot of marriages?) I gave her a hundred-and-fifty dollars in yen and breathed a sigh of relief when we cast off our lines for thirty days of SEATO exercises.

After that there was Yumiko—"Sarry"—who'd been

Carmichael's girlfriend before the cruise. She was eighteen, fresh and stunning—unquestionably the most beautiful hostess I would ever encounter in Yokosuka. Her hair was teased up into a stylish bouffant bubble, her eyelids were heavily outlined, but otherwise she wore no makeup. I was a sucker for that beatnik poetess manner. She had uncommonly proportioned legs for a Japanese, too, long-boned and trim. I was proud to be seen with her. Sailors would swivel their heads in admiration and Japanese men follow her with their eyes as we strode through the cobbled alleys, the neon-lit dusk thick with the clack of clogs and the chatter of Pachinko balls, the air perfumed by charcoal and soy sauce, ginger, raw Suntory whisky and cloying Peace tobacco.

Yumiko breasted the stares haughtily. She was alternately impassioned and perfunctory in bed. Sometimes in the bar she would giggle and jitterbug with manic joy, but part of what made her beauty so haunting was a lurking melancholy. I wonder if it had something to do with the status among her chauvinistic countrymen of women who consorted with *gaijin*. When I came back after two weeks chasing the *Ranger* on carrier quals, I found her missing from the bar. I went to the building she'd lived in, but managed to learn nothing from the dismissive grunts and hand-gestures of her former neighbors. Later, one of her coworkers told me she'd tried to kill herself. Another pooh-poohed that intelligence and intimated she'd simply ducked out of sight for a routine abortion. Whichever, the lovely, *triste* Yumiko had vanished.

Finally there was Martha—Masa. We sat in the grandstand cheering for the Taiyo *Whales* (after the game we turned in our ticket stubs for a can of whale meat) and expressed our own athleticism trying to emulate the positions illustrated in erotic Japanese woodcuts. She kept a book of out-of-register reproductions at bedside, rather the way orthopedists stock their waiting rooms with ski magazines. At first I was somewhat daunted by the enormity of the penises displayed by these smugly rooted *samurai*. She assured me it was artistic license, a hyperbolic convention. And we did, indeed, fit quite nicely. She had one major reservation, nonetheless: she resolutely defended her anus against my mild efforts to discover what D.H. Lawrence had been so perfervid about.

Masa waved me off from dockside when we departed for Rangoon. Within hours, I knew, she'd have exchanged her brocade kimono for a silken *cheong sam*. And she'd spend the night entertaining the Marine Phantom pilot from Atsugi I alternated with as her "*boy-furendo*." But at least I had acquired the rudiments of a repertoire by the time I met Victoria.


## She was proving the least reticent of the women I'd known.

Victoria's were the first kisses slowly to stray down my neck to my nipples, to my navel, to my scrotum. Among the most intense sensations of my life was the astonishing, unanticipated slither of her parted lips to engulf the shank of my taut penis. I groaned aloud, writhed in ecstatic anguish at the unctuous caress of her palate and tongue. She crouched over me, breasts pendant. I fondled her puckered aureoles. I reached down and plunged my middle finger into the jellied socket of her vagina. She squirmed and hunkered to settle more deeply on it—I could probe the alien solidity of her diaphragm. Clutching my tumescence like a fleshly popsicle, she doggedly, deliriously licked, sucked and teased me with arch scrapes of her incisors until I warned her with a strangled, "No!"

But Victoria wasn't stopping. And I couldn't now. My entire musculature tensed. A tidal constriction swept inexorably from my straining toes to my locked knees to my knotted buttocks, arched spine, quavering belly and loins....

"Aaagh, Christ!" I gargled.

And only at that instant of climactic, spasmic release did she disgorge me.

A clot of opalescent fluid spurted and sailed to splat on my left shoulder. She breathed a little "ooh." As the salvos diminished in force and trajectory, she directed them playfully across my twitching abdomen. Most of the milk-blue ooze puddled in the declivity of my navel. She stirred it with her forefinger and sampled it fastidiously with the tip of her tongue.

"A good year?" I gasped. My breath and composure were slowly returning.

"Prime vintage," she nodded. "Haven't you ever tasted yourself?"

"Nope."

"Care to?" she asked.

With a mischievous tilt of eyebrow she bowed low over me and slathered the cloudy exudate on her nipple. Then she crept higher across my chest and dangled the glistening pap above my mouth. I gaped obediantly.

My semen was bland, I found, slimy like oyster juice, with a faint odor that reminded me of Clorox.

Victoria's essence, on the other hand, was pungent, saline with a bitter tinge—muskily ammoniac. Always before, hygienic reservations had stayed me from indulging the cunnilingual impulse. But I responded with alacrity to her urging, "Lick me, Richard! It's my turn now."

To be frank, I didn't even know how to find the clitoris. But the gentle steering of her hand beside my ear, the crescendo of her breath and the convulsions of her abdomen soon made me an expert on the erectile bud's location and utility. My jaw had begun to ache, though, before she finally thrashed and cried out. I was stiff with desire again. I salivated and glazed the roseate frills around her vulval slit with my exhausted tongue.

"Come in me. Come in me, Richard. Fuck me," she exclaimed.

I knelt and eased bayonet into scabbard. The room sounded like a swamp being crossed by a platoon of Marines—loud, rhythmic slurps as our pelvises slammed together and her breasts flattened under my chest. I averted my head and picked a pubic hair out of my teeth. I wondered about the noise and the maid. And then I lost myself in the knead, knead... need....

Victoria and I were intensely wound up in each other for those few days, but although I felt the high-keyed preoccupation often called love, I had no real sense of a future to the relationship. I harbored no possessive fantasies, no anxious premonitions of impending heartbreak when the interlude would end. We bobbed determinedly on the physical surface of the days and nights, what conversation we exchanged equally superficial. For all her enthusiasm in the bed and on the tennis court, Victoria remained, by nature or preference, a biographical mystery.

She'd grown up in Melbourne, I learned. Her tennis career had effectively ended when she'd married and had a baby. She'd spent a succession of dreary exiles in military outposts in Australia and abroad. And Philip, her husband, wasn't due back until Sunday morning, the day before we were to sail.

That was about it... which, in fact, was okay with me. I wasn't in the market for a complicated dependency. As to the morality of the situation—well, I was troubled briefly during those busy silences in the bunk when the mind puts its affairs in order for sleep. But my resolution was uncomplex and pragmatic: I was still free to react to any woman who attracted me. The responsibility the woman felt to her pledges, her responsiveness to my transmissions, those were her concern. The obligation to an absent husband didn't devolve on me. (As a husband, later, I must admit, my ideas would undergo some revision.)

Friday night I'd drawn the duty. Saturday morning I got off early again. That flag-bedecked black Caddy that Victoria could cause to idle at the foot of the gangplank carried a pretty persuasive panache.

Although we hit the ball for about an hour, it was hitting the sheets that was foremost on my agenda. Victoria assented to my proposal of an early lunch. We grappled in a fierce silence. It was the last opportunity before the evening, with its awkward goodbyes, its obligatory hypocrisies meant to assign some kind of overriding proportion to this essentially self-contained, carnal episode.

Afterwards we lay for a long time side by side, not touching, listening to the crackle of the noon sun beyond the blinds, the heavy whisperings of the *pipal* trees ringing the lake. Slowly I became aware of a slushiness to her breathing. I turned my head on the pillow; she stared at the ceiling in profile, rigid. Her fair nostrils had flared pink. A tear abruptly oozed from the corner of her eye and trickled down her temple, losing itself in her sweat-damp sideburn. I started to twist on my elbow, solicitous. And then I froze. I wasn't sure I wanted to know why she was crying. A woman's tears in bed were new to me. In my egotism I was sure I must be their cause, I the focus of her emotion—and I was afraid of the burden she might place on me if I made her articulate it. But I was gallant. Dutiful. After a moment I reached out a finger and gently caressed her arm.

"You're crying," I murmured. Brilliantly perceptive. "What's the matter?"

She didn't answer me at first. I watched her swallow, dilate her raddled nostrils. Then, to my surprise, she virtually sneered, "Nothing!" And suddenly a flush of anger suffused her tanned face. "Nothing you'd understand... or that bloody well has anything to do with you, don't worry."

I drew my finger away quickly.

"Come on," she snapped. She rolled out of bed with a flurry. The sight of her white breasts and buttocks, nipples and pubic thatch leeringly emphasized by the keylight pallor of bathing-suit modesty, rekindled hopeless lust in me.

"I suppose you want to be fed," she snarled.

I wasn't altogether sure at that point. But I slunk obediently into the kitchen, where she put together a couple of Vegemite, cheese and lettuce sandwiches. The maid was off this afternoon, she explained. We ate on the verandah and shared a giant can of Swan Lager. She was impatient to get back to the court. I'd have preferred a longer interval for digestion. But talk was strained and I was anxious to accommodate her moodiness. We drove to the embassy and began at once to rally.

# 2

**My shoulders and arms were heavy, my swing mushy.**

I shuffled my feet with maximum economy. She, on the other hand, was wired, and my temporizing nonchalance made her increasingly angry.

"Come on, Richard, damn it!" she piped as I lazily failed to stretch for a hard backhand. "Move! Don't waste both our bloody times!"

"How come you Aussies say 'bloody' so bloody much?" I taunted. The ball kicked off the fence and rolled toward the net. I ambled for it and leaned to tap it off the clay with my racket. As I did I caught the peripheral sweep of her serve.

I glanced up in time to hump my back protectively. The cannonball grazed my shoulder.

"Hey!" I protested. "What are you doing?"

She stalked a couple of paces closer and fired a second overhead at me. I pirouetted defensively. It ticked my elbow.

"Cut that out!" I squawked. I could still feel the sting where the first shot had rasped me. A full-on blast from a tennis ball, while not exactly lethal, can leave a pretty painful bruise.

"Well, you do have a bit of energy, I see. For self-protection, at least."

She wasn't smiling. She turned on her heel and paced to her right. "Serve!" she commanded.

"What are you, my coach? My mother?"

"Serve and play seriously or I'm going home," she said.

Mildly piqued, a glint of vengeance in my eye, I strode to the line and lashed my first intended ace into the net. Double-faulted off the tape with my second. That was really annoying. We exchanged corners wordlessly.

I netted my first flat smash again, but popped the twist into her backhand. She hammered it down the line, a chalk-puff winner.

"Nice shot," I acknowledged. Jaws set, I lugged the sandbags that passed for my feet back to deuce court. I lost my service on four straight.

Although that sluggishness continued to plague me for the next few games—she eventually won six-four—it was soon apparent that Victoria was in a form I hadn't thus far encountered. Devoid of expression, almost blinkered in pure physical concentration, she slugged, nipped, attacked, dinked with the precision and unpredictability of some flawlessly programmed tennis automaton. I was awed, and in my admiring determination to uphold my responsibility to such finesse—dig to keep each point alive, extend her—I gradually transcended my own lunch-and-lager-sodden lethargy.

Lungs pumping, vision tunneled by heat and exertion, I became as unconscious as she of all but the loom and departure of that whirring spheroid, the scramble to protect the thousand square feet of pink clay yawning on my side of the net and the tactical dissection of the shallow strait in which she weaved. She won the second set too. Eight-six.

"Jesus, you're really on today," I panted.

"Three out of five," she said.

"Won't hear any objections from me. Only let me get

a drink firs...."

I'd turned toward the lawn table and chairs outside our fenced enclosure, where we'd left an ice chest with a flask of fresh lemonade and a handful of Swan cans. There were two people sitting under the umbrella. I hadn't been aware of their arrival—obviously they'd been watching us for some time. One was young, a very pretty woman with dark skin, the other a burly Western man of middle age. Both wore tennis togs.

Victoria saw me start. She too had been oblivious to the spectators, whose presence had been masked by the flowering tendrils twining up the fence and our own single-mindedness.

"Phil!" she exclaimed.

The man sat spraddle-legged, clutching a liter-can of Swan. "Afternoon, love," he replied.

I swallowed uneasily and squinted at him. I'd confronted no photos among Victoria's furnishings, and whatever nebulous mental image I might have been carrying around was instantaneously swamped by the reality.

He was barrel chested, meat fisted, with forearms like hawsers. His face was broad and florid under its tan. He had a flat nose and a lantern jaw. He looked to be in his early forties, his dark hair, thin above the forehead, combed back neatly on the diagonal. It was a fashion that reminded me of his princely English namesake, but there was an air of domesticated toughness about him, like a handsome, weathered prize fighter. What was most arresting, though, were the ornate, serpentine blue dragons tattooed on each of those Alley Oop forearms.

I followed Victoria through the gate, smiling tentatively.

"Sharp as a tack today, I see," the man declared. "Who's your playmate?"

My ribcage stiffened.

Victoria indicated me with her racket. "Lef'tenant Junior Grade Richard Schubert, United States Navy...."

"Naval Reserve," I corrected her.

"...Who's been gracious enough to give me a game or two while you were away. He's with the *Busby*, the American destroyer that's...."

"I know. Most gracious of him indeed."

"My husband," Victoria told me. "Commander Philip Cashman. R.A.N."

"How do you do, sir," I nodded.

"Thank you, lef'tenant, for taking care of my wife. Tennis is her passion, you might say. As you've no doubt discovered." His mouth spread to display teeth that were remarkably regular and white.

"An honor, sir," I managed.

"Hello, Gillian," Victoria said.

The young woman bobbed her head.

"Lef'tenant Schubert. Gillian de Souza."

She extended her hand. Although my nervous attention had been directed primarily at Commander Cashman, I hadn't failed to appreciate this striking female presence throned cross-legged in the adjacent wrought iron chair. She looked Indian, despite the surname (quite common, I later learned, among upper-crust Anglo-Indians): fine-boned, with huge, dark-lidded eyes framed by bangs and modishly turned-under shoulder-length hair—so lustrously black it was haloed by a shimmer from the blue spectrum. Her complexion was set off by her tailored tennis dress. She was very brown, but almost completely Western in features. She projected a languid hauteur that also seemed characteristically Indian. I pressed her slender fingers, suddenly aware of my hanging shirt-tail, rumpled hair and sweat-soaked armpits.

"I called Gillian when I came home and found you out, Vicky dear," Cashman said. He grinned lazily, making me wonder about that last phrase.

"How fortunate for you you were able to get back early," Victoria replied. "You should have cabled me or something."

"From Lashio? I'd be surprised if it arrived next week."

"Yes, well, now you're here, perhaps we should let you two have the court."

I'd pinched my racket between my knees and was busy stuffing my wet shirt-tail back down my shorts. It kept snagging on my jock-strap. "Sure, go ahead," I agreed. "She's been running me ragged. I could use a breather."

"No doubt. But I wouldn't dream of it," Cashman smiled. "You both seem to be in finest fettle. Be a shame to interrupt it now. Tennis *interruptus*... never do, eh?" He rumbled at his own humor.

"Where are you from in the states?" the girl inquired. I realized her onyx eyes were trained on me. Her accent was pure high Raj—Cambridge except for slightly elongated vowels and faintly trilled r's. I sidled closer to her chair, removed the racket from between my legs and combed my fingers through my cropped hair.

"Cincinnati," I said. "Ohio. In the Middle West. Originally, anyway. I went to graduate school in California for a year, though. Before I went into the Navy."

"Oh? I attended Stanford, actually. For two years."

"Really? I'll be darned! I was at Berkeley. Cal."

"Oh, yes?"

"When were you there?"

"Do pardon me," Cashman broke in, "if I spoil this touching little reunion, lef'tenant. But I've been cramped inside a very small plane for a very long time today. Would you two Wimbledonians stoop to sharing the clay with a couple of hackers like Jill and me? Just for a game or two? We won't interfere with your cozy communion too long, I trust."

Cashman lunged to his feet, grabbed his racket and drained his outsize beercan with a noisy, head-back swallow. The dragon on his muscle writhed.

I glanced at Victoria. She stood impassive.

"Fine," I shrugged. "You and Vict... your wife... uh... could stand Miss de Souza and me, I suppose. Or...."

"I think not," Cashman said. "I think Vicky would prefer to be paired with her guest. Hospitality and such. Correct, my sweet?"

Victoria scowled. She genuflected for the thermos of lemonade in the ice chest.

"Give us," she sighed, "a chance to recuperate for a moment at any rate. Why don't you two go ahead and warm up?"

As they walked away, she poured me a cup and I drank. "So that's Phil," I whispered, handing the cup back.

She nodded. "Damn his bloody eyes. I hadn't made the bed, you know. Stupidly careless of me."

I winced. "Well. Nothing we can do about it now, I guess." I was experiencing new dimensions—the ramifications of extramarital sex. More than trepidation, I felt a kind of bemused curiosity. "Either he knows or he doesn't."

"Bloody keen in the philosophy department, aren't we?" she sneered. She tossed back her lemonade.

"Who's this Gillian?"

"Touch of interest, have we? She *is* beautiful, I must agree. Phil wants me to think he's sleeping with her. And maybe he is. Though it seems a bit out of character."

"What, for him? You mean... for her, huh?"

"Mm. I can't imagine what he has to offer. No prize in the bedroom, that much I can assure you."

"Well, he's got a kind of earthy... I don't know. Animal magnetism. Those tattoos...."

"Had 'em done at eighteen, when he was a rating, in Singapore. They're a terrible embarrassment to him now, if the truth be told." She chuckled harshly. "But I think they're one of the main reasons I married him."

"So. Is Gillian... what? Part of the diplomatic community or something?"

Victoria gave me a hard look and shoved the thermos into the chest. She squinted at the court, from which the *tup... pip... tup* of ball on clay and strings counterpointed our conspiratorial murmurs. "Couldn't you mask your enthusiasm just slightly?" she growled.

"Hey, come on, Victoria," I protested. "Don't be silly. All I did was ask a simple question. I don't care...."

"Her father's some high muckty-muck in a steamship agency. She teaches at the English school. Beyond that I can't help you very much, I'm afraid." She snatched her towel from the back of the chair. "Why don't we go get this over with?"

Scrubbing her racket grip, she strode toward the court.

## As we entered, Cashman circled the net to join Miss de Souza.

We began to rally. The Cashmans instantly lashed baseline drives at each other, as if in resumption of some longstanding, bitter routine. With a good deal more hesitance, I tested Miss de Souza's capabilities.

She seemed to be a reasonable weekend club player, though she showed a tendency to react late. She took the first few forehands too close to her body and punched at them, falling away. But she had a graceful backhand—evidence of lessons and a natural coordination. In fact, the backhand was her best stroke. She swatted the first one with a velocity

I hadn't anticipated—I picked it up on the short-hop and netted it. When I suggested she come forward to practice volleys, she giggled reluctantly. And indeed she displayed the tardy reflexes of a sometime player, more intent on self-defense at the net than aggression. In short, she possessed the basics for an adequate game, but she lacked consistency and thus confidence. Easily intimidated, I judged—really, she was way, way out of her league against Victoria and me.

So was Cashman... at least on form. I was assessing him carefully from the corner of my eye. He was thick-set, bandy-legged and invincibly unorthodox. But I noticed he hit the ball with tremendous force and, for all his choppy stylelessness, seemed to have excellent control. He also had a court sense that enabled him to appear very deliberate, even clumsy, yet somehow to pounce on each return as if he'd willed rather than reacted to its placement. I had a hunch he'd be the kind of opponent you couldn't look good beating... and who just might cause your own game to degenerate so terribly he could lull you into a defeat you'd be grinding your teeth over for months. If not refinement, the years pitted against Victoria had certainly given him an education. I could see he'd probably become quite an adequate foil for her. That obstinate inelegance, though, must, I'd bet, be a constant gall.

While Cashman rounded up balls, I invited Gillian—she'd told me at the net to call her that—to practice her serve. Her motion was jerky, but she gave the ball spin off a high toss and seemed to know what she was about. If not a particularly fast serve, it appeared dependable. I was relieved and complimented her.

Cashman took his place beside her at the line and rocketed one at Victoria—low, flat and so far out she had to skip to avoid being struck on the fly. He served again immediately, almost before she had time to recover: a wicked skidding drive delivered with a curious contortion that was unquestionably the nadir of his idiosyncratic arsenal. And this one was in. Moreover, he repeated the serve with accuracy six or seven times—arms flailing, body pretzeled, the interval between toss and racket contact grotesquely accelerated, like an ancient film clip run at modern speed.

"Right-o, we're warm as we'll ever be, no doubt," he grinned. "Eh, Jill? Since we know you two are... *hot*... care to spot us a couple of games? Might help keep it interesting."

I looked at Victoria. She shrugged. Face sour, she flicked her racket at a speck of loose clay. I started to reply when she abruptly grinned up at him, "Have you no pride, Phil?"

"I wouldn't know, Vicky, love. What's pride? It's a question I've asked myself...."

"We'll give you as many games as you want, won't we, Richard? Three? Four be all right? Five better?"

"Two should do," Cashman drawled. "Wouldn't want to take unfair advantage. Even if you are the bloody champion."

"No, Phil. Unfortunately, that is one thing I most definitely am not. And never, alas, have been or will be."

"Alas, alas," Cashman echoed. "Call for serve."

He spun his racket.

"You may as well serve too," Victoria said. She showed him her back.

Cashman strolled to Gillian, turned her racket face horizontal and placed the balls there as if on a platter. She'd stood stiffly, wincing, through the acerbic exchange over handicap points. Pride was no equivocal matter to her, I could see. I'd bet she'd rather have lost six-love than suffer the near occasion of its questioning.

Her serve, as a result, was perfunctory. Victoria smashed the return at her husband, who crouched at the net. He managed to throw up his racket and tick it with the frame. The bloop arched over my head and fell into the extreme corner.

"Sorry, cobber," he grinned. "Luck."

Gillian netted my gentlemanly return, and then Victoria chose once again to drill hers at Cashman. He put it away between us with authority. On her third try, though, Victoria did finally succeed in passing him, and on Gillian's errors—in spite of the fact that I was alone in hitting to her, and conscientiously offering soft, fat returns—we won. We erased their advantage on my serve: three aces, even though I was still throttling back.

Cashman got a measure of revenge in his turn. He had only one service speed, I discovered. Most players try to overwhelm you with a mighty cannonball on their first effort, then, having faulted, opt for security with a much timider second. So when Cashman's first profligate swat sailed awry, I shuffled forward—only to have him sizzle the follow-up full-bore down the middle. It handcuffed me, and I popped up a clay pigeon he neatly dispatched.

I didn't repeat the mistake. Even so, he'd mastered that awkward, disjointed semaphore and was capable of putting the ball in as deceptively hard as any journeyman club pro. He knew how to follow it, too. He won his serve. And then, on a series of grim, point-blank rat-a-tat volleys with Victoria, he eventually broke hers.

I was beginning to feel like the forgotten man. I played Gillian's serves back to her, but Victoria insisted on poaching and, instead of going for the point, went invariably for her husband. Here Cashman's canniness told. He had a way of keeping the ball in play—teeth bared in an intent and tauntingly gleeful grimace—until Victoria's unrelenting musketry produced a misfire. When Gillian held her workmanlike serve, we were down two-five. I won mine, and then Cashman went into his threshing act again.

Victoria, face mottled, bristling within a cocoon of fury, shelled him for alternate winners and mistakes while

I backed her with courteous placements to Gillian. After a seesaw skirmish through a litany of deuces, I carelessly netted one of Cashman's better bombs. Nobody's perfect. Victoria glowered at me, and—in what I could only interpret as an effort at winning in earnest—uncharacteristically slashed a booming topspin return at Gillian, who had stayed back. Victoria sprinted toward the net behind her shot, but Gillian curtseyed perfectly, head down, and lined the backhand at Victoria's feet. So it was their set, six-three.

"Super shot!" I exclaimed, beaming at Gillian, as congratulatory as a coach to a protege.

"Attagirl, Jill, love!" Cashman chortled.

Victoria pondered her shadow. For a second I thought she might hurl her racket. But she was disciplined. She looked up and in a quiet voice said, "Very nice, Gillian." There was a pallor around her eyes, though. Her flush was suddenly as splotchily defined as rouge spots on a Dresden doll. She wheeled and walked off the court.

"What, quitting, Vicky dear?" Cashman roared. "What about that vaunted pride? Pricked?"

He strode past me, dogging her, his face sweat-sequined and ruby red.

**Whatever Victoria might have had in mind, she stood now under the umbrella fumbling at the canister of lemonade.**

Cashman lumbered to her side and I could hear them muttering at each other in harsh staccatoes. Gillian and I hung back, allied in mutual discomfort. We stood at the edge of the court and exchanged slightly stilted chat: about Stanford—where she'd studied comparative literature—Berkeley, San Francisco, the private school for English-speaking foreigners where she was teaching sixth-form boys.... I couldn't fail to respond to her riveting eyes, the lightly perfumed heat of her slim body. I found myself trying to exude charm like some additive musk I could secrete through my already streaming pores.

Both of us kept glancing uneasily at the Cashmans. Impelled, I suppose, by some sense that our presence might have conciliatory value, we drifted toward the table. A ponderous silence now prevailed there. Cashman sucked thirstily at another huge can of Swan.

"Would you like some lemonade, Gillian?" I asked, exercising my new familiarity.

"Yes, please," she nodded. She edged close to me to accept the cup I filled for her. I poured one for myself.

"Good Christ," Cashman chuckled at Victoria. "Don't you even pick 'em old enough to drink now?"

He swung his leer at me and winked—a look, apparently, intended simultaneously to disarm and intimidate.

"Does it always give you such pleasure to act the swine?" Victoria hissed at him.

Cashman squinted at her for a cold moment. "The loo-tenant knows I'm only ragging him. Don't you, loo-tenant?"

"I guess I'm sort of unfamiliar with the Australian sense of humor, sir," I replied. "I appreciate the chance to get to know it better."

"Ah, charm to the gills. Serve you well up the ranks, I dare say. As it has here, mm? Hands across the sea and all that? Busy, busy those hands, too, no doubt. Wager you've become quite familiar of late with certain of our Australian traits."

"Your women's tennis is impressive, yes, sir, if your wife's any indication," I countered. I found I was having trouble catching my breath. My diaphragm was taut, and my hand trembled when I raised the cup to my lips.

Cashman swilled from his beercan. "Jesus, that bloody plane ride gave me a ferocious bastard of a headache," he grumbled to no one in particular.

"We really should let you and Victoria have the court back to yourselves again," Gillian said to me. "It was an imposition on our part. I do thank you for being kind enough to let us play. You were very tolerant...."

"Come, come, Gillian," Victoria smiled. "You aren't going to deny me... deny *us* the opportunity for revenge, are you?"

"Oh... I've had a tiring day already. And of course so has Philip. I think...."

"Mm," Victoria agreed. "Perhaps you're right. Age beginning to tell and all, eh, Phil?"

"Age bloody hell!" Cashman exclaimed.

"Darling, you're the color of a mandrill's bum," Victoria said cheerily. "And you're puffing like a bloody rhino. I wish you could see yourself. Gillian's right. You should go home and... well, I was going to say go to bed."

"Yes, that would be your regime, no doubt, wouldn't it? One you've followed vigorously yourself, I dare say. I noticed when I arrived this afternoon the bed seemed to be in singular disarray."

"The...? Phil! For God's sake. It's Nellie's day off. And are we about to start squabbling in public about the tidiness of our bedroom? This, Richard," she said, turning to me, "is a man who is in the diplomatic service of his country. Difficult as that may be to credit."

I narrowed my eyes at Victoria. I didn't appreciate being drawn into their fray.

"Victoria. Philip," Gillian exclaimed. "You can imagine how uncomfortable all this makes one. I'm certain Lef'tenant Schubert must find himself at a complete loss.

197

Surely...."

"Oh for Christ's sake," Cashman growled as I flashed her a look of gratitude, "let's just get on with it. One more set."

"As a matter of fact," I demurred, "it is getting sort of late. I think probably I should call it quits."

"I'd be perfectly happy to give the lef'tenant a lift to his ship. If that would be more convenient for you two," Gillian offered.

Victoria eyed her with hatred.

"Sure, that'd be fine with me," I nodded.

Victoria's baleful gaze swung my way.

Suddenly Cashman heaved himself up and seized her shoulder. "Come on, love. Another go. Jill? Loo-tenant?"

Victoria shrugged. "Whatever you say, dear. Just one more set? I suppose we do owe it to him. I certainly must acknowledge a tremendous debt to you, Phil, darling. All right, Richard?"

I sighed. I glanced at Gillian. She nodded, brow furrowed. I made my own dubious but acquiescent face.

"Would you like two games again, you two?" Victoria inquired archly as we filed into the court.

"Maybe we should split up this time," I proposed.

"Whatever for?" Victoria said, peering at me with a hard gaze. "They butchered us last set, didn't they?"

"And will again," Cashman chortled. "Without any help, either. I believe I overestimated you, Vicky sweet. A function, I suppose, of my encroaching senility."

**"I don't know what you're acting so upset about,"
I muttered to her as we rounded the net.**

"You didn't exactly play to win, you know."

"Nor you," she hissed, "with your oh-so-genteel little lobs to the Maharani of Mysore. My sore arse."

"*She* can't play with you, Victoria. I...."

"She's a deceptive little whore. And I'm not interested in standing here listening to you analyze my play."

"Bullshit!" I let slip. "This is ridiculous."

"I'm happy you think so." She had been refusing to look at me. Her face was sour, puckered and abruptly very unattractive to me.

"All right, what?" I said. "Is it gonna make you happy if I just pick on her and win every point? Why aren't you going for her? That'd make it a big, meaningful victory, right?"

"Frankly, I doubt you could. Do whatever you please."

"Thanks."

"I would appreciate it, however, if you would bloody well shut up."

I flashed her a forbearing grin and took my position in the forecourt. I smiled at Gillian, hunched forward and squinted at her sleek brown thighs through the knotted squares of twine—waiting for Victoria's serve to whistle overhead.

But, like the incoming shell that gets you, it never whistled. I rocked onto my toes as I heard the twang of ball on gut—and instantaneously lost all video to an intense, painfully localized explosion behind my right ear.

Two or three seconds were neatly scissored from my consciousness. Apparently I lurched forward a pace before jerking upright and reaching out to brace myself against the wire-spined net-tape. Bubbles of blindness gradually yielded to sensation. I felt the last reverberations in my throat of the gasp that had been jarred from me.

My racket lay at my feet. Waves of pain began to shimmer across my skull.

"Ow," I moaned. I grabbed the throbbing protuberance in the lee of my ear and massaged it, blinking hard, rotating my neck.

"Dreadfully sorry, Richard," I heard Victoria say behind me. "Perhaps you should crouch lower."

I turned and grimaced incredulously at her.

She hadn't even taken a step forward from the baseline. "Are you all right then?" she inquired impatiently.

I slitted my eyes at her. My weight shifted forward angrily. And then I caught myself. What could I possibly do to her?

"Yeah. I'm fine," I snarled. "No problem." I swallowed down a brief chop of nausea. "Luckily you hit me in my least vulnerable spot. Oughtta be pretty obvious."

I bent, still tenderly fingering the knot, and retrieved my racket.

"Don't worry, I'm okay," I assured everyone. My brain felt as if it had come unmoored, and was sloshing around with my footfalls like tepid jello. The bitch! Not that she could have had that kind of pinpoint aim, though. God damn lucky shot. The bitch!

"Dangerous to turn your back on her," Cashman commiserated. "Should've warned you. Glad it's you over there, cobber, and not me."

Victoria, never having moved from service stance, bounced the ball at her feet wordlessly. "Serving second," she announced.

I flexed my brow to dissipate the mists and bent at three-quarters angle to her this time, swaying warily to keep her in the corner of my eye. The ball arched over me. Gillian returned it cross-court. Victoria hit a drop shot shallow to Gillian's forecourt. Cashman, who was at net, scrambled across and scooped it to my backhand. I slapped the ball behind him. Gillian managed to get to it and lift a deep lob. As Victoria drifted back under it, arm cocked for the overhead smash, I dropped to my knees with a clatter of racket and tucked into a fetal crouch.

Cashman let out a bellow of laughter. Victoria must have been distracted too. Instead of hammering the ball as it descended, she allowed it to drop behind her. Then, back to net, she flicked her racket at it disgustedly. The sharp bolo stroke caught the ball on the rise and launched it into a stratosphere-scraping trajectory.

"Bloody clown," she snarled at me.

I unwrapped my arms from my head, snatched up my racket and scampered back to the baseline. "Just protecting myself," I grinned.

Victoria's circus lob actually stayed in. It was so high that Cashman too let it bounce before throwing himself at it. He was only a foot or so behind the service line, and his whole weight went into the sharply angled smash. But somehow Victoria managed to lunge headlong and extend her racket face to meet it. Her unflexing wrist and the ball's own momentum clothes-lined it back past her gaping husband before he'd even untangled himself from his follow-through.

"Afraid you'll have to better than that, dear," she scoffed.

"Oh, I will, love, never fear," Cashman replied. "Try me again."

Victoria put her first service to him in, and Cashman rifled it back. Again Victoria undercut the shot. It plinked softly into Cashman's forecourt. He pounded for it at full tilt and, as I danced at the ready in front of him, thrust his outstretched racket under the dying carom. The desperate spatula kiss wiped almost all spin off the ball. It floated up lazily in front of me... just as Cashman, windmilling futilely for balance, lost his footing and sprawled into the net at my feet.

I put the ball away with a perfunctory tap.

## Cashman rolled on his hip and sat for a moment shaking his head.

His breath came in phlegmy bursts. He heaved himself up slowly, in ponderous sequential bursts, like a capsized water buffalo. He brushed abstractedly at the clay dust caked on his belly. It instantly turned an ugly scarlet from his sweat. Rivulets of blood-like red clay trickled down his shins. He lumbered to his place for Victoria's next serve.

Gillian netted it.

"Forty-love," Victoria called. "All right, here's your opportunity, darling."

She gave him a hard first serve. He drilled it deep to her backhand and this time barreled for the net. She looped up a high cross-court lob. Cashman back-pedaled under it and swatted a line drive at her. I'd retreated, but Victoria—contrary to normal tactics—had advanced squarely into the mouth of his fire.

"Out!" I shouted.

Maybe it was too late to check the reflex. At any rate, she ignored me. Still on the run, she swerved and in the same motion chopped viciously at the incoming shoulder-high blast.

Hers was almost a mirror of Cashman's swing—an amazing display of neural circuitry, of instinctive hand-eye coordination. Gillian, at the net, didn't even have time to flinch. The ball ricocheted off her body with a sharp, muffled thud, like a punch in the stomach.

The sound seemed to hang in the hush that followed—amplified by her stricken motionlessness. I wasn't sure where she'd been hit until her brown hand snaked almost furtively to her breast.

"Jesus bloody Christ, Victoria!" Cashman roared in outrage. "You're a bleeding menace!"

"Dreadfully sorry, Gillian. Really," Victoria said.

I seemed to have heard those words before. Nor was there the animation in her voice that sincerity requires.

"I think maybe we better stop," I suggested. "It's getting kind of dangerous out here. Everybody's tired."

"Oh, come now," Victoria muttered in sullen self-justification. "Things like that happen. Surely you don't think it was intentional."

"Bloody damn well *count* on it with you around," Cashman rebuked her.

"*You* can say that!" she sneered.

"Believe I just did."

"You, whose negligence...."

"Don't say that, Vic! Ever again! I warn you. I mean it. You bloody cunt, what on bloody earth...?"

"Please!" I exclaimed. "My God...!"

But immediately I bit my tongue. Who was I to insert myself, chiding, between an irate senior officer and his wife? Abashed, I returned my attention to Gillian. She huddled neglected through all this acrimony. "Do you want to sit down?" I sympathized. "We better quit. This is ridiculous."

She shook her head. She was game all right. Tears glistened on her cheeks, but she hadn't complained or whimpered. She ducked her face and blotted her eyes on the shouldertops of her tennis dress. It occurred to me that as much as pained she was probably embarrassed—about having been struck on one of the most sensitive and vulnerable parts of her anatomy, a private sex differentiation that modesty suggests not be advertised with public kneadings.

"No, I'm... okay," she said. She smiled at me with a puzzling intensity. And suddenly I understood that she was searching for approval, that she'd meant that Americanism for me.

"Attagirl, Jill," Cashman boomed. He veered over and braced her with a tattooed arm around the shoulder. "Shake it off. Got you in the tit, did she? Nasty. I'd offer to give it a rub...." He chuckled. "No fear. Just take your time."

Gillian seemed to shrivel—all entreating eyes, appealing to me for tolerance from within his enveloping grasp.

I could scarcely believe the grossness of the man. Tit. I was sickened. "I've had it," I said, shaking my head. "I gotta go."

"No, not on my account, please," Gillian said. "I'm quite able to go on. Really."

"No, it's not on your account," I assured her. "Things just seem to be getting a little too... I don't know. Earnest, or...."

"Earnest, lef'tenant?" Cashman echoed.

Some ominous timbre to his drawl reminded me of my position: a subordinate, on foreign ground... a junior officer who'd in fact justified his superior's fairly blatant suspicions of cuckoldry. While I couldn't specify the mechanisms by which he might make trouble for me, I didn't doubt there was a plenitude in the military. Even across national lines. It seemed best not to provoke him further. Making me squirm through this unpleasantness was, apparently, his form of retribution... a reminder of my comparative impotence in, at least, the career realm. Just because I was so inconsequential he could indulge in as rude, as brutish a display as was his whim.

"I just... mean... I thought this was supposed to be for fun," I muttered, scowling at my feet. "But all...."

"Yes, having 'fun' is a primary consideration for you, I shouldn't wonder. I'm sorry if this isn't as much 'fun' as you were anticipating, lef'tenant. Or perhaps you hadn't given it very much thought at all. Dear me. Are *you* having 'fun,' Vicky?"

Victoria had been pacing in small circles, brooding down at the scuffs her rubber soles were leaving in the clay, like a skater working on school figures. She didn't raise her eyes or answer him.

"I'm talking to you, you bloody bitch," he persisted. "Are you enjoying yourself? Shooting at people like gallery ducks? Can we console ourselves that in this, this somewhat twisted way, one of us, at least, is having 'fun'?"

"For pity's sake, Philip! Stop it!" Gillian remonstrated. She wrenched herself out of his arm.

"We've just won the first game," Victoria sighed. Her voice was thin, uninflected, a memory of speech squeezed out airlessly in some ultimate contraction of ribs. "Are we going to continue or not? If so, it's your serve."

"Yes!" Gillian declared. "Mine! Balls, please!" She beckoned impatiently. "Change courts!" she commanded. "Come on! Let's just play," she pleaded, "can't we?"

# 3

## Signaling reluctance or assent seemed useless.

I shuffled with a prisoner's resignation to the opposite baseline. "You want forehand or backhand court this set?" I mumbled.

"No matter," Victoria grunted. "Play the way we are."

She about-faced and slouched with her hands on her knees, a weary parody of readiness. Her husband's vituperation, I mused, had finally truncheoned her into listlessness. This would be a wonderful set, a thrilling experience... the grotesque conclusion to a week that now seemed to have occurred years ago.

And with a person whose appeal I'd have been hard pressed at this juncture to account for.

I exchanged a few sulky baseline forehands with Gillian off her serve. She was hitting her ground strokes well now, actually. I began to experiment with little increments of speed and topspin, and she answered each with a resolute addendum of her own. When it became clear that she wasn't going to falter, I sliced the ball shallow to bring her up. There was a brief flurry at net until Cashman scooped one wide to give us the point. It had been a surprisingly good one, as a matter of fact.

Gillian and Victoria repeated the opening cadence. Victoria was less studied than I'd been in shifting to fortissimo, but Gillian wasn't cowed. The kinks in her game seemed to have vanished. Forehand, backhand, she oscillated from one to the other with oiled precision. My own gloom began to dissipate in the pleasure of watching her. Anger usually tenses me, but for her it seemed to have acted as a release. Too preoccupied with her disdain to worry about her physical image, she was freed to risk the errors her freedom paradoxically diminished.

When she won her service and then helped extend mine through five ads—I'd stopped holding back so much to her on the first, too—it was obvious she'd ceased to be the glaring Achilles heel of that twosome. Maybe Victoria had been right. There were depths to Gillian's game she hadn't revealed. She even started rushing the net and holding her own there—slashing at the ball with a purposeful frown instead of dodging it with a flustered titter.

Five ads were enough, though, I decided. I bounced the ball for concentration, rocked forward, peered at a spot down the middle while my brain held kinetic rehearsal—mustering axons and dendrites, marshalling serotonin. Then, sinking on my haunches, I flipped the ball into the blue with a fluid underhand. I sprang at it, rising on my toes to full, forward-arcing extension. My arm whip-cracked—I tried to see the actual instant the felt-clad rubber flattened against the strings of my racket-head. And even as I heard my own remote grunt, I caught myself with a sprinting step and pursued the ball on its flight.

My serve vaulted Cashman's racket before he could even waggle it.

Okay. Ace. Two-one. Four to go, at least, before the ordeal was over.

We changed courts. Cashman's odd service motion hadn't changed—it was hard to imagine what a degeneration would have looked like—but he'd definitely lost something. Which wasn't altogether surprising. He was expending a lot of energy for a big man. He was still Victoria's almost exclusive target, but the bite seemed to have gone out of her game too. Where before she'd crowded the net and pelted him with a hail of bullet volleys—as if the object were to bludgeon the ball through him rather than around him—she was tentative now. She hung back a pace, picked up half-volleys or checked the ball with her racket face instead of directing it with a deft snap of wrist or twist of hips. Which meant she had to scuttle more on the defensive. Her attacking shots were off speed enough or poorly angled enough to allow him to get to them. And doggedly he did.

As a matter of fact, now in the middle of the fourth game of the set, I realized that I couldn't remember her having put a single shot past him. If she dinked, he barreled to it and sent her on the chase in turn. If she lobbed, he clambered back under it. If she pinged a volley at him he ponged it back. I had to admire his ponderous dexterity. It was wearing, though. He was in almost constant motion—and the resultant fatigue was starting to tell.

But if Victoria's demoralization had taken the burr from her game, it hadn't leached her of tenacity. She continued to race, stoop, slide, pirouette, somehow grittily recover to return the counters she hadn't quite been able to deny him. By the time he punched his thirty-forty volley wide—his errors or hers, after long scrambling exchanges, the way most points were being scored—they were both lathered.

Cashman clapped his hand over his eyes when he lost his serve, threw his head back and groaned theatrically. The sudden blind snap of neck must have disequilibrated him. He staggered sideways and had to catch himself with a hasty grab for the net. He stood clutching it, blotting his forehead with a dragon. Beadlets of sweat dripped from his nose and chin as he waited for the heavings of his ribcage to ease.

"Ready to chuck it in, dear?" Victoria inquired in that toneless voice.

"Not... bloody... likely," he croaked. He combed his thick fingers through his sparse, now wildly disarranged hair.

Victoria served—another long seesawing game. Every time she got an ad Cashman fought back to deuce. This was certainly not the Victoria I'd played against earlier in the day. I could see by the relentlessly ticking tendon at the corner of her jaw how frustrating she must have been finding it. The hours we'd put in on the court already that day, her bitter mood and the exertion those last few long games were demanding seemed to have dessicated her. It was as if the fleshy softenings of frame I'd once responded to had been rendered away. Her legs and arms had become ropy bunches of muscle and sinew filmed by viscous sweat. Her breasts were anomalous bits of fatty padding, encumbrances... her eyesockets, cheekbones and chin as pinched and angular as if hacked by a hatchet blade into a skull dotted with greasy tussocks. This was the ugly caricature of the woman athlete I must admit, to my chagrin, to having once harbored. And I recognized—because in Victoria I'd transcended it before—how dependent that image was on the temper she was projecting.

Meanwhile, it was Gillian who'd replaced her as my ideal of athletic beauty. Gillian wasn't working as hard, true, but her postures seemed more balletic now. Her glossy hair undulated languorously with her movements and the sweat on her copper skin was like an unguent anointing supple arms, tapered thighs, sinuous calves. I was entranced. And at every opportunity I hit the ball to her—justice anyway, evening out the game—so that what we had going amounted to parallel singles matches.

Nevertheless, for all my indifference to the cosmic implications of its outcome, I definitely preferred not to lose this match. Winning is a personality trait one acquires quite apart from skill. I'd put a lot of effort into cultivating it over the years—perhaps even against my own inner grain. And as Elmer, my childhood coach, had counseled me, each willing betrayal, each acquiescence to losing, eats irreparably at the tenuous instinct no matter how casual or negligible the occasion.

So I had a strategy—and in this company it could have been effective. If not for Victoria. The approval I sought from Gillian depended only on my being steady, on my allowing her to realize her ability—but ultimately to make the errors, with dignity. And there were lots of obvious points to be taken, preferably at Cashman's expense.

Oddly enough, though, it was his indefatigable scurrying that was setting up Victoria for the lapses that kept them alive. His rancor and her spite had destroyed her competence, it seemed. She insisted on trying to twist him off balance, to slant the ball just beyond his straining reach... and almost inevitably failed.

He broke her serve that way—avoiding me as much as possible and running Victoria to better effect than she ran him. That made it three-two with Gillian serving.

Our shadows canted gawkily at our sides in the ruby afternoon. The sun had sunk almost to the top of the vine-laden enclosure now. Victoria and I took divergent courses around the net. I paused beside Gillian.

"Little better now, anyway, isn't it?" I murmured. "You're really playing well."

"Thank you," she responded. "Very much." There was a warmth to her voice that made me shiver. She intensified it with a laser look, as if beaming her marrow at me through those liquescent ebony irises. Good God, she was beautiful—responsive to me, it seemed, too. Where had *she* been the night of the dance?

Cashman, laboriously gasping, brushed past us and collapsed on the wooden bench by the net post. He buried his face in a towel. He was sweating so hard he gave off a palpable aura several degrees denser than the ambient humidity.

"That's it for you, is it, Phil?" Victoria called.

Cashman peered up over the sodden, clay-smeared terrycloth. He collected breath for an answer, couldn't seem to amass enough, scrubbed his incandescent brow again and snapped the towel to the bench at his hip.

"Damned... anxious... for an excuse... aren't you, love?" he panted. "Why don't you... just... come right out and say it... if we're... too much for you?"

"Too much! Oh, don't be daft," Victoria snickered. She tapped a ball impatiently. "You're done for. I'm just wondering why you prolong the agony so? But... go ahead, lie about as long as you like."

Cashman was slumped behind his pulsating gut. Abruptly he squared his shoulders and lumbered up off the bench.

"I sit... for a mo... and she calls it... bloody lying about," he snorted. "Bloody begging for it... isn't she? Can't wait, eh, Vicky? Well. It's one... pleasure...." He snatched the towel and swiped it across his forehead. "...I'll be happy... to indulge you."

He flung the towel into the vines and swaggered onto the court—a bit jelly-kneed I thought. Gillian's eyes left my glance to follow him. The rift I felt could have generated a thunderclap.

*Et plus ça change....*

Victoria and I won the first three points, but with the score love-forty she tried once again to loop the ball over Cashman at net. He caught it with a leaping swing and drove it between us. On the next point, Victoria cheated into my terrain, volleyed at Cashman and allowed him to bat a crossing shot into the forecourt she'd vacated. I hadn't had time to circle behind her to cut off the angle.

"That wasn't too smart," I grumbled.

"Not with you mincing around back there with your

bloody head up your bloody arse," she hissed in reply.

"What?"

"Just fuck off," she snarled.

She went for the low back-spin lob over Cashman again, and again he smashed it behind me with a wild jumping overhand. It was a terrible shot on her part—stupidly chosen and almost impossible to pull off on a service return. I snorted in disgust.

Cashman had bellowed at the strain of launching his two hundred or so aching, exhausted pounds off the ground, but as he'd come down and watched the shot puff chalk, he'd punctuated that feral groan with a bark of glee.

"Deuce!" he cried.

Only suddenly his legs quavered, twined lamely and wobbled out from under him. He sat on his shadow.

"What's the matter, then?" Victoria said instantly. There was no urgency to her tone. Rather, it was detached, even taunting in its rising inflection.

Cashman's head lolled. He shook it in a spasmodic, disjointed way.

"Nuhne," he mumbled. Then, with more force, he pronounced, "Nothing!" He blinked around, eyes vacant, disoriented by this odd new worm's-eye perspective.

I started forward. Gillian hovered there already, looking concerned and uncertain. Before I could kick my leg over the net, though, Cashman turtled onto his knees. Using his racket as a crutch, he cranked himself to his feet. He staggered a few steps before regaining his balance.

"Dizzy. Li'l dizzy... 's all," he said. His tongue clacked thick and dry.

"Philip...," Gillian frowned. "Really...."

"Shut up, Jill," he snapped. Then, "Sorry," he added. "Go on, serve."

I looked at Victoria. I expected her at least to say something. To protest. Instead, she simply tapped the loose ball she'd picked up back across the net to Gillian.

"Hey, wait a minute," I objected. "Commander?"

"Please, Philip," Gillian implored.

"It's been a hot afternoon," I said. "We're all feeling it. This sun, the heat... it's not something you should just take lightly. It's time...."

"You're... a bloody... sawbones?" Cashman wheezed contemptuously. "Along with... your other... bloody attainments?"

"He's right, you know, Phil," Victoria chimed in. "You're not a young man any more. It's stupid to go on pretending to yourself...."

"Oh, for God's sake," I exclaimed. "Age isn't...."

"I applaud... your concern... both of you," Cashman gasped. "However... I'm quite capable... of taking care... of myself."

"The way you've always taken care of everything," Victoria sneered.

Cashman ignored her. He raked his fingers across his scalp and bent forward, glowering at me.

"Serve, Jill," he instructed over his shoulder.

She stood for a long, thoughtful moment at the baseline... staring down, racket arm poised stiffly behind her. Finally her shoulders heaved decisively. She pumped, flicked the ball up and belted one of her hardest serves of the afternoon at me.


**I sent it back deep with a full sweeping swing.**


All my misgivings and disgruntlement once again miraculously evanesced in the satisfaction of that shock up my arm. Gillian took the shot well herself, aiming for my backhand as I bolted to the net. I whirled just as Victoria

213

hurtled across my field of vision. The ball popped weakly off her intruding strings—another shallow bloop that Cashman clawed himself out of gravity's grip for. He swatted it down: three tries, three points for them. Victoria's pigheadedness—and her inept execution—were killing us.

Cashman shuffled across court as if in a daze. His soiled shirt had ridden up as he'd leaped and stretched. The milk-blue flesh of his hairy spare tire remained exposed. His face and neck, by contrast, were the color of raw steak. He looked awful. His torso was clamshelling desperately, the long congested sucks for breath so raspy I wanted to clear my own throat. He sagged at the waist to face Victoria.

"What? No crowing, dear?" she needled him. "You certainly seem to have my number now, don't you?"

Fatigue had wrung Cashman's expression into a gargoyle leer. His eyelids fluttered and he worked his tongue as if trying to speak.

"What's the matter?" Victoria persisted. "Run out of ugly little quips to entertain us with?"

"Oh, come on," I said. And suddenly...

My God. The suspicion kindled.

Victoria returned Gillian's ad serve with a gently scudding forehand. Cashman lurched to his left to intercept it, but couldn't quite get his backhand around in time. Gillian, rushing forward, picked the ball up behind him and instinctively avoided me at net. Victoria took the shot waist high and dropped it into the alley at Cashman's right. He stumbled for it, bent, straining, and managed to scoop out a feeble floater. Victoria stiffened for the put-away... but instead relaxed her wrist as she met the ball.

"Lob!" she announced. "Rover go fetch!"

Cashman swayed, flatfooted, almost off the court where his momentum had carried him. Victoria's gently arching shot and her warning had given him an utterly improbable chance at recovery. He spun in impulsive pursuit.

He'd taken three steps before his legs tangled. He pitched prone, racket skittering.

I turned, aghast, and stared at Victoria. "Oh, Jesus," I breathed.

She smiled.

Cashman was on his knees, creeping in groggy circles, searching for his center of balance like a boxer working with his last kernel of instinct against the count.

"All along...," I muttered. "Right?"

How, I wondered, could I have been so dense? Not to have seen it from the beginning. "What in the world are you trying to prove?" I demanded. "My God, Victoria, that's...!"

She looked away coldly. "Have you taken a fancy to it down there, then, dear?" she jeered. "You seem to be spending more time rooting in the dirt than standing on your feet!"

Cashman thrust one knee off the ground and tottered over it, poised to rise. With a groan he hobbled erect.

"Commander?" I said. "You'd be... we'd all be nuts to keep on playing! Really! It's time to call it a day. For me, anyway, if nobody else. I have to get back to my ship."

I stared at Gillian for support.

"Yes!" she exclaimed. "I must be going too!"

"Oh, Philip never quits," Victoria interrupted. "He doesn't know the meaning of the word. Do you, love?"

"Score," Cashman mumbled.

"That doesn't...," I began.

"Three-two yours," Victoria said. "And we're at deuce."

"Finish... game," Cashman gasped.

"She's making a fool out of you!" I said. "Sir? She's been doing it the whole time. Can't you see that? She's got you running back and forth, jumping... over and over. Like a puppet on her string! It's all she cares about! She's not even trying to win. Just put you through as much...."

"Is that what I'm doing, Phil? Making a fool of you? Goodness! I didn't think that required *my* assistance."

Cashman stooped for his racket and almost toppled sideways.

"I... I didn't mean that!" I exclaimed. "I'm sorry, sir. Forget the word. All I...."

"Three-two?" Victoria cooed. "Two good points and you're up four-two, Phil. Not bad at all for what my partner considers a 'fool.'"

"Victoria!" I squawked.

"Not that you're going to get them, I might add. At least not without...."

"She'll let you!" I warned him. "Or something. Anything, just to keep it going," I insisted. "You're beat... bushed, I mean. And she's...."

"My, how diabolical of me!" Victoria laughed. "But he's right. You might as well quit now. We *shall* win."

"Rot!" Cashman croaked.

"Look, if it comes to that I'll concede right here and now," I said. "Great game. Great set! Commander? You really showed us."

"Philip...," Gillian nodded.

"Finish!" Cashman lowed. "Jill?"

"Sir, listen," I said. "I won't play another poin...."

"'S 'n order! Lef'tenant?"

"I'm not in your Navy, sir! You can't...."

"Oh, I can't? Are you bloody sure about that? Insubordination. Oh," he spluttered, "innocence! Just you see, you bloody... buggering little puppydog barst...."

Gillian hurled the ball she was holding at Cashman's feet. "Goodbye," she said quietly. She tucked her racket under her arm and strode toward the gate.

"Jill! Back here!" Cashman roared.

She opened the latch. "I'm sorry, Philip. What can you threaten *me* with?" She walked out.

216

"Ji...i...!"

His bellow died with a wheeze. His chin snapped forward disconsolately.

"Thanks for the game, sir, " I muttered. "For everything," I added, glancing grimly at Victoria.

I turned on my heel and followed Gillian.

## "Very nicely done, Phil," Victoria chuckled behind me. "Let's you off the hook once again, I'd say."

As I reached for the gate latch I heard a grunt, followed immediately by the thwack of a ball.

I flinched and wheeled defensively, having been a target often enough that day. But it was only Cashman— serving, apparently. He plodded off the line as Victoria smacked a return down the right side. I watched him stumble to the backhand. By some telepathic concurrence, they seemed to be engaged in finishing the game on their own. Maybe even the set. Whatever their perverse private agenda no longer interested me. I gave Victoria's white-pantied butt under the flaring tennis skirt a last bloodless appraisal as she sprinted to Cashman's cross-court chop. She sliced it down the sideline. Still relentlessly running the poor fagged-out meathead, of course. Well, he was clearly her accomplice now, so I needn't drum up much sympathy.

It occurred to me that in its own twisted way, her performance of the afternoon had been among the most skillfully camouflaged and finely calibrated tennis exhibitions I'd ever seen. Each of her shots had been within his reach— but only barely. And on top of that, she'd consciously left herself open to returns demanding the swiftest recoveries, yet time and again repeated the deft placements... all with only his half of the doubles court to work on.

217

The whole thing was so utterly depressing, though, I could feel the tear-ducts brimming behind my eyes. What a waste! What a squalid end to this most potentially precious of experiences. Love. In Rangoon!

Frittered away, walled inside a tennis court, mooing after an implacable shrew.

I swung the gate closed and trudged across the lawn toward Gillian. She was hastily gathering her gear. The day was fading, the air heavy as molten wax. The greasy heat seemed to damp all sound except the muffled thud of their shoes on the clay behind me, the agonized sibilance of Cashman's gasps. I looked at Gillian unsurely.

"I wonder if I could maybe hitch that ride you...."

I'd raised the pitch of my voice but not its volume. She didn't appear to understand me. Rather than repeat myself louder, I fixed her with a tentative smile and quickened my stride....

What made me turn I'm not sure. Some subliminal apprehension, some belated awareness of the abrupt absence of sound at my back... or perhaps I sensed that Gillian's gaze was directed through and beyond me, that the composure on those dark features was undergoing a subtle metamorphosis. I swiveled my shoulders.

My eyes found Victoria first. She stood erect and motionless, the white of her dress vivid through the screening flowers and verdure. And then, after an instant of confusion, I deciphered the second smudge of soiled white—formless as a carelessly strewn bundle of laundry.

It was Cashman. His stocky body sprawled, splay-limbed, on the garish clay across from her.

I didn't move for a second or two. None of us did. And then my racket fell from my hand and I sprinted toward the gate, fumbled clumsily with the catch and shouldered through.

He lay with his face in the dirt. His mouth and eyes

were still open, as if he'd hurled himself down to gnaw apoplectically at the earth itself.

Sneering in dread, I squatted and rolled him over. The clay crusted his forehead and cheeks like fresh scabs. His irises had almost vanished around the enormous, vacant pupils. I could see no evidence of breathing. I mashed my fingertips into the spongy flesh around his Adam's apple—wringing his massive neck in search of the carotid pulse.

Nothing. Desperately I tried to conjure the first aid I'd learned at OCS.

"Jesus," I muttered, looking up at Victoria. "He's in a bad way!"

She remained where his collapse had rooted her. She was still poised for the return he'd never make. She stared at me and began to nod.

"Go get help!" I blurted. I dropped to my knees by Cashman's shoulder, cradled his nape to tip the lolling skull back, pinched his nostrils closed, bowed and planted my open lips over his. I exhaled until, in the corner of my eye, I saw his ribs expand. I sank back urgently on my haunches.

Victoria hadn't budged. She was still nodding dreamily.

"Gillian?" I screeched.

She'd dashed up behind me. "Yes?"

I wiped the back of my hand across my mouth, spat, bent and gave Cashman another humid kiss.

"Run up to the house," I told Gillian, "as fast as you can. Get a doctor here. Emergency equipment, ambulance, whatever they've got. It's critical. I think he must have had a heart attack or something. Then get back. I need you."

She whirled and I bowed over the livid cadaver again. I screwed my lips to the rubbery male flesh—wincing at its torpor—and hissed a half-dozen full breaths into the dank recesses of Cashman's lungs. They rose and fell with my inflations, but when I groped again for a ticking artery

I failed to find one. I began external cardiac massage.

Hunched across his chest, elbows locked and flat palms crossed, rocking forward and back while obsessively counting off the throws of my weight into his creaking breastbone, I was aware only in the remotest way of Victoria's presence. She seemed totally detached. She watched me unhelpfully for a few minutes as I crept between her husband's yawning mouth and his rigid sternum. Finally she strolled to the bench by the net stanchion and sat.

Gillian returned quickly, accompanied by two servants in white jackets. They were small but strong-shouldered, and understood English. I explained what was to be done. They slid in beside me and took over. We alternated in teams—they pumping Cashman's chest, Gillian breathing into his lungs while I knelt with my hand up the leg of his shorts, fingers pressed into his hairy groin, monitoring the arterial stroke of blood the heart compressions were forcing through.

Within about ten minutes a squad of Burmese soldiers squealed up in a Land Rover bearing Red Cross insignia. They trundled out their resuscitation equipment and hooked Cashman up at the instructions of a combat-uniformed doctor who'd arrived in their wake in a jeep. Elbowed aside, relieved of our tasks, Gillian and I stepped back to squint anxiously at their professional efforts. My arms ached. The gossamer mustache on Gillian's upper lip bore microscopic crystals of sweat. She sagged into me, weary, despondent. My hand found hers. I gave it a squeeze. Grief clears away barriers.

While we'd worked on Cashman, the ambassador and his wife had trotted down from the house. They'd been followed in trickles by others of the embassy staff. Shirt-sleeved consuls and attachés had paced around us, leaning closer to frown at Cashman or inquire if we needed help, craning their necks for the ambulance, drifting over to murmur uneasy condolences and reassurances to Victoria.

She'd perched on her bench affectless—back straight, one leg crossed over the other at the thigh, hands folded demurely in her lap. She'd nodded polite acknowledgments when spoken to, but her attention had never—when I was watching—wavered from Cashman's inert form. If it was, to me, a display of repugnant coldness, it was probably to others, I realized, a textbook example of keeping a stiff upper lip. Her behavior would no doubt be the subject of much retrospective admiration by those who were now witnessing it.

Anonymous under an oxygen mask, Cashman was belted to a gurney and hoisted into the gloomy innards of the Land Rover to be whisked away. The cortege straggled off the court and broke up into hushed little groups. The ambassador's wife and several men escorted Victoria solicitously to the house. The ambassador himself accompanied Gillian and me across the lawn. He praised us repeatedly for our quick-witted life-saving actions. Some months later I received a letter of commendation for my efforts, in fact, from the government of Australia.

Victoria allowed herself to be sequestered in an inner room. Gillian and I each drank the stiff Scotches the ambassador offered. Badly shaken, cowed by his presence, we didn't say much. He had his car sent round for me.

"Would you mind if I called you tomorrow?" I asked Gillian in the hall as we were leaving. "Maybe we could have lunch or something. God, I'm sorry...."

"Yes," she murmured. "Yes.... Awful."

# 4

## Thursday night was Steak Night in the wardroom.

For most of the eighteen of us whose pooled dues provisioned the officers' mess, the prospect of a grilled T-bone with mushrooms and mashed potatoes by now outweighed the dwindling shoreside allures of Rangoon. Even the captain appeared at his customary setting in the center of the kidney-shaped table that dominated the space.

(That had been his brainstorm, an utterly non-reg accouterment he'd finagled from the Yokosuka shipyard during post-typhoon repairs the previous August. A thirty-foot wave had slammed into our deckhouse and crumpled its armorplate like a karate master dispatching an aluminum beercan. I'd been down below in the Combat Information Center at the time, trying to ride a heaving stool and keep track of the scattered blips—translated into penciled dots by the green-gilled radarman clinging to the dead-reckoning tracer table—that marked our supposedly semicircular anti-submarine screen formation. No bronco could have thrown me any more decisively than that stool when the wall of water broke against us. Fortunately, I only suffered bruises; bloody divots or fractures put four of our crew into sick bay. Force Twelve weather can be pretty exciting when you're tossing in a tin can.)

I hadn't planned to eat aboard. This night was supposed to have featured my bittersweet parting from my voracious Road-to-Mandalay lover. But Dumalag, the ebullient Steward First Class who tended the wardroom pantry, assured me it would be no problem to dish up an extra steak. He liked me for my appetite. It had become a standing wardroom joke. At breakfast after a four-to-eight bridge-watch underway, I'd been known to down a bowl of hot oatmeal, six eggs, two pork chops, whatever sausage links or bacon crisps might be scrounged from others' plates, a mound of hash browns, four or five pieces of toast with butter and jam, a couple of tumblers each of juice and milk and, of course, lots of freshly brewed coffee to dilute the NSFO I'd been slurping to keep me alert while night and stars dissolved into sunrise and blue horizons. (Navy Special Fuel Oil, the gunk destroyers burned, also gave its initials to the black sludge that steeped in department coffee urns twenty-four hours a day.)

I wasn't exactly on my feed that evening. I dutifully cleaned my plate but passed up the strawberry sundae. Its appearance on the menu always reminded me of *The Caine Mutiny* anyway. I'd virtually memorized that novel as a teenager—next to sports stardom, my keenest adolescent fantasies had come to center on some day wearing an eagle and fouled anchor on my cap, like Ensign Willie Keith. Or Mr. Roberts... issuing flawless orders to my admiring men as the plucky vessel pitched and the guns roared and the blazing kamikazes fizzled into the sea around us. (In reality, I found I dreaded gunnery exercises because I was unable to suppress a violent flinch every time one of the ship's main batteries went off. When the forward mount was firing abeam, especially, the muzzles were just below the pilothouse windows—spewing cataclysmic noise, flame and cordite fumes with each wrenching salvo.) It made me slightly ashamed to have my romantic fatuousness recalled— to recognize the banality of so significant a determinant of my destiny. Oddly, strawberries with ice cream also held special nostalgic power for the Annapolis graduates among us. They liked to eat it for breakfast on special occasions— apparently an Academy treat. That was another instance in which I found the dish resistible.

I excused myself and went aft to read in my bunk. Dostoievsky's dense *Idiot* proved something less than the ideal antidote to the afternoon's residue of tragedy. I spent at least an hour on the same two pages. I might as well have been sounding Cyrillic.

Cashman was dead. Of that I was almost certain. But there was always a microscopic possibility he'd been revived. I didn't know how to find out which. Except perhaps to call Victoria. And I couldn't steel myself to that ordeal.

Eventually I took a stroll forward along the outboard rail. I could hear the familiar theme melodies of *Victory At Sea* as I passed the wardroom porthole. Gray reflections from the screen flickered on the fireproof tiles of the overhead. It was a film staple that the XO and Ungerer never seemed to grow tired of. Now they had a novice enthusiast in Barlow, too.

A cooling breeze ruffled the river. Wavelets slapped softly against the hull. The mooring lines creaked to the lazy swells. I sat on the anchor windlass and smoked a cigarette. I was sobered, of course, by the most vivid reminder of mortality I'd confronted since the deaths of my mother and grandmother when I was thirteen... but equally troubled by my equivocal role in the afternoon's events. What guilt did I bear?

I slept badly. Strange dreams jerked me about my narrow pallet as if we were in a sea. Tennis, interminable tennis... and then Cashman's leering, empurpled face. I felt pity for him. I came closer, opened my mouth to kiss him, reached up the leg of his shorts and felt his thick, slack penis against my hand. Slowly he was transformed into Sublieutenant An. Dark, slim as a woman. I was aroused.

Tenderly I opened An's shirt and bared perfect breasts. He was Gillian. Or perhaps—the confusion was part of my dream—the torso I leaned forward to caress belonged to that first Manila whore.

I floundered awake. I could almost taste my revulsion, perplexity and shame. I had an erection.

Reveille sounded at oh-six-hundred. A few minutes later, Dumalag bustled into the pantry to start breakfast. He found me slouched blearily over the wardroom table in front of a heaping ashtray and a mugful of dregs from the overnight coffeepot. I was trying to submerge myself in *The Idiot* again. Nothing in my Midwestern upbringing or my latter-day experience had prepared me for my own lurking polymorphous perversities.

## I'd drawn the forenoon quarterdeck watch.

At seven-fifteen, slightly improved by a couple of poached eggs, a shower and a shave, I relieved Barlow. I was five minutes early, and I made sure he recognized the fact. We reviewed the log and the plan of the day. He handed over the ceremonial OOD's telescope.

"I relieve you," I said according to the formula. I nonchalantly cocked my cupped hand to the bill of my cap.

"I stand relieved," he drawled. He braced his shoulders and snapped off a reproving return salute of impeccable Prussian precision. Too bad, I mused, the little asshole hadn't been assigned to a cruiser, where the white-sidewalled Marines and snotty, aiguilletted admirals' aides could've tested his mastery of military etiquette all day long.

(One cool September morning at Officers Call in Yokosuka the XO had surveyed the *Busby*'s department and division heads and wryly observed, "Do you guys realize that not a single one of you is in the same uniform?" Blues, khakis, tunics, ties, open collars, short sleeves, long sleeves, foul weather jackets—we'd taken the motley as a tribute to our ingenuity. Aboard the *Busby* we prided ourselves on informality and individualism. There was a consensus—percolating down from the captain, I guess—that job performance was the measure of a man rather than the insignia pinned to his collar or the stripes sewn to his sleeve. A tin can, especially, is too familial for officious insistence on rank and ceremony. It only undermines morale. As it happened, Barlow proved chronically seasick. To no one's regret, he was reassigned to a desk at ComCruDesPac on our return to Japan.)

The initial details of morning routine helped divert me from my waxing melancholy. The bosun's mate of the watch had just blown his whistle and announced "Attention to colors" over the 1MC when the quarterdeck telephone rang. I gestured to the messenger to take it inside the companionway while I remained frozen at the head of the gangplank in salute to the fantail. (For this expeditionary occasion, the duty signalman on the bridge was playing our worn tape of the National Anthem over the loudspeaker.) The messenger pantomimed that it was for me. At "Carry on," I beckoned for the receiver.

"This is the Officer of the Deck," I acknowledged.

"Listen," the voice at the other end blurted, "I want to talk to Captain Rogers. But first, don't let anyone off the ship until further notice. Got that?"

"Uh... who's this?" I demanded.

"Yeah, sorry. This is Leffler. Naval attache's office. U.S. Embassy. Here, Rangoon? Lieutenant Commander. I'm your liaison officer."

"Yes, sir," I said.

It was about Cashman, I thought. My heart did a flutter beat. Now what? My God, some kind of diplomatic brouhaha. My illicit relationship with Victoria must have been uncovered, loosing awesome international sequelae. Was he dead or alive? And which was going to be worse for me...?

"There've been, uh... developments, overnight," Leffler confirmed. "Political... stuff.... Look, we don't really know what's going on yet, but it appears there's been a coup. Or an attempt. The Burmese Army's got blockades up, and until we sort it out.... Anyway, I can't talk too much. Just keep your crew aboard. And stay on the alert."

My ears buzzed with adrenaline. Relief and incredulity were followed immediately by the realization that my routine watch suddenly yawned as a morass of uncertainties in which I would be called upon to function responsibly, improvising God only knows what crucial decisions according to procedures and training I would later be judged on as either having credited or betrayed.

"What, are they Communists? You think the ship's...?"

"We don't know what to think. But we don't want to take any chances. Now gimme the captain."

"Well, the thing is, sir," I winced, "he's... not aboard." Barlow had passed that word. I fumbled at the clipboard where Captain Rogers had left a telephone number. "You can reach him," I said, "at...." I read off the number, wondering who might be lying alongside him when it rang.

"Okay. Gimme the XO then. And don't let any unauthorized folks aboard."

"Gee, really, sir?" I replied, unable to repress irritation.

"You know what I mean," he conceded.

The XO looked pretty nervous when he'd finished mumbling into the telephone in the midships passageway. I was tremendously grateful for his more senior presence, though.

"Christ. Better start the gyros and have the engine room watch light off the other two boilers," he said. "Pass the word that all liberty and shore leave's canceled." Burmese Navy buses were scheduled to arrive at oh-eight-thirty to load a group of sightseers for a trip to Pegu. A few of the most ardent camera fanatics, bristling with souvenir Nikons and Bolexes acquired in Hong Kong, were already lounging in fresh whites nearby. "And uh... maybe we better break out the firehoses."

"The...? Ah. Roger," I nodded, stifling the apprehensions his agenda triggered. I visualized a horde of crazed Asiatic revolutionaries suddenly appearing on the dock, brandishing pistols and rifles and curly-bladed krisses, storming up the narrow, canted gangplank at me, shinnying across the mooring lines in fanatic disregard of the rat-guards.

"Pass the word," I rehearsed my instruction to the bo'sun at such a pass, "to stand by to repel boarders." He would dart to the 1MC, pipe shrilling, and echo the command. It had a quaint charm, an antiquated ring that evoked "Old Ironsides" and the days of the Barbary pirates. And maybe we could indeed simply spray off Burmese assailants with our firehoses like so many swarming ants.

After all, I reminded myself, they're reputed to be gentle people. Imbued with Buddhist pacifism and neutrality. Frankly, the idea of personal combat—of squeezing a forty-five automatic's trigger at someone face-to-face, and being the object of whizzing leaden slugs in return—was about the most frightening scenario I could imagine. I'd chosen OCS and a forty-month stint in the Navy to avoid being drafted into the Army for twenty-four months. A goodly part of the calculus, I used to admit good-humoredly, hinged on the lagniappe that "at least nobody's gonna have *me personally* in his sights. I'm a whole lot more comfortable with the idea that they're only aiming at a nice impersonal target like a ship." (But when President Kennedy put us on wartime alert to bring the Cuban missile crisis to a head seven months later, I found—as I looked around CIC for a place to cower safe from shells and H-bombs—that the distinction offered pretty weak balm.)

I rummaged hastily in the drawer of the quarterdeck desk for the loose-leaf binder that contained the Ship's Organization & Regulation Manual. I wasn't sure which bill covered the manning of firehoses to keep boarders at bay. General Quarters, all hands buttoned up at battle stations, seemed altogether inappropriate—designed for full-scale warfare, equal-against-equal: five-inch guns whanging skyward to down swooping jets ("bandits" and "bogeys"), depth charges crumping off the fantail to flush seam-sprung submarines, our roostertail proudly frothing as we heeled and zigzagged ("Left full rudder! All ahead flank! Make turns for thirty-five knots!"—absolutely the most exhilarating commands an officer at the conn could sing out) to evade torpedoes and homing rockets.

"No, uh, GQ or anything like that, right?" I confirmed.

"Geez, no. Not... yet, certainly."

"But you think we might...?"

"Christ, Rick," the XO winced, "fuck me if I know." He doffed his cap and scratched his scalp. Flakes fluttered down on his khaki-shirted shoulders. He suffered from psoriasis. He gave me an uneasy, apologetic grin.

"Firehoses...." He shrugged and snorted. "Those intelligence bastards have their heads up their butts as usual. Who the fuck knows what might be going down?"

"Break out small arms?" I proposed.

He nodded. "Yeah, maybe you better have the duty master-at-arms stand by the locker. The thing is, though, we want to keep it low-key. Just look like we're goin' about our everyday business as usual. 'Cause probably it's nothing that involves us. Who's ashore besides the Old Man?"

"Uh, Bob Mueller and Chief Gonder went over with a couple of storekeepers just after I came on watch," I recalled. "They were gonna get some fresh milk, I think." Mueller was our Supply Officer. I glanced at the clipboard. "Otherwise that's it."

"Okay. Well, instead of knock-off work we'll belay holiday routine. Have the chiefs figure out some kind of training drill or something. Let's keep people below decks and out of sight as much as possible. 'Case somebody gets it into his head to take a pot shot at us. Have the messenger tell the division officers and department heads to muster with me up in the wardroom. *Hayaku.*" (The *Busby*'s two years of permanent deployment to the Asiatic Squadron were reflected in our distinctive Japanese-peppered shipboard patois.)

"Aye-aye," I acknowledged.

"And gimme a jingle the minute you see the captain coming," he grimaced. "Hope we don't find out he's the one that started this thing. Dickin' around with the wrong guy's wife."

I accorded a grunt. The comment struck a nerve, needless to say. And while I was flattered to have apparently achieved a status where the XO would indulge a criticism of the captain with me, I was extremely uncomfortable about being placed in a position of supposed concurrence with a negative assessment of a superior. It was dishonorable, *infra dig*, the Navy had successfully indoctrinated me, to voice complaints about a senior before a junior—to undermine authority by behind-the-back grousing. Even this mild, ribald grumble shocked me. It seemed uncharacteristic—and suggested just how annoyed and flustered the XO was at having been abandoned to command in such a nonstandard situation.

Which didn't exactly hearten me for the stint ahead.

I told the messenger and the boatswain's mate of the watch, who at least wore a sidearm, to stand inside the passageway. Shelter themselves. A good officer always puts the welfare of his men foremost. In the interest of maintaining an appearance of normality, however, I had to remain at my exposed station on the quarterdeck, supervising the gangplank that bridged the splintered quay-lip and the waist of the *Busby*, moored port-side- to.

I squinted anxiously at the warehouse. Its cargo bays were shuttered by corrugated doors. I surveyed the roof-line—brick parapets, a perfect vantage for snipers. I stiffened and almost ducked for cover when, about twenty minutes later, a cab hurtled around the warehouse corner. But it braked to disgorge Captain Rogers, who bounded out, in civvies, and hauled himself at a trot up the gangplank toward me.

"Heard anything new?" he frowned, nodding perfunctorily at the stars and stripes flying from the fantail flagstaff.

"No, sir," I replied, saluting. "Sure glad to have you back aboard, though. What's it like out there? Any signs of trouble?"

"No. No," he shrugged, "it's real quiet. I noticed a few Army vehicles around, coming back. But that's about it. Still, keep your eyes peeled. Tell Les to come see me in my cabin."

"Aye-aye, sir," I nodded. Even as I beckoned for the messenger, the XO darted through the hatch to greet the old man with a profusion of briefing.

For the next three-and-a-half hours, I was the most conspicuous human presence on the *Busby*. I hoped someone was taking note of my courage. Resplendent in brilliant white from cap-cover to shoe-soles, braided shoulder-boards clearly advertising my officer's rank, my only weapon the ridiculous, anachronistic telescope I cradled—and nervously screwed to my eye every now and then for a precautionary sweep of that potential rooftop sniper's vantage—I dutifully stood my post. At any moment, I mused, the snowy breast of my tunic might blossom with a crimson stain. There'd be a faint report, a distant poof of gunsmoke—not that I'd ever see or hear. I'd stagger, clutch my heart in dying reflex, topple—the most glaring target, the first casualty if anyone had aggressive designs against us. Well, if dead no pain. And there was just as good a chance, I soothed myself, the shot would miss.

"He was a hero," my shipmates would declare in the alternative. I hoped. I wasn't sure how much heroism attached to being a clay pigeon. Rationally, of course, I figured the probability was minute that I was in any real danger. You sure as hell wouldn't have found me strutting around in the open like this if I believed there was a *likelihood* of sniper fire. And as the watch stretched on, even more placid than usual without comings or goings, the city hushed and invisible beyond our warehouse redoubt, the garish reveries were actually a pleasurable distraction. The uncertainty, the sense of peril palliated the tedium, whose only interruptions were the return of Mueller and his party with a truckload of milk canisters—they'd been blissfully unaware that anything was out of the ordinary ashore, although now that they thought about it the streets had seemed awfully empty of traffic— and a couple more telephone calls from the liaison officer to the captain indicating that we should remain on alert but probably not be too apprehensive.

So I can't say I was unhappy when Donicht, the Damage Control Assistant, presented himself as my relief at twenty minutes past noon. He didn't need much explanation of why the decks were puddled—swollen canvas firehoses, oozing at couplings and mains, snaked across the nonskid— or why I told him to check with the XO before piping sweepers.

"When I first came on," I confided, "I was a little

worried about standing out here like this, you know—sort of the designated bull's-eye. You get used to it, though."

"Yeah. I noticed you were all hunched sideways behind that stanchion."

"Not gonna do *you* much good, though, is it?" I countered. Donicht was chunky. I left him edged deep under the lifeboat deck overhang, almost within the hatch, peering intently at the dock. I sauntered forward to the wardroom. I had, I noticed, developed an appetite.

## A gutful of Dumalag's lasagna and the release from the morning's tension made me drowsy.

After all, I'd had a ragged night following a grim day. I stretched out on my bunk with my shoes on and propped the pillow over my eyes.

"Phone call for you, sir."

The messenger's cautious touch pummeled me out of my oblivion. But you learn not to swing back. I must have been asleep for ten or fifteen minutes. That was enough for the weight of the pillow to have flattened my eyeballs. I fought up onto one elbow and grimaced confusedly at the twin strangers hectoring me from inside a tunnel veiled with Spanish moss. I blinked them into more or less single register, nodded in recognition and kicked my feet over the edge.

Years of untimely arousals train your body to respond before your mind engages. So I'd grabbed my cap and caromed through the passageways to the quarterdeck before my curiosity even gelled. I cleared the phlegm from my throat and lifted the receiver to my ear. Somehow I expected to hear Gillian's voice.

"Hello?" I said tentatively.

"Hello."

"Vic... toria?"

I was startled and unnerved. I glanced around furtively. Donicht and Farmer, the tall black boatswain of the watch, idled together near the hatch. The quay and the padlocked warehouse shimmered silent and unpeopled in the midday glare. I tugged the cord as far forward as it would stretch comfortably and hunched into the mouthpiece, my back turned for privacy.

"Richard?"

"Yeah, I'm still here."

"I thought I'd ring you up and tell you. Phil.... Well, is dead."

"Oh. Can't say that's exactly unexpected news. I'm sorry."

There was a long silence.

"Are you free? Could you come over?" she said.

"God, *no*, actually!" The idea took me aback. "I mean, it wouldn't exactly be proper, but... and even if I wanted to, which frankly I don't... the main thing is, there's a revolution going on! Haven't you heard? Everybody's confined to the ship."

"What? You're joking."

"No, really. I can't tell you much more than that, though."

"What do you mean, revolution? Where?"

"Here! Burma! Maybe the better term is *coup*. *Coup d'état*. I don't know."

"How? Who?"

"Don't ask me. Seems pretty peaceful so far, at least, whatever it is. A few of our people were ashore...."

"There must be some... confusion."

"You're telling me."

"My God. I'll have to call the embassy. Phil...."

"Yeah, he's not gonna be around to keep you filled in

on the latest poop any more, is he?" The blurted slang word surprised and embarrassed me. Not the acrimony.

"Mm," she acknowledged. "That's... what... had come to mind."

I sighed. "I'm sorry," I repeated.

"So am I," she said. "In a way."

"Gosh, that's a touching outpouring of grief, Victoria!"

"He was a royal bastard, if the truth be told, Richard."

"Your husband. So you keep insisting."

"Do you think I meant for it...? What happened? That I... well, deliberately...?"

"Tried to kill him or something?"

"Yes!"

"Well, no. No, I don't think you could plan a thing like that. Although, you certainly.... Anyway. I'm sorry for you. It's a hell of a... you know. Thing to live with, anyway."

"He had a heart attack. 'Massive coronary... something.' Words they used. He'd always been in perfect health."

"Yeah. I'm sure he had. You didn't exactly do him any good though."

"No. I know. You're absolutely right. At some level, I... *did* want. What happened. To happen. I *wasn't* sorry. Then."

"I noticed."

"And... well, I'm not really sorry now either, I must say. In fact. Might as well admit it."

"That's your business."

"Are you sailing tomorrow?"

"Mm. Still the plan, anyway. Far as I know. Unless this thing turns bloody or something. In the literal sense. Or changes the schedule, whatever."

"I can't imagine.... I mean, everybody loves Nu, they say."

"You'd better be careful," I cautioned, softening. "Do

call your embassy. See what their advice is."

"Precisely what I mean. If there were any danger, I'm sure they'd have contacted me long before this."

"Maybe so," I shrugged. "Hope you're right. I'm sure you are."

"Will... will I ever have a chance to see you again? To talk to you?"

"I... guess not," I said coldly. "Why would you want to? I didn't think I was exactly your favorite person yesterday either."

"And will you... be seeing Gillian?"

"Jesus! I don't know! Aren't you feeling even the slightest little twinge of remorse? Sorrow? Anything? To ask me *that*? Christ! I mean, a man is *dead!* He was your *husband!* Even if he was a so-called... 'bastard!' Yesterday he was running around full of life. Then all of a sudden...."

"I hated him."

"Clearly."

I caught flickers of white at the margin of my vision and realized I was being overheard. I lowered my voice and bowed deeper into the mouthpiece. "Couldn't... wouldn't it have been a lot simpler just to have left him? Gotten a divorce?"

"I didn't know what I felt. How much I despised him. Until I watched him crawl. Spewing his venom. Mocking me, always mocking. With his tarts and his...."

"Look," I interrupted. "I'd rather not really discuss this. It's over. You have yourself to live with. It's your conscience. If you're satisfied...."

"Oh, I did kill him. You knew it. What I was doing. Deep down... it *is* what I wanted. And he deserved it. Deserved it, the bloody...."

"Victoria! Listen...!"

"He killed my baby!"

"What do you mean? Why do you say that? On the

236

court yesterday...."

"My little Robin. Only five years old. All I asked was an hour. Just an hour, for me. For a set or two. Do you know how often I had a chance to play with anybody who was halfway decent in those years? 'G'wan, I'll watch him,' says Phil. So bloody magnanimous. 'We'll go to the beach.' Robin loved the water. He could swim already... he wasn't a baby any more, really, you know. Beautiful, blond hair. Sweet, soft skin, all bronzed from the sun. I'd taught him to swim. Little lifeguard in training. Spent virtually every moment of my life with him from the day he was born. Why I married Phil in the first place... he got me pregnant. Wife and mother at eighteen. Him away at sea half the time. Leaving me to rot in boredom all by myself in a Navy cottage in Broome. God, it makes me sick just to think about it! And then he starts chatting up the nearest sheila in a two-piece. Forgets to keep a lookout for his own son...!"

"Victoria, gee. I'm sorry, really I am. But...."

"That's what went through my mind yesterday. The way they came and told me. And him standing there with his head hanging. Criminal negligence! What it was."

I sighed.

"I scarcely had the stomach to look at him. He knew it. Fortunately, I didn't have to do for a year, after he went back to sea."

"I'm not blaming you, Victoria. I can't put myself in your shoes."

"I'd been right on the edge! Almost a champion, Richard! You've played there. You understand. And then... here comes this bull of a man with his big toothy grin and his stories about typhoons and his dragons. Love!" The word ended on a harsh snort. "The only love I'd known then was a tennis score. My whole life could have been different."

"Yeah. But that's a useless kind of speculation...."

"Oh, you're so wise, aren't you? At twenty-five."

"No."

"You don't realize."

"That's true."

"The sorts of... accommodations... one makes. What that can do to you."

"Yeah, I guess. I'm sorry. So what are your plans now?"

"I don't know. They'll probably be sending me home soon. Funeral, military honours...."

"You'll look great in black. You do in white."

"Oh, what a smarmy, tasteless thing to say," she moaned. "That's beneath you, Richard."

She was right. I was ashamed. "Yeah. Listen, I better not keep the phone tied up. Somebody might be trying to get hold of us."

"Richard...? Couldn't you...? No. Never mind."

"There's nothing really more to say, in fact, is there?"

"I suppose not. Except... I'm not sorry for what we had."

"Mm." The phrase made me squirmy. "Anyway, maybe you can get back on the circuit again now."

"At my age."

"Sure, why not? You still have a murderous game."

I wished immediately I hadn't succumbed. There did seem to be a fatal inclination to the cheap cliché in my disapproval.

"Listen, I take that back too," I said. "I'll always remember you, Victoria. Good luck."

**General Ne Win's ouster of Premier U Nu had been so surgically tidy it was barely a topic of conversation in the cocktail bar of the Strand Hotel that evening.**

I was there with Gillian, who seemed as unruffled by the change as the rest of the citizenry. (She thought it signaled a further leftward tilt that would make the *Busby's* visit even more of an anomaly. And she was right.)

After a couple of gimlets, we went to catch the last rays of the sunset in the golden roofs of the Sule Pagoda. She drove me around the city, and then we ate chappatis and vindaloo in a tiny Indian restaurant. Afterwards we walked along the riverbank. Points of light danced like fireflies where boatmen worked their sternsweeps furiously against the current. Usually it's been cowardice that has kept me from kissing a woman goodnight. This time it took all the wise resolution I could muster.

Two years later, in Hong Kong on my last WesPac cruise, I happened across a tournament box score in the *South China Morning Post.*

"QUEENSLAND OPEN," read the agate type. "Second Round Singles – M. Smith d. V. Cashman, 6-2, 5-7, 6-0."

Good God, I thought. It *had* to be her. She'd made it through a round, drawn Margaret Smith (later Court, the top woman player in the world of that day) and taken a hard-fought set. I made a point of scouring sports pages from then on. I never saw her name again.

In the months that followed, I wrote Gillian maybe a half-dozen letters. She replied, but eventually the correspondence petered out.

Rangoon is a long way away from the rest of the world.

*Halftime Report*

# Cricket

**It seemed, for the times, to be important— something worth knowing about.**

So I agreed to let my friend Jay, an aspiring poet and longtime apostle of the drug, guide my initiation into the mysteries of lycergic acid diethylamide.

We lived then, Susan and I, in a eucalyptus forest high in a fold of hills behind the Claremont Hotel. Our deck looked out across a green canyon on whose far ridge, a mile to the north, perched the complex of laboratories where Susan farmed cells and dissected their nuclei under the haughty direction of a misogynous Nobel laureate.

She'd been a doctoral student in bacteriology at UCLA when we'd met. I was a lame-duck Naval Reserve lieutenant a week shy of release from active duty. My ship had just returned from WesPac to Long Beach, where my captain—whose wife and family lived in San Diego—was having an affair with Susan's divorcée mother. They thought it would be cute to fix us up.

The tawny-haired girl with corruscating eyes who greeted me at the door on that first blind date destroyed every stereotype I'd harbored of the bespectacled, plain-Jane scientist. Her esoteric smarts were pretty daunting, though. The most taxing intellectual challenge I'd confronted in recent years was translating sextant readings into lines of position from the tables of the *Nautical Almanac*. Still, I gave her another call before packing up for Berkeley and a renewed attempt at earning my own doctorate, in English literature.

The chemical reaction we catalyzed when I ventured

to kiss her goodnight stunned me.

"I just might," I heard myself assert, "end up marrying you."

We took turns commuting for the next six months between the apartment I shared with two other grad students below Memorial Stadium and the maid's room in her mother's house in Bel Air, where for propriety's sake I was accommodated on my weekend sojourns. (Susan would tiptoe in after lights-out to help me keep the sheets warm till dawn.) Pacific Southwest Airlines flew between SFO and LAX for $11.95 in those days. Nevertheless, simple economics eventually recommended action on my half-jocular prophesy. Anyway, when I held her in my arms I felt as faint with emotion as any popular song had ever promised. I guessed that *was* the touchstone of true love. After weeks of mounting agony, I surrendered my future to fate. I wrote my father and asked him to send me the engagement ring he'd given my mother. He'd promised it to me when she'd died.

The flinty little diamond glistened on Susan's finger as she crossed a campus stage one June morning wearing her mortarboard and powder-blue hood. Three days later I submitted to the formal wedding her mother had planned at the Westwood Presbyterian Church. There was a garden reception under a translucent tent next to the tennis court in her back yard. My brother Paul, then in his second year of medical school, was my best man. My father, my stepmother Anne and my ten-year-old stepsister Frannie came out too, on their first visit to California. They lapped up the Cadillac-and-chateaubriand L.A. dazzle provided by Susan's father, an affable vice president in a big commercial real estate development company who favored burgundy slacks, white shoes and pinky rings. He knew a few second-tier celebrities and awed my family by introducing them to Milton Berle in the parking lot of the Beverly Wilshire at our pre-rehearsal dinner.

I liked him a lot. And he approved of me, after I helped him complete the *New York Times* Sunday crossword puzzle he was laboring over the first time we met. But his was exactly the sort of would-be *riche* taste both Susan and I shuddered at in Southern California. We headed up the Pacific Coast Highway in my Volkswagen convertible. The radio told us three civil rights workers were feared dead in Mississippi. We stopped overnight in Santa Barbara and Carmel—our honeymoon—and settled into the new apartment I'd rented overlooking a gas station at the corner of Alcatraz and Telegraph Avenues, on the Oakland-Berkeley line. Susan had received a postdoc in Cal's prestigious department of molecular biology. Fatally unable to rekindle an interest in the literary Milton, however, I'd wangled a job as a cub reporter sifting police blotters and synthesizing zoning board hearings for a Hayward newspaper. At least it gave me a chance to write.

And over the next two years, my byline was appended to some increasingly interesting stuff. I covered Mario Savio's harangues of the waxing Free Speech Movement. I interviewed a local Navy pilot who'd dropped the first bombs on North Vietnam. (The provocation cited by President Johnson—an alleged torpedo attack on U.S. destroyers in the Tonkin Gulf—sounded dubious to me in light of my own shipboard experience with perennially malfunctioning electronic gear. I could just picture the hysteria in Sonar as the ships tracked each other's propellers. Technological complexity teamed with routine, jumpy incompetence means modern naval battles are more likely, I was convinced, to be won by fluke than facility.)

When Watts burned I was sent to query two or three among the handful of "Negroes" living in Hayward's manicured foothills as to whether it could "happen here." The answers were predictably soothing. I celebrated the

247

caterwauling, swooning teenage girls who welcomed the droll Beatles to San Francisco's Cow Palace. Notepad in hand, I stood between antiwar protest marchers led by onetime University of Cincinnati acquaintance Jerry Rubin and baton-fondling Oakland cops ranked to bar the marchers' southward passage from tolerant Berkeley into red-neck Oakland. Susan looked down on the confrontation from our apartment window.

If the times were metamorphosing, as Bob Dylan croaked, they were also altering me. Oh, I'd always been a liberal. Receiving the ACLU newsletter in the wardroom mail aboard the *Busby* had been a source of provocateurish pleasure. And of course, one of the best of American traits is sympathy for the underdog. (Nazis and torturers blindly, cravenly glory in power, so terrified are they of their own weaknesses. I've always suspected something of the same characteristic may be necessary for champion athletes, too.) So when those pistol-packing, riot-helmeted androids in blue refused to acknowledge my press pass or even to meet my eye at that first demonstration against U.S. involvement in Vietnam, I experienced only mild surprise. They'd recognized much more clearly than I which side of the line I belonged on.

Soon I'd pasted a peace symbol on the bumper of my VW. During vacation I let my whiskers grow. The editor of my newspaper summoned me into a side office. Beardedness did not accord with editorial policy, he told me. The publisher had just endorsed Ronald Reagan for the governorship. Shave, I was admonished. No, I retorted, I'd rather quit.

Susan's career was in ascendance. She'd been invited to continue her research into glucose metabolism as a full-fledged staff scientist at Lawrence Berkeley Laboratory. So she supported, even encouraged me in this act of bristly conscience. We'd recently bought a down-at-heels one-bedroom cottage on a canyon slope high above the freeway that tunneled into Contra Costa County. We paid $18,750 and worried about meeting the monthly mortgage nut of $106.

"Go ahead," Susan urged. "This is your chance to write that novel you've been talking about. We can make it."

Trouble was, I'd been talking generically. I hadn't conjured a plot or characters. I muscled my desk into the living room to face the picture window, sharpened a dozen pencils and sat down to twiddle my mustache over a yellow legal pad. On which the morning sun slanted distractingly. And I craved another cup of coffee. And there was one more movie review I'd forgotten to read in the newspaper. Discipline was as hard to curry as inspiration. In the intervals when one can't continue to tax one's brain any longer anyway, I began to build a deck. And through Susan I landed a few free-lance editorial projects translating scientific jargon into common English. That's where I met Gail, Jay's wife. She was a cancer epidemiologist at the lab.

The obvious parallels drew us together as couples in extracurricular friendship. For a long time, Jay and I maintained a certain wariness. Writers are quintessentially jealous of each other, as if the Muse were indeed a fickle lover always susceptible to a rival's superior attributes. Faint as those might be to descry. There was a flesh-and-blood analog to the Muse in this case, too—Gail. She was the svelte, Radcliffe-educated daughter of a Kuomintang official who'd fled China for Manhattan in the 1930s. Like Susan, she was the official breadwinner in their family. Eight years out of Princeton, Jay—the son of a New York investment banker with a prominent Jewish surname—had yet to publish a line. I think Gail was a little fed up, despite periodic grants in aid from her father-in-law. She admired my pragmatic ability to turn a buck at the typewriter, hang belletristic glory. Jay suspected our attraction. But after a business trip to San

Diego together, in which Gail and I barely but finally spurned the temptation to create havoc in our lives, a comfortable, mostly platonic ease developed among us.

By now I'd scaled back my literary horizons to the short story. In accordance with the law of the conservation of energy, however, my manual arts ambitions had aggrandized proportionally. Afternoons found me snapping chalk-lines, sawing two-by-fours and clambering among the fragrant rafters of the addition I'd studded out in the rear of our cottage with the help of a graph-paper sketch by Susan and the illustrations in *House Carpentry Simplified*. As I worked, mule deer foraged in the nearby brush. Bluejays flitted through the gum trees, raucously chiding squirrels. The house was sheltered by a wooded hill that screened San Francisco Bay. If we trudged the several hundred yards to its crest, threading blackberry creepers and poison oak, we could gasp at the hazy urban littoral suddenly splayed panoramically beneath us. Here in the bulldozed clearing of our side yard, though, surrounded by tall old rosebushes gone wild, we might as well have been ensconced in some remote Mendocino aerie.

So I wasn't altogether overjoyed when Jay, whose paeans to LSD had finally piqued my curiosity, insisted on Tilden Park as the ideal setting for my experience.

"I know that place like the back of my hand," he explained. "There are more different kinds of terrain there. I can control the trip, program it. You can get a whole range of mood changes."

**On the day we'd appointed—it all seems touchingly naive now, so earnest, almost reverent—Jay arrived as Susan and I were finishing coffee and the Sunday newspaper.**

Susan had consented to drive us to a spot Jay had selected in the vast regional wilderness. She would then return home to wait for our phone call, late in the afternoon. Meanwhile, Gail and their two small children would also locate to our house, to keep Susan company during the vigil. She was being stoic about it, but Susan had real trepidations. She was afraid I was going to be transformed in some watershed way—that I would return to her a stranger, either a burnt-out zombie or a mystic, blissed on chemical *satori*.

I was much more casual in my expectations. Jay and I each bent over the drinking fountain in the parking lot and washed down one of the four foil-wrapped tablets he'd brought from the supply he always kept in his refrigerator. I don't remember the dose, if I ever knew it. Susan kissed me goodbye—she wore a parting smile of grave, apprehensive cheer, and I tried to wave reassuringly as she drove away in the VW convertible whose top I'd painted a garish paisley when its seams began to split.

Jay and I started up a long dirt trail flanked by tall grasses. Minute wildflowers baked in the June sun. I had, of course, smoked marijuana before. A young assistant attorney general of the state of California, no less, had provided the materials for that introduction. When he and his wife, Susan's lab assistant, departed at the end of the evening, Susan and I had reeled back to the couch to polish off a bowl of fruit, chortle uncontrollably over the bananas and finally undress each other for a bout of clumsy but memorably heightened love.

Jay and Gail had also fed us pot in a numbing

251

confection they called "the White Cookie of Marrakech." Its pungent, grassy pith took effect slowly and subtly, but the waves built inexorably, like combers crashing in from some distant oceanic storm. After waiting as long as I could for the vortex to pass, I finally had to drive home while still under the sway of those fiendish pre-dinner cookies. That two a.m. trek across Berkeley—mesmerizing stoplight after stoplight, grotesquely-lit intersection after intersection after intersection—was one of the longest trips of my life.

And I expected something of the same chemical crescendo now as Jay and I trudged across the Tilden uplands. The cloudless sky was an electric blue against the golden knolls; our shirts were knotted around our hips; insects careened in the sweat-mist off our bare torsos. So far, though, all I felt was a mild buzz. I might just as well have taken a couple of tokes from a not particularly potent joint.

The sun sizzled toward its zenith. We doubled back. Jay and I were both cultivating private reveries. We hardly spoke. We turned off the trail and followed a creekbed. Thick trees canopied the banks. Sparkling water sluiced between the rocks and jeweled the ferns that flourished in the moist shadows.

There seemed to be more and more people around, though. Red-armed women were spreading tacky blankets in the clearings. Raucously they hailed one another, set wooden picnic tables with hoppers of glutinous potato salad, ripped open cellophane packages of balloon buns with their teeth and talons, prodded charred lumps of mystery meat and blistered hotdogs that oozed grease into petroleum-scented barbecue flames, distributed handfuls of thermoplastic resin extruded to resemble knives, forks and spoons sized for dwarves. Bulbous-nosed men with tumorous bellies and varicose veins fungoed softballs to obese, butterfingered children. Slavering dogs frolicked and humped. The creekside path had become a thoroughfare for roistering louts in frayed cutoffs who clutched aluminum beer cans you knew they were about to toss into the water or the underbrush....

"Listen, are you feeling very much?" Jay inquired.

I shrugged. I wasn't sure how I was supposed to be feeling.

"I'm not," he declared. He dug the remaining tabs out of his pocket and frowned at them. "Maybe this stuff is a little old."

He was my mentor, the expert. We found another fountain and downed a second tablet each. We resumed our peregrination.

The world was definitely taking on an unaccustomed intensity. Beams of sunlight burned like lasers through the tremulous foliage overhead. We lingered to stare in distracted wonder at hovering bees, scurrying ants, the dappled nuances of the chlorophyll cycle and the retina-stabbing bursts of pigment in blossom and bloom....

Our legs had begun to tire. We emerged from the trees onto a broad field. The green expanse was dotted with men in spotless white duck pants and poplin shirts, sleeves rolled to the elbows. They were young and lithe. Most had brown East Indian faces, others were fair. Beyond them, at the far end of the meadow, an audience of demure women in pastel dresses or vivid saris clustered in canvas lawn-chairs. Plump, docile children toddled among wicker hampers. The incongruous tableau might have been transposed intact from the pages of *Country Life*.

What we'd stumbled on, I realized, was a cricket match.

Jay and I sprawled on the grassy fringe of the field to rest. The acid was really working now. My brain pulsed like a stressed muscle under its freight of consciousness. I found myself utterly absorbed, transfixed, by the Olympian pauses and punctuating flurries of incomprehensible action on the pitch.

I recalled once having defended a "wicket" chalked on the wall of Harmon Gym while a fellow graduate student—English, of course—trotted toward me flailing stiff-armed, and suddenly let fly a tennis ball. My Knothole baseball days had proved adequate training to wield the flat bat against even his fastest and most distractingly delivered pitches—he termed what he was doing "bowling"—so long as they traveled in the air or bounced well in front of me. I proudly swatted line drives all over the gym. But then the ball started plunging at my feet, skittering up beneath my awkwardly cocked bat to leave a damning smudge on the chalked rectangle (proving the horizontal "bail" would have been dislodged in a real game). I was reduced to uncoordinated swipes and xenophobic mutters. Aside from that limited acquaintance, however, I'd learned almost nothing about the structure of the sport. I knew you scored runs (in the hundreds for each game) by running back and forth between wickets. But I wasn't at all sure who was supposed to scamper where or when or why.

Cricket, on the evidence of the match I was now observing, is a languid pastime. Something obscure and altogether negligible would happen, there'd be a polite spatter of applause from the spectators and then minutes would ebb as the players sauntered to new positions, exchanged shin pads and bats, readied themselves in stately, perplexingly impenetrable rituals. There was a tremendous benignity about it all. I watched with a widening grin. I was bemused—and loving it. Unhampered by any distracting sense of the rules, I could peer through with crystalline acuity to the ultimate absurdity of the enterprise. That this elaborately codified set of muscle twitches could so engage so many sober men, women and children through a long summer afternoon seemed suddenly to reveal for me the futility at the heart of all human endeavor.

Nowhere could cricket exist except in a vacuum. And that alone conferred on it a sort of tragic nobility.

I might perfectly well have been enthralled for the rest of the afternoon if Jay hadn't coaxed me away. He failed to share my fascination. We slogged off in pursuit of new acid revelations.

By now I'd started to experience the cheap effects of the drug. And it was indeed amusing for a while to recognize the LSD signatures one had always suspected in the Beatles' later albums—the minutely protracted attenuations of sound, the mushy distancing and reverberation of voices. I noticed an archer's lost arrow in the weeds beside the trail. I stooped to pick it up. The arc of the shaft in my hand as I rose imprinted itself on my optic nerve in distinct, disparate images, like a series of stop-action photographs.

But soon enough the sensory gimcrack lost its novelty. I followed Jay around Lake Anza. The shoreline was riprapped with humanity. Every jutting boulder, every wedge of hardpan had its perchers. Across the muddy water was a sandy semicircle of beach, with an offshore raft bobbing inside a ring of boundary floats. The entire swimming area—beach, raft and shallows—swarmed with bathers. They were thick as lemmings. It was the first hot weekend of the year. Tilden Park, we later learned, had drawn its biggest crowd of the season.

I was growing more and more uneasy. The emanations from all these alien nervous systems assaulted mine. It was as if LSD had dissolved the protective sheathing around my neural fibers. Peeled bare, dendrites wriggled in the aggressive currents of ambient energy like the tendrils of a sea anemone. Passssersby had only to glance at me to grasp me by the soul. And I winced in turn with unwanted knowledge of every grubby secret fibrillating in their thoughts. To be in this state of exposure permanently would, I shuddered, be hellish.

Not that I was ever in serious doubt that I'd be marooned there. I kept reminding myself that all the trivial distortions, all the warped—and for that troubling—mental perspectives were only temporary. I knew I ought to keep a grip on that fact to defend myself against the bleak panic that can carry away suicides and freak-outs.

Still, I wasn't at all happy about the complexion things had taken.

"Let's go home," I said to Jay. I was anxious for what solace I could find in my own secluded rose-garden.

"Not yet," he urged. He shook his head, vexed. "I can't understand it. I've never *seen* Tilden like this!"

To leave now, I understood his implication, would be to repudiate his judgment—and to capitulate to the yahoos who'd expropriated territory he considered his own. He was very indignant about their presence.

"I drop acid here every *week*!" he wailed.

We doggedly scrabbled up a steep slope, huffing to distance ourselves from the lake. We traced a faint deer path zigzagging through the scruffy live oak and prickly, waist-high underbrush. Out of breath from the clamber—we must have been three hundred feet higher now—we burrowed into a patch of shade and collapsed.

A pristine amphitheater of hills spread before us. We were finally alone.

There was only one flaw. Focused and clarified by the contours of the bowl, the entire symphony of human recreational babble—shouts, laughter, screams, splashes, squawky radio music, tortured revs of hotrods, squeals of tire rubber, infants' mewls and the gnarring keen of police sirens—blared up at us from the basin below.

I squirmed in misery. All I wanted was a little peace and solitude. Not this jangling proletarian cacophony. In my acid-sodden state, I began to mull—appropriately enough for the locale—Bishop Berkeley's conundrum: Does the world exist outside my own mind? If not, I mused, I should be able to control it. And believe me, I was trying hard. But since I didn't seem to be able to, the objective realm must possess an independent existence, I concluded. Because after prolonged consideration, painstaking circumanalysis, I was convinced that my mind had neither the motive nor the inventiveness to inflict anything so weirdly and profoundly unpleasant as all this on itself.

I studied Jay. He sat with his eyes closed, face tilted to the sun. He was slighter than I, paler. But we both had dark hair and beards. There was a resemblance. Was he simply my mirror image? I felt a moment's disorientation. Was I he? Was he I?

Or were we both one—a single thought in the great Nous, the collective Mind. Perhaps the mind of God that Berkeley had reasoned to... the support of substance....

My philosophic vertigo was broken by grunts and rustlings. Two figures suddenly loomed trough the tall grass, struggling toward us up the dim trail we'd just broken.

They were teenagers. Both were dressed in black—studded leather jackets, military caps, grease-impregnated denims, square-toed motorcycle boots: the full Marlon Brando kit, from the *The Misfits*. One was white, the other black. The latter wore a makeshift bandage wound around his lolling forehead. He sagged weakly in the supporting embrace of his pimply blond companion. Both were smeared with incandescent gobbets of fresh blood.

"You can make it, pardner," the white youth croaked. "Just a little more. You can make it."

Suddenly he noticed us.

"How ya doing?" he nodded. That's all—an absurdly conventional greeting. As if the surreal apparition of which he was a part—casting and dialogue out of some preposterous Grade D "affirmative action" remake of "The Spirit of '76" set to a biker theme—were normal, unremarkable back-park traffic.

"Good God!" I goggled. "What... happened?"

"Jumped us. Down at the lake," he replied. "Big rumble in the parking lot. Buncha *chollos*. Stabbed my buddy. Ain't too bad, though. Come on, fella. We're almost there."

Without any hesitation, still panting cliché encouragement, he hobbled with his moaning burden past us, on up the hill and out of sight.

Jay and I looked at each other. Then we scrambled to our feet, picked our way to the nearest pay-phone and called Susan.

## I relaxed somewhat back at home.

But even contemplating the glow of my roses in the balmy dusk, I continued to feel the resonating acid discords.

Susan and I slept outside on our deck that night. Watching the stars pullulate overhead, I felt totally estranged in the cosmos. All was bizarre. It was at least two weeks before I could write a sentence that didn't grate in my inner ear as if it had been translated from the Suomi.

A couple of years passed. An overhead mirror allowed me to see the sodden head of our first child loom into the world from between Susan's quavering thighs. For eleven hours I'd fed her ice chips, daubed her sweating forehead, cooed distracting conversation, timed the interval and duration of her contractions—hyperventilating in sympathetic mimicry of the gasps she'd rehearsed with six other ballooning matrons on our Lamaze instructress's living room rug.

"It's a boy!" I announced. The obstetrician displayed him for me like a fresh-caught snapper. The nurses weighed and swaddled him, and the pediatrician put a stethoscope to his chest.

That's when they heard the heart murmur. It turned out to be "tetralogy of Fallot." Two surgeries in ten months ruddied Matty's lips each time they faded to cyan. But the prognosis, we were told, was poor for his survival much past adolescence. Not with four such extreme congenital cardiac malformations.

And then one autumn afternoon, as we waited in the glassed lobby of Children's Hospital for the surgeons to stitch still another, larger shunt into Matty's tiny withered pulmonary artery, the anesthesia failed to yield its grip.

Susan and I took our grief to Europe. Jay and Gail arranged for a friend to rent our house. They too were planning to travel—to Japan, where Jay had been offered a job teaching English.

We found a postcard from our renter in the American Express box in Paris. Jay's routine pre-departure physical had diagnosed acute leukemia.

He was given five months to live. Chemotherapy blasted him hairless. But, great advances having been made since my mother's day, the radiation triggered a remission. (On his doctor's recommendation, ironically, he fought the nausea his treatment produced by constantly smoking dope.) Meanwhile, he and Gail split up. The divorce was amicable; it took courage and clarity. A film-maker recorded Jay's poignantly articulate reconciliation to the imminence of his death. It was shown on PBS. Incredibly reprieved, a wry Jay hosted a theaterful of friends to a preview screening in Berkeley. Soon he moved to rural Oregon. He began building a cabin for himself with his own hands. His first book of poetry was published.

Arid then he too was dead. Age thirty-four.

"I lived well into my thirties," Jay wrote. "I can always say that."

It occurred to me that he'd done better than Jesus.

259

Sometimes I wonder—although no link has ever been shown—whether his marrow might not have been fatally rendered by the lycergic acid that was his communion sacrament.

As for me, once had been enough.

"It's like drinking five thousand martinis," I told Susan. I'd consciously chosen the banal simile. "I just don't think the human brain was meant to handle that kind of punishment."

Still, if nothing else, my brief spate of psychedelic detachment left me with an indelible image of mankind's desperation, gallantry and whimsy. Jury-rigging fretworks of meaning to conceal the great, encompassing void.

Jay's life—like my mother's, like our infant son's—guttered out sooner than the actuarial tables had promised. He faced its loss with anguish, fear, resentment... and then ultimately with a sense of calm and freedom. Because no matter how short a conscious life is, it's a terrifying stretch in the fathomless ocean of time. And so we have to throw up what rudimentary ramparts we can—pick sections to maintain among the labyrinthine levees of custom and duty, the rickety scaffolds of *soi-disant* purpose our ancestors have improvised and left for us.

You can rant, implore, shake your fists at the mute sky, read a libraryful of philosophy texts or theorize over cups of hot coffee and cold pizza until dawn. You can jubilate or mourn in hospital corridors, hiss prayers in echoing sacristies, squint wordless into the purple chasm of the Grand Canyon... but you almost never remember that you're still clambering around on the old bulwarks. So busy minding your balance you can't feel the arctic chill sucking at you through the framing.

Paul, on the road to Damascus, was nicked by a lightning bolt. I dropped a little acid. Our visions were rather different. He saw Being. I saw nothingness.

Held at bay for another sunny afternoon by a plucky band of cricketers.

*The Third Quarter*

# Downhill Skiing

# 1

## Marc-Yves arrived in the dark, puffy-eyed and redolent of aftershave.

He parked his rented car in our garage while I fitted the skis to the Peugeot's roof-rack. We kissed the kids goodbye as they slept in their beds. Noelle, our gangly nineteen-year-old *au pair* from Le Puy—upright, incredibly, at this barbarous hour, even more incredibly mascaraed and lipsticked *à la Parisienne*—padded after us in her best embroidered bathrobe, gasping pathetically each time she rammed a toe into a piece of furniture. She'd forsworn her thick glasses in Marc-Yves' presence.

I drove. We sucked black coffee from thermos cups and shelled hard-boiled eggs. Pretty soon Susan stretched out across the back seat and slept. Marc-Yves rode next to me, impervious to the intense golden dawn behind aviator shades so authentically detailed you wouldn't have been surprised to learn they'd logged several hundred hours in the cockpit of the SST. We made diffident small-talk in English. After a while I ventured French. I understand it faster than I can find words, but I like the practice. He told me about his daughters, who were at the Lycee Henri IV... about his wife, who produced *Actualités* for *Antenne 2*... and about his cars. A Mustang and a Ferrari. I think he found my stodgy seventy a bit nervous-making.

A beautiful spring morning flushed awake around

us. The fields, the freeway embankments, the distant hills defining the Central Valley were still spongy and verdant. Higher up, in the foothill orchards, blossoming fruit trees sighed petals on a carpet of yellow mustard. The sky was clear—a ripple of pink cloud faintly scrawled on the horizon soon solidified into the Sierra. We made the summit by nine.

Because he was only in the United States for two weeks, primarily to attend the Triple-AS meeting in San Francisco, where Susan had delivered a paper on selective protein secretion in mammalian cells—it was a line of work similar to his own at the Institut des Recherches Biochimiques at the Université de Paris—Marc-Yves was without ski gear of his own. He was dressed for the slopes in a pair of tailored designer jeans, an American-style ecru button-down shirt, a pale blue vee-necked Shetland pullover and a metallic silver Ferrari racing jacket. A figured maroon handkerchief was knotted cowboy-fashion around his neck. With that exception—and its practiced flair was quintessentially exceptional—Marc-Yves might have been any novice flatland American up for a day of pratfalls in the April corn. In fact, his casual wardrobe and the apparent ease with which he wore it were part of what made me like him. At the same time, its impeccable styling and trig accessories, as I believe they're called—the neck-scarf, for example, an affectation I've experimented with once or twice, but never for more than the moment of glum mirror assessment required before I snatch it off—were catnip to Susan. How, I've always wondered, can Europeans get away with stuff like that: suavity that on an American would make most compatriots gag?

We'd decided to ski at Squaw Valley. I found a parking place within easy walking distance of the lift-ticket booths. For some reason, the weekend crowd I'd steeled myself for—and the weather merited—hadn't materialized yet. I guessed a lot of the regulars were jaded by this point in a long season. I dropped Marc-Yves off at the first ski-rental shop we passed. Then Susan and I grunted into our boots at the car. We shouldered our skis and poles and clomped off bent-kneed through the slush, loose buckles jangling and upper lips puddling at the sudden nip of frost. It was the first time that year we'd skied without the kids. We exulted over the amazing ease with which we'd accomplished this usually prolonged and tumultuous logistic transition.

"You get the tickets, Richard, okay?" Susan said. "I want to go find Marc-Yves and see if he thinks I should rent myself a pair of shorter poles."

I nodded, eager. The adrenaline was already pumping as I grimaced up at the dazzling snowfields splayed against the sky, the tree-stippled gullies and ice-ribbed cornices that divided the mountain into its component topography. Diminutive chairlifts were strung at precarious angles along blue-shadowed slopes, still only sparsely flecked with skiers. I breathed a silent "yahoo!" into the credit-card line.

We rode the tram to the upper lodge standing, pressed shoulder-to-shoulder. The seatless aluminum tube was crammed to capacity. We clung to overhead straps and staggered in unison when wind-gusts swayed the car—eternally damned commuters. Marc-Yves had rented the most expensive skis available, all day-glo stripes and numbers. He and Susan chattered away about their length and flex while I smiled sympathetically beside them. Marc-Yves stood about five-nine. Susan is five-four. I towered into their stratosphere. I hunched my neck and frowned at their lips, but as often happens in these situations, I couldn't share most of the conversation. The ambient babble was too high. I entertained myself by peering out at the granite ledges we were skimming and easing myself discreetly into the warmth of the blonde who cushioned my flank.

Unlike most couples we know, or have encountered in lodge bars, Susan and I ski together. Always have. I suppose we'd be categorized as intermediates, and fairly strong at that—there's a running controversy between us, in fact, as to who's better. She'll grudgingly yield to me on speed and stamina, but never on form. She may be right. Not that I willingly admit it. But I *am* basically self-taught. Which is why I'm always a bit uneasy when direct comparisons loom between what I recognize as my bad, serviceable habits and the flamboyant grace of an expert.

"Oh, I don't worry about getting down anything any more," I'd chuckled in self-deprecation when Marc-Yves and I had discussed this trip. "But I might not look very pretty doing it."

Unfortunately, however, form is about as close to the essence of downhill skiing as it is to that of any sport save maybe diving or figure-skating. Or gymnastics. You'll find guys in the NBA—Larry Bird or Chris Mullin as notable examples—who don't look all that pretty yet have an uncanny knack for getting the job done. Still, whether shooting baskets or driving nails, form generally informs function. And in skiing, "getting down"—mere survival—is only a beginner's concern. It's quickly supplanted by the desire to get down with style, because style enlarges the compass of what you can get down. Even utilitarian-I must grant that my every run is gauged by how it feels it looks—a matter not just of shallow narcissism, but of meeting a standard of coordination... satisfying an internal esthetic.

So when Marc-Yves had mentioned over coffee at our house three nights earlier that he always took his family to the Alps for Christmas—modestly acknowledged that he skied *assez souvent*—Susan had seized on the idea of this weekend not only as a chance for hospitable sharing of enthusiasms, but also, more pragmatically, as an opportunity for self-improvement. And sure enough, as soon as she saw him carve his first fluid S off the top of the tram slope, she was his admiring student.

## We spent the morning in the back bowls—Marc-Yves leading and Susan undulating in his tracks.

The two of them stopped frequently so he could observe her poling rhythm or posture over the skis, maybe suggest a line of descent that would exercise some particular element of technique. From long habit I brought up the rear. It was I who had taught her to ski in the first place—right here, as a matter of fact, where we'd spent a brief second honeymoon. As her mentor (even though I'd only learned a couple of years previously myself), I'd become accustomed to supervising her from above and behind. That way I could stand scout and plunge to her rescue when she fell—which, in the early days at least, she did often enough to recommend the practice. (My own wipeouts, consequently, occurred well behind her. She'd be left to gape anxiously upslope for five or ten minutes until I slogged ignominiously out of the trees crusted with snow, carrying my splintered ski and skewed pole but well rehearsed in some exculpatory tale of catastrophic equipment failure even Jean-Claude Killy would have been hard-pressed to survive intact.)

Marc-Yves, wisely, confined his instruction to Susan.

"But you ski very well!" he declared when we veered to a stop, spraying powder, at the bottom of our first run.

"Oh, that was easy," she demurred. "Wait till you see me on moguls or really steep stuff. I always get scared and go to pieces."

"But you have taken many lessons, I think."

"No. No," she panted, "only a couple." She smiled.

I craned over my poles and scowled at my bindings. There was justice, I suppose, in excluding my amateur

271

attentions.

"Then you make me feel very bad," he laughed. "I have spent *milliards* of francs to learn. And more years than I care to count."

"Don't worry," Susan grinned. She touched his arm. "It shows."

It did. He outclassed me, for sure. So I eavesdropped and applied his hints, though he was scrupulous to avoid any focus of eye or direction of comment that might suggest they were intended to extend to me as well. It made for a certain superficiality of bonhomie.

"I'll ride up with Marc-Yves this time," Susan announced as we herringboned toward the chairlift. She was radiant in the brilliant sun. The ski down, the exertion, the frosty morning air had burnished her high-boned cheeks under their sheen of tanning lotion. Snow crystals glinted in her hair. It was pulled back under a white woolen earband. She wore a dazzling pair of hip-molding white bib overalls, a matching quilted jacket and a crimson turtleneck the same shade as her boots and the palms of her tri-colored leather mittens.

"Why not?" I replied. I fluttered my eyelids. My moue and accent plainly mimicked Marc-Yves. It was one of his characteristic phrases.

"Why not?" Susan echoed. She poked her elbow into Marc-Yves' ribs. *"Pourquoi pas?"*

He acknowledged with a chuckle.

I turned to the ramp line behind me. "Single!" I yelled.

**We worked the sunny upper crescent of a broad bowl, its top hummocked by yesterday's moguls.**

The snow was still creamy and forgiving, though.

"That was great!" Susan bubbled on the chair as we ascended once more. She'd favored me this time.

"Yeah, you looked very confident," I said.

"Marc-Yves told me to lean forward more and really concentrate on staying in the fall-line. I always have this tendency to sit back into the hill, you know. Chicken out."

"You weren't tentative at all that time," I assured her. "At least not from what I could see."

She rested her mittened hand on my thigh. "How about you?" she inquired. Her eyebrows knitted earnestly above her mirror sunglasses. I saw my own reflected. "Are you having fun?"

"Sure," I nodded. "Of course I am."

"Good. Because I'm having an absolute ball!"

She swiveled in her seat and surveyed the view emerging from the serrated ridgeline behind us. Snow-mantled firs framed Lake Tahoe. It was puddled blue as antifreeze in the basin far below. Even the usual winter haze of woodsmoke and auto exhaust was missing.

"What a glorious day!" she exclaimed. She waved at Marc-Yves, who was in the chair following ours. "Look at the view!" she called. She pointed. He beamed and circled his thumb and finger at her.

"That guy's pretty amazingly Americanized," I observed.

"He did a post-doc at Harvard, you know. And he's been a visiting scientist at the Lab a couple of times."

"Yeah? 'D you know him before, then?"

"I met him. But this is the first time we've had something really in common."

"Scientifically speaking, I suppose. Mm?"

"Mm," she nodded. She looked away from me. I noticed the unsunned creases at the corner of her eye. "But he certainly is very attractive, isn't he?" She gave me a smile. "I admit it, I enjoy comparing notes on enzyme metabolism with such a handsome and attentive colleague. Wouldn't you?"

"Community of science," I muttered. "Heads together. Hope I'm as cozily accommodated next time I get away...."

"I'll bet you're cozily accommodated," she snorted. "Little odd moments in the busy round of cocktails and dinners and press conferences you somehow neglect to fill me in on?"

"Yeah," I agreed. "You've got it scoped. In what free time I have left over from toadying, I'm a real bear with the local geishas."

She wrinkled her nose and mimed me a kiss. "I'm sure you are, dear. 'Prepare to Unload.' Better get your tips up."

"Funny," I said. "That's almost exactly what those geishas tell me. 'Tip' in the singular."

"Ooh," she sneered. "Boo! Not only is that *not* funny, it's *disgusting!*"

## We ate lunch alpine-style, reclining on the snow against our crossed skis.

The midday sun was so warm we took off our jackets and pushed up our sleeves. We'd found a glade of pines on the side of a gully to shelter us from the wind. There we picnicked on the dry salami, crusty rolls, oranges and dark chocolate I'd carried in my fanny-pack. We squirted Chianti from a goatskin *bota* into our upturned mouths.

Our tastes, Susan and mine, had evolved toward the European, you will have noted. Francophile, I suppose would be more specific. The Ursuline nuns had taught me *Frère Jacques* in kindergarten, my mother the *Marseillaise* before I was ten. And I'd minored in French as an undergraduate. The Indian summer we'd spent in Paris after Matty died had proved, in retrospect, effective therapy. Rebecca was conceived there. And after I went to work for PML, boosting our economic status, Susan and I had begun to vacation in France every couple of summers. Recently, she'd started looking for an appointment that might allow us to spend a year or so there. I was getting a bit fed up with the corporate life anyway. The only rung left to climb was vice president-public relations, and the guy already there—my boss—only had a year or two on me in age: youthful fee-nom. We could put the children in French schools, we fantasized—no cost, as opposed to the small fortune we were forking out in tuition to Berkeley's Ecole Bilingue. That would make up for the loss of my income. I'd work on the novel I'd never finished—sitting in a leafy courtyard in some stone village on a sun-baked promontory overlooking the Cote d'Azur. ("Do they have a biochemistry department at the University of Nice?" I'd prompted Susan. "Try there.") Or maybe I'd emulate Hemingway. Hunch over a back table at a Left Bank cafe shrouded in Gauloise smoke, the windows steamed, a hard rain falling, saucers clinking and my notepad filling while Susan did her cell biology thing at... the Institut des Recherches Biochimiques.

Hm. Her best shot too, probably. Hm.

The afternoon recapitulated the morning. Most of the exposed runs had turned glutinous, and then, as the shadows lengthened, the undersides of the moguls iced hard. Edges chattered as we pivoted. I had a couple of runs where I just couldn't force my legs not to splay.

"Knees together, you jerk," I muttered to myself.

"Parallel, parallel!"

I tried to copy Marc-Yves, in front of me. Lunge, plant pole, unweight—always attack, but maintain a smooth, sinuous rhythm. Mine was ragged. And my skis insisted on stemming when I turned—spreading pigeon-toed, like a craven tyro's.

Then, just before the Ski Patrol swept us off the trails and the lifts shut down, I got it together with back-to-back runs so effortlessly and fluently conceived they wrung yodels of glee.

The three of us were almost abreast as we dipped into the last long pitch. We weaved, converged, suddenly arced away on exuberant high-speed tangents.

"Yee-ha!" I chortled at Marc-Yves. I waggled my hips.

He grinned and returned the *wedeln*. He lifted a pole in salute. Somehow he carelessly shifted his weight too far onto his outside edge. He sat suddenly, slithering down the hill in a shower of snow but managing to keep his skis together. He bounced upright within a few yards.

"Perfect," he snorted as I braked alongside him. "So I end this day."

He showed me a wry expression—behind which, for an instant, I thought I saw the constricted pallor of real anger. It startled me. He swiped perfunctorily at the snow on his jeans and skated off after Susan, who hadn't seen the mishap.

I poled hard, but I couldn't catch him. Still, I did maintain the interval.

Zigzagging my weary way through the old snowbanks—yellow as urinals—and the milling *après*-skiers at the bottom of the mountain, I was elated, all in all, by my day's performance.

# 2

**The cabin we'd rented was on the lakeshore, screened from the road and its neighbors by a thicket of sugar pines.**

The lot was unusually large and private, probably bought for further subdivision since the house itself was an undistinguished A-frame finished in cheap, knotty peckerwood. Inside, there was a sleeping loft over a shag-carpeted living room, a fake fieldstone fireplace and precariously tracked sliding glass doors that opened onto a partially-roofed deck facing the lake. There was a big bathroom with a cultured-marble counter and a plastic tub-shower unit. The kitchen was all-electric, but the size of a broom closet. Its drawers were stocked with mismatched bowls, Pay 'N' Save china and Army surplus mess-hall utensils. In short, this was a typical Tahoe vacation rental except for the setting—phenomenal—and the price: right. The place belonged to a colleague of Susan's who'd intended to use it with his own family that weekend until chickenpox struck. He'd offered it free, but Marc-Yves had insisted on paying—and treating us in return for the two dinners we'd fed him. And oh yes, there was one other remarkable feature: a redwood hot-tub on a five-day timer that waited simmering between the deck and the water's edge.

We were pretty wiped out by the time we arrived. The

drive along the Truckee from Squaw had stiffened our ski-worn muscles. Our faces burned from the day's unremitting sun and wind. The tops of my boots had chafed my shins and somehow I'd wrenched my shoulder in craning to grab a fast chair.

It all felt delicious. My head pulsed pleasantly from the can of beer I'd drained on the ride over. I creaked inside, lugging our boot-trees and shared suitcase, and while Susan stowed the groceries Noelle had packed for us, and Marc-Yves unloaded the rest of the stuff from the car, I dug out the gin bottle.

"An acquired taste, perhaps... one you may have no trouble *not* acquiring," I chirped. "But one you should experience at least once if you're to understand us, M'sieu de Tocqueville."

I handed Marc-Yves a martini.

"*À votre santé*," I toasted.

"Cheers," he replied. He clinked glasses with Susan and me. She watched with fond, amused expectation as he sipped. He flared his eyebrows, pursed his lips, turned down the corners of his mouth and cocked his head from side to side—all quintessentially French.

"Awful?" she laughed.

"*Pas de tout*. No way, José," he replied. "No no. Quite interesting." He tried another cautious swallow. "Yes, this will do. Very, very nicely." He rubbed his hands. We'd clicked on the thermostat, but it was still frigid inside the high-ceilinged room.

"And now," he twinkled, "I wonder what other instructive experiences you have in store for me."

"Well," Susan smiled, "for starters, how about a nice California hot-tub?"

"Why not?" he bowed.

"Why not? Why not?" we chimed.

Susan took the first shower and came out hugging

herself in her terrycloth bathrobe. Her hair was combed back wet and close against her skull. Marc-Yves and I had got a fire going in the fireplace, and heat was beginning to radiate noticeably from the baseboards.

"Next?" Susan said. "Hurry up. I want to get in."

"Go ahead," I said.

"You go first," Marc-Yves deferred to me. It was an awkward moment—one of us was going to be alone in the hot-tub with her. I appreciated his *délicatesse*. At least, that's how I read it. I was trying not to read much of anything, though.

"I'll see if I can build up this fire some more," he offered. He fanned at the anemic blaze we'd kindled with the crumpled grocery bags.

I undressed quickly, showered and furled the damp towel around my hips. We'd already checked the temperature of the tub and found it piping. I flip-flopped into the living room on my rubber thongs.

"So what are we waiting for?" I said to Susan, who still lingered above Marc-Yves. "*Allons-y. N'est-ce pas*? We'll start the water bubbling out there and await your imminent immersion, M'sieu Perrier. *D'accord*?"

**I set aside the wooden covers and the foam insulator that floated on the dark, aromatic surface while Susan shucked out of her bathrobe.**

Steam billowed from the vat like Old Faithful erupting. Twilight was approaching and the ambient air temperature was probably below thirty. Moving about in it bare-skinned offered a peculiar, masochistic sensual pleasure. Not one to be prolonged, though. I dipped in quickly beside Susan, yelping at the sting of the scorching broth, and sat on the submerged slat-bench.

The tub was equipped with air jets. We had the water foaming merrily when Marc-Yves appeared. He was wearing a white silk Algerian-style *djellaba* that set off his tanned face strikingly. It was only when he peeled it over his head that his winter-pale chest and shanks were revealed. We all had that odd skier's pigmentation. He clambered in and eased himself, sucking breath through a grimace, into the flow from a jet.

At first we just sprawled silently. The churning water rippled flaccid muscles as its warmth seeped into our marrows. Fragrant steam wreathed our lolling heads. We sniffed its redwood tang—oleoresins and esters faintly laced with chlorine. We exchanged heavy-lidded, beatific grins.

"*Merveilleux,*" Susan sighed.

"Far out," Marc-Yves agreed. Something about the atmosphere was making us keep our voices hushed.

"Phew. I've got to cool off for a minute, though," she said. A fine sweat misted her forehead and upper lip. She rose, streaming water from nipples and pubic hair, radish-bare body flushed radish-red, and pushed herself back on the decking.

Hot-tubs were the raging fad then in California. You couldn't live in Berkeley without being exposed in one. And I'm not confusing my prepositions. So although I wasn't altogether crazy about Susan's waxing chumminess with Marc-Yves—which made this *bain à trois* rather less innocuously hygienic than a lot of others we'd taken in mixed company—I was sufficiently accustomed to companionate nudity to suppress my misgivings. And curiously, as I looked at Susan displaying herself before a man whose interest she clearly reciprocated, I found myself mildly, perversely stimulated.

Not that there was any overt flirtation going on—we

were all making it a point to act blasé, casual... civilized. After fourteen years of marriage, though, I thought I knew my wife pretty well. I could sense the mingled hesitance and daring, the exhibitionism indulged against prim instincts. Her conversation had an electric eagerness, and her cheeks a high color. She was turned on. And so, watching her that way, was I.

Susan's body, at thirty-nine and despite having borne three babies, was still admirably firm. Good genes, evidently. Her breasts had been nursed flatter than when I first, reverently, bared them—fumbled at the straps of her bikini top in the bathroom of her mother's house, after a day on the beach in Santa Monica. I could hardly breathe as I contemplated their beauty—a tracery of fine blue veins underlying the milky flesh, perfect circles of pink ringed by minute bumps of arousal, the soft central nubs rising firm to accept my first kisses. And if the aureoles' pigment had darkened slightly by now, they remained pert and resilient. She had a couple of faint stretch marks on her lower abdomen. But only a summer's sunning rendered the tracks of puckered skin noticeable. She was broad-hipped and broad-shouldered, with a narrow waist and generous buttocks. She worried they were sagging to flab. They weren't. Her belly was taut, with a saucy navel and a central feathering that flourished into a perfect triangle of chestnut fuzz. The water had shaped it into a neat crest over the pink vaginal dimple as she rose.

Although she lounged modestly with her thighs together, Susan couldn't help offering new flashes of herself for scrutiny every time she moved. I saw Marc-Yves' eyes flicker discreetly over the spectacle.

He too was an extraordinary physical specimen for a man who'd cracked forty. I think I'm in reasonable shape only ten or fifteen pounds over my collegiate playing weight. But Marc-Yves didn't carry an ounce of fat. He was compact, lean and smooth, as sleek as a twenty-year-old swimmer. Besides that, to my atavistic chagrin, he possessed a stout bockwurst of uncircumcised penis that looked a lot longer than my own shyly retiring, tonsured stub. I wondered if Susan was tantalized.

**We'd sloshed in and out of the tub a few times each—the chemistry, it seemed to me, growing palpably more concupiscent.**

Susan jiggled and posed and began to tease Marc-Yves with coquettish underwater kicks and nudges. He responded with courtly good humor and intense eye-contact. He caressed her without extending a finger... told her wordlessly she was beautiful, funny, incisive, fascinating. Yet he never violated the bounds of formal politeness as patroled by a present husband. I knew his manner was practiced. I suspect Susan did too at some level. But he struck no false notes. He was just M. Sincère, our mutual friend from Paris. I had to admire the urbane son-of-a-bitch.

Still, there was that undercurrent of erotic tension. We probed it like kids teasing a snake with a stick. Our banter had a risqué edge and our laughter was just a bit too raucous in pitch. For an instant I did toy with *Penthouse* fantasies: Susan writhing under Marc-Yves, me slithering in to meld our three slick bodies in some contorted interpenetration....

The actual imagining disgusted me. There was a time-honored antidote.

"Hey, Marc-Yves," I said. "Think you're man enough to join me for a dip in the lake?"

"The lake?" Susan exclaimed.

"Yeah. Like a sauna, in Finland. Let's see," I grinned,

"if we can stand it."

"Good grief," she said. "And you ripe for a coronary as it is at your age."

"'Ripe!' Me?" I protested. "How can you say such a thing? I don't smoke. Maybe two cigarettes a week. I eat rabbit-food for lunch. And I play tennis. Swim laps. See? Look at all this extra muscle I'm developing." I grasped the girdle of flesh that padded my pelvic crests. "What's more, I'm a totally relaxed, laid-back personality. Not a care in the world, not a furrow on my brow. Mr. Couldn't-Give-A-Shit. Obviously. Ice water courses through my veins."

"You've got ice water *on* the brain, more like it," she muttered.

"All that icy water out there beckoning." I swept my hand toward the lake. "Like unto like. A challenge to be met. In the immortal words of that great Amurrican patriot, General Electric, 'Give me frigid air or give me death.'"

I squared my shoulders and vaulted off the decking into the ankle-deep snow. "Lafayette," I taunted Marc-Yves, "are you here?"

I started running. At the high-water mark I had to slow, to stork-dance gingerly over the beach pebbles. But as soon as my feet splatted into lakewater I lost them. One, two, three desperate hops on numb, shrinking stumps until I could fling myself flat out into oblivion.

The shock hammered me senseless. The effect was too instantaneous for a scream. Cold pierced my ears like an awl. My breath was flash-frozen inside my lungs. The fiery surge paralyzed me—I was a ribcage, a nub of flayed skull and a few squibs of cartilege shriveling in an acid sea.

Then, with a stentorian gasp, I broke through the stupefaction.

"*Ho-o-o-ly CHRIST!*" I bellowed. I flailed erect and spun to look for Susan and Marc-Yves. Needless to say, they still reclined on the tub platform, peering at me curiously.

"So how is it?" Susan called with a sweet, nonchalant inflection.

I hopped and jigged and pumped my arms, puffing like a marathoner. "De-de-dee-licious!" I squeaked. "Whoo-ee!" My voice was shrill and already I was wracked by violent shivers. "Oughtta t-t-try it! Oooh... *GAWD!*"

I flopped under once more to confirm my ding-nigh superhuman power of will, beat out two or three wild strokes and then scrambled to my feet and stumbled up the rocky slope toward shore. I could see my toes splayed blue-white on the bottom. The water was pellucid. My scrotum was so tight my testicles had retreated halfway up my spine. My dick had practically puckered itself inside out. I was trembling too hard to coordinate running. But I was thoroughly proud of myself. I'd always wondered if I could do that.

A few minutes poaching in the tub were sufficient convalescence, too. "Chickens," I sneered. "*Poulets.*"

"*T'es brave type, Richard*," Marc-Yves conceded. "*Mes compliments, Herr Viking.*"

"Herr Shirt. Hairball," Susan punned experimentally. "In any case, definitely *un dindon.*"

## I'd broken the spell, anyway.

We hung around the tub a while longer, draining our martini glasses and watching the lake lour from purple to black. Immense stars dusted a limpid sky. The blanched Nevada mountains luminesced in their thin light.

We were reduced to whispers by the time we toweled off and went inside. We put on sweaters and jeans—Susan her furry mukluks—and cooked dinner. It was a group project. Marc-Yves uncorked a bottle of the Bordeaux he'd brought, and then began expertly chopping vegetables. I stirred oil and red wine vinegar, garlic and mustard and salt and pepper and tarragon and a dash of Worcestershire sauce, for the salad dressing. Susan cooked. We had *entrecote* topped with a sauté of mushrooms, red bell peppers and onions, pan-fried potatoes and, for dessert, apple compote. Susan and I by long habit kept referring to it as "compost." We had to explain the joke to Marc-Yves.

Afterwards we sat on the floor by the fireplace eating camembert and sipping cognac out of lo-ball glasses.

"Ah, I porked out," Marc-Yves sighed.

"I love it," Susan grinned.

"'Pigged out' is the expression you hear more commonly," I informed him.

He dimpled sheepishly. "*En tout cas, t'es cuisinière extraordinaire, Madame Suzanne.*"

"It was pretty basic," she shrugged. "And you were my coauthor, after all."

"Ah, no no," he exclaimed, lips pursed in that Gallic manner. "I do nothing. *Mais*, excuse me, Richard." He always pronounced my name "Reechar," giving it the hard "ch" the French perversely apply to Chicago. "The *vinaigrette* you make was also *excellente*." He pinched the air with thumb and forefinger. "*Néanmoins, à toi, Suzanne, mes applaudissements.*"

"*Et les miens aussi*," I nodded. I hoped I'd used the correct gender form. My French seemed to have flowed through dinner swimmingly, to muddle a metaphor, thanks to its vinous lubrication. But I was a little uneasy about Marc-Yves' *tutoyer*-ing of Suzanne. Susan! Jesus, now he had me doing it. The question was, were there innuendoes—innuendi?—to a *tu* to her from him?

I sat brooding, slightly fuddled, as they began to talk about people at the Lab. Although they both made occasional perfunctory efforts to include me in the dialogue, it was once again obvious that I was an appendage to their absorption. All I had to do was look at the glint in Susan's eyes, hear the lilt in her voice, to recognize how long it had been since I'd struck the same resonance. We made a familiar kind of love with satisfying regularity. We spared each other few details of our daily encounters, coups, frustrations and aspirations across the dinner table. We took care of Rebecca and Christopher, the new house, the bigger garden, the social calendar and the weekend errands side by side in the time not consumed by two fairly demanding jobs and vigorous ambitions. We were, in sum, paragons of marital accommodation... a solid couple who, except for a few stormy hours every week or so, basically liked, loved, each other.

And yet... the rub of that long shared life had worn off most of the astonishments that are the key to passion.

I inhaled cognac fumes and stared at the flames sputtering between my stockinged feet. My legs were propped on the hearth amid a litter of empty, groping gloves and hissing socks. If the kids were here with us, they'd be badgering us to toast marshmallows about now. I pictured them at it: Becca fussily tending her skewer, proudly exhibiting the perfect, symmetrically inflated, uniformly golden-crusted *objet d'art* she'd lavished twenty minutes on. Meanwhile, Chris would be fidgeting, sniveling, cursing, howling with glee as he fished his leprous chunks of carbonized sugar from the ashes, or watched them ooze and dribble off his flaming brand. Our volatile, marvelously differentiated offspring. I wondered what they were doing at home right this minute. Past nine, bedtime. Noelle would be trying to corral them for the ritual story. I almost missed that puppy turmoil. Hell, I *did* miss it.

Unlike their oblivious mother over there, I grumbled to myself. Giggling and batting her lashes, radiating musk like some pepper-pantsed teenager.

I clacked my toe-knuckles together in indignation,

and heaved myself upright. I lurched into the kitchen for a brandy refill.

## Susan and Marc-Yves were on their feet too when I came back.

He was arching his neck, stretching and twisting. He reached for his jacket.

"We're both feeling a little stiff," Susan said. "How about you? Marc-Yves suggested we all go out for a walk. Get a breath of fresh air."

Marc-Yves nodded and beckoned. "Take a gander at the moon."

"Hoo," I smiled, "you really are gettin' our language down, aren't you, bud? Unfortunately," it occurred to me to point out, "*il n'y a pas de lune ce soir.* Anyway, who's gonna stay and watch the kids?"

"Huh? What are you talking about?" Susan frowned.

I flashed her a mean smile. "Nothing. Just wondered if their existence ever crossed your mind."

She gave me a calculating squint and tossed her hair. "I'm not sure what that's supposed to mean. And I don't think I care to find out. You coming or not?"

"Not, I believe. You two go ahead. Go-ho o-on without me," I croaked in a wounded-cowboy quaver. "Ah kin make it. Jes' lea' me be here, with a tot o' whuskey t' take away the pain. Oooh...." I collapsed on the sofa. I was careful not to spill any of the three fingers of cognac I was clutching.

"Looks to me like you're already pretty much beyond pain," Susan observed. "I'd cool it with that stuff if I were you."

"There are hurts and there are hurts," I leered.

She wagged her head and stalked off.

So I'd given them rope. And from some strange, almost generous instinct. *Noblesse oblige*—the *noblesse* of the odd man out.

They certainly proceeded to take it, too. At first I scarcely noticed their absence. I turned on the TV set that lurked in a corner, nursed my drink and tried to lose myself in *Fantasy Island*. The comedy was unbelievably inane, but there was an actress who kept appearing in wispy tops, obviously *sans* bra. I can get a lot of mileage out of playing peek-a-boo with nipples.

But not enough to distract me indefinitely from my sulk. I began to shudder, to snarl an obscenity every few minutes—wrenched by sudden bitter recollections of the lapse in judgment by which I'd compliantly volunteered to be put in this horrible position. I mean the whole weekend! Anger, self-pity, self-contempt kept bubbling up out of the psychic muck that seethed below my alcohol-glazed, TV-coagulated consciousness.

Pretty soon I realized they'd been gone for close to half an hour.

Well, that isn't so long for a walk, I rationalized. I began to pace the room. Christ, I sneered at myself, I was nothing *but* rationalizations. I started gesticulating with my glass. Muttering aloud. "*Le cocu.*" The cuckold, I rasped. What an ugly word. Especially in English. And the French have an equally ugly gesture to go with it—to waggle behind the poor sap's back.

I jabbed the air with horned fingers. "*Cocu, cocu!*" I taunted myself.

Marc-Yves must hold me in utter disdain, I mused. For my passivity, my acquiescence.

Now going on forty-five minutes.

And what about Susan, I thought? How dare she flaunt her total disregard for my feelings this way! My obvious awareness of the demeaning situation. Rub my nose

in it: "'Bye, dear," she'd winked coyly, "we'll be back in a bit."
Yeah, shit. After a fucking little roll in the fucking hay, no
doubt.

I grabbed my parka and slammed out of the cabin. I
carried my drink with me, after decanting three more fingers.
I started up the long driveway toward the road, searching for
their footprints. But the snow was old and trampled. There
were too many branching furrows to decipher. They'd be
more likely to stroll the lakeshore, anyway, I decided.

I plowed back around the house, bucking through
deep, crusty drifts among the trees. The pebbled beach gave
no clues as to which direction they might have taken. So I
chose one.

## I guess I walked for about twenty minutes.

I snuck past other beach-front chalets, some dark and
shuttered, some warmly lit. Here and there a rickety dock
fingered into the lake. Offshore swimming rafts wallowed
under incongruous cargoes of snow.

When I was near habitation I skirted wide around the
crunchy pebbles to mask my passage. I hunched into myself
and tried silently to attenuate my field of raging energy. But
once out of earshot again, I let loose—swilled from my glass,
shook my free fist at the water, ranted and harangued the
stars with gobbets of French and English punctuated by fits
of sardonic chuckling.

I moaned, sobbed, moaned some more for dramatic
effect as I dredged up every past grievance I could catalog
against my errant wife. I argued my own forbearance, my
devotion, my earnestness... all the wonderful husbandly
traits I personified. Not to mention my spotless, stupid and
now emphatically unreciprocated fidelity.

I blocked out scenarios for the confrontation. Quiet dignity followed by a punch in the beak. Or maybe the stomach since he was shorter. Anglo-Saxon vengeance, fists as opposed to lead or steel. His good luck I wasn't a Frog, eh? A Corsican, say. Whoo! Slice off his balls and stuff 'em in his ears. Eye-sockets. How would *she* feel, I whined, if I were doing this to her? If I'd brought some doxy along on one of our trips, pitched woo undisguisedly....

*Pitched woo? Doxy?* Just a second here. Even as I pled my case to the pines and the Big Dipper, I sat in the jury-box snickering. My florid eloquence was impressive—you have to take my word for that. It was. Seldom except in other, similar drunken perorations has the circuitry between brain and tongue operated with such hability. I was a glib Clarence Darrow and a wildly cheering, foot-stamping audience in one. Not to mention the gavel-wielding judge and the snide opposing counsel, constantly reading into the record the ridiculousness of all this hysterical posturing.

Nor was it much of a catharsis. I just got angrier and tireder. And of course I never found them. Nearing town I realized the hopelessness of dragging from one motel to another in hopes I'd turn them up. Maybe they'd just tugged their pants and jackets open and humped in the snow anyway. I hurled my glass at a tree—missed—then threw rocks at the lake until my arm got sore and I lost my breath. Then I sauntered into the lights and the first bar I came to.

I drained a quick Scotch while I rested my feet. I scrutinized the terrain furtively for a woman, unattached, who might conceivably be read as attracted to me. The best looking were two muscular young blondes in cowboy shirts and Levis playing pool between sips of draft beer. They might not have been the lesbians they appeared—who can tell with women? But otherwise the distaff clientele was plain or paired or sullenly oblivious. The customers all looked blue-collar and local. Lodge waitresses, snowplow drivers...

I got hostile stares when I entered, then the acceptance of being ignored. I was none too comfortable with myself there anyway. I slurped and ran.

The Scotch hit me about halfway back. Cold, fatigue, the altitude and the load I was already carrying potentiated it. The sky began to wheel like a planetarium show suddenly kicked into fast-forward. I grabbed a passing tree, clung to it for a moment and then squatted and retched in hacking spasms. It was the first time in years I'd drunk to the point of being sick. At least I still had the presence to avoid my boots. Hard-won Navy skill. It was a while before I could totter up and walk again. The rest of the trip seemed an eon of head-pounding, putty-legged determination not to succumb to the yawing and pitching of the beach.

At least I finally had my catharsis.

## I could see Susan and Marc-Yves through the glass doors as I approached the hot-tub.

He was in his *djellaba* and she in her bathrobe. Exactly as I'd dreaded. I cringed and spied on them while I collected myself for my entrance.

They were on the couch side by side, twisted to face each other—their near arms draped over the back so that their hands were almost touching. Susan is an outgoing person, lively in conversation. But I saw a special intensity in the way she inclined toward him. She devoured his eyes, displayed her broad repertoire of facial expressions, flounced her hair and reached out once to pat him—a glancing caress to underscore enthusiasm. Jealousy seared my gullet—as acrid as the residue of my recent cookie-toss. And then I just felt hollow.

"Oh, hi!" Susan exclaimed when I clattered through the doors. "Where've you been? Must've decided you needed that walk after all, huh?"

"Mm. Gr' p'w'rs d'duction...."

"What?"

I cleared my throat. "Nothing," I managed.

"You must've gone a long way. It's beautiful out there tonight, isn't it?"

"Mm-hm." I pushed off from the wall against which I'd steadied myself and crossed to a chair without, I thought, noticeable difficulty. I fell into it.

"Where...?" I croaked. I coughed and cleared my throat again, baffling any transmission of fumes with a curled fist. I started over. "Where'd you go? B'lieve it or not... went looking for you."

"We made a *promenade,* of the lake," Marc-Yves smiled.

"Hell of a promenade," I muttered.

"You were gone quite a while yourself," Susan declared. "Actually, I was even starting to get a little worried...."

"Looked it," I grunted.

"Marc-Yves suggested we should maybe send out a St. Bernard," she grinned.

"S' B'nard... not what I needed. Thoughtful of you, though, g' buddy." I braced myself to rise. I couldn't stifle a complaint before leaving, however. "Christ, I waited here almost an hour...!"

"You must have left just as we were getting back," Susan blinked. She sounded uneasy. Guilty.

"I wouldn't know about that. Listen...."

"We found the TV set blaring," she said. "No sign of where you'd gone. We finally went out and had another soak. We kept expecting you."

"I'll bet. Sorry if that put a damper on things." I

cranked myself out of the chair. I felt lighter somehow, as if a weight I couldn't specify had been removed from my shoulders. "Bit of a pun, eh? Soak, damper. Heh, heh. Listen, I'm going to bed."

"I'll be right there," Susan assured me.

"No hurry. Take your time. Don' lemme interrupt anything. G' night, all."

"I am sleepy also," Marc-Yves said. "And if we want to ski early tomorrow...."

"Mm," Susan agreed. "I'm about ready to nod off right here where I am, actually. It's been a super, super day, though. Hasn't it?"

I left them simpering to each other as they doused lights and policed saucers and glasses. I went into the bathroom to scour my teeth and tongue. I sluiced down three aspirins. The bed took off like a crop-duster when I climbed into it. I lay with the pillow over my eyes and one bare sole planted on the floor, riding out the death spirals.

Susan recognized my condition when she burrowed in beside me.

"Good God," she whispered. "What'd you do, go and get yourself snockered?"

I was cultivating a precarious catatonia.

"I don't believe you're asleep yet," she taunted. She peeled the pillow off my forehead. "Comatose or dead, maybe. Not asleep."

I snatched the pillow back and exhaled irritation.

"As I suspected. Aren't you going to kiss me good night?"

I didn't stir.

"Good night, then," she said. She bent over me and kissed me wetly on the lips. "I love you," she breathed. "Even if you do smell like a distillery and act like a drunken toad."

"And you like a shameless trollop," I hissed.

"Oooh, *trollop!* And shameless! How Dickensian!"

293

"Tart. Hussy. Prick-teaser. Have I found the era and the idiom you prefer? I just wish you had the decency and the respect not to make me have to watch!"

"Rick...."

Marc-Yves was in the downstairs bedroom but the sleeping loft was open. Who knew what he might overhear? I didn't want to argue now. "Just put the pillow back, okay, Susan?" I whispered. "Please?"

"I'm sorry if I've hurt you," she said. "I haven't meant to. And no matter what you think, you don't have anything to worry about."

"Great."

"I do love you."

She smoothed the pillow over my eyes again tenderly. Then she curled hard against me. I lay supine, rigid. Her palm began to creep down my abdomen.

"Don't," I muttered.

"Wouldn't you like to relax?"

"Not that way."

"How out of character. I'm sure you would," she cooed.

"I would," I snarled, grabbing her wrist and removing it, "*not!*"

But damn it, she knew my body. And my mercurial ambivalences. She was not usually the aggressor. We both had sexual hang-fires to discharge, though. I was aggrieved, nose out of joint—in no way, I mocked myself, the author of her arousal. Merely the convenient beneficiary of its displacement. But I was betrayed by my indiscriminate flesh. If you've got 'em by the balls, as the Marines used to roister, their hearts and minds will follow.

Susan's soft, skillful attentions assuaged me. Soon we were locked together in muffled thrashings our efforts to keep clandestine only made more exciting. I took out my frustrations in harsh service. Afterwards I clasped her tightly.

"I love you, Susan," I exclaimed into her hair. "I...."

I wanted to justify my possessiveness. But I was suddenly wary.

"...Really do," I detoured lamely.

The fire made cozy crackling sounds from the room below. Its orange reflection played on the ceiling and walls. I heard the faint metallic creak of a bedspring. So, I guess, did Susan.

"Poor Marc-Yves," she sighed. "I hope we didn't make too much noise."

She laced her fingers into mine, gave them a squeeze and rolled over.

# 3

**The sky was pewter when I woke up.**

Desultory snowflakes sifted out of the overcast. I smelled coffee and heard Marc-Yves rustling around below. Susan tunneled deeper into the blankets but I pulled on my jeans and gentled my throbbing head down the staircase. I frowned through the glass at the grey lake. The light, even flat and diminished, made my eyeballs pucker. I withdrew into the kitchen.

"Morning," I said to Marc-Yves. "*Bon jour. Vous avez bien dormi?*"

"*Bien assez,*" he nodded. He was in the *djellaba* but shaved already. I caught the perfume of his French cologne. He was reading a paperback.

"*'Y a du cafe?*" I asked. I fingered my stubble. The headache was growing worse by the moment. My mouth tasted like apple compost.

"*Ouais.*" He indicated the pot with an invitational gesture.

I poured myself a cup. "*Quelle heure est-il?*"

So far this was all simple stuff, but I found the illusion of French domestic fluency enjoyable. My animosity toward him had pretty much receded in the final triumph of last night.

"*Neuf heures. Environ.*"

"*Si tard!*"

"Suzanne sleeps well?"

"Ah, *oui. Elle... descend dans une minute, je crois.*" I dumped a teaspoonful of sugar into my coffee and poured milk out of the carton until mine matched the khaki of his. I usually drink it black, except in France. "*Mauvais temps, ne?*"

That last particle was Japanese, I recognized with a start—a woman's interrogative at that. The shreds of my seldom-used languages tend to plop out of the attic willy-nilly once I open the trap-door. "Enh?" I corrected.

He shrugged. "It will be not so bad, I think." He elbowed the book aside, ostentatiously according me undivided attention. "You do not want to ski today?"

"Oh, no, no," I assured him. "*Si*, yes, I do. Don't you?"

"Of course. If Suzanne wish. Wishes. And you. Whatever." He smiled. "I am your guest. I amuse myself either way, at your pleasure."

"Ah, but we're *your* guests," I corrected him. "For which we thank you very much."

"Ah, no no. You buy my ticket for me even, yesterday. I must repay."

"Hey, you rented those poles for Susan. Call it even."

"Oh...." He pooh-poohed with his lips. "It is nothing. She has been so good to me all the week."

"She respects you. She thinks you're a top-notch scientist." She hadn't said as much, but I could infer it. And I thought the prosaic explanation might be mildly galling. "I'm sure she'll want to ski too when she gets up. It just looks a little chilly and inhospitable this morning, that's all."

"We should build up the fire, perhaps."

"No, I meant outside."

"I under... stood."

"Well, if it's almost nine we probably ought to be thinking about getting going pretty soon. And there's no sense coming back later. So we might as well make it as easy on ourselves as possible to clean up...."

"It is not so much to do."

"No, true. But...." I shrugged and shifted subjects. A reminder. "Your, uh, wife... does *she* ski?"

"Oh. Yes, in fact. Mm."

"Compared to Susan," I proposed, "how well? Better?"

"Oh... my... wife ski very well. Skis. She is... how should one say... more... classical, perhaps. She always want to have the good form."

"And what do you think about Susan's form?"

"Ah. It is... quite good! She has taught herself for a long time? She is *athlétique*, of course. Very amazing, not to have taken a... whole raft of lessons."

I smiled at his awkward slang. "And how about me?"

"You." He shrugged. "You ski as you ski, very good for you. Like many Americans, I think. What can I say?"

"You could probably say plenty," I smiled. "If you weren't trying to be a diplomat. I know, I've got room for improvement in technique. But I just do it for the fun...."

"What were you guys saying about my form?"

Wry with curiosity, Susan was descending from the loft. She looked deliciously rumpled and tumescent from sleep. She was knotting the cinch of her bathrobe.

"He said it's amazing," I replied.

"I'll bet," she laughed.

"Ask him."

"Amazing I haven't broken my neck by now or something."

I'd been about to tease her along exactly that line.

"Amazing for one who does not ski so often and has taken few lessons," Marc-Yves interjected. "And nevertheless quite, quite good. For anyone. There. Are you satisfied, young lady?"

He'd risen politely, and his smile had incandesced at her appearance in a way I doubted I'd matched since... well, since the moment Christopher had popped out.

"Don't I wish it were true," she sighed, "Either the 'quite, quite good' or, for that matter, the 'young lady.'"

"Not to mention," I mumbled, "the 'satisfied.'"

**We ate toast and jelly, dressed, measured chlorine crystals and soda ash into the hot-tub according to a two-page list of instructions, left water trickling from all the faucets so the pipes wouldn't freeze... and made the tram again by ten-thirty.**

Which wasn't bad. The abrupt shift in weather seemed to have discouraged a lot of yesterday's skiers as well. We found ourselves braking directly onto the chairlift's wooden loading slats at the bottom of most runs.

We retraced a few favorites as warmups and then worked our way across the mountain to a network of trails under a long, looming cornice. The snow was perfect. To top it all off, the overcast began to curdle. Soon there were capillaries of blue threading distinct, velutinous clouds. By noon we were in full sun again.

"Let's go get some lunch after this one," Susan said as I joined them off the top-ramp.

She'd ridden up with Marc-Yves. Alone on my double-chair—watching them suspended in front of me in happy, animated discourse while I vacantly dandled the weight of the elongated staves clinched to my boot-bottoms—I'd suddenly lost the zest I'd been feeling only moments earlier.

Maybe it was purely physiological—a need for fuel,

my gauge nearing empty. Whatever, I experienced a sour twinge of last night's... envy. Helplessness. Jealousy. The whole duke's mixture. And though the latter may be virtually inescapable, the natural validation of a relationship, it is certainly destructive to the impotent sufferer, I decided.

Lonely chair-rides are great for introspection. Who, I asked myself, was I really jealous of? Marc-Yves up there? Because he could bask in her arousal, exult in the virtue of his novelty? All *his* charm was unfreighted by the years of tawdry modifiers I'd gained.

Or was I jealous of Susan? Galvanized by the scintilla of possibility he'd rekindled. Alive to something I was not. Poor me.

The leisure for further rumination was interrupted by the warning placard: "Prepare To Unload."

Ah, if only I could, I chuckled. I wriggled forward to the edge of my seat, unlimbered my poles and hopped off the chair as it grazed the lip of the scaffolded receiving platform. I rode the deep track down the ramp-curve to where my problematic companions waited.

"Go ahead, lead the way," I told them. I adjusted my sunglasses and slipped my pole-straps over my gloved wrists.

To the left, off the top of the lift, there was a steep convex tongue of snow between shrubby outcrops of bare rock. It was in shadow most of the day, deceptively moguled and, as far as I was concerned, thoroughly unpleasant. We'd tried it on our second run off this chair—dropped over the brink at Marc-Yves' heels in blithe disregard for the black diamond "Most Difficult" symbol nailed to a pine at the trail-fork. We'd often skied black diamonds. But once out on the appallingly sheer face, I'd stiffened. I'd forced myself through two clumsy switchbacks—prolonging each traverse until I was almost into the bordering rocks. And then, as might have been anticipated, I'd mistimed a mogul.

In part it was the fault of the overcast, which washed

out contours. Mostly, though, it was my own timidity. I was reluctant to carry the speed such a pitch demanded and hesitant to unweight into the fall-line—to offer myself for that crucial instant to gravity. So I equivocated with my pole, shot across the mogul's crest, pivoted too late and buried my ski-tip in the mushy base of the hummock next below it.

Fortunately, I suppose, my binding didn't release. I tilted headlong, writhed instinctively, felt only a mild tug on the ligaments of my left ankle as the embedded tip shucked loose. I soared for an astonishingly protracted interval before absorbing the frigid blow I was hunched for.

I took it as prescribed, across the shoulders. I slithered a long way on my back—momentary shock followed by disgusted surrender to just punishment—before collecting my wits enough to somersault. My skis bit and brought me up sharply. Even with a modicum of aplomb. If aplomb can be salvaged from ineptitude. At least no beginner could have caught himself so cleanly, I consoled myself. It takes a lot of falling to get this skillful at it.

Anyway, that accounted for about two-thirds of my descent of the summit pitch. One way to go about it. I spat snow, dug a plug of it out of my ear, brushed it out of my hair and jiggled a pound or two out of my Norwegian sweater. Most of what had funneled down the collar, though, seemed to have melted immediately. I was sodden, humiliated, contemptuous of myself. But unhurt. Although my ankle may have been weakened, because I managed to fall a second time trying a little jump on the much less demanding lower section. It was not, needless to say, my favorite route.

Susan had had her troubles too. So from then on we'd traversed the ridge below the milky cornice and peeled away to descend one or another of several steep but well-groomed fingers—marked with blue "Intermediate" squares on our trail map—cut between sun-dappled clumps of Ponderosa pine. They were good runs for technique. I'd regained my self-esteem. But now, skating to catch up, I was suddenly apprehensive. Instead of cruising toward the familiar cornice traverse, Marc-Yves was taking us out on that nose again.

He pulled up by the lone tree with its diamond signboard.

"I get it," I grinned when I drew alongside. "You liked my cartwheels so much the last time we went down here you want to see a replay."

I was trying hard to be cheery. But I was distinctly unenthusiastic about the prospect. My tongue snapped drily when I spoke and my chest was tight. I was conscious of my heartbeat, sluicing adrenal courage—and dilute enough at that—through the constricted filigrees in toes and clammy fingertips. My turtleneck was pasted damply against my armpits and spine, and my empty stomach was shrink-wrapped so tightly around the vertebrae from the front-side I could almost count the spurs.

I shivered. A breeze was gusting up from the valley below.

Suddenly I was very, very anxious for lunch.

Marc-Yves leaned on his poles and peered over the precipice. "If you want, you can go here, Suzanne," he said. "Or we can circle around...."

She nodded.

"We found an easier way on the map," she explained, turning to me. "We could try it, so you won't have to go down the face again."

"Which do you want to do?" I asked.

"I don't know. In some ways I'd like to try to master this. Although...."

"What the hell," I said. "I'm game."

Marc-Yves had been studying the terrain thoughtfully. "On the other hand," he drawled, "maybe you would be interested, uh, to try a different challenge, Reechar."

I shrugged. I'd already steeled myself for an ordeal.

"Sure," I agreed. "Why not?"

"Why not?" he smiled.

## I imitated Marc-Yves' nimble step-turn and followed him out along the rim of the promontory about fifty yards.

At first I thought perhaps he was heading down the easy route after all. But he halted abruptly and I swiveled to a stop too. Susan was behind me.

"Here," he said. "This should be a good *preuve* for us." He bobbed his chin and flashed his teeth. "I will show you. This remind me of Bonneval. How we ski *aux Alpes*."

I sidestepped closer to the edge, where he stood. I was incredulous. I realized now what he was proposing. To my right was a scattering of jagged boulders, the top of a long granite buttress scoured bare except in its lee by the updrafts. To the left was another skeletal outcrop whose descending facets were crusted with lichens so strangely and vividly colored they looked like the defacing blotches left by spray-can vandals. Cascades of icicles glazed the column—little sun fell into this chasm. Between the sheer walls formed by the two pillars was a narrow, almost vertical snow-chute. It formed a kind of side-entrance to the midpoint of the face. Merely gaping down along it from my fragile perch was dizzying. The idea of leaping into it on skis was beyond serious consideration.

"You're kidding," I said to Marc-Yves. "That's straight down. There's hardly even room to turn."

"No no. You can do. It. Not zoom, but short, sharp." He pantomimed with the flat of his hand, like a carrier pilot describing a series of dogfight stalls. "Edge, edge. That control you. Controls. Just little...." He bounced on his flexed knees and waggled his hips. "You have tell me... told me, 'I can get down anything,'" he grinned. "I think?"

"Mm. 'S what I said, all right. Christ."

"I will go first. So you can see how I do. Suzanne?" He pointed back at the tree. "You go there, like before. I will watch from below. When I say."

"Are you really going to try this?" she frowned at him.

"*Mais oui! C'est egayant. Allons-y...!*"

Leaping suddenly off his planted poles, he canted almost horizontal before plummeting. A puff of white spray erupted around him as he struck the incline below us. He sank into a crouch, sprang, alternately checked his momentum and swooped free—rhythmically tapping his pole-baskets in front of him with the staccato precision of a deft blindman feeling curbs. His back and shoulders stayed square to the mountain while his knees buckled and his legs swayed below the hips like two strands of spaghetti pasted together.

And then having dwindled almost as quickly as if he had fallen, he shot out of the strait onto the open face. He hopped a mogul and skidded to an exuberant stop, pirouetting. He semaphored his arm at us.

"God, isn't he beautiful?" Susan said.

I flared my eyebrows. His skiing was. I mean... there are people who could've done it better, I was sure. His upper body was a little too rigid, I thought. His technique was mechanical. But the fact that I knew enough to criticize didn't mean I was anywhere near his class myself. All I had were the rudimentary skills enhanced to some degree by long familiarity and a bullish willingness to rely on them. Against most slopes.

"Well, what do you think?" she said.

I shook my head. What I thought was: This

proposition scares me spitless. And it was a terrible sensation. Because I'd never felt it before.

The summer of my sophomore year in college I got a job as an assistant to the tennis pro at a posh tourist lodge in Grand Teton National Park. I spent my off-hours riding horses and scaling the craggy scarp framed by the cathedral windows of the main lounge. My cautious father, I thought, would have shit a brick if he'd seen me—inching along exposed saddles between thirteen-thousand-foot pinnacles... spidering up basalt chimneys... rappeling off cliffs... clawing for handholds on crack-riven sheer walls a thousand feet above talus. Never mind that a personable bellman from the University of Tennessee was dashed to bloody meat on the rocks below the Teewinot glacier one sunny Saturday afternoon. Or that in assaulting Mount Moran, my ropemates and I slogged through a field of baby-shoes, rumpled clothing, Bible pages and women's cosmetics strewn among the boulders of the skillet-glacier's terminal morain. Several winters before, a DC-3 had slammed into this mountain in a blizzard. The remnants had been eerily preserved by cold and altitude    awesome reminders of the abrupt deletion we might suffer on the treacherous slabs and snowfields above.

It wasn't that death didn't scare us. It wasn't that we stupidly considered ourselves immune or immortal. Quite the contrary. Yet, having figured the percentages and assessed our capabilities, we'd elected to pit ourselves against that ultimate possibility. Later, I would brave Hunters Point at two a.m. when the bus routing left me no alternative—stride alone from Third Street to the Naval Shipyard through a deadly black ghetto... fling myself into blue nothing with only a swatch of wadded silk strapped to my back... push a motorcycle to a hundred and ten on the freeway... swim a mile to a tiny island through frigid waters so remote a cramp would inevitably mean drowning. Not to be exhaustive, or suggest I qualify for the Red Badge of Courage. But the point is, all my life I'd coolly subordinated misgivings to joys enhanced by rational risk.

And now suddenly it was different. I couldn't see beyond the fear. Worse, I considered the grounds for my trepidations insufficient. Sure I might fall. So what? I'd done that hundreds of times. Sure I might hurt myself—I might hurt myself tripping down the lodge steps in my ski boots with a lunch tray in my hands. Or, as happened to me once, pull a hamstring crossing my tips on the iced rut of a snowmobile track. I was even halfway convinced I *could* ski the damned notch if I wanted to. Simply tuck and schuss it, if nothing else. Blast out through that needle passage without a wiggle—a hundred and thirty miles per hour and four hundred yards of roostertail when I finally curled to a stop somewhere east of Reno. Talk about exhilarating. *Égayant*, as Marc-Yves had crowed.

Trouble was, I didn't for an instant *feel* the allure my mind was trying to foist on me.

"Think I should?" I temporized.

"Depends," Susan said. "Is your life insurance paid up?"

"Life insurance! Ha! You think I'm about to leave you in comfort for the rest of your life so you can pick up with some suave, debonair type like that Frog? Fat chance! When I go, I want *everybody* to be sad. And stay sad."

"Then you better not go yet."

"Sort of what I was thinking. Wait a minute. Are you trying to tell me...?"

"I'm only trying to tell you that I think this is really more than you can handle. That's all. And it's no big macho...."

"Yeah. Well, thanks," I muttered.

I scowled into the couloir. She was right. Or maybe she wasn't. Christ! In the past, the simple curiosity aroused by that question would have nudged me over. Or so I believed. But now I simply didn't care if I found out. I was light-headed with apprehension. This, then, was cowardice.

Over a ski-run?

Well, one thing it was, I realized with a poignancy that seared the moment into memory, was age.

## "Tell you what, though," Susan announced archly.

"*I'm* gonna try it!" She waved and shouted. "Marc-Yves...?"

"Are you kid...? Hey! Wait a minute!" I blurted.

But to my astonishment she eased herself over the edge and, with a breathtaking surge in velocity, hurtled down the corridor between the two shroud-gray parapets.

I saw at once that she was sitting too far back. The tense over-rotations of her shoulders as she tried to slow her descent broadcast alarm. Suddenly she shrieked and folded heavily on her hip. Her skis windmilled, snow detonated and she bounced, threshed, skirred down the chute as flaccid and formless as a load of towels tumbling in a drier.

"Oh God," I breathed.

She lay on her side where she'd come to rest, near the foot of the buttresses. Her arms were wrapped around her head. She hadn't, at least, caromed off any rocks that I'd seen.

"Sue! Sue!" I bellowed. "Are you all right?"

She'd popped out of both skis. They were equipped with brakes rather than safety straps—little spring-loaded spikes that stay cocked under the bootheel until boot departs binding. Then the brake-barbs snap downward like anchor-prongs to prevent the ski from sliding away. They're safer in a fall than the old-style straps—no flailing six-foot machete tethered to your ankles. But they can mean a weary hike back uphill to retrieve a ski that you've tumbled far beyond. In this case, Susan would almost have had to be a mountain goat to clamber to where she'd shed her skis, athwart the couloir.

"Susan!" I repeated, more urgent. "Are you all right?"

She was motionless. Unconscious? Marc-Yves too was calling her name. Now he leaped forward and began the arduous herringbone trudge upslope from where he'd been waiting.

She stirred, slipped, squirmed into a sitting position and kicked herself a perch on the snowy incline with her boot-heel.

"Of course I'm not all right, God damn it!" she snarled. Her voice, though low, rose clear. "Do I look all right to you?"

"What's the matter?" I cried. "Are you hurt? How bad is it?"

"How bad would you be satisfied with?"

"Jesus, Sue!" I exclaimed, though her sarcasm seemed a hopeful sign. "What's wrong?"

"Well, I seem to have twisted my knee."

"Can you use it, you think? Should we get the Ski Patrol? Here... I'll come down."

And so, into the Valley of Death I ventured. Finally. Propelled by gallantry. On me, as usual, had devolved the mission of mercy. Not that I made any valiant attempt at grace or *élan*. I just side-slipped cautiously most of the way. And even that was scary. There were one or two places where I lurched into the fall-line, but I snow-plowed in panic immediately. Even so, I almost chattered out of control. I only barely avoided tangling in Susan's first jettisoned ski. I grabbed for it and hugged it to my chest, tippy-tippied down to the next, then snatched up the sunglasses—earpiece bent—and tube of sun-lotion she'd parted with in plummeting. By the time I made it down to her she was flexing the injured knee with only a mild grimace.

"Well, you do got guts," I said. "That much I'll grant."

"If not sense. Damn it all!" She whacked the snow angrily with a pole. The movement started her sliding again. She scrabbled for a new footing. "I wanted to show him I could *do* it!"

"And you did. After a fashion," I winced.

"Mm-hm. Hardly the one I had in mind, though. I guess this just goes to prove that I should really stick to the same old nice safe runs we always take. Huh?" She glowered at me accusingly. "That'd be your advice, wouldn't it?"

I squinted away. Shreds of vapor scudded across the ridge above us, clouds in birth. From this perspective, the slope seemed even more impossibly vertical.

"Afraid I'm not giving out advice any more," I sighed. "I've reached a point in life where I need the whole supply for myself."

## 4

**Susan skied to the upper lodge under her own power.**

She was clearly in pain, but said she thought she'd be okay after a rest. Marc-Yves and I flew solicitous formation on her wings.

The lunch crush was over by the time we stabbed our skis into the snowbank off the deck. We separated and mismatched the pairs to thwart thieves. We found a table and then I went to the taco kiosk while Marc-Yves bought cups of beer.

There was a family at the adjoining table who were merrily taking pictures of one another with a fancy Polaroid camera. Marc-Yves, an admitted "freak" for gadgetry, was fascinated. He'd always wanted one, he said. Now he was reminded to indulge the desire before he left the states. Somehow his obvious interest insinuated itself into the family's effervescence. Before long he and Susan—I sat at the end of the table, beyond them—were being passed prints to examine and join in the chortling over.

"Here, let me take a picture of you two," the father offered. He trained his camera on Marc-Yves and Susan—the obvious couple.

"Oh, wait," Susan exclaimed. "Be sure to get *him* in." She indicated me with a pat on the forearm. "He's with us too."

Uncharacteristically, she decided not to ski again, even after a break of almost an hour.

"You guys go on," she urged. "Don't waste what's left of the afternoon. I'm perfectly content to just sit here and work on my spring tan."

"No no, not without you," Marc-Yves said. "Why don't we go home?"

"Yeah, if you're hurting, honey," I concurred. "We can get a jump on the traffic."

"Listen! I told you it's nothing serious. I really could ski if I wanted to. I just think it'd probably be better for me to give the knee a little rest. Okay?"

"You should see a doctor," Marc-Yves declared. "Have a *radio*... an X-ray. Eh? We must take you...."

"Darn it all, you most certainly must not. Hey! Will you two old maiden-aunt worry-warts quit fussing and fluttering over me? Give me a little peace? Go on, get out of here! Go use those lift tickets we paid for!"

"Pouf!" Marc-Yves snapped. He waved his hand in dismissal. "What does that matter?"

"It matters sixty bucks-worth! Or whatever. Listen, you may have an entirely different idea about money than Richard and I do, but there's no point in wasting something that's perfectly good. I happen to be frugal. And anyway, wouldn't you like to get in a few more runs on a day like this? You say you enjoy skiing so much."

"But I do! I simply appreciate the charming company of a beautiful woman so much more. I tell you what. I will stay here, and you can go, Reechar."

I shook my head.

"Oh, for Christ's sake, all right!" Susan grumbled, bracing herself to rise. "I'll ski."

"No no. No no," Marc-Yves hastily interjected. "I'm sorry." He leaped to his feet and bowed. "I will do as you wish, *madame*. Rest here, take it easy, we will ski. A couple of quick runs, and then come back. Okay?"

"Yes, for God's sake! It's what I've been saying! Only ski as long as you want. Why don't you see if you can't find some nice new cliff to go over somewhere and *both* break a leg! 'Cause Richard'll follow you. It's a question of his manhood, or something. He's as stupid as I am where his pride is concerned. Right, dear?"

She gave me a smile that managed to combine both reproach and conciliation.

"On the evidence of this weekend," I smiled back, "I could not but agree with you, my dear. Yes, indeed. Maybe even stupider."

I wrinkled my nose and puckered her a kiss.

## Why we stuck together I'm not sure, except that we were under commission from our liege-lady.

Marc-Yves and I rode the lifts side by side, exchanged civil inanities, politely solicited each other's opinions about which routes to take down and then skied them in silent, self-absorbed tandem.

Without Susan to pace him, Marc-Yves gobbled up each run in a single top-speed, non-stop plunge. It was good for me, because if I wanted to keep up I had to be less deliberate. And concentrating on speed forced me to be less precious about form. That, of course, worked the paradoxical athletic magic. Because I was skiing on muscle-instinct rather than brain, I was looser and suppler in form. Then too, once into an aggressive rhythm I was maintaining it from pitch to pitch and across the level transitions rather than constantly stopping to catch my breath and think, which interrupts the flow.

I found this kind of skiing very tiring, though. At the bottom of the third run I hung over my poles for a long time—exhilarated but gasping for breath, hoping the twitching in my calves and thighs would subside into a nice dull ache before I shuffled toward the lift line.

There wasn't much of one. The sparse crowd meant I was getting less time than usual for R&R between exertions. Marc-Yves dutifully attended my brief tarry for recuperation. Then we took our positions abreast to mount the chair. One of the oddest things about that weekend in retrospect is that I never, except during my drunken stumble of the previous night, focused significant anger on him. I was just so God damned civilized and understanding. And he was so oleaginously courteous and soft-spoken. Even while trying to seduce my wife right out from under my nose, trying to run me over crazy sheer drops where the best I could hope for was some mild comparative humiliation....

Right now, for that, he might be taking his pleasure watching me compete myself to utter exhaustion, I realized. Shades of that Australian... Navy commander, whatever-his-name was—Cashman. Victoria. Jesus. I hadn't thought of her for years. Victoria Cashman. Love of my young life. Virtually killed the guy on the tennis court playing to his vanity. Dead there on the clay. Heart attack. Artificial respiration. Breathing into his lifeless maw watched over by... Gillian. Something. The one who might really have changed my life if we'd spent another day or two in port. Or not. Or Gail, for that matter, if I'd let myself knock on her hotel-room door in San Diego that night. Ah, well. Life is such a two-edged sword. What goes around comes around, they say.

See? There was the perfect demonstration. Every time my id started to hurl itself snarling, hackles bristling, against Marc-Yves as the source of my troubles, the namby-pamby superego hastily began strewing drugged biscuits, all these dumb distractions and equivocations.

313

"*Couloir*," Marc-Yves said, interrupting my reverie. He nodded at the face as we ascended past it. "What do you call that in English?"

"Um. Corridor? Actually, we use the same term. In geology, if that's what you mean. Couloir." I nodded.

"Shall we try it again? No? Eh?"

I snorted in surprise. I squinted beyond him at the spindly arm of the Y emblazoned on the mountainside by the two narrow, converging strips of snowfield.

"It test... tests me," he shrugged. "I like hard things." He stared into my eyes with a closed-mouth smile that could have been affability... or contempt.

"Me too," I said. "Did at one time, anyway."

I'd decided to meet his challenge with frankness. Superior maturity is the last refuge of cowards, after all. He who fights and runs away, I could hear my father reciting in singsong, lives to fight another day. "Now I'm very particular, though, about which hard things I like."

"Only if you push, push, can you live," he grinned. "If you stop, you are beginning to die. I think."

"Ah. Pascal? Des Cartes? Or our own devilishly incisive Dr. Joyce Brothers?"

He bowed. "It is not, perhaps, *la sagesse des philosophes*."

"No, in fact I agree with you, to an extent," I acknowledged. "But there's pushing and there's pushing. And there's also 'beginning to die' and actually doin' it."

"Here we are," he interrupted. "I go right. *Hup*."

We clattered out of our moving seats and zipped down the grooved incline elbow to elbow. I usually stop just off the ramp and out of traffic to slip my pole straps over my wrists, draw a breath and compose myself. But Marc-Yves kept skiing. And by habit I pursued him—threaded my gloves through the leather loops at the ends of the pole-grips while on the fly, allowing his undulations to mesmerize me, beckon me to the face... and then out beyond it, to the lip of the couloir again.

"See you later, alligator," he called. *"Amuse-toi bien."* He flashed his ivories at me and cut into the chute. *"À toute a l'heure,* Reechar!"

I skated out as far as I could without committing myself irreversibly. I wanted to be in a position to fully appreciate the tragedy if he crashed and burned. Plastered bits of himself, clack-splatter-plop, all along the chimney walls. Hammered a gaping ding or two... or twenty... into that slick *cinématheque* façade of his.

But, of course, it didn't happen.

## So there I was.

I surveyed the notch. I'd gone down it once already, hadn't I? After a fashion, as I'd ragged Susan. Who, in attempting the feat, had shown the willfulness I loved—the backbone that had enabled her to forge a career in a man's field, the grit that had made her my closest friend as well as my wife, lover and sturdiest antagonist.

All of which was why I had such a hard time denying her a little temporary deviation on the sexual compass. Marc-Yves' plane ticket and waiting family presumably assured it would only *be* temporary. I could empathize with the quiverings of their needles: his—away from home, alone, miraculously presented with a succulent, responsive, intelligent colleague... hers—mother of two, slightly anxious matron suddenly courted like Cendrillon in lab-coat. Ah hell. What a curse it is to be modern and reasonable.

Or was it more accurately the case that I was simply unmanned? *Frightened* to make a scene, force a confrontation, insist on my prerogatives. Which were what?

315

Who was I kidding? Does a husband have *prerogatives* any longer?

No, maybe I was just too lily-livered to throw a punch, stomp off to the car or even voice unminced words. Any of which might rock and capsize my precarious emotional life-raft.

Just as I stood here now, I taunted myself, choking on my lead-pipe tongue and listening to my intestines writhe. In contemplation of a skiable run.

I'd lost my tolerance for risk.

So I *had* to go down it, didn't I? Either that or finally piss away my last microgram of self-respect.

I settled my glasses firmly over the bridge of my nose, tensed to leap, clamped my jaws, stared down the shroud-white strait and sucked in my breath, rehearsing the first, second, third moves....

And abruptly I blew it all out in a ragged curse that disintegrated into laughter.

What a hopeless ninny I was, I chortled. I put my head back and guffawed at the clouds. Of *course* I was afraid. But not in any demeaning, soul-riddling way. This just wasn't right. Did I ski to prove something? Or, as I'd always maintained, for the simple fun of it?

The idea that I would somehow be tempering my mettle by blundering down a dangerous pitch I quite obviously didn't have the technique for—or at least lacked confidence in—was absurd! Pure adolescent hogwash. Sure I could negotiate it. I'd done that when I'd side-stepped and snowplowed to Susan's side. If style didn't count, I could manage an even woolier descent. But style *does* count.

I back-tracked eagerly to the Black Diamond pine. Now this, the face itself, this *was* within the upper limit of my technical range. It was a run that had buffaloed me badly the first time around. I stood at the crest and scouted the snowfield below. Tricky moguls lay in wait to snap at my ankles, bow my skis, flip me out of control. I would have to keep my poise and flexibility. I tried to anticipate in my mind—and transmit to my sinews—the kinetic sensations I sought:

Knees solidly together, as if pinching a coin... body curled and loose... head and shoulders jutted unflinchingly out over the fall-line.... Think ahead, I instructed myself. Choose the pivotal crests, lean forward, plant pole, unweight. Then edge down the frontside. But always attack. Stay in that fall-line.

I licked my lips and hurled myself underway. I didn't stop until I reached the lodge-steps.

This is the climax of the story. Art and my epiphany demand, it seems to me, that the run turn out to have been the most nearly perfect I'd ever managed.

But life isn't art.

Still, I didn't do badly. Really not badly at all.

# 5

## Going home, Marc-Yves offered to drive.

My legs felt like waterlogged hawsers. My ankle was puffy by now too. I accepted.

Susan, naturally, rode in front. That was okay with me. I lay across the back seat, sipped beer from cans and listened to the freeway breeze flute through the rubber window gasket by my ear. I was trying to be mindless.

Noelle and the kids had just finished a hotdog dinner when we limped through the door. There was the usual hugging and shrill questioning. Susan invited Marc-Yves to stay for potluck. Noelle, who'd snatched off her glasses, chimed in with enthusiastic endorsement. I smiled vaguely and worked at staying upright while Christopher joyously tried to dislodge my arm from its socket.

Marc-Yves, who'd accepted after appropriate reluctance, sat by the piano and listened to Becca perform her repertoire of simplified Bach. Then he settled Christopher on his lap and read a Babar book in English. His accent gave the household chestnut a charming new dimension even I had to grudgingly enjoy. He complimented Noelle for the omelettes she'd helped make—she sat at the table with us nursing a glass of wine—and helped me trundle in the skis and our other gear while the kids were being pajamaed and bedded. He declined an after-dinner drink but stayed until ten-thirty. Actually, he got up to leave with effusive thanks for the weekend long before that. He and Susan took at least a half-hour getting from the doorway to his car. I resolutely remained inside.

They spent the next day—his last in Berkeley—conferring in her lab. That evening he took her to dinner at the Carnelian Room. The dollar was low then—it was one of those dauntingly elegant rooftop restaurants in San Francisco you had to be traveling on yen or a Northern European currency to afford. He gave her about a liter of her favorite perfume as a going-away present. Of course, he'd asked the brand. The whole thing was precisely the sort of thoughtful, intimately suggestive, flamboyantly over-generous gesture I'd have expected of him.

I found out about all this when I got back from L.A. on Tuesday. I'd had to fly down there, to our San Pedro terminal, for a cocktail reception Monday night. The line's newest containership was making her first Southern California call after delivery from the Mitsubishi Heavy Industries yard in Kobe. The maiden voyage party for the local shipping community is a bit of *de rigueur* maritime sociability I don't normally dread. There are good *hors d'oeuvres* and liquor (I always station myself by the oysters on the halfshell) paid for by a round of increasingly painless handshakes with strangers and fifteen minutes or so of ceremonial picture-taking whose supervision has been my ticket to most of the ports of the Pacific Basin.

This time, though, I'd marched off to the commitment with a lump in my gut that, by every right, should have set off the airport metal detector. I knew Susan and Marc-Yves would use my absence for a final *tête à tête*. All through the shipboard *soirée* I was schizophrenic—one minute frantically stalking the nearest pretty woman, introducing myself and exuding personality as I sized up my chances of promoting a retaliatory one-night stand (zilch unless she were ready to wrestle me into the cab)... the next withdrawing into monkish aloofness, on the wishful premise that my behavior would magically influence Susan's—that we were some kind of double entry on the cosmic ledger.

I could have caught the midnight plane back to Oakland if I hadn't made an appointment to talk to a writer from a regional business magazine next morning. I could just as easily have done it in my own office, but I'd lashed myself to the mast this way to counter the abjectly custodial instinct. Give 'em rope, my motto. I fell asleep in my airport hotel room with the sports channel droning (a sparring match between two Panamanian flyweights who couldn't have bruised a princess), an L.A. *Times* tented over my face and three of those minibottles of Scotch from the minibar standing empty on the bedstand. Still I couldn't stop thinking about Marc-Yves and Susan, and what they might be doing.

By dinner next night, he was out of my hair. Physically, anyway. Aloft somewhere over the Pole, *en route* to Paris and the sleek, olive-skinned blonde and two pert, pig-tailed daughters in *lycée* uniforms he'd proudly dealt us pictures of from his wallet deck.

"He said to be sure to tell you what a generous host you were," Susan said. "He wanted you to have this." She pointed to a glossy coffee-table book on the sideboard. It was a survey of French Impressionist painting. "He also said to tell you he thought you were certainly well above average as a skier."

"Boy, he knows how to turn a mean compliment, doesn't he?" I snickered. I riffled the color plates in the book. "This is pretty appropriate, too. He left a strong French impression on me, that's for sure."

After that I shut up. Sniping at Marc-Yves was so transparently self-serving, I realized, it would only tarnish me in Susan's sensitized regard. Besides, what was there, on the immaculate surface, to knock? If she was intent on preserving the fiction that he'd earned our mutual affection, had wormed his way into the familial bosom as our dear joint friend... well, I wasn't going to argue with her. Out loud.

## In the days that followed I was especially solicitous.

We usually ate late—*à deux*, over a fresh tablecloth, with candles and wine. Susan was a sucker for romantic touches. We talked about trying to get away for a brief vacation, just the two of us—something as simple, maybe, as a long weekend at a bed-and-breakfast in Carmel. I looked into her eyes a great deal. Our sex life even improved—in frequency, at least.

In fact, things seemed to be going so well I was caught off guard by her moody distance at Saturday breakfast two weeks later. I figured she was tired— she'd had a rough week at the lab. I took a shower and put on my sweat-shirt and old corduroys.

"Okay, the mortar's mixed," I announced loudly when I came in to refill my coffee cup. We'd decided to extend the brick patio. Susan was always full of *Sunset*-inspired home beautification projects, and I, despite a lot of grumbling and a severe distaste for being nagged to start or finish jobs, derived my own pleasures from maintaining my calluses. "You gonna help?" I shouted.

There was no answer.

I stuffed my gloves into my hip pocket, drained the pot and stalked her through the house. I found her upstairs in our bedroom staring out the window.

"Hi," I said quietly. "We're all ready for the big push out there."

"Mm."

I started to drink, hesitated. "Here," I said, extending the cup. "You want some of this? Coffee?"

"No, thanks."

"What's the matter?"

"Nothing."

I came up close behind her at the window but didn't touch her. She hadn't turned. Framed between the boughs of our two tall cypresses, distant Mount Tamalpais hovered over a hazy blue Bay. Fog was breaking into cumulus puffs behind the red arches of the Golden Gate Bridge.

"I thought we were going to work on the patio together today," I said.

"We were, I guess."

"So?"

She shrugged.

"This *was your* idea, you know."

"Mm-hm. I know. I just don't want to do it now. That's all. I was standing here realizing that."

"Oh. Okay, then." I sipped. "Just like that. So. What *do* you want to do?"

"I'm not sure. Go to the lab, I guess."

"Mm. All right. Whatever. Meanwhile, I've got a hundred pounds of wet mortar out there slowly turning into …"

"I just have such a tremendous bunch of work to catch up on, Richard!" she wailed. "There've been seminars all week. And people barging in and out because it's budget review time. You know...."

"Yeah, okay. I understand. I mean, I won't pretend I love it, but...."

"I'm sorry."

"No, it's okay."

She looked at me. The rims of her eyes were pink.

"Oh, jeez," I said. My stomach knotted. "Are you crying?"

"No," she replied. She shook her head. She sucked her lower lip under her teeth and combed her fingers through her hair. Technically, I suppose, she was being truthful. But I could see the crystal glint of moisture in the web of fine, untanned creases by her temple.

I sighed and put my arm around her shoulder. I cupped her gently. "Okay, what's the problem?"

She swayed against me rigid, a pillar of stone. She shook her head wordlessly.

"You can tell me...."

"Look. Just let me go about my business. All right? I promise I'd be no good company for any of you today. Just lay your bricks or... whatever. Do something fun. Do whatever you feel like. Go play tennis."

I smiled. "I've got Christopher down there with a trowel, smeared to the eyebrows already...."

"That stuff's not good for him to get on his skin!"

"Figure of speech, figure of speech," I hastily assured her. "He's got gloves on, and long sleeves and everything, don't worry. But the point is, he's out there goin' crazy, pestering me: 'Now, Daddy, now? Can we start?' So I think I'm pretty well committed. Anyway, I don't mind."

"Good."

"Boy, we're really up today, aren't we?"

"I told you." She shrugged. "I'm just not in the mood. For family stuff, or...." Her voice dwindled. "I apologize."

"No need to." I dropped my arm. "Don't worry, we'll stay out of your hair."

"Oh, Richard. You're trying to be considerate, I know that. And I appreciate it." She smiled at me sadly. "I'm sorry I'm such a poop."

Now that I'd released her she eased her weight into my ribcage.

I squinted at Angel Island. There were white specks of sail on the water.

"No problem," I murmured. "Listen, I better get back outside...."

"I miss him, Rick."

## The words caught me like a sneak punch to the solar plexus.

They took away my breath for an instant. And yet I was not surprised, somehow. I knew exactly what and who she meant.

"So there *is* a problem," she admitted.

"Mm."

"He called me last week. From...."

"Called you!"

"Yes. I didn't tell you. From Paris. Wednesday morning. I was in my office and the phone rang. Just like that. It was Marc-Yves."

"*Quelle surprise*," I drawled. I managed to sound sarcastic, but I was shaken. Telephoning from overseas! It was completely unforeseen and, in my view, an unforgivably perfidious tactic. It made me very, very angry. And very scared.

"Yes, it was."

I waited for her to go on.

"So," I said when she didn't. "What'd our *cher ami* have to say?"

She shook her head. "I shouldn't be telling you any of this."

"I take back the question," I agreed somberly. "It's your business, not mine."

"I wish I hadn't even brought it up."

"Frankly I'm glad you did. I'd rather know...."

"The only reason I did is because you're always

saying you're my friend. Always at me to tell you what's on my mind."

"Yes I am. I'm evil incarnate, I admit."

"So all right. So we had a very nice conversation. Very low key. He said he kept thinking of me."

"Real originality. A breakthrough in the annals of romantic...."

"Richard. Don't."

"Sorry." I clamped my hand over my mouth. But I didn't grin. I removed it and waited patiently.

"The thing is... you have to recognize it's very hard to spend such an intensive period of time with someone. Come to care very... much. For that person. Him for her and her for him. And then just... bloop." She made a chopping motion with her hand. "Suddenly forget it. Break off all contact. Know you'll never see each other again. At least not for... years and years, probably. A long, long time, whatever. And not have all that... affect you. Deeply. Disturbingly."

"Yeah. I imagine."

"So. I'm just finding it... a little tough today. That's all."

"Mm-hm. Okay. Well...." I'd withdrawn deep inside my bones. Susan's shoulder was only a dull, annoying pressure on the external leather—an itch that made me nervous. That I wanted to squirm out from under, yet at the same time perversely hesitated to interrupt.

It was Susan who brusquely wheeled away.

"So enough of this," she snapped. "I'm off. Goodbye."

"What?"

"Better get back to your brick-laying. If that's your chosen activity for the day. I'm going down to the lab to see if I can't accomplish *something* constructive, anyway."

I trailed her to her dresser. "This, I suppose, not being considered constructive."

"You think it is? God. Look at my eyes." She bent

close to the mirror and rooted among her cosmetics.

"Look, oddly enough...," I said. I sampled and rejected phrases. "...Well, what I'm trying to say is, I think I *can* appreciate what you're going through. And I actually do sympathize."

"That's very generous of you."

"Yes. You're God damn right it is! Especially since I also believe, my dear sweety, that this fucking out-of-sight-but-not-out-of-mind *amour* of yours is nothing but a conniving, four-flushing, underhanded grease-ball son-of-a-fucking-bitch! Who'd tell you anything he thought you wanted to hear if it'd help him get inside your pants. I wouldn't trust that smarmy line of bullshit of his any further than I could throw the little French cock-sucker... which would not be that inconsiderable a distance if I ever do manage to get my hands on him again. I hope you don't mind all these technical terms."

"Oh, wonderful! Marvelous," Susan said. "Yes, that's exactly the calm, mature attitude I expected of you, Rick."

"You want honesty? I'll give you honesty."

"Indeed. I think I'd rather have strawberry," she said. "And the thing is, you're just plain dead wrong about Marc-Yves."

"I doubt it."

"You are. I can assure you of that. But it doesn't matter. He's ten thousand miles away. Happily married—he loves his wife. I love you. Neither of us... neither one of us has the slightest intention of jeopardizing our present situations...."

"Oh, thank you. That's very reassuring. Speaking as a situation."

"He is just not, no matter what you think, a threat, Richard."

"Oh no. No threat whatsoever. But why is it, my dear, that you think I'm so threatened?"

"I wouldn't know. Your actions."

"I act it?"

"Oh, Rick, please. This is pointless, isn't it? Maybe I'm... just projecting. Does that satis...?"

"Maybe you are. Maybe you're confused, uncertain, guilty...."

"How penetrating. I certainly am all those, all right."

"If you say you love me so much."

"Did I use the term 'so much?'"

"No, you didn't."

"Rick...." She put down the mascara brush she'd been dabbing distractedly at her lashes. She turned to face me. "We've been together almost fifteen years. When I met you I thought you were the handsomest, wittiest, most intelligent, most interesting man...."

"But what did you know then?"

"Exactly. And everybody changes in subtle ways over the years, obviously. You and I are habituated to each other by now. We take each other for granted. At the lab, men come on to me all the time. I'm such an anomaly—female. Feminine, at least moderately attractive. And a senior scientist! Sure that scares off a few, the old school. But it's catnip to a lot of others. I could have my pick of about a dozen men right this minute if I wanted... or at least so they keep insinuating. If I were really available, they might change that tune a bit, I recognize that. But what I'm saying is... I've never yet met a man who has the qualities you do."

"Even now? Faded beauty that I am?" Her compliments excited and pleased me. "God, poor bastards."

"Yeah. It's a pretty sad commentary, isn't it?" she nodded.

"But then, into your life waltzes Marc-Yves."

"Mm-hm. Into... well, there you have it."

"I don't want it."

"Well, you got it. You asked for it."

"Maybe if I took skiing lessons...."

"Actually, he's a lot like you."

"What? How's that?"

"Okay, on the surface there are all kinds of differences. You're tall, he's not. He's much more my size, actually. You're dark-haired, he's blond. But those are only superficial things. The real parallels are that you're both strikingly good-looking, successful, elegant, charming...."

"You consider me charming?"

"When you put your mind to it. You still *can* be. I mean, one thing you do have to admit—no matter how much you resent Marc-Yves—is that I have good taste when it comes to men."

"I don't got to admit nothing," I grumbled.

"I chose you, didn't I?"

"Fluke, possibly. Performance over the long haul, that's the test."

"Yes, well. Maybe our haul has been dragging on just a little *too* long."

"I guess that's what you've got to decide, isn't it?"

"No... Richard, look. I've told you. I still love you."

"'Still.' Sounds so tenuous."

"Well, isn't love always tenuous? What do you expect?"

"I expect permanence. Total and absolute commitment forever. Till death do us part. I expect you to gaze on me with fawn-eyed rapture, the way Nancy Reagan does on Ron. Even on his *picture!*"

"Joke away."

"Hey, I'm not joking. Or if I am, it's just to keep from whimperin'."

"I... yes, I know that. Not that you have anything substantial to whimper about."

"Sure I do. I don't fill your every waking need and desire. I'm not the be-all and end-all of your existence. The way I once was—or at least thought I was. And you gave me to believe. And I still consider myself deserving to be."

"I don't doubt that."

"As does everybody, I'd suggest. Everybody who's in love. If they're honest."

"Okay. Don't you think we've pushed this about as far as we can?"

"I'm afraid so."

"You'll just have to accept for a while that I'm... making adjustments. Working things out in my mind. I'll get over it. I mean... God! Richard? To suddenly discover there's somebody else in the world you could... okay, be happy with? It seems. Who understands you? Another person you could... yes. Love, if things had been different? You think that isn't unsettling? To say the least? I wasn't looking for it. But suddenly I got it. There it was. It's something I've got to... well, get my head on straight about. It's something that's never happened to me before."

"Hasn't happened to me yet," I muttered righteously.

"I'm not sure at this moment which if us is better off."

"You bettah off," I said.

I smiled ruefully and sipped a mouthful of tepid, bitter coffee.


## Susan called at five-thirty to let me know she wouldn't be home for dinner.

She wanted to finish a run on the computer now that she had the program up. I said fine, I could handle it. Noelle was going out, so Rebecca and Christopher and I fried chicken. I told 'em it was an adaptation of my mother's secret recipe. I sprinkled a bunch of herbs and spices into the paper

329

bag with the flour and cornmeal, by way of demonstration.

"Colonel Daddy's," I called it. I'll bet my mother would have been aghast to find thyme, rosemary and marjoram in her batter. But the kids smacked their lips and loyally agreed ours surpassed Colonel Sanders'. Afterwards we watched KQED, and then I tried to translate a chapter out of the LIFE "Early Man" book into kindergarten English without affronting Becca's fourth-grade sensibility. Mostly I just played digressive riffs on the picture captions.

Once they were tucked in I cracked another beer and found the tail-end of a Warriors game to watch. My shoulders ached from the brick-laying. A lot of nervous energy is burned shepherding a pair of kids through an evening, too. When the game was over, I went upstairs and took a long hot shower. My next installation, I decided, should be our own *al fresco* redwood tub.

It was nine-thirty when I went into the bedroom with the towel around my waist. I caught a glimpse of myself in Susan's mirror. I was startled by the grayness of my muzzle and the raddled spare tire puffed out above the terrycloth. God, I looked old, I thought.

I flung off the towel and strode closer to study my image. The veins in my forearms seemed more prominent and gnarled than I remembered. The skin at my gills was puckered and inelastic. It was the first time I'd noticed that. I drew myself up and tried to will all the slack flesh back into the taut discipline of its prime.

There was some improvement. Maybe I was being too hard on myself, I mused. Every so often I used to be struck by a recognition that I was indeed a handsome man. I seldom felt I knew how to trade on it with women, though. Certainly not like a Marc-Yves. I should work out harder, I resolved. Jog, do push-ups and sit-ups to flatten the abdomen, play more tennis and basketball. Maybe swim laps daily, the way I did for a while in high school. Still, you can't help getting older. Can't stave off indefinitely that mortal downhill slump.

"It's nine-thirty-five," I said to myself in the mirror. "Do you know where your wife is?"

"Kind of," I replied.

Partially obscured behind the bottle of *Je Reviens* on her dresser was a color photograph. It was the instant print, I recognized, documenting our ski-weekend with Marc-Yves. I picked it up. There, in garish hues, our diminutive likenesses had been frozen like waxwork effigies: Marc-Yves and Susan side by side, their faces all glowing cheeks and perfect ivory, alight with health and voluptuous cheer... me in the middle distance, the lurking *éminence grise*, a doughy blur with a dead grin punched into it: "He's with us too."

I tucked the picture back where I'd found it. I resisted the impulse to crumple it. Well, I was here now, and Marc-Yves wasn't. That was my trump card.

I suddenly found myself sinking into a skiing posture. Thighs together, the big knuckle of my right foot snuggled into the instep of the left, my right knee firmly butted against the other's lee. I squared my shoulders, bent at the waist, cocked my fists at my hips and bounced lightly on flattened heels. Did a slightly deeper squat and pendulumed from side to side. Nice liquid waggle. "Shwii...shhh," I whispered. I appraised the effect in the mirror.

The thing to do is to go downhill with style, I reminded myself. Don't be afraid of the fall-line. Work the bumps, edge judiciously and always lean out over that fall-line. Use gravity. Otherwise it'll use you.

I flexed my knees. "Shwiii...shhh," I purred at the mirror. I wondered what Susan would think if she walked in and saw me now.

"Shwiii...shhh," I murmured. My incantation. "Shwiii...shhh...."

*The Fourth Quarter*

# Swim Practice

# 1

**Of course there would be traffic on Highway One on a summer weekend.**

I probably should have detoured inland and taken the freeway. But the serpentine coast road is the most direct point-to-point route from our house in Mendocino to Point Reyes. I'm a sucker for direct, even if the broken line on the map signifies a dirt track that'll take an extra hour to negotiate. Elisabeth and I usually opt for scenic too; Highway One is nothing if not that, even with a high morning fog blurring the forested ridgetops and casting a chilly pall on the barren bluffs and the gray ocean breaking against the offshore rocks below us.

It was a Saturday in July, balmy but hardly the tourist-brochure ideal of beach weather—although you can never tell in Northern California. Indeed, by ten o'clock the western horizon was striped with azure and gold; here and there shafts of sunlight slanted down to jewel patches of ocean surface. By noon the day might well be magnificent.

We'd made good time to Gualala. But then, as the morning matured, the dawdling sightseers materialized to clot the road. It's two lanes all the way, and opportunities to pass are few and far between. Every time a stretch of dotted centerline finally loomed in front of me I'd edge left eagerly... only to confront oncoming traffic. And none of the pokey drivers I was trailing deigned to use the turnouts. That's really infuriating.

I muttered and sighed, sank into my seatback, rolled my shoulders and stretched my neck muscles, working to contain my impatience.

"Aren't you following that guy kind of close?" Elisabeth murmured.

"Yeah," I acknowledged. I lifted my foot and let the interval slowly lengthen. "I'm in third gear! He brakes every time there's a fucking *wiggle* in the road!"

"Hey," she chided.

"Yeah," I apologized. "Sorry."

"Enjoy the ride," she counseled. "It's beautiful. We'll get there when we get there. We're not in any hurry."

"Oh, no?" I said. "Speak for yourself."

It was a meaningless retort. She was right—at our age there's no reason to rush... anywhere. All good moments should be protracted. But I *hate* wasting speed potential. The limit along here was fifty-five. For all the twists and dips, you could do sixty, sixty-five without breaking a sweat on this well engineered course—a little slower here, a little faster there: it would be exhilarating.

Fortunately I'd decided against adding another hour to what would be a long day of driving: I'd foregone my Saturday morning swim. The pool in Fort Bragg is a half-hour from home. According to the map I'd printed off the Internet, the trip to Point Reyes would take us four hours. Same coming back in the evening. Eight hours behind the wheel at a minimum. And so far, at least on this leg, I'd underestimated. We trailed along, sandwiched among the meek and the cowed, the gawking and the oblivious, past the upscale rusticity of Sea Ranch, the faded wooden towers of Fort Ross, across the sandbarred mouth of the Russian River at Jenner, past Shell Beach, Portuguese Beach, Schoolhouse Beach, Bodega Bay, inland through eucalyptus stands to Valley Ford and out again to Tomales Bay, past the catwalk piers and oysterbeds around Marshall to Point Reyes Station where we stopped for gas, then back up the opposite side of the narrow finger of saltwater that traces the San Andreas Fault, through Inverness and into the wind-scoured National Seashore. Historic G Ranch, Historic B Ranch, a few weathered buildings huddled behind lonely cypress windbreaks....

It was almost two by the time we nosed into the North Beach parking lot. We'd left at nine.

I'd come here every summer for four or five years when I'd been married to Susan. One of her colleagues, Jack (his face remains vivid but I still have to think to retrieve his last name), and his wife Deirdre hosted an annual picnic for friends and coworkers whose main feature was all the oysters you could eat. They'd buy burlap sackfuls of jumbo Pacific oysters—several hundred—from the commercial farm a few miles back on Drake's Estero. Then they'd build a charcoal fire under a grill at the base of the sandy cliff below the parking lot, set out lemons and hot sauce and let guests—who supplied the drinks and the side dishes—choose between raw or barbecued oysters... or, like Susan, none at all, thanks, oh, okay, maybe just one to be polite.

The more the better when it came to squeamish abstainers, as far as I was concerned. I'd down a dozen or so on the half-shell *au naturel* to savor the straight thalassic tang—I think of it as eating the sea, I once explained to the kids, like swallowing a barely solidified mouthful of the amniotic fluid of life. Not that I used those big words. I'd also put away a dozen or so seasoned with a squirt of lemon or a splash of horseradishy seafood cocktail sauce or both, and another dozen or so, similarly doctored, piping hot and plumped up after a few minutes over the coals.

To assure free access to this bounty I usually volunteered to serve a stint as shucker. On my knees in the sand, protective leather glove on my left hand, stubby broad-bladed knife in my right, I'd probe for a slot between the bivalves' gnarled, calcareous jaws, wriggle the point in, twist and pry at the resistant hinge until the tendons surrendered to yield the little lump of gray treasure cupped in its bed of iridescent nacre. Then I'd look around for a taker. Or if no one spoke up quickly enough I'd slide the blob of concentrated protein and its delicious, briny liquor into my own mouth. The Schuberts were usually among the last guests to leave; for helping with the cleanup I'd be rewarded with a take-home bag of leftover oysters. Next morning I'd whip up a hearty Hangtown fry—bacon, oysters dredged in seasoned flour, sliced shallots, scrambled eggs. Susan's aversion notwithstanding, the kids grew up to share my appetite for bivalves. Even Susan developed a taste for mussels and clams when I steamed them in a broth of garlic, lemon and white wine. But it was Becca who actually listed oysters among her favorite foods at the age of ten—which blew the mind of the playmate's father who'd asked her what she most liked to eat and reported her precocious response; his own daughter, he laughed, had managed with difficulty to propose spaghetti and pancakes.

Both Rebecca and Christopher, with their spouses and my grandchildren, were going to be at today's reprise of those oyster orgies *d'antan*. Elisabeth's two sons and their families—she had one granddaughter, Julietta—had been invited but they lived too far away: Scott, Julietta's father, in New York City and Jeremy, a set designer, still single though hetero, in Hollywood. Still, Elisabeth was an oyster fancier, a second mother to my two kids and an acquaintance of Deirdre and Jack from many years back.

There were a lot of reasons we cranked ourselves with happy expectancy out of the car.

# This was not an altogether joyful occasion, however.

It was a kind of wake, a celebration of Jack's life by and for his friends on the West Coast in a tradition he'd inaugurated and maintained more or less regularly on summer visits to the Bay Area even after he'd accepted a prestigious offer from Michigan and moved with Deirdre and their twin boys from Berkeley to Ann Arbor twenty-some years earlier. Jack had died there in February, of pancreatic cancer. Age sixty-six. I'd learned that from Susan when she'd called to invite me and Elisabeth to come to this memorial event. Susan and Deirdre had maintained their friendship and Susan was helping with the arrangements. Susan herself had been widowed two years earlier.

Life gets complex as you put mileage on it. After Susan and I split we kept in very close contact as we shepherded the kids through middle and high school. We had joint custody—it was one of those "amicable" divorces, with no major squabbles over money, no alimony (a straight fifty-fifty division of assets, meaning Susan volunteered to sell the house and move so I could have my fair share of the equity), no vicious recriminations, no snide insinuations about who was at fault to poison the kids' minds.

Although she was at fault, all right.

Oh, she maintains the contrary. I was the one, she says, who brought it on through my inability to... I don't know, meet her emotional needs, blah-blah. We'd grown apart. All those clichés... nebulous dissatisfactions I'd have been hard pressed to rectify. And that I didn't, in those feminine terms anyway, sense or share. She claimed I'd become violent. That she feared my temper. Now there, at least, was a complaint I could get my hands around. And throttle until it was dead, dead, dead.

Seriously, I *have* always had a propensity to go light-headed with rage and, consequences be damned, bellow obscenities or suddenly hurl whatever's in hand at the nearest inanimate surface. Then pick up the pieces. Or, on occasion, drive a fist into a locker, smash a racket or club, lash out with a foot the way I kicked in that little bedside chest when I was a kid. I've never forgotten that. It's like the surge of lightning that dispels the charge. A coping mechanism, albeit both destructive and self-destructive... but, in a way, that's the point. To punish yourself, for your sin (anger itself one of the Seven Deadly), to supplant the frustration of a stymied argument or an unassuageable sorrow with the mundane need to sweep broken glass into a dustpan, tidy and reorder the crime scene or run cold water over the bloody, throbbing knuckles. And apologize, abjectly apologize.

But those outbreaks were rare occurrences. Susan had tolerated them for years. From one of our earliest dates, when a drive-in hamburger kept dribbling catsup on my lap and I finally jumped out of the car and dashed it against a tree, she'd been aware of my irrational volatility. She'd come to terms with it. Even once or twice responded in kind—shrieking, semi-hysterical escalation... although that was uncharacteristic. Her own usual response to turmoil—learned, she said, from her divorced parents—was to clamp her lips, spin on her heels and stalk out of the room. Or out of the house. And it wasn't a good withdrawal, as I saw it. It was a punitive withholding: passive aggression. Those absolute refusals to engage, to play out a shouting match through dénouement to healing resolution—my fantasized course of a disagreement—drove me incandescent. Often they were the provocation for my projectile detonation. But I'd never assaulted her or anyone else. Well, until the night I slapped her.

I can't even recall the exact circumstances. I just acknowledge I did it. I was at the end of my string. Another night when she'd left after dinner and hadn't come home until two. With no explanation other than a hard-faced "I had things to do." The implication was that she'd gone to her lab—and it's true, she did periodically have to work late into the night on an experiment, or calculations, or a journal article, or a report. So I had to try to balance that. But how *naif* would I have to have been not to recognize that something was fishy? Particularly when she wouldn't give me the satisfaction of an answer: Are you cheating on me or not?

Yeah, cheating. I'm as conventional as the next guy. Insecure. Possessive. Jealous and envious. I guess those were in there as well. Proud, lustful... oh, I admit to the full complement of Seven. If she were getting it on I should be freed to play the same game too, no? Except that reciprocity wasn't what I really wanted. Not at all. I wanted her to love me, without reservations, or at least no more reservations than any two human beings always harbor about each other. The way I had always and still loved her.

The little interlude with Marc-Yves had, of course, put me on the *qui vive*. Hard to ignore a warning shot like that across the bow. But I thought we'd worked through it. More than a year had passed. I thought we were pretty happy. And she'd been honest with me back then. Brutal but straight-forward... well, except when it came to acknowledging how far things had actually gone. I'm betting she'd slept with him. Still, I'd come to expect something of the same kind of heads-up. Instead she'd turned secretive—*transparently* clandestine. I guess there was a certain honesty to that too. In fact, in retrospect I think she was very conflicted—she wanted the excitement of the affair, the heightened emotion, the hot illicit sex, the novel praise and admiration of an unfamiliar man, but she didn't want to lie to my face and she wasn't ready to break up our marriage. That's a unique scenario, isn't it? So anyway, words led to more words that night, and in an agony of uncertainty, desperate for candor,

I grabbed her by the shoulder and slapped her across the cheek.

Slap some sense into her.

It doesn't work that way, does it? I'd just proved that the trepidations she would later allege had been justified. Appalled, regretful, I allowed that I was sorry. I was *sorry.* I *was* sorry. I paced around sullenly—alternating remorse, accusation and self-justification—while she jammed a few clothes and toiletries into a duffel bag and drove off, never having said another word to me, to spend the rest of the night, no doubt, with Dan. He was the eminent physician-researcher at the University of California San Francisco she'd fallen for over drinks and meals at a conference in Boston a few months earlier. We'd had him over to our house for dinner shortly afterward, not surprisingly. ("I think you two will like each other," she'd chirped. Where had I heard that before? As previously demonstrated, Susan was given to cutting me in on her enthusiasms. Until, I guess, things got too enthusiastic.)

Anyway, she was back next evening for the kids' sake, and slept in the room I'd added on by the kitchen for Noelle when she was our *au pair.* One of us had to go, she declared. Within a couple of days she'd found me a month's house-sit a few blocks away and I'd moved out. Honor requires, etc.

But I didn't demand a divorce. I didn't give a shit what happened. I started smoking again. I hunched over the phone at night with a Marlboro in my claw and a couple of martinis under my belt calling up people like my brother and Susan's mother to whimper about how unjustly I was being treated, how shabby her daughter's behavior was ("I'm sorry, Rick. This makes me very uncomfortable. You did hit her, she said." "No! All I did...okay, see....").

Six months earlier I'd quit my job with the shipping company to freelance again. I'd lined up several assignments from business magazine editors whose good will I'd curried in the years of PR pitches and press releases. Once it's in your blood, working for yourself.... But more to the point, I'd been offered and accepted a book contract to research and write the text of an illustrated maritime history of San Francisco Bay. Every morning I'd crawl out of my lonely bed in the basement guest room of the alien house I'd been exiled to, make myself coffee in a strange cup and scuff to the desk I'd cleared in the bamboo-slatted solarium, to spend the next six or seven hours at the luggable word processing computer I'd just bought myself. Some days I'd bicycle to the Bancroft Library on campus to search out journals, obscure reference works or microfilmed 19th century newspapers. The publisher's deadline was nearing. It was to be a popular, not an academic, history, but still... I felt a journalistic obligation to accuracy (at least to the secondary sources; I wasn't going to try to puzzle out Colonial Spanish, German *fraktur* or Cyrillic in manuscript).

Susan later added the indictment that I'd become obsessed with the project, that I'd absented myself even further psychologically from her and the children in the months before she'd succumbed to Dan's unfreighted charm. Maybe. How can I say? I hadn't thought that was the case. I wonder if she wasn't also bothered more than she admitted, possibly even to herself, by my once again having given up a steady job. She'd assured me she was okay with it; God knows she was earning enough to support the family by herself, if maybe not quite in the style to which we'd become accustomed if I couldn't continue to pull my weight. Anyway, at least I had something to keep me from brooding too much on the *ménage* that was now bubbling along without me only a few blocks away.

And I had basketball.

**Nearly every afternoon around three-thirty or four—but as early as noon on Saturdays and ten on Sundays—my nerves would start sizzling with anticipation.**

I'd push away from whatever I was doing, bungee my gym bag to the luggage carrier behind the saddle of my bicycle and pedal eagerly downhill for a few sweaty, exhilarating hours of running, leaping, woofing and athletic self-validation.

The Sunday morning game was at Live Oak Park, where the nets were made of chains and some of the flimsy hoops sagged from too many aborted dunk attempts. But the competition was always ferocious and occasionally at a very high level. My home court six days a week, however, was on the roof of a university parking garage on the north side of campus, next to a trio of tennis courts where I'd first glimpsed the permanent floating pickup game I tentatively joined one partnerless afternoon. Soon it became the literal pole (topped by a full-size backboard perfect for bankshots from deep in the corner, and strong orange hoops with nets woven of real string that we regularly replaced ourselves) around which I ordered my shattered life.

Like a sitcom, the game featured a rotating cast of core characters with, especially on weekends, guest appearances by players who had real—meaning nine-to-five—day jobs. The regulars were a mixed bag of grad students, non-tenured junior faculty members and counselors on break from a nearby drug rehabilitation program. Then there were the occasional-workers and hard-to-classify "others" like me. There was a novelist in his mid-thirties whose first book had won some acclaim. (I was a bit jealous, I'll admit; we paced around each other with wary cordiality, like two unneutered dogs.) There was a photographer who showed up between exotic assignments for National Geographic. There was a sous chef at a new three-star restaurant on Solano Avenue; a late-night radio deejay; two parolees (one a disbarred lawyer, one a union carpenter with a record of ADWs).... You found these things out from dribs and drabs of reluctant conversation when joints were passed between games (except when the drug counselors brought their charges around for a scrum) or while waiting a turn to run. The rule was losers out, a new set of three or four or five to challenge the winners. If ten or more guys showed up we usually played full court, otherwise half. On really crowded Sunday afternoons we broke into A-level and B-level four-man half-court games. Racially we were about equally divided between white and black. There were a couple of quick little Asians—a Japanese-American gardener and a Chinese-American chemistry teacher at Berkeley High. We knew one another only by first name or nickname. Since I was among the taller players I got the sobriquet "Stretch."

Most of us were pretty good; a couple of the black guys were more than that. I'd kept my hand in to some extent over the years—intramurals in college, Navy and rec leagues, lunch-hour games at the Embarcadero YMCA near my San Francisco office. This was the fastest company I'd ever consistently run in—at least often it was—and I was invariably the oldest guy on the court. But in my own mind, anyway, I yielded nothing: my hands were still fast, I still had hops, my outside jump shot was streaky but the deadly sequences outnumbered the slumps. I could still strip, swat and out-rebound twenty-four-year-olds—moments of triumph that warmed me in recollection through the empty nights. Soon I'd given up the cigarettes. The dinners I made myself in the borrowed kitchen—muscle-weary after two or three hours of pounding and banging on the court, then the uphill pedal on my bike back "home" with the evening's groceries from the Co-op—were mostly hearty mixed salads, lots of garlic, boiled eggs and red potatoes, tuna or shrimp, garbanzos or green beans, Niçoise olives, tomato wedges, red onions, peppers, cucumber, leaf lettuce or baby spinach, fresh basil and oregano, splashed with virgin olive oil and lemon juice and sometimes sprinkled with blue cheese or feta, fresh-baked whole-grain bread from the Cheeseboard, pasta, fish, roast chicken, green chile pork and occasionally a steak. I still drank a martini as I chopped, and I washed the food down with a beer or two, or a couple of glasses of wine. But fifteen pounds almost immediately evaporated. I started living in my warmup suit and basketball shoes. Physically I was fulfilled—well, if we leave out sex. Mentally I was distracted when I wasn't engaged by my writing and reporting. Emotionally, in the long dark diurnal dregs, I was a mess.

Susan found me a place to take refuge when the housesit elapsed. It offered slightly more permanence: the home of one of her colleagues that I could rent while he and his family were on a six-month sabbatical. It had three bedrooms so the kids could stay with me on weekends comfortably. She asked if I wanted a divorce and I said yes. What else? She agreed to start the paperwork. Dan had been married when they'd first hooked up, although he was already living apart from his wife. Now his divorce had come through and he was, I learned from Becca and Chris, apparently a regular fixture in the evenings at "my" house.

One night, having stewed for an hour or so in solitude while the afternoon's exertions wore off and the preprandial alcohol soaked in, I stabbed the point of my chef's knife into the cutting board and stormed off to confront the motherfucker who was usurping my wife and my appointed place. If it's violence she expects, I thought, it's violence she'll get: Maybe it's what she really wants—manly proof of the depth of my love.

Sure enough, when I burst through the kitchen door

I found Dan at one end of the dining room table, Susan at the other and the children, goggle-eyed at my thunderclap appearance, between them. Mercifully I've since forgotten whatever profanity-laced idiocies I was spouting. As I loomed into the happy domestic tableau Susan yelped at the children to leave the room and interposed herself when I strode toward Dan, who paled and shrank back in his chair but didn't clamber to his feet. Fists balled, I ordered him to leave.

He was shorter and slighter than I—Susan always seemed to be attracted to smaller guys, which made me wonder why she'd married me. His size actually worked against my assaultive intent. I was brought up not to hit people who're smaller—unless they strike first. Otherwise it's an unfair match. It's bullying. (I couldn't hit him if he stayed sitting down, either, could I? A breach of the honor code. I wonder if he was counting on that?) And as much as my brain was clouded by rage and self-pity, cocked to go off in a paroxysm of violent mischief (I mean, taking a swing at Dan, bloodying his nose and loosening his teeth, sweeping all the crockery off the table onto the floor, grabbing a silver candlestick, say—a wedding present—from the sideboard and flinging it through the mocking reflections in the big central windowpane... all of which flashed through my mind within a neuron's breadth of activation... bing-bang, *sturm und drang*, a sufficient shitload of mess to be dealt with as a sequel for my trouble but still only peanuts, minor, childish crime, if that, compared to the timeworn vengeance of plunging a knifeblade into your unfaithful spouse or firing a slug into the swine who seduced her, both of which had a strong momentary appeal)... there was still a ghost of superego on guard. It took the form of a mind's eye, a consciousness of my actions apart from and a beat ahead of my actions. I observed myself playing this tawdry, demeaning scene... and I withheld the dramatic punctuation.

No, no, no, no, no, no, no. No good was going to come of it, I recognized.

Firmly, like a skillful parent, a grownup, Susan steered me backwards into the kitchen and talked me out the door while I continued to fulminate half-heartedly at Dan over her shoulder. She reminded me in parting that this kind of behavior would not play well in the children's psyches. I sighed and nodded and slunk back to my lair, my exile.

That was the nadir. In later years Dan and I achieved a civil relationship. But we never did really warm to each other, for some reason.

## I ached for a sex life beyond *Penthouse* and my right hand.

Even my masturbatory fantasies featured Susan's intimate parts. Pathetic uxoriousness, I scored myself, and now without even the *uxor*. I needed replacement parts. I needed a warm female body to fondle, a female mind and sensibility to spar with, the musk of female companionship I'd grown so accustomed to and dependent on, the yin to equal the yang Susan had the benefits of, God damn her.

One night as spring dusk gathered over the court the other three guys who were still hanging around taking desultory shots in the fading light indicated they were about to repair to LaVal's for pizza. They grunted some signal that I'd be welcome to join them. I was surprised to be included—I didn't know them or anybody else at the court beyond a name you barked when you were open and wanted a pass, and I was both older, as previously noted, and of a different (slightly more elevated, if you want my candid assessment) social station. But I had no friends, so why not?

Mike, the gardener—Inagi, I would learn—turned out to be a freelancer like me, just in an earthier trade. He seemed bright and witty—he'd apparently gone to Cal—but his speech pattern was, for some reason, High Ebonic. The others were an odd pair, a burly, shaven-headed white guy closer to my own age who was one of the clumsier players on the court, and the pal who always showed up with him, a taller and considerably younger blackish kid, pate also shaved (this was before the style was ubiquitous), only a little better at the game mostly because he had the flexibility of youth and that basketball/negritude thing working for him. Turned out the older guy, Jerry, was a plumber and his sidekick, CC, was his apprentice.

We talked sports as we drank mugs of beer on the patio and split two "everything" pizzas. Then as we were divvying up the bill they mentioned there was some kind of party—at this remove I don't remember the details, only that I ended up going home, shucking my sweaty basketball clothes, showering, putting on clean jeans and a fresh Oxford-cloth shirt, getting into my car, driving to the address in deep West Berkeley they'd given me and ringing the bell at a door behind which music thumped. That was where I met Maartje.

Time has erased the memory of exact dialogue: I find it as hard to imagine chatting up a strange woman now as to piece together why and how I pulled it off then. I guess I figured I had nothing to lose. The "party" consisted of a handful of guys in the kitchen, including Jerry and Mike, smoking dope and playing poker while others including CC vaguely kibbitzed. A tape-player pumped rock in the living room, where two couples lounged with beer bottles in hand—the only two females in sight. A dingy refrigerator— CC waved me to it—held a pair of depleted six-packs. I realized with chagrin that I should have brought some kind of alcoholic beverage of my own to contribute but I helped myself to a bottle. I watched the poker for a couple of hands—I'm not a gambler so I had zero interest in joining. I declined the proffered tokes. I was, of course, by far the oldest person in the place and distinctly out of place. As soon as I'd sucked down the beer, I decided, I'd leave. I drifted to the living room. There, previously invisible around a corner, sat Maartje alone on a worn, possibly grimy couch.

She was very slender, very blonde—her hair was cropped mannishly short—very pretty in a severe, unmade-up (except for the eyes) Northern European way. She was also very tall, I discovered later when she stood; we were almost eye-to-eye. She looked as bored and as lost as I felt. She blinked up at me from the couch without much expression when I shuffled into range. She was in her mid-twenties I'd have guessed—actually twenty-nine it turned out. She looked way too young for me but at least old enough to have crossed the robbing-the-cradle threshold. I once made a pretty spectacular back-handed catch of a screaming line-drive foul down the third-base line at a Giants game in Candlestick Park—the crowd around us gave me an ovation and I was told they'd replayed it on television. The point is, I'd simply thrown up my left hand at the last instant to protect Susan next to me, and I'd fully expected a ball that hard, traveling that fast, to carom painfully out of my grasp; to my astonishment it stuck. (I didn't brandish the prize, I just bobbed my head in acknowledgement of the cheers, vouchsafed a modest smile and wordlessly handed the souvenir to Susan, as if I were a seasoned professional for whom that play was routine; it was how I chose to react whenever I sank a thirty-footer or a flying, spinning, last-second switch-hands-in-midair lay-up through heavy traffic on the basketball court—"act like you've been there before," as the old football adage has it about touchdown celebrations in the end zone, although these days most guys jig madly, point a finger at God or pound their hearts.) Anyway, that's what happened with Maartje. Cut to the chase: she actually came home with me that night.

The fact that I'm a sucker for foreign women and obscure languages gave me a conversational handle; curiosity sustained me after the halting opening. I asked her how her name was spelled; she'd pronounced it something like "March-ya." She was a painter, she allowed—you could scrabble out a living as an artist in the Netherlands, she later explained, because the government subsidizes your work by buying what you can't sell—and she was on an extended travel break that had taken her to Greece, Israel, India, China, Japan and now the United States. She had a capacious backpack, a sleeping bag, a shoulder-tote crammed with conté crayons and sketch pads, a notebook listing addresses of friends or phone numbers of friends of friends in strategic cities, and an adventurous nature. This was the farewell tour for her youth, what with thirty and its trappings of maturity and propriety louring. To her dismay, the girl she'd counted on staying with in Berkeley had had to go away that week. In a roundabout way she'd ended up here where she'd been told she could crash on the couch for the night, although she'd wasn't too comfortable with the guy whose place it was. She had a ticket to Chicago out of SFO five days hence; did I have any suggestions where she might find cheap or preferably free accommodations in the meantime?

Well, I said....

So somehow I convinced her that I wouldn't jump her bones, that she could sleep in the master bedroom I'd promised the owners of the housesit I would not intrude into while they were gone, that we could share the kitchen, that I'd be working quietly in the solarium in the mornings (she perked right up when I told her I was a writer), that I'd be out most afternoons so she'd have the place to herself and that I'd be tucked chastely into my own bed two floors below by night. Which is pretty much how it worked that first one.

And a damned uncomfortable night it was. The owners had told me to help myself to anything that was in the liquor cabinet. I found a half-full bottle of blended Scotch and poured us each a couple of fingers over a couple of rocks, to smooth the nervousness about the arrangement we were about to share. I was charmed by her accent. She had a cheerful manner and a way of giving back your—my— gaze full in the eye. She laughed easily and appropriately, a mellifluous sound. We seemed to be in temperamental synch as we told each other little revealing bits about ourselves. She widened her eyes when I said I was in my mid-forties; she assured me she'd guessed I was a decade younger. If true, and if an asset, credit the lifetime of calorie-burning, endorphin-spritzing, stress-relieving, childish athletic *divertissement,* I suppose. She didn't have a boyfriend, she said; the guy she'd lived with for several years, a sculptor, had moved out some months earlier to join a male lover, which was pretty demoralizing for her and another impetus for her mini-*wanderjahr.* My story... well, if anything she acted as if that baggage, carried gracefully—at least in the telling—added depth to my character. It was age-appropriate, anyway. I wasn't some weird middle-aged lifelong bachelor.

Then it was bedtime.

## I manfully refrained from trying anything.

I didn't want to make a false move because I was dizzy with hopeful attraction. As advertised I repaired to my basement cell to squirm and thrash until morning, bristling with awareness that a nubile young woman lay barely clad if at all—I got an erection every time the image flickered—only a few meters away (to be European about it) under the same

354

roof.

I must have been *crazy,* I berated myself, not to have pushed harder. How was it that Susan could pitch so readily into sexual dalliance and I couldn't—even in the most obvious of circumstances? I thought of marching upstairs and into Maartje's room... which maybe was what she really expected and was counting on me to do, no? Seize the initiative, be male... probably that was how Susan's thin defenses had been breached. I mean, this was ridiculous! Adults *sleep* with each other! Any other man and woman like us in this world, having so clearly struck it off... and from the way she'd smiled and her color had risen and by her general body language, every tilt of that swanlike neck, each dip of those lightly tanned shoulders toward me the absolute opposite of distancing, I was all but certain I'd kindled a spark in return... any other pair of serendipitously proximate human beings of our prime reproductive age (never mind the reproduction) would be locked together right now fucking their brains out. She was *Nordic,* for God's sake! *No* inhibitions about sex, right? She was an artist on top of it all, unconventional, a free spirit, *épater les bourgeois*—and I was one now too, sort of.

But I'd been brought up to be such a *gentleman!* Phaugh!

I got out of bed before she did, made coffee and repaired to my computer. I was finishing up a chapter on the world's last great windjammer fleet, the four-masted *Star* ships of the Alaska Packers Association that had sailed out of Alameda every summer until 1930; I'd interviewed a couple of surviving octogenarian crewmen. When I heard her bare feet slap on the kitchen floor—she was in shorts, hair tousled and damp from the shower, huge Delft-blue eyes carefully lined—I went in to show her where the breakfast stuff was. I forced myself back to my desk although I was too distracted by her vicinity to concentrate effectively. She sat curled up in the living room quietly drawing the view of the bay framed by the window. Around noon, since she hadn't left—another good sign—I asked if she'd like to go out with me for lunch. I splurged and took her to the new upstairs cafe at Chez Panisse. Afterwards we strolled to Peet's so I could buy a pound of French-roast beans, then climbed the hill to the Rose Garden, wound down Hearst—close by the basketball court where I *wouldn't* be lining up for the first-game qualifying free-throw that afternoon, thank you very much—and crossed the campus to the University Art Museum. We completed the slow circle at the Co-op, where I'd left the car parked. I'd gotten the idea of cooking her a *rijsttafel* dinner. (I didn't mention that it used to be one of our specialties, Susan's and mine.) I asked her the Dutch words for the ingredients as we loaded them into the cart. "Mmm, *lekker!*" she exclaimed as they accumulated. It was an all-purpose Dutch superlative, she told me—literally "delicious," but with all sorts of applications. My attempts at reproducing her gutturals occasioned much laughter.

It was among the most memorable meals of my life. We worked flank-to-flank in the kitchen, sipping sauvignon blanc, brushing elbows often, while we chopped and assembled the "boys" to go with the chicken breasts I sautéed. We boiled eggs and rice and used the host's blender to grind up an assortment of chiles, garlic and milk from a fresh coconut I cracked open on the doorstep with a claw hammer to make a fiery sambal oelek. We set the kitchen table with a candle and ate by its light—the heaped rice, diced chicken and overspiced sauce topped by raisins and peanuts and shredded coconut meat and bits of fresh lime and cilantro and Major Grey's chutney from a jar, washed down by icy bottles of Anchor Steam. For so slim a drink of water she certainly put away her tucker like a horse. We blotted the tears from our cheeks and talked for a long time about all sorts of things. To quench the lingering interior blaze we broke out a wedge of Edam and two Granny Smith apples to quarter. We drained the bottle of Scotch. By the time we'd risen from the table and finished washing up it was almost midnight. I was practically faint with desire. And suddenly I was once again struck by the key motivating calculus of my life: Why the hell not? What have I got to lose?

As she unbent from slotting a ladle into the dishwasher I grasped her shoulders, drew her to me and pressed my parted lips firmly against hers. I was braced for a knee in the groin.

She sagged into my embrace and returned the kiss. Her arms laced around my back, her lips yielded softly, our tongues tentatively caressed... and then abruptly she jerked away.

"No," she said. "I am here too short, Rick. I go back to Amsterdam too quick. You have a wife, two little ones...."

"I'm getting a divorce!" I protested.

She shook her head. "I know. But it's very... complicated? I don't want to go to that place. It would be trouble, maybe, for both of us."

"Maybe," I said. "But trouble's okay. We can deal with trouble if it comes. Hell, I've got all kinds of trouble right this minute! You're about the only thing that hasn't spelled trouble for me in months."

"I'm sorry," she said. "Really, you are very nice."

"Ah. Okay. Never mind," I scowled. "I get it."

"I go to bed now. The dinner was super. *Lekker*. Thank you so much."

"Yeah, yeah. Great. Good night," I snapped. I wheeled and strode to the stairs.

All the quandaries that had haunted me the night before returned in force but now in addition I was angry. Why had she led me on? Or had she? Had I been misreading common sociability for romantic responsiveness? Apparently.

I'd been rebuffed, hadn't I? In no uncertain terms. In the most demeaning terms, in fact. I was "nice"—what a devastating judgment. Clearly unappealing as a lover. Why had she kissed me back that way, though? Out of pity, no doubt. Let this sad old lecher down easy. Well, screw her. Which is one thing I could be sure I wouldn't be doing, I snarled at myself, so get over it.

I flopped onto my back and smashed the pillow over my eyes.

### I awoke with a start.

Something had brushed my arm. The room was dark but I realized from the focal warmth and the scent that Maartje stood beside the bed. I felt the blanket being lifted; she sidled in beside me—skin catching skin. I edged against the wall to make room.

"I am cold tonight," she said. "I'm sorry if I have made you angry. I wasn't... ready, really. For... this. You know?"

"It's okay," I allowed eagerly. My heart hammered with groggy surprise and sudden, surging surmise.

She cuddled tightly against me. She slept naked too, apparently. She shivered and I simply held her. Then I kissed the top of her head. Her mouth found mine. For what seemed a long time we clutched each other and sighed into each other's lungs, her small breasts flat against my chest, thighs against thighs, my erection flat between our clammy abdomens. When it seemed appropriate I rolled apart enough to insinuate my hand between her legs. Gently I brushed the soft mat of pubic hair and the moist portal to prepare....

"You... have a rubber," she murmured.

"A... rubber," I repeated inanely. My God, after sixteen

years of marriage the notion of protected intercourse hadn't even flitted across my obsidian brain. Birth control had always been Susan's concern—at least since the earliest days of our dating, the first time she'd agreed that withdrawal was risky and less than fully satisfying. Before the next weekend visit she'd had herself fitted for a diaphragm. Then came that marvelous invention the IUD, and when it proved problematic the pill—interspersed with planned pregnancies. How clueless was I not to realize Maartje wouldn't just open herself blithely to getting knocked up or catching who knows what venereal disease I might be harboring?

"No, I, uh, don't," I stammered. Rubber. The very word sounded prophylactic. "You're not taking the pill or anything?"

"No. I have stopped. I have no need any more, I think, for now. Without a boyfriend."

Yeah, maybe, I thought. Though that still wouldn't have eased any concern she might harbor about contagion by a stranger. Which I hadn't considered for myself. AIDS had only begun to infiltrate public consciousness, thanks in large measure to Randy Shilts' articles in the *Chronicle*. But it was thought to be a disease that struck gays and heroin addicts. Still, there were the old favorites, syphilis, gonorrhea, genital herpes.... What a blockhead! Of *course* as a single man, if I hoped to bed women, I should have some rubbers on hand.

So that killed that. We lay enmeshed for the rest of the night making do with the primal comfort of flesh glued to flesh. She seemed perfectly satisfied. I offered to use my hand or mouth but she demurred, and she didn't offer her own relief for the unabating hard-on I endured. I now know what priapism feels like. We talked some and dozed and kissed and dozed, innocent as kittens except for that concupiscent intrusion. Finally we fell into a deeper sleep and didn't stir until mid-morning. When she rose to go to the bathroom I asked her to stop at the door and turn around. She hesitated, then shyly consented. My innards did a flipflop.

"You... are... *lekker*," I whispered.

"No, I have no breasts," she blushed. "I think I have too much hair here." She gestured at the red-blond patch between her groins. It was lush, all right. Wilder than Susan's neat dark triangle. (Thongs and waxing had not yet been popularized.)

"You're absolutely beautiful," I assured her. "Your breasts are perfect." I've never understood the appeal of giant, bobbing melons. "They're cute. Pert! Your nipples are *very* cute and pert," I smiled, "you know that? Hasn't anybody told you that?"

She waved her hand dismissively and covered them. "I am too tall. Too much bone," she insisted and dashed into the hall.

Talk about bone. I creaked around in a half-stoop until noon. I learned that the fabled high school affliction "blue balls" is a real condition. All my equipment throbbed from the night's prolonged, unrelieved congestion. (It was actually my introduction to my prostate, apparently.)

The morning was pretty well shot for work, but I was in no mental condition for anything except Maartje-worship anyway. I had that dazed, giddy, grinny sensation—"walking on air," the popular song lyric so aptly describes it—that comes with the first detonation of love. Well, at least its precursor, infatuation reciprocated. It was a heightened aliveness I hadn't experienced since those first weekends with Susan eighteen years earlier, the astonishing intensity long since forgotten. Everything about Maartje, the curve of her hip when she sat with her feet tucked under her, the way she gracefully ran her long fingers through her tight cap of golden curls, the way she licked a crumb of buttered toast off her lip and wrinkled her nose when she sipped her steaming coffee-with-milk, absorbed me, made me woozy with admiration and desire. I tried to mask it, to go about the ordinary business of showering and dressing and making small talk and silently forcing my eyes to trace the lines of type in a *New Yorker* article while she sat at the other end of the couch absorbed in sketching me—how reciprocal a sign of affection was that?—until hunger knelled.

We walked down the hill clutching hands. We ate lunch at my favorite, idiosyncratically mediocre Mexican restaurant on Telegraph. Then we wandered among the street stalls and the bookshops—Cody's, Moe's—before I led her afield to a drugstore, which was a long, pretty uninteresting walk through commercial Berkeley. That, of course, was my overarching destination before the afternoon was out.

Condoms were still mostly kept behind the pharmacist's counter in those days—or dispensed from coin-machines hung between the stained washbasins and reeking urinals in gas station men's rooms. I had to ask for them specifically while Maartje stood apart surveying the cosmetics. Needless to say the clerk out front was a woman. Notwithstanding the worldly aplomb I'd gained with age, I had to suppress a tinge of adolescent embarrassment at voicing so unambiguously and vividly penile a request. I chose plain from among the several varieties she matter-of-factly spread in front of me. There were others too, she noted. I said these would do. Maartje loomed at my hip and set a tiny bottle of eye-liner on the counter in front of the packet of condoms.

"And this one," she said. "I pay." She delved into her shoulder bag.

"Don't be silly," I objected. Her apparent willingness to take ownership of the rubbers too startled and discomfited me. It didn't seem right that she should buy them for me. At the same time I was elated.

"It's nothing. I've got it all," I insisted. I smiled into the clerk's eyes as I handed her a twenty-dollar bill. *Look, I* tried to telegraph proudly; *look* at this incredibly beautiful young woman I'm about to use these things on!

It turned out somewhat differently.

## We were both tired from the afternoon's hike and the previous night's sleeplessness.

We plopped into the puffy cushions on the couch and after a moment she swung around to lie supine with her head on my lap. I stroked her arm. Soon she was breathing regularly. The rubbers were burning a hole in my pocket and I had to squirm to make sure she wasn't disturbed by the hard protuberance in her pillow. I resisted the pull of the breasts at hand and surrendered my expectations. I dozed off too. When I woke I was squarely in the beam of the low sun lasering through the windowpane. The room was sweltering and I was damp with sweat. Maartje was gone. When I rose to look for her I heard the shower running upstairs. I thought of joining her, sliding in beside her—surprise!—but decided against it. Too banal, too intrusive, potentially a fatal turnoff. I went down to my own shower. Afterwards I introduced her to the martini—she wrinkled her nose dubiously in that way I loved and coughed when she swallowed. Brows touching we looked through the movie listings, skipped off downhill once again hand-in-hand, ate hamburgers and fries at Kip's and saw something or other we enjoyed. Back home we made coffee. We agreed it kept neither of us awake, another confluence. At last we headed to bed—upstairs, to the big queen.

It was then, after the usual preliminaries, that I called time-out to don my crucial new armor. But as I fumbled in haste to unroll the clammy little powdered disk over my throbbing manhood, as the euphemism has it, I found myself unaccountably losing interest. Well, not interest, to be sure, but the dynamic physical tension it's supposed to generate, the rigor that's necessary to... well, you get it. Slowly, inexorably my penis went limp inside the latex sheath. And much as I temporized, rationalized, willed and confidently assured her and myself that the inexplicably lost vigor would restore itself after a brief hiatus—this had never happened to me before! What the fuck was going on in my head?—I was done for the night. Once again we made do with fervid cuddling and smooching. And indeed, periodically the pressure in my loins would build to the required peak. But the instant I reached for the latex the erection would begin to wither. And a slack condom, as last-ditch experiment proved, is worse than useless.

I was distraught. But, of course, I bravely tried to mask my anguish. Hell, I knew from literature if nothing else that this kind of thing can happen. If to other men then certainly I was vulnerable. Romantically I could only soldier on. A soldier gravely wounded....

That was the sad state of affairs for the next two nights.

I must say Maartje handled it with calm and the requisite sympathy. She assured me it absolutely didn't matter to her. Physical closeness was what she waxed on; sex had never been that important. She didn't think she'd ever had a proper orgasm. So she pretty surely hadn't. There went my stereotype of libidinous European women. (Didn't say much for the guy she'd fallen in with... but if you lie down with men who love men... except who was I to talk? And had she never masturbated?) When I gnashed my teeth, rolled my eyes, hurled myself on my back and grimaced in frustration she suggested it must be her fault, she must be doing something wrong. It was *not* her fault, I groaned emphatically. I resumed my caresses of her supple flesh.

We spent the remaining days much as we had the

first. I wrote, she drew, at midday we excursed. We went to San Francisco to ride the cable cars, visit the museums and eat. We took the Forty-Nine Mile drive, from China Beach to Sausalito and points between. One night we went to the Oakland Symphony, both of us underdressed in jeans (although I wore a blazer and she wore high boots with heels) because no fancy clothes took up precious space in her backpack. At intermission we noted that we towered a head above everyone else in the Paramount's crowded lobby. I loved the way being with her forced me to walk tall, shoulders squared and spine unkinked to the max. I loved the attention, the sidelong glances—admiring, certainly, for her—our height and our glow drew. Once someone actually posed that hoary question, "How's the weather up there?" Another time when we walked out of a record store the middle-aged black proprietor, who'd been watching us browse and coo, asked hesitantly, "Are you... movie stars?"

We both nodded. "Oh yes!" Maartje exclaimed.

"You guessed it," I told him with a toothy grin. I put my finger to my lips. "Don't tell the press we're in town." Outside we broke into laughter at the exorbitant flattery and our mutual response.

I was absolutely smitten with Maartje. I'd started mulling scenarios for our future. I wanted to, needed to, introduce her to the kids, and vice versa. Introduce her to Susan, and vice versa. Heh. I could follow her to Amsterdam, I fantasized. We could live on a houseboat in a canal! I could do magazine pieces from Holland as readily as from California. Or almost, no? Maybe I could get a job again with, say, one of the many Dutch shipping companies. Or the Port of Rotterdam, Europe's largest. She wouldn't really have to be a mother to Rebecca and Christopher, just a kind of older, wiser sister. Who was Daddy's... girl friend. Wife, perhaps, eventually. We'd have them with us for three months every summer, take trips down the Rhine and the

Seine, make them fluent in Dutch and French.... Maybe we'd produce our own giant half-siblings for them, with Olympic volleyball or high-jumping or NBA careers in store.

I was awash in *folie d'amour*.

On the night before she left I suffered the familiar humiliation. Out of obligation and forlorn gratitude I insisted that she allow me to try to show her what she'd been missing, using my lips, tongue and fingers. She'd been resistant, but this time she acceded. Very tenderly, very carefully, I applied myself until she let out a rising series of sighs and finally a long, convulsive *"ah... ah... aaaaaahhh!"* At that I was hard as a ramrod. I grabbed for the rubbers, slapped one on, knelt over her and eased inside. I had plenty of staying power too. She came again.

She let me make love to her next morning. She lay astonished by a new sensation and I almost sobbed into her neck with relief as we clasped each other, decompressing. So that dam, whatever it was, had broken. (I've never quite figured out the source of my problem. Susan and I had made love at least once a week all the way until our abrupt caesura, and I'd always been up for it. Which, come to think of it, explains that figure of speech. I think my initial shriveling with Maartje may have had to do with the fact that for the first time in years and years I had an unfamiliar partner. And the interruption and imposition entailed by gearing up for sex turned the condom into a deadly symbol of the unacknowledged performance anxiety it subsequently justified. Or something like that.)

We killed the last day in the usual way—she enthusiastically milking her remaining hours in the amazing city, I in cloudland but dreading the trip to the airport and the parting. The flight was delayed so we had plenty of time to hang out in plastic chairs gazing moonily into each other's eyes. I hadn't told her I loved her yet; I considered it. I don't know how I could have been any more in love at that moment. She clearly returned... what? Affection, even strong affection. Or else she was a world-class dissembler and I a hopelessly self-deluding dupe. But I'd always recognized in her a withholding, a background dubiety. She'd parried my one suggestion that we take Rebecca and Christopher out with us to a restaurant... she was afraid to meet them, she admitted, because either way—whether she liked or disliked them—there would be troubling ramifications.

She'd had it right from the beginning: Fate was against us. Or at least reality, circumstances. What did I have to offer? I'd paid for everything while she was here— why not? I could afford a brief splurge, she was a penurious young traveler. But I'd made it clear my prospects were iffy—I was hardly a reliable long-term sugar-daddy. I believe she'd slept with me because she wanted to, because she got real satisfaction from it, felt real... affection for me. It wasn't just a crass, manipulative, commercial transaction. On the other hand, there may well have been an element of grateful *quid pro quo*; if sex didn't mean all that much to her, why then not reward the generosity of an older guy with impotence issues anyway? Whoa, *there* was the recommendation for future happiness *I* brought to the table. Nope, the age difference, my children, the continental gulf... our planets were not in alignment.

We kissed fervently at the boarding gate. Her eyes glistened as she pulled away, brilliant as the North Sea. My heart swelled into my craw. We vowed to call daily, to write. And for a time we did.

Then we didn't.

# I am now going to risk offending Elisabeth.

I am not going to describe in equally clinical detail the courtship—just as red-hot and starry-eyed, I can assure you—of the woman I actually married, the true love of my latter life. She'll approve the reticence, I'm sure. But I apologize if I've lavished disproportionate gush on what was, after all, an interlude.

More than a year had passed before Elisabeth and I... well, not *met*, since we'd already done that many years earlier, when she was the wife of a post-doc in Susan's department. We'd see each other occasionally at colloquia and pot-lucks. Then her husband got a job at Penn State and she vanished from my orbit. I'd had several animated conversations with her, the last at their going-away party—safely flirting, I guess you could say; I'd always thought she was very attractive. Susan had recognized that and even, one night driving home, displayed a little jealousy. But she was in no danger. All the less so with Elisabeth bound for Happy Valley, where she would give birth to two sons and, at about the same age as Susan, be jettisoned by her husband in favor of one of his students. That was a common occupational hazard facing faculty wives in a less enlightened (some would say less politically correct) time—and without very much opprobrium accruing to the errant mate. It was expected. Elisabeth had grown up in Palo Alto, where her father taught American history at Stanford, so she'd returned with her young boys to California.

I'd had a desultory dating history after Maartje. For a while, reminiscence, the round Dutch script on blue airmail stationery and a renewed immersion in basketball sustained me. But as the exchange of *billets doux* between Berkeley and Amsterdam slackened in frequency and fervor, I grasped at the fix-up suggestions that occasionally wafted my way. Including from Susan, who felt sorry for me and promoted a couple of single acquaintances. Nothing ever worked out. I became the kind of guy who shifts from foot to foot on the doorstep, tells women he's had a great time and will call them and doesn't. The impulse is charity—but the weaselly self-protective kind, insufficient to motivate a second ordeal of doomed sociability or uncomfortable telephone excuses. Surely, I rationalized, they'd shared my strain, understood the futility.

The divorce had come through. Our erstwhile family nest had been sold. I'd found a Craftsman bungalow, a fixer-upper in the flats whose down-payment I could afford with the check Susan had enclosed with the final decree. She'd married Dan and with their combined incomes moved into a rather more substantial pink Mediterranean on a wooded slope above the lab. In that house the kids had their own rooms; in mine they slept in beds I'd built for them out of two-by-fours and plywood, in a room divided by a wall I'd slapped up so Becca could have adolescent privacy. A block away hookers strutted University Avenue. Staying with Daddy was an adventure. They shuttled back and forth for a couple of weeks at a time depending on Susan's and my schedules. She and Dan had scientific conferences to go to, for example, often in exotic places like Paris, Venice and Athens. But I wasn't doing so badly by comparison. I'd finished the book and done an author signing arranged by the publisher at the Maritime Museum in San Francisco— the sole promotion. The paltry advance had long since been spent, of course, and I didn't expect much in the way of royalties. But I was getting more assignments from a couple of magazine editors, and they occasionally involved significant travel. I flew in luxurious business class to Hong Kong, Melbourne, Singapore, Tokyo, and in coach to a lot of places around the U.S. The pay was lousy but the expense accounts were nice. I did some destination pieces for airline magazines, which allowed me to eat every so often in a four-star restaurant or stay at a cushy Wine Country spa. On every one of those trips, for some reason, there was a moment when I'd think to myself, "Wow, Susan would really enjoy this. Too bad she's not here with me." Yeah, not Maartje. Of all people, Susan. Old habits die hard.

Then in Mendocino village, in an art gallery I'd sauntered into on a note-taking reconnaissance for the delectation of Republic Airlines in-flight readers, my gaze kept returning to the voluptuous woman minding the room. She was a knockout, with lustrous chestnut hair falling loose to her shoulders and big, lively dark eyes in an oval face that looked intelligent and amenable to laughter. She resembled Susan a bit, to tell the truth. There was something else about her....

I was more than intrigued. After a brief turn among the seascapes—realistic rocks and foam, rugged headlands and gnarled cypresses at sunset, or abstract eddies and stormclouds, all of a quality that accorded with the eye-popping prices—I concocted a few questions with which to engage her. It turned out she was one of the artists on exhibit. When I asked which were her works she led me to a wall hung mostly with watercolors. They brought to mind Mary Cassatt—although I was too shaky on art history to be sure that was the right reference: impressionistic landscapes in pellucid washes that were nevertheless saturated with color, a few human studies that brought the subjects to life in a way that transcended photorealism. To put it tritely, I thought they were really, really good. I jutted my chin, nodded and murmured cool approvals—"Mm-hm! Mm-hm!"—as I appraised them one by one. It crossed my mind to buy one, although the cheapest was really more than I could in good conscience afford. A small placard identified the artist represented by this grouping: Elisabeth Conrad. The last name was unfamiliar. But when I raised my eyes and turned to speak to her again the new context jogged recognition. Not absolute certainty—just enough years had passed and fine lines begun to appear at the margins of her bare features to disguise the twentyish face that had swum up from dim memory.

"Elisabeth! With an *ess!* I *remember* that! I *know* you! Or at least I think I do. Elisabeth... MacIntyre...? I thought it was?"

"Why... yes!" she said, eyes widening. "That was my married name." She screwed up her eyes to study me.

"Rick Schubert," I said. "I was married to Susan. Susan Schubert... she was, then. Who was in your husband's department... in Berkeley. Long time ago."

"Of course!" she exclaimed. "My God. You had a beard!"

"I did, didn't I?" I recalled. "Off and on. Right now it's off."

"That's why I didn't recognize you. *Rick!* How nice to see you! How *are* you?"

And so on. We filled each other in on intervening developments over dinner at the Seagull. She hadn't been sure she could get a babysitter on such short notice, but did. We hit it off, to say the least. It was as if we'd hardly broken stride since those teasing conversations so long before, and only gained momentum. And we were now both unhitched. It was a Thursday. I'd been planning to head back home along the coast next day, but instead I leaped at her invitation to have dinner at her house on Friday evening.

**The address proved to be a comfortable cedar-sided two-story in a clearing surrounded by slender new-growth redwoods on a dirt lane about two miles up Little Lake Road, east of town.**

She taught classes and painted at the Art Center, I learned, tended the gallery three afternoons a week and sold enough of her work to maintain a middle-class life style what with alimony and child support. She'd won a few awards. Over a juicy roast chicken fragrant with fresh tarragon and rosemary, washed down by the tart Anderson Valley pinot noir I'd brought, I bantered with Scott and Jeremy, who were just a couple of years younger than my kids. They were well mannered, lively and saucy with each other and their mother, but more diffident with me, the way kids in divorces always are before a parent's suspicious new acquaintances.

Elisabeth and I sat for long time at the table after the boys had polished off dessert (apple pie, home baked including a cinnemony scratch crust, and fresh-churned vanilla ice cream, I still remember). Then I helped her gather and rinse the dishes. I offered to go when she called upstairs to quiet the boys for the night, but she waved me to the couch. We nursed our wine glasses in front of the simmering metal fireplace until almost two. I couldn't believe it when I glanced at my watch. I hated to leave, I was so comfortable and, more important, she was so exhilarating a presence. But finally I did, even though she'd shown no sign I was overstaying my welcome. In the doorway I ventured to touch her arms and give her a peck on each soft cheek along with my profuse thanks—the kind of gesture that could be excused as French. She leaned into me lightly and kissed me, quickly but firmly, on the lips.

I don't think I used any gas driving back to Heritage House, where I was staying—my little Fiat Spider's tires never touched the asphalt. That had not been merely a polite kiss.

I popped in and out of the gallery all day Saturday just to be around her—she had to work. She seemed happy for my company. And we were on again for the evening when I returned from one of my forays to announce that I'd wangled a precious table at the Cafe Beaujolais on the strength of my assignment and a fortuitous last-minute cancellation; it was an opportunity she couldn't, or at least didn't, resist. I'd seen no ethical breach in trading openly on my credential as a journalist—I was not writing a review, I'd made clear, only reportage. And of course I'd be paying. In the afternoon I drove to a pharmacy in Fort Bragg to equip myself on the remote chance I might somehow, before I had to go back home to Berkeley, get as lucky as I would have prayed to get if I weren't afraid just thinking about it too much would provoke the gods. Once again I was head over heels, drunk on the endorphin-flood of fresh, seemingly requited romance.

Her appearance at the door in a simple black sheath dress she said she seldom had occasion to dig out of the closet—every generous curve lovingly molded—made my chest ache. According to the clip I just went out to retrieve from the rusting file-cabinet in the pumphouse, we ordered an appetizer of Dungeness crab cakes, a salad of baby spinach leaves and baked goat cheese and respective entrées of pan-roasted filet of sturgeon and roast duck. The meal was "Lucullan" and "fully justified [the chef's] reputation," I wrote. (What a stylist.) I still recall how good even the coffee was. When I took her home she invited me inside. She'd arranged sleepovers for both boys, she told me. In her bed, when we got there and the time came to tear open the little foil packet, she covered my hand and whispered, "That's okay. I use the pill. Unless...."

No unless.

And was it ever.

For the next four years we maintained a bi-communal relationship that only grew stronger with time. Rebecca and Christopher still needed me in Berkeley, I agreed with Susan; ditto for Scott and Jeremy in Mendocino where Elisabeth had constructed their three lives. We talked for an hour or more almost every night on the phone. As often as I could, several times a month, I'd drive up to spend a few days with her. Regularly, but less often because it was harder for her to arrange, she'd come down and nestle in with me. Usually there were a couple of weeks in the summer when Scott and Jeremy were visiting their Dad that we seized to get away together. Both of our sets of kids came to accept the new cohabitant of their parent's bedroom, the new bleary-eyed coffee-drinker in the morning kitchen and sharer of the toothpaste tube in the steamy bathroom. Both Elisabeth and I took pains not to act *in loco parentis* to the other's kids; we told them explicitly we were not trying to supplant their real mother or father, but that we *were* their father's or mother's new companion and would be there for them in any way they wanted us to be. Which, of course, was no way at all at first.

Elisabeth turned out not to be as unattached initially as I was. On that first postcoital Sunday morning after brunch, threading our way hand in hand through the driftwood on Big River beach in a drizzle, she revealed to me that there was a guy she'd been going out with for a while. Sleeping with, to put it bluntly. (A real estate agent in the village, she would eventually let fall.) The liaison was more of convenience than commitment, she assured me. Still, given their history and the geographic flaw in my personality profile, she wasn't prepared to swear off the trysts. She thought in all fairness I ought to know where things stood. Her gold-flecked brown pupils earnestly plumbed mine for reaction.

I withdrew my hand to consider the news. But what

right did I have to set conditions? I appreciated the candor, something I still faulted Susan on. I shrugged. "Okay. I can't say I'm thrilled, obviously. But... thank you for being honest." She was too luscious to lose because of petulant pride. I took her hand again, pulled her close and kissed her. "I'll win you over," I warned.

I'd become a lot less conventional in my attitudes, a lot less possessive since the split with Susan. Or at least I was conscious of trying to be. If the price of making love to the delicious Elisabeth regularly was knowing that something I didn't want to know about was happening when I wasn't around to know about it.... Well, that was adult business. But, like the burr under the bronc's saddle, the irritant slowly worked its way deeper. Maybe four months in, as I stood against my car with her pliant body pressed to mine, about to tear myself away for the three-hour drive back to Berkeley, I bucked.

"I've fallen in love with you," I declared. "I don't want to share you with anybody else. It tears me up. I know I'm being unenlightened....

"You are," she murmured. "He doesn't mean anything to me the way you do. I've fallen in love with you too."

"You have?"

"Mm-hm. Seems to be the case."

"Not 'two,' as in tee-double-you-oh, right?"

She laughed. "No! 'Too' as in... us. You. Just one, you. You've swept me off my feet, the way you said you would."

"Jesus. That's great to hear. So why do you go on seeing him?"

"Well, he's... here. You're there. A lot of the time you're there and he's always here. We were... together... before you showed up."

"Yeah, well." I shuddered at that kind of talk, at the flick of mental picture it unavoidably evoked... not that I had any idea who the guy was or what he looked like. "Maybe

I'll just stay *there*. Not show up again. I don't know. I'm not giving any ultimatums. Ultimata. Ol' tomatoes. I'm just saying. How much it tears me up...."

"All right. I'll have to still *see* him. Around. But otherwise...."

"Otherwise...?"

"I'll stop."

"Stop...?"

"Seeing him. Okay, *sleeping* with him!"

"Ah." I flinched again at the phrase. "You will?"

"I will, if that's what you're asking."

"Of *course* it's what I'm asking! *Jesus!* But I mean... only if you're okay with it."

"I'm okay with it."

"Really?"

"Really."

"Wow! That easy!"

I kissed her with such zeal it was all I could do to sidle between the Spider's bucket seat and the wheel. "You won't regret it," I promised jauntily.

## In the years ahead I would broach the subject of marriage a couple of times.

Not proposing, just asking if it was something she wanted. She said it wasn't. There were the relocation issues, of course, and also the economic consequences—she'd lose her alimony and child support. I said I'd make it up, but we both knew my attitude on money matters was a blithe and not altogether realistic optimism. "God will provide," I parroted, my motto. "She always has."

"Yeah, well, I'll never match *Susan's* income,"

Elisabeth noted acerbically, twisting my badinage back at me in a way I hadn't intended. "That gravy train left the station a long time ago, I'm sorry to inform you."

Susan sat between Dan and me listening proudly as Becca gave a valedictory at her high school graduation. Then my talented daughter was off to Brown. A year later I sat beside Elisabeth at the Mendocino High graduation as Scott collected an impressive trove of awards and small scholarships offered by local businesses. Then he was off to UC Santa Cruz. Christopher went through a rebellious phase and Susan and Dan packed him down the hill to live with me full-time. We almost came to blows a few times but overall we developed a solid father-son bond. One rub was that my girlfriend could stay overnight in my bedroom but I was hypocritical enough to deny him the same latitude.

Susan called to inform me that Dan had been offered a high-level post at the Salk Institute; as a two-fer she was promised a tenured professorship at UCSD and her own lab.

"That's fantastic!" I exclaimed into the phone. "Good for you! I always knew you had it in you!"

She'd branched into a burgeoning science called proteomics. In fact, she'd become a leading researcher into a recently discovered process known as ubiquitination. There was a time early in our marriage when I'd decided I needed to get up to speed with her scientifically—bring the superior intelligence evidenced by my Phi Beta Kappa in English to bear on the technical stuff that had left me cold but had engaged her since high school. In the evenings, I imagined, we'd chat about mitochondria and Golgi bodies and what she was doing with her little cell colonies, and I'd nod and maybe offer an insightful suggestion or two about how to solve some nagging experimental problem. How hard would it be? A little reading, some classes to fill in the requirements I lacked like, um, chemistry. And calculus. Well, maybe I'd do the reading anyway. Since the public language of science is all analogy to the visible world we inhabit, it's easy to think you could handle the insider mechanics if only you boned up on the basic concepts as described in common language.

The DNA molecule is a "double helix," for example—okay, I can picture that, especially with the help of a TinkerToy model, something like Watson and Crick constructed with input from Rosalind Franklin to depict their brilliant insight. The intertwined arms of the structure are dotted with nucleotides: adenine, thymine, guanine and cytosine, in varying patterns of which specific "packets," identified as genes, represent a "set of instructions," or a "code," for the "production" of the particular proteins that characterize a specific kind of cell, and from the constellation of cells a particular organ, and from the collection of symbiotic organs a specific organism. And so on. But that's just superficial babble. It has as much relationship to actually understanding how those complex ingredients exist, interact and can be manipulated—in the chemical gumbo, the atomic swirl that's life—as a glance at a diagram in a car repair manual has on my ability to rebuild my transmission.

So I know from Susan's explanations that ubiquitin is a molecule that attaches to a protein within a cell to signal that the unlucky recipient, which may be damaged or superfluous, is to be ushered into the cell's proteasome, its "death chamber." There the doomed protein will be "disassembled" and its parts "recycled." (More glib analogy.) Teasing out the nuances of this process has implications for treating conditions like Parkinson's and Altzheimer's diseases and some cancers. Twenty minutes clicking Web links and I could probably distill a pretty decent outline of current knowledge in the field, using the vigorous verbs and household metaphors that give lay readers the illusion I'm an expert and they're now semi-enlightened. Fact is, I really had no idea what Susan was about, puttering in her professional kitchen among her glistening electronic apparati, mixing and stirring her little soupbowls of biochemicals. (Come to think of it, *apparatus* is probably fifth declension in Latin, so the plural would be just more apparatus.)

Anyway, I appreciated that for her to refuse the deal she'd just described was almost unthinkable. And with Chris already out of the house, she and Dan had no reason not to skedaddle to professional glory in San Diego with my blessing.

I couldn't jerk Chris out of Berkeley High in his senior year—he was on the football and lacrosse teams besides. So Elisabeth and I continued our conjugal commute until I'd deposited my wiry wide-receiver/middy son in his room in the athletic dorm at Colorado College on the eve of pre-season practice. Then, at Elisabeth's urging, I put my little Berkeley house on the market. It sold almost immediately. Thanks to blind-luck timing, the appreciation netted me an amazing fiscal cushion. I joined Elisabeth and Jeremy full-time on the North Coast.

Jeremy was a fun kid to be around, sunny of nature and a devilish caricaturist, art editor of his yearbook. But soon he too collected his diploma—wearing Groucho Marx eyeglasses-*cum*-fake nose under his mortarboard, the scamp—and trundled off with his portfolio to the Art Center School of Design down south. Like mother like son.

With the nests now empty (can you write about this mundane stuff without falling into cliché?—maybe, but it would only be putting lipstick on a pig) we decided finally to go the official route. Elisabeth arranged an informal June wedding in a garden still thick with late-blooming rhododendrons. All four of our children, who'd come to know and like one another, even acknowledge one another as semi-siblings, were there along with Elisabeth's parents, my brother Paul and his wife from Chicago—where he now had a neurology practice—my stepmother Anne from her native Santa Fe where she'd moved back from Cincinnati after my father died, my stepsister Frannie and her new husband Tom, from Albuquerque where they both practiced law, and what to me was a surprising number of Elisabeth's students and friends. I guess I hadn't fully realized how popular she was in the community. I shook the hands of at least two guys who were identified to me as local real estate agents. One of them was my height and pretty good-looking, if I'm any judge.

I always wondered... but, of course, was circumspect enough never to ask.

# 2

**We stood at the metal railing above the beach and scouted the destination of the potato salad, the two six-packs of Scrimshaw and the bottle of sauvignon blanc in the cooler I was holding.**

The day was indeed glorious. Not a cloud in the sky. Great lines of waves slowly heaved in from Japan, the long swales trailing one another at perfect intervals, finally to peak, fold inward, collapse in a fury of froth, spume and noise and anticlimactically tail up and back down the wide, gentle slope of open sand that stretched straight for as far as the eye could see. A continuous rumble filled the air, as if an endless freight train were in passage. Miles to the south Point Reyes shimmered above the salt haze that billowed off the churning surf. Far to the north hovered the spine of Tomales Point.

The wind was steady but moderate, just brisk enough to take the sting out of the blazing sunlight but not so strong as to wrench off the wide-brimmed New Mexico-style sombrero I'd clapped on my head. In the old days I'd attended these oyster roasts bare-headed, bare-armed in a tee-shirt, bare-legged in tennis shorts. For years I'd assiduously cultivated a tan. Now I'd been careful before getting out of the car to smear pungent sun-screen all over my face, neck and the back of my hands; I was wearing a long-sleeved white cowboy shirt and jeans. My forehead, my jaw under my carefully trimmed beard and my scalp under its receding white ticking (I hadn't gone bald, but the thatch had undeniably faded and thinned) were mottled with scaly brown actinic keratoses. Periodically I'd visit the dermatologist to have the little blemishes spritzed with icy liquid nitrogen that made them blister and crumble away. And I'd had three tiny basal cell carcinomas sliced off my shoulders and back. That's what my fair-skinned youthful pursuit of pigment, my perverse Anglo-Saxon repudiation of my unique genetic heritage, had won me. (Hey, only white people can be *really white*, it occurred to me one day while I watched a Goth girl cross Main Street. She was dressed in black to emphasize a complexion so devoid of color she might almost have been a cadaver, or floured like a Kabuki dancer. So why, I mused, don't all of us Caucasians embrace our pallor like that, if we truly honor ethnic diversity?)

The beach in the vicinity of the parking area was well peopled by Point Reyes standards. That meant there were a few umbrellas here and there, and every fifty yards or so a sunbather stretched out on a towel, a family hovered over an ice chest, kids sailed Frisbees or kicked soccer balls. A couple of toddlers shepherded by a parent dabbled their toes warily at the tideline. It wasn't hard to locate Susan and Deirdre and the group we were to join, clustered beside a big pan of smoldering charcoal—I could smell it on the breeze from where I stood. The grill was sheltered between two huge driftwood logs near the base of the low sandstone cliff only a little to the left below us. We could have ducked through the rail and clambered down directly, but with the cumbersome cooler to ferry we took the paved walkway that descended to our right.

A big maroon sign with white letters warned that no lifeguards were on duty, the surf was dangerous—"enter at your own risk"—and dogs on leashes were permitted from this point south but prohibited to the north, which is nesting habitat for snowy plovers, an endangered species.

Deirdre was the first to spot us plodding toward them. At the car I'd exchanged my cowboy boots for flipflops, but once the pavement ended I'd slid the rubber sandals into my rump pockets; it's less painful on the web of the big toe to negotiate loose sand barefoot. Deirdre waved and strode to meet us. I put down the chest to give her an embrace and to say how great it was to see her, how sorry I was to learn of Jack's death and how grateful I was that she'd invited us. She and Elisabeth knew each other from those earlier picnics and expressed pleasure at seeing each other after so long, notwithstanding the bittersweet circumstances. Elisabeth offered her condolences.

Susan had trailed up close behind and I greeted her with a hug and a cheek-to-cheek air-kiss, a little awkward and self-conscious as always, especially in Elisabeth's presence. But the two of them had long since come to terms with each other and the odd turnabout in their circumstances. They smiled readily and embraced as Elisabeth offered her commiseration over Susan's loss of Dan. (He wasn't lost, I thought reflexively whenever I heard the euphemism; he was dead.) Becca and Chris had attended the funeral but we had not.

"Thank you," Susan acknowledged simply. Then, turning to me and suddenly brightening, she exclaimed, "You won't believe who's here!"

I glanced over at the people scattered in the vicinity of the grill. I saw Chris, his wife Élodie—the only black person in sight—with their two sons, my bubbly, brown-skinned little grandsons Olivier, seven, and his three-year-old brother Patrick (pronounced, *à la française*, "Patreek"); Rebecca and her husband Joel and their daughter, my precocious stick-figure nine-year-old granddaughter Molly. The children scampered among a handful of others I couldn't identify. There were a lot of elderly faces I half-recognized from those picnics a quarter-century ago, and many others, mostly younger, that were unfamiliar.

My eye, I must admit, kept flicking to a bare-legged teenager in an oversized diaphanous white shirt with the collar turned up, the sleeves shoved to the elbows and the buttons open to reveal the three tiny triangles of a scarlet bikini underneath. She was a real Lolita: mature breasts, taut tummy, perfect coltish stems, smooth olive skin, a heart-shaped face stylishly masked by wraparound sunglasses, pouty lips and elaborately braided dark blonde hair pulled high to underscore the gazelle-like length of her neck. She was raking furrows in the sand with a raspberry-painted big toe as the taller, angular woman who stood beside her waved a plastic wine glass in animated conversation with Élodie.

Élodie is from Côte d'Ivoire. Educated in Abidjan, Paris and Geneva, she was earning her management stripes at a five-star landmark hotel in Denver when Chris met her while teaching high school math and coaching lacrosse there. (He's doing the same thing now at a big private school on the Peninsula.) She's tall and svelte and has an elegant fashion sense. She was dressed in tight white slacks, a skinny purple tee-shirt and a purple-and-white-patterned headscarf tied African-style with the flaring bow cocked over one ear. The woman who was conversing with her eye-to-eye was equally put together. She wore orange-lensed sunglasses identical to the young girl's, crisply creased designer denim jeans, a short-sleeved white silk blouse and a large, colorful scarf loosely knotted and thrown over one shoulder. Something about her, some chic she shared with Élodie but that the American women I know seldom cultivate—Elisabeth in her shapeless, rough-cotton white Guatemalan peasant sundress, Susan in khaki shorts and a polo shirt with UCSD stitched above the breast, Deirdre in a floppy bush hat and olive-drab cargo pants rolled to mid-calf—suggested she was... wait a minute!

"Holy moley!" I exclaimed. "That can't be... is it? Is that Noelle?"

"That's who it is!" Susan confirmed.

"Noelle! Look at her! She's in her, what...?" I did a quick mental calculation. "Good God! Her *forties! Late* forties! How hard is *that* to believe? Our little Noelle. And yet she still looks... pretty much the same, wouldn't you say? Bit older, bit wiser? But so... so totally *soignée!* Who'da thunk it? She was a kind of a klunk as a teenager, as I recall."

"Still thin as a reed," Susan noted—a bit enviously, perhaps. Susan had put on weight since I'd last seen her. She and Elisabeth, who'd always been plumper (but in all the right places), were now women of substance. Both of them, favored by natural beauty, vivacity and vigor, wore the flesh well.

"I recognized her right off," I said. "Even with the sunglasses. Noelle was our *au pair*," I explained to Elisabeth. "Long long time ago. She was, like, nineteen at the time. I wonder, did she come to any of these oyster roasts with us back then?" I asked Susan.

Susan nodded. "She said she *did*. I couldn't remember either. She found my e-mail address and wrote me out of the blue a couple of years back. *I* told you that."

I shrugged. "Maybe."

"We've kept up a correspondence ever since. It was great to get back in touch."

"So she's up on all the history."

"Yep, fully up to speed," Susan assured me. "And when it turned out she and her daughter were coming to the U.S. and gonna be in San Francisco this week it was serendipity...."

"Noelle has a daughter!"

"That's who's standing next to her. Gaby's her name.

She's fourteen."

"A *fourteen*-year-old daughter! Wow, and going on twenty-four!" I added. "What a stunner! Gaby, huh?" The quintessential French name for a *fillette*.

"Pop the eyeballs back in, grandpa," Elisabeth needled.

"I am just stating the obvious," I defended myself. "Don't worry, I know my place. I'm not Humbert Humbert."

"Noelle says she's a handful," Susan acknowledged.

"Yeah, well, fourteen. Remember Becca at that age," I said.

"There's a boyfriend in the picture. Eighteen. Inappropriate."

"Tell me about it," I said. "Remember Becca at that age?"

"Noelle already has her on birth control."

"Well. Blame Mother Nature," I said. "It's *Her* that... it's *She* who turns these teenyboppers into bombshells before their time. Hard for a sexed-up eighteen year-old guy to resist. Is there a M'sieu Noelle?"

"Not recently," Susan replied. "She's been divorced for several years."

"Lot of that going around," I said. "Wow, whole life story, our little *au pair* has. Who was she married to?"

"Some English guy who worked for the same company. He was older. They were having an affair for a while before that, she said. That's all I know. Noelle's actually an executive! A V.P. Marketing."

"Really!" I exclaimed.

"She says it's because of her English. She started out shuttling between London and Paris as a translator and kept getting promoted. That's where she is now, Paris."

"We'll have to go visit her," I said with a playful cock of my eyebrow to Elisabeth. "Come on, I'll introduce you. I don't think she's recognized me. I think the hat and the shades have thrown her off."

Noelle erupted with a huge smile when I hailed her.

"Richard!" she exclaimed, using the French pronunciation. She whirled away from Élodie and jumped at me. We gave each other exuberant French kisses, the Platonic kind. "This is my wife Elisabeth," I said. Noelle clasped her hand warmly. It was immediately apparent Noelle still had the openness and sweetness about her we'd appreciated when she was nineteen—a complete contradiction of the cold, supercilious stereotype of the French. With a flush of pride she presented her daughter, "Gabrielle.... Everybody calls her Gaby."

Gaby observed the etiquette of meeting our eyes in turn and offering a pleasant if dutiful, "Hello."

*"Enchanté, mademoiselle,"* I said with a playful bow of my head. *"Parles-tu anglais?"*

"Aah... yes," she replied. "Mm... little bit?" She glanced at her mother. "We study English in my school." She had a much stronger accent than Noelle, not surprisingly. It was, of course, devastatingly charming.

"Here is a very good chance for her to practice," Noelle noted. "You should talk to people," she urged Gaby. "She is very disappointed," she added. "She wants to swim, but the water is so cold and rough. This is not like the beach she imagined. Not like St. Tropez. I told her it wouldn't be, but...." Noelle shrugged.

"Do you like to eat oysters?" I asked Gaby. *"Huitres?"*

She scrunched up her nose and shook her head. "I am not... so, ah... 'ungry... 'ungry for them," she said.

"Well, I am," I declared. "Hey! Élodie, hi!" I exclaimed, turning to her. "I didn't mean to neglect you."

I grabbed Élodie and gave her a peck on the cheek, which she returned. I've always been very fond of my trophy daughter-in-law, but also a little in awe—so striking, so capable (fluent in five languages; she was now an assistant manager at one of San Francisco's toniest hotels), so humble and eager to please within the family while so dignified and commanding (her natural shyness harnessed as self-possession and sometimes mistaken as *hauteur*) in public. And from so different a background. Africa. A poor family—at least comparatively. Her late father had been a middle-level civil servant. She still sent support money every month to her mother and occasionally to her brothers' families. It felt odd to be on so different an economic, social and cultural plane (okay, and racial, although I try to deny the whole malignant construct of race) from your counterpart, the mother-in-law of your son, the fellow grandparent of your grandkids. Neither Susan nor I had ever met her and probably never would. Sometimes I feel a little guilty about that. Chris had made the difficult trip after Patrick was born, judging that it was finally safe—off-and-on political violence in Côte d'Ivoire perennially complicating the already formidable planning, distance and expense factors. I had to admire Chris's guts in wooing and marrying this woman. Knowing her, and, yes, looking at her, there was never any doubt why he had.

"Okay, I'm going to grab myself a beer," I announced, delving into the cooler, "and then I'm gonna go over there and do some serious damage to those *huitres.*"


**I spent the next couple of hours drifting between the mollusks, the salads, the sides, the mollusks, the cooler, the mollusks and the people I knew or half-knew and the strangers whose names I failed to register when I was introduced.**

And the mollusks.

But if I do say so myself, I'm a fairly gregarious guy in situations where I'm called upon to act the part. At least I'm inquisitive by nature, a trait that serves one well both as a journalist and as a conversationalist. I ask people a lot of questions. And I've gained just enough knowledge about a lot of stuff to keep the pump primed. Usually I take a genuine interest in the subjects they reveal themselves to be most interested in—high on the list of which is themselves. Not that I can say I'm any different. Each life detail, each amusing or instructive anecdote recounted to me excites recognition of a personal parallel or prompts a recollection of something similar I experienced. I struggle not to let my attention get sucked inward into rehearsal and anxiously await an opening to regale the audience with *my* story. Occasionally the opportunity passes. Often I suppress the impulse. What I've noticed is that many people's eyes almost immediately glaze over when they're not themselves occupying the conversational spotlight. You can just watch their focus wander off... to some external business in the wings, or some "pssst" from their own little mental prompter—away, in any case, from... *hey, listen!* It's *my* turn! This is about me, me, *me!*

So maybe it's preemptive revenge, in a sense, that I indulge by failing even to *hear* people's names the first, oh, say, three or four times they've wafted past my earholes. Talk about self-involvement. There could be another factor: I'm putting so much psychic energy into projecting cordial sociability—which is apparently a strain on my nature—that I don't have any in reserve to devote to catching something so ephemeral, so non-definitive, as a name. I've always been a visual, not an aural, person anyway. I learn languages by reading grammars and vocabularies, not by listening to foreign gabble. If I don't know how a word's spelled I have no confidence in pronouncing it. (Which is why I was frustrated by the *kanji, katakana* and *hiragana* encoding Japanese when I was based in Yokosuka in the Navy; I only learned to construct a few of the most rudimentary sentences.) What I do pride myself on, however, is a memory for faces and an ability to place the context in which they belong.

Nearly everyone who'd come here in tribute to Jack was or had been involved in some way in the sciences, primarily the life sciences. The ones I knew were people I'd encountered many times on campus, on Cyclotron Hill or at social gatherings over the years with Susan, lo those many years ago. The oldest had long since gone to pasture, of course. Some were just more grizzled, haggard or bloated versions of the incarnation I remembered. A few were shockingly wizened and infirm now, clearly pushing their physical limits to have staggered this far across a breezy beach on their canes or walkers, or in at least one case probably to have been carried from the parking lot, since the folding wheelchair in which one woman slouched at an alarmingly stricken cant, a blanket tucked up to her chin, wouldn't have rolled well on sand. Then there were the hale emeriti, still voluntarily in some kind of research or professorial harness or, like Susan, on the cusp of that last phase of an academic career. Not that it couldn't be an astonishingly busy and productive one: Consider her UCSD colleague Francis Crick, who after winning the Nobel Prize for his elucidation of the structure of DNA moved from cloudy Cambridge to sunny San Diego, tacked into neurobiology and had been finishing up a paper on the cellular mechanics of consciousness when he died two years shy of ninety.

The ones I classify as "half-knowns" were people from far-flung universities or non-academic corners of Jack's and Deirdre's lives—their accountant when they'd lived here, for example—whom I'd encountered only on this beach in the distant past and could probably not have identified on the street but whose faces seemed more familiar than not in the setting. Then there were the children, now unrecognizably adult, and the complete strangers, who tended to be younger, Jack's ex-students from Michigan or friends of Deirdre's sons.

Increasingly fortified by beer and many times my recommended daily dietary allowance of magnesium, phosphorus, vitamin D, vitamin B12, iron, zinc, copper, manganese and selenium—the nutritional payload of an oyster in the raw, now massively enriching my bloodstream—and with Elisabeth on point to lead and then lend moral support at my elbow, I dutifully waded in and out of the mix.

My granddaughter, meanwhile, was wading literally. So after a while I took a turn at Molly's supervision. Jeans rolled to the knees, I spelled Becca so she could make another pass at the oysters. She and I might well have been the biggest oyster eaters in the crowd. Becca's a triathlete, among other accomplishments, and burns off every calorie she consumes. That's one thing I've given my kids—a love of sports, more particularly a love of physical exertion.

Becca was co-captain of her soccer team in college. She'd become a bruising defender who liked nothing better than muscling an attacker off the ball and, when the rare opportunity presented itself, sneaking up to boom a cannon-shot into the goal. I saw her do it twice against Harvard on a parents' weekend—to my astonishment at the fierce on-field exuberance of the self-effacing, self-questioning teenager I'd known in mufti. She still plays in coed pickup games but mostly she runs, swims, bikes and works out—for several hours nearly every day—to stay in shape for feats of endurance I wouldn't come within 10K of. (She raises sponsorship money to fight leukemia and lymphoma in the bargain.) She's broad-shouldered, with smooth but distinct muscular definition in her upper arms, a taut hour-glass waist and powerful legs that show to advantage in miniskirts or, as today, in flared white short-shorts. She walks with a kind of strut, arms swinging. This is a woman you would obviously mess with at your peril.

Joel, her husband of twelve years, seems devoted to her despite some rocky patches in their marriage. But what else is new? I know my kids' idiosyncracies, shall we say, and *I* would be hard pressed to live with them. So I admire their spouses for their pertinacity. (I wouldn't be altogether surprised to discover Joel had a less complex inamorata stashed somewhere on the side, not that I'm condoning it or believe it to be actually the case.) Rebecca makes no bones about how embittering and destabilizing it was for her when Susan and I split. So I'm not sure what transgression it would take for her to divorce Joel. Fortunately he's a stoic, even-keeled, patient guy, a labor lawyer kept busy and fulfilled representing wronged union workers. Cheerful is his default mode. He seems to be unquenchably in love with Becca and she with him. What's more, he's a runner too. The family that....

Molly cut her teeth (literally, again) in a stroller on bicycle wheels being shunted along the jogging trails of the East Bay Regional Park District. That's where Becca had kept encountering and being passed by the handsome young guy with the remarkable mop of curly black hair (he's from one of North Oakland's pioneer Genoese families) and the very brief track shorts. One day she decided to keep pace and ran with him shoulder to shoulder until they both collapsed in exhausted laughter. (She says she suspects and he claims that near the end he hadn't been going at full tilt.) She'd dropped out of Brown in her junior year, never at home in the East, and bounced around for a while before taking a ceramics class at Laney junior college, where she discovered her life's passion. Like Elisabeth she now teaches her art, works in a home studio, has had shows in some prestigious venues and is developing a characteristic *oeuvre* recognized by peers and, as important, museum curators and buyers.

Notwithstanding her parents' solid body types,

Molly is all sinew and bone. That's how I was at her age. My mother, no doubt on my pediatrician's advice, tried to pad my corrugated ribcage by sliding nasty spoonfuls of cod liver oil between my pursed lips and serving me eggy between-meal milkshakes. To no avail. I remained skinny—but very fast on my feet (until they suddenly outgrew the rest of my body in puberty), deceptively strong and resilient. And that's how Molly is. She plays youth soccer and is probably, from the few times I've watched her, the star of her team. She's ebullient, coordinated and like her mother aggressive and unafraid. But she's skinny as a colt. Every time she's in a collision you worry that something's going to get broken. (So far, so good.)

Without any insulating blubber, Molly succumbed soon enough to the nip of the Pacific. Her game—and mine if I wanted to stay within grabbing distance—was to prance down the band of hard-packed gray sand below the high-water mark in pursuit of the receding wash of a spent wave. Then, cheekily waiting until the moment the incoming surge met the undercutting ebb—a split-second's seething grace for escape—she'd wheel and shriek and flee toward dry sand. More often than not the flood outraced her. Swirling around her calves or thighs depending on how far she'd pushed her challenge, the dying wave would whisk her off her pins. Which was pretty much the point of the exercise. She'd topple and splutter and pretend she was a jellyfish dragged willy-nilly by the shallow *va-et-vient*. Before long she was crusted from toes to blond crown with sand. Before much longer I noticed that underneath the grit she was goose-fleshed, blue-lipped and shivering. But still game. I had to drag her to dry land where I brushed off as much of the wet sand as I could and bundled her tightly in a beach towel. I led her to the lee of a low dune and nestled her into its protective warmth to bake for a few minutes out of the wind.

I was feeling the chill factor myself. Not only had

I allowed myself to be caught in water deeper than I'd anticipated when I'd rolled up my pants, but I'd managed to lose my balance completely while dancing backwards from an in-coming spate whose velocity and reach I'd misjudged. The translucent current suddenly scudding between my legs was disorienting, and the cant of the beach and the water clutching at my ankles combined to trip me up. The seat of my pants hung heavy, soaked. I knelt beside Molly with the evidence of my pratfall aimed seaward (windward) to hasten evaporation, and encouraged her to regale me with plot summaries of the books she'd recently devoured. She's a torrid reader. The list surprised me for its classicism—Laura Ingalls Wilder, C.S. Lewis, Lewis Carroll, Baum's Oz books—leavened by Harry Potters, of course, and even a biography of Amelia Earhart. I asked her if she thought she'd like to be a pilot and she said yes, she thought it would be fun to fly a Navy fighter jet and land on aircraft carriers. I wondered where she'd got that notion. TV, of course. It's a realistic ambition for a girl these days, I acknowledged—but she'd be catching the hook over her militantly anti-militarist mother's prostrate body, I thought to myself.

When Joel hove up to relieve me of baby-sitting duty I chatted with him for a few minutes about his latest cases. That segued almost immediately into our customary call and response in which we fanned each other's outrage at recent atrocities (not altogether figurative) committed by Republicans and their enablers.

Joel and I see eye to eye politically—as, in fact, does everyone in my extended, blended family. Elisabeth and I sometimes comment on that—we think it's remarkable: Rebellion against your parents' politics was almost *de rigueur* among the flower-power generation that swept us along with it, even though our births pre-dated the postwar baby bulge by a couple of years. My brother and I both broke with our conservative father on party identification. I find it hard to believe my Dad's fundamentally egalitarian, individualistic values wouldn't have long since disassociated him from today's degraded party of Lincoln, however. Watergate, in fact, outraged him, soured him. Not that he didn't hate taxes and unions with the best of 'em. But I can't imagine he'd condone state meddling in matters of conscience, personal autonomy and privacy. As a patriot and a good lawyer he'd gone so far as to confess full sympathy with the ideals of the American Civil Liberties Union. And in his cosmology it was Democrats who ran up the national debt and got us into wars. Once again a Republican shibboleth, history inconveniently notwithstanding. Elisabeth's father too, even though he was a college professor, was a Republican. It was Stanford, after all. And he was a native Californian, a reasonable Warren kind of Republican until his latter days, when he shriveled into a bitter, crabbed know-nothing....

In any case, every one of our kids, and every spouse, is a flaming liberal. That, at least, is one less cause of friction around the holiday dinner table.

## I fetched another Scrimshaw and offered myself as an oyster shucker.

After a half-hour or so of that I noticed Chris tossing a rubber football with Olivier and Patrick and two other little boys. I handed over my knife and gloves to the theoretical physicist who'd been graciously fielding my stupid questions about unified field theory while we shared unclaimed hot oysters off the grill; I sauntered across the beach to join the fun.

Chris had just managed to round up a wild, end-over-end pass launched by Olivier. "Heads up, Pop-pop!"

he called, using the name Molly had bestowed on me and was now my universal grandfatherly appellation.

He reared back and let go a long, looping, tightly spinning spiral. Chris prides himself on his strong arm.

The wind caught it and it started to flutter, but Chris had allowed for that. The ball was perfectly aimed to force me to trot a few strides to haul it in. Chris was mischievously running the old man. Shades of our afternoons in the middle of the street—"okay, hitch-and-go, eight yards out, shoulder fake, quick look back, then take off for the pole..."— Chris practicing the patterns that would eventually earn him varsity playing time, me trying to lead him just right. I wasn't much of a quarterback. I'd always been a receiver myself when I'd played touch football in college and the Navy. But I did my best and I think his eye and hands even benefited from my errancy. I enjoyed the reciprocal pitch and catch. I tried to teach by example—any ball you can get a fingertip on, I parroted the cliché, you should be able to stretch another inch or two for and snag.

So I shifted the beer bottle into my left hand and darted right—staggered is more like it, the loose sand and the crackling adhesions in my aged joints reducing my effort to slow motion—eyed the ball's descending trajectory, flung my right hand up, fingers splayed, and gentled it out of the air.

You've got to let your arm go slack: cup the ball and yield to its momentum as you control and redirect its fall— like feathering the brakes rather than standing on them. Even so, about half the time the object will simply thump off the interposed flesh. Not this time, though. I guided the ball snugly against my ribs one-handed... just as my broad-brimmed hat flew off behind me.

"Sweet!" Chris called with a grin.

I stumbled to a halt. Beer foamed out of the neck of the bottle and ran over my wrist.

"Still got 'em!" I crowed. "Million-dollar hands, baby!"

He was way too far away for me to fling it back to him. I'd had a sore shoulder for several months. Possibly it was arthritis but more likely bursitis from wielding a heavy nail-gun overhead while installing siding on Elisabeth's studio behind the house. My semi-daily morning mile in the pool probably hadn't helped. They say you're supposed to give an inflamed joint rest, but after the first few strokes the pain always muted and I figured the benefit to my cardiovascular fitness and Adonis-like physique outweighed any putative damage. Joel and Becca and the boys had stayed with us for a few days earlier in the summer; we'd taken them to a swimming hole on the Navarro River about halfway between Boonville and the coast, where I'd discovered my throwing arm was too tender to skim a rock. It had been feeling better lately—that is, I'd realized there was no longer a sharp twinge when I rolled onto my right shoulder in bed—but I didn't want to risk straining it again. So I retrieved my hat and then walked the ball in closer until I could lob it underhand to Olivier, who cradled it into his breadbasket.

"Good catch," I approved. "Try to use your hands as much as you can."

"Okay, Pop-pop," he acknowledged. He cocked his arm and fired the ball at his father.

Olivier's big for his age. Brown hair cropped close, *café au lait* skin and pale hazel eyes. He has a winning grin gapped by lost baby teeth and the emerging crescents of their permanent replacements. It reflects the joyful disposition his father too had until... well, I guess until shortly after Susan and I got divorced. He's sturdier than his older cousin. (It's interesting how both kids are physical opposites, at least at this stage, of their mothers.) And he's less cerebral, I guess you could say. But maybe that's just a boy-girl thing. Molly was already tearing through books on her own at his age, but Olivier still isn't comfortable reading. Fortunately he still enjoys being read to, as, of course, does Patrick; there's nothing more tranquilizing than settling onto a couch and having a warm child snuggle against your flank as you crack open a familiar storybook. Or, in Olivier's case, one of his favorite illustrated taxonomies of dinosaurs. He's amassed a lot of lore about prehistoric fauna from picture books —not to mention about pirates and African animals. And superheroes. He has a vivid imagination. And a good spoken vocabulary. He's also bi-lingual. Chris and Élodie decided they'd each speak their own language to the children at home, so both Olivier and Patrick respond to English in English and French in French. (She figured they wouldn't get much mileage from Ivoirian Dioula, the language she'd grown up in, although Olivier came back with a couple of phrases after their visit to *Grandmère*.)

I watched Chris being a good Daddy. And devoting equal attention to the other two little boys—he has a way with kids, genuinely likes them, even when they mutate into adolescents. That's why he enjoys teaching and coaching— and, I'm sure, is outstanding at them.

Patrick's just a bit young for football; he would square himself up at the ready, squinting bravely in anticipation of a faceful of rubber and sand, knees locked, arms extended like a returner waiting for a punt, but the ball would almost always squirt between his elbows or thud off his chubby hands even when it was carefully shoveled to him from only a few feet away. Not that he wasn't fine with that. He'd chortle and scramble to corral the dropped ball so he could "pass" it back. In contrast to his butterfingers, he has a strong, mature throwing motion; you were wise to scuttle rearward as quickly as possible and keep your hands in front of your crotch when he wound up.

Patrick is the child movie star of the family. I wouldn't hesitate to call him beautiful. He's a shade closer in color to

Élodie, a kind of baby Sidney Poitier whose round cheeks dimple when he smiles and whose enormous onyx pupils glisten through lush lashes. He's as temperamental as a movie star, too—willful, sly, manipulative, aware of his charm and quick to turn it on... or off if the world thwarts his expectations. I think they call that being three. (Or maybe terribly two—his birthday was four months earlier, and I'm describing past behavior I'd observed. In fact, I think he has begun to mellow. Childhood character is a moving target.)

But Patrick's attention span, at least for an exercise in which six people were now sharing the rotation, pretty soon lapsed. He and the little boy who was about his age (he belonged to one of Deirdre's sons, I believe) wandered away to the miniature buckets, shovels, toy dump trucks and bulldozers they'd been plying earlier under Molly's guidance in the construction of a lumpy sand "castle."

Being a good grandfather myself—actually, I'm not, at least not nearly as doting as my children think I ought to be—I scanned the beach periodically to make sure all the little kids were safely in range and under some kind of chaperonage. Molly, I noticed, was back cavorting at the water's edge—now with Gaby. Who'd doffed her shirt and was, I admit, an eyeful. It's unseemly for a man my age to stare lustfully at a nymphet barely into her teens, but you can't escape biology. And it wasn't really lust, it was appreciation. And I wasn't really staring, my eyes just lingered for a few extra beats before I reminded myself that ogling is unseemly. I was wearing dark glasses, so no one could be absolutely sure, I told myself, whether I was focused appropriately on Molly or inappropriately on the wet, nubile, nearly nude Gaby. (The suit was no skimpier than ordinary on a public beach, but still plenty revealing. I wondered if she'd be topless in St. Tropez. Probably not with her mother around. I remembered Susan shyly baring her breasts to do as the Romans were doing thirty years earlier on the Côte d'Argent.)

Three brown pelicans flew into my field of vision from the left. I watched them skim the break in close file only inches above the foam.

Elisabeth, Rebecca, Élodie and Noelle sat a few yards away from the girls on the crest of the beach. They were nodding and laughing and gesticulating to one another with their plastic wineglasses. It was gossipy, womanly camaraderie that was cheering to see. Joel and Deirdre's oldest son, also a lawyer, were on their knees intently shaping turrets and deepening a moat with the boys—two generations of boys absorbed in play. I saw Susan among one cluster of guests, Deirdre in another by the grill where the physicist still crouched in charge.

I drained the last warm swallow of bitter beer and set the empty bottle at my feet next to my hat, which I'd temporarily doffed, to remind me to take it over to the recycling bag when we were done tossing the football.

Chris zipped a pass to me. I snared it and lateraled it to Olivier.

That's when I heard the women's shrieks.


## They're called sneaker waves, or sleeper waves, or sometimes rogue waves.

Visitors to the National Seashore are warned to be wary of them. We're very familiar with the phenomenon on the Mendocino coast: Almost every stormy winter the *Beacon* reports the loss of a hapless tourist who wandered too far out on the headlands to gawk at the spume or snap a picture and was swept to sea.

Because they were upwind, the cries rang in all their shrill immediacy to me; I turned my head so quickly I saw

399

Élodie and Noelle still floundering to their feet, flinging drops of water from their hands as it eddied around their ankles. Elisabeth and Rebecca had already hopped upright. They were slapping at their sopping backsides. Elisabeth's cotton dress was semi-transparent, molding her panty lines, buttocks and thighs.

Ten or fifteen yards beyond them I saw Molly flailing in slack water that had flushed her inshore but was already gathering momentum to suck her out again. Half swimming, half staggering, squealing at the chill of the dousing, she fought against its drag. But the current was too powerful. She was hoisted on the deepening ebb, flipped and sluiced backwards toward the base of the white cliff of wave that reared over her flimsy body.

Near the surf line she rolled under. The incoming breaker crashed down with a thunderous boom, boiled atop her....

...And as suddenly coughed her up! There she was, prone, arms windmilling, riding the flood inshore once again. When she was able to gain a footing she scrambled erect and wallowed toward safety, knees pumping high, a frown of determination on her face. She splatted through the retrogressing wave—diminutive in comparison to its anomalous predecessor and now gurgling in retreat toward Mother Ocean—and kept running to Becca. All four women had dashed toward her when they'd seen her in distress. So had I, I now realized, slowing. An autonomic reflex.

Before she flung herself into her mother's embrace Molly started laughing—prancing, capering, kicking up sand, flapping her arms, chortling in high glee.

"Mommy!" she shrieked. "Mommy! Did you see me? I was *body surfing!*"

I said the kid was dauntless.

I hadn't even thought about Gaby. I hadn't noticed her....

...Because I hadn't focused out far enough. Out into the ocean. Out into the heaving dazzle, past the surf line! Which was where I now spied the cap of golden braids glinting in the sun.

It was Gaby, all right. Her head bobbed in the trough just beyond the turbulent break... rose on the approaching comber, disappeared behind its crest and reappeared in the new trough. She crooked her arm, a wave at the beach. Her eyes were saucers but she was smiling. She buried her face and kicked into a smooth crawl, headed toward shore.

The wave washed over her. Again she slid away, out of sight. When she reappeared in the declivity she was still swimming. She showed confident form. She was breathing over her shoulder, her stroke was fluent, her beat measured, her fluttering feet churning up a little froth behind her. But she hadn't made any discernible progress. In fact, she was further out than before.

She paused and trod the heaving water.

"Gabrielle!" Noelle shouted. "Gabrielle! *Reviens!*"

Gaby waved again.

"*C'est interdit!*" Noelle called, beckoning with imperious sweeps of her upturned hands. "*C'est dangereux! Il faut revenir! Maintenant! Reviens! Tout vite!*"

The wind was blowing pinpricks of spume into our faces. I doubted her mother's shouts carried to Gaby over the surf's pounding din. She was at least thirty yards out now.

I sidled alongside Elisabeth and slid my arm around her waist, which startled her. She flinched, looked up at me and then scowled back at Gaby.

"She didn't go in on her own, did she?" I asked.

"No. I don't think so. There was a sneaker wave," Elisabeth replied. "We all got drenched. Even up there on the beach."

"Yeah, I saw," I said.

"Did you see what happened to Molly?"

"I did."

"She almost got pulled in too."

"I know, yeah."

"Thank God she's okay."

"It was just a fun little two-way ride as far as she was concerned."

"We should have been watching them more closely. They were too near the water. I think we were depending on Gaby to be responsible."

"Yeah, well, hindsight," I said. "She's old enough. Wasn't her fault anyway. It was a fluke wave. And I probably started it, by letting Molly play too close to the surf. I don't like this, though. She looks like she's a good enough swimmer, but she's not making any headway."

"Gaby!" Noelle cried. *"Ah, mon Dieu. Elle n'écoute pas.* This frightens me."

Beside her, Susan, Becca and Molly were reinforcing the urgent hails. The commotion had caught the attention of others among the picnickers; people started to filter down toward us, shading their eyes, grimacing out at Gaby. Everyone knew no one's supposed to be in the water at this beach. Chris had sprinted over with the football in hand; Olivier and his little friend stumbled close after him. Chris shouldered up alongside me. Joel arrived at Becca's side and scooped Molly into his arms. We all squinted anxiously at Gaby, who was definitely further out now, even though she'd resumed swimming toward shore.

"Fuck," Chris muttered. "She's in a rip. You think?"

"Could be," I agreed. "Not that strong, it doesn't seem. But still...."

"She's not gonna make it back that way."

"Not if she's in a rip current," I nodded. "She needs to swim out of it, to one side or the other. Right?"

"You think she knows that?"

"You do. Don't you?"

He hitched a shoulder—meaning "obviously," or "not really."

Gaby's face rose. You could see her sputter, blink the seawater out of her eyes, swivel her head to check her bearings. You couldn't really read her expression. So far there were no signs of distress or panic, though.

I ran forward to separate myself a little from the crowd and yelled at her, even though I doubted my voice would reach her, "Gaby!" I raised my right arm as high as I could, my forefinger rigid. I started jabbing the air, pointing right.

From a little more panoramic perspective I might have been able to read the water. They say you can sometimes spot the edge of a rip by the difference in the color of the outflowing current, or by a line of foam or flotsam, or by a break in the pattern of the combers. This close to the surf the ocean's blue-green surface seemed to bulge over me, sea-level looming higher than the sand that rimmed it. So it was a toss-up which direction, north or south, offered the fastest escape. I shielded my mouth with my left palm, fingertips against my nose, and bellowed, "*This* way! Swim *this* way!"

I jogged a few steps down the beach along the wave line to illustrate. I started hopping to attract her eye, still pumping my arm emphatically. I brought the other arm up into play, pantomiming an Australian crawl. "Swim *parallel...!*"

I realized how hopeless that instruction was for a French girl. No doubt a frightened French girl... and it would be inaudible anyway against the wind and roar. I just looked like a crazyman.

I saw no response that suggested comprehension. She arced her palm again, her wrist barely breaking the surface. It was hard to tell if she meant to reassure us, to acknowledge us as her audience, to signal that help would be appreciated...

or to solicit it.

I glanced back and saw Chris unwrapping his tee-shirt over his head.

Uh-oh, I thought.

## I spun on my heels and retraced my steps as quickly as I could.

I almost lost my balance when a wave tail slid in, surged to mid-shin, shackled me for a precarious moment before retreating.

"Wait!" I barked out at Chris. "Wait a minute! Chris? Don't do anything stupid!"

I reached him, panting, and stretched out a restraining hand. My fingers stubbed on his bare chest. I felt a sudden, almost embarrassing current of intimacy—the male flesh of my flesh.

"I'm gonna go in," he announced. "She's in trouble. Somebody's gotta help her."

"*You* can't," I argued. "You're not even that much of a swimmer." I pointed at his satiny nylon lacrosse shorts, baggy and knee-length in the current fashion. "Those things are going to weight you down as much as a pair of cement shoes."

"They're light. I swim okay," he insisted. He hooked his thumbs into his waistband to slide the shorts down.

I grabbed his wrist. "No!"

He flicked his forearm brusquely and shucked my grip. Chris lifts weights. His pecs and biceps—and abs and all the other muscle groups—show it. His is not a swimmer's body.

"No!" I repeated. "Not you."

"*Somebody's* gotta do it," he maintained. "I'm not gonna just stand here and watch. While she gets carried out further and further until it's too late."

Becca had recognized his intention and rushed nearer too.

"Forget it, Chris," she snapped. "You practically *drowned* at scout camp."

"I did not," he defended himself. "That's ridiculous."

"There's a grain of truth there," I concurred, briefly picturing the soggy little muskrat, quavering uncontrollably, who'd been dragged by his patrol leader out of the frigid Sierra lake in which he'd flailed to narrowly pass his second-class swimming test on Parents' Day.

Now Becca was peeling *her* tee-shirt up over *her* pony-tail. She had on a black sports bra underneath. In the breeze her nipples were raised.

I looked away. At Gaby, who was—no question— more distant than she'd been just a moment before. Probably a hundred yards out now. Shit, I said to myself. My heart was pounding and my throat was tightening. Shit. This *was* becoming a serious problem.

"I'm used to open water," Becca said. She flung the balled shirt at her feet.

I seized her upper arm. There was no spongy give to the daughter-flesh beneath. Muscle of my muscle, toned at the throwing wheel and the Nautilus machine.

"I swam the Escape from Alcatraz last year!" she reasoned. "That's a mile-and-a-half! This is nothing."

"You had a wetsuit. And you haven't had lifeguard training," I objected.

"She doesn't need a lifeguard," Becca said.

"No, not yet," I agreed. "But the last thing we want is to take a chance on losing somebody else. You're both young, you have families. You have little kids to raise. This stuff's dangerous, and the worst thing... you read about it all the time. Somebody goes in to try to rescue somebody... and then they get caught in the rip too... and you end up with two or three people drowning"

"Well, I'm not going to just stand here and let some little girl drown," Chris glowered, "in front of a bunch of spectators. While we all discuss it."

"*Nobody* is!" I agreed. I ripped open the plastic-pearl snaps on my shirt cuffs, unhooked the Navajo silver buckle on my horsehair belt, unbuttoned the waistband of my jeans and zipped open my fly.

"What are you doing, Daddy?" Becca demanded.

"Nothing," I said.

"Who is it?" I heard a voice pipe.

"Why is that child out there, for God's sake?" asked another.

"Gaby! Gaby! *Reviens à l'instant!*"

Noelle was still calling—echoed at supportive intervals by others including Elisabeth, Susan who'd joined them and Élodie—as if she believed, or wanted to believe, or needed to believe that her daughter was simply being foolish and stubborn.

"Oh, my God! Nobody should be swimming here! There's an undertow!" somebody observed.

"And sharks."

"Great whites," another specified helpfully.

"Who's got a cellphone? Call nine-one-one."

"No coverage out here."

"Don't anybody else go into that water!" an imperious baritone commanded.

"Why aren't there any lifeguards?"

"Somebody's got to drive back to Park headquarters! We need a helicopter!"

"It'll be too late!"

"Isn't anybody going to help her?" a soprano fretted.

I'd managed to wriggle free of my pants—the wet,

rolled-up legs bound my calves tightly, which made shucking out of them more difficult and awkward than usual.

"I've got nothing to lose," I told my kids. "I've had a good long life... and I'm not going to lose anything anyway!"

I popped the row of snaps and shrugged out of my shirt. I was momentarily abashed about baring my septuagenarian physique. My stubby penis (shrunken by chill and fight-or-flight adrenaline) was contoured clearly in the pouch of my gray cotton bikini briefs. But this was no time to dwell on modesty. Or body image.

"No, Dad, that's crazy," Chris sputtered. "No no...."

"She just needs somebody to show her how to swim out of it," I insisted. "A little moral support."

"Yeah, that's why *I* should...," Becca declared. She lunged for the water.

"Stop!" I bellowed. I reacted quickly enough to catch the top of her shoulder with my claw before she started gaining on me. It threw her momentarily off-stride. I caught up, thrust my bare knee in front of her and pivoted. I blocked her with my leg and arm. "Think of Molly!" I blurted. "Think of Joel. Please, Becca!"

I leveled a finger at Chris, who'd leaped after us. "Think of Élodie, and...." I had to pause for a beat to pull up the names of my grandsons: "...Olivier, and Patrick! I swim more miles a week than *you* do, Becca."

That might not have been true but was close.

"I was a lifeguard once, if it comes to that," I added.

Technically a lie. But I almost believed it when I said it.

"I'm the logical one for this. I'm older than anyone on this beach... well, most of 'em anyway... and I'm fitter... well, I'm fitter than all but you two, probably. Nothing bad's going to happen. It'll be okay. Whatever you do, though, don't you or anybody else come in after me. Okay? Promise? No matter what!"

Somebody, maybe Joel, was going to beat me into that water if I didn't act fast. And the longer Gaby struggled the more exhausted she'd get. That's why people drown in rips.

"I love you both," I said. "And my grandkids!"

I realized I still had on my watch. Waterproof but clunky, an impediment. I clicked open the clasp, stripped it off my wrist and tossed it to Becca. Sunglasses too! I ripped them off my ears and flipped them behind me. I broke into a canter.

This was nuts, I knew. I really didn't want to be doing this. My last act, my last minutes on earth, maybe.

Although it was just water, I told myself. Just a swim. Little rougher than usual, little colder, but just a swim.

I'd been eyeing the set of the waves while tracking Gaby. They purled in at a slight angle to the beach and there was a kind of diagonal lane between the trailing edge of one breaker and the nose of the swell cresting alongside but a little behind. That offered a less resistant entry.

I looked around over my shoulder for Susan and found her.

No! I should be looking for Elisabeth, I realized.

I saw them both. Gaping at me. Then lifting their hands, calling my name....

I turned, hit the water, gasped, ran as far as I could on the ebb, got almost to chest depth, spread my arms for balance like a tightrope walker, waddled a few more paces against the frigid surge, took a deep breath, squinched my eyes....

...And lunged.

# 3

**I was on my hands and knees gouging at dry rot under the sill in the doorway to Elisabeth's studio when the phone rang.**

She got up from her easel, went to the workbench and answered it. She brought me the handset. "Doctor," she mouthed.

I sat back on my haunches, laid the chisel aside and accepted the phone. "Hello?"

"Richard?"

"Richard Schubert. This is," I acknowledged.

"Doctor Jacobs here."

The petty pomposity annoyed me, I have to say. First name for me, "Doctor" for him. In first person yet.

"Listen," he said. "We got the blood work back on your retest."

"Ah," I said. I'd straightened fast and I suddenly felt light-headed.

"Your PSA's definitely on the high side."

"Ah," I said. "Great."

"I think we ought to do a biopsy."

"Great," I repeated.

So I had cancer.

I humped my back and hung my head to let the blood wash back into my brain. My heart was racing. For a second

I'd been really dizzy.

Of course, there was an equal chance—even a better chance—that I *didn't* have cancer.

I waited for the doctor to continue. I was pleased by my phlegmatic response. The sarcasm had popped out unrehearsed. But I was disappointed in my physical reaction. Had I grown faint upon hearing the pronouncement of my death sentence? Or had I just had a physiological reaction to an abrupt change in the relative position of head to heart? I'd experienced the latter often enough. And not only was the former not necessarily the case—I'd done plenty of reading on prostate specific antigen tests and what they do and do not prove—but I'd been bracing myself to confront my mortality with equanimity for almost sixty years. When my mother died I'd sworn I wasn't going to give God, or Fate, or What-Have-You the satisfaction of catching me with my guard down ever again.

"We can make an appointment right now if you'd like," Jacobs offered.

I'd read up on biopsies too. Googled and surfed all over the web sifting information on cancer of the prostate and mere benign prostatic hyperplasia (the piss-inducing enlargement that affects a lot of men my age, although I could still go for hours, including all night, when I needed or wanted to).

I'd reluctantly unclenched at a biennial checkup to allow the doctor to poke his gloved and copiously Vaselined index finger up my ass. He'd argued for it—flattering me that I was remarkably lithe and healthy for my age and thus had a life expectancy that made early detection and treatment of so curable (no, more accurately "treatable") a disease worthwhile.

And then he'd detected it. Or at least something out of the ordinary in the little gland—"a nodule," he'd explained, trying hard not to alarm me yet convey the severity of

411

his concern. While by no means a sure sign of cancer, he emphasized, it made it wise to do a PSA test. And then, when that came in at eight-point-five, to do another one six weeks later for corroboration. ("Normal" is under four. "The gray area" is from there to ten... ten somethings... nanograms of antigen per milliliter of blood, if I'm not mistaken. [And I'm not, because I just checked.]

So here we were.

"How would you do the biopsy?" I asked. I knew there were a couple of approaches.

He explained. Another nasty invasion through the tensely defended posterior portcullis, as I'd anticipated. Outpatient procedure. "Not a big thing," he assured me. "Little momentary discomfort, maybe, but...."

I told him I'd get back to him after I checked my calendar. I clicked off the phone and picked up the chisel.

The thing about having prostate cancer and not having prostate cancer is that there's not much difference. Something's going to kill you. Something lethal is ticking inside you no matter how old or healthy you are. Sooner or later it's going to explode—go metastatic, start eating out your organs, blow a hole in a critical membrane or a fuel line—unless a careening car or a lightning bolt does the job first. (Something like fifty unlucky people die in electric storms each year on average in the U.S., I've read.) Accident, disease... we're here to be taken out.

Which is hard, it seems, for most people to come to grips with. Especially in this age of medical wonders, of vaccines and drugs and fancy technologies that postpone death or remove it to the privacy of hospitals so that a majority of citizens of the developed world may live into ripe middle age before actually knowing, as opposed to being told or reading about, a dead person. And except on a television or movie screen—where it's usually fake—they may never *see* anyone die. Until it's themselves.

So, although I obviously can't say this with certainty, I think death's invisibility, its unfamiliarity "up close and personal," makes it more rather than less frightening to us than it was to earlier generations. Losing a wife in childbirth, losing two or three or four children—or six or seven or *all* of them—to contagions (measles, diphtheria, smallpox, cholera, scarlet fever, whooping cough...), losing a husband to tuberculosis or galloping consumption or a trip and fall under a threshing machine, all were commonplace. (I use the word "losing" in the sense that a loved one is wrenched out of one's life.) Sitting by a bedside clutching a clammy hand, listening to the last gasps, the rattle, watching the rictus slowly harden upon the pale, beloved features... those were the rule rather than the exception. Death was part of life.

This is all really original stuff, no?

Anyway, uninvited and unwelcome, death became part of my life at a comparatively early age. I experienced it as an exceedingly nasty trick—a broken compact between me and God. Which, of course, was ridiculous. And precisely the point when it dawned on me: there was no compact. There was no God. At least None Who made compacts with His— Its—hapless creations. Death was the condition under which we live—the terms set Unilaterally. So the only question is timing. And since we have no control over timing—unless we take the matter into our own hands—the only satisfaction we can derive is from *not* being astonished when the buzzer blares. React with stony disdain. Forewarned is forearmed. It could happen at any moment. You've got to remind yourself constantly of that. Paradoxically, it doesn't make life grimmer, it makes it sweeter. Freer. When you know you're going to lose it you've got nothing to lose.

Although I'll admit there's another, more prevalent, take on that proposition: When you know you're going to lose it you'd better hang on to it for as long as you can.

Well, I'm in no greater hurry than anyone else to

413

shuffle off this endlessly entertaining coil. Still, there is a question of grace, of panache. Desperately *clinging* to what you've got, timorously sequestering it, muffling it up against risk, squealing and puling and scrabbling with white knuckles and dug-in fingernails when you finally sense your grip beginning to slip... that's craven. That's *infra dig*. Wear your life at a jaunty tilt, I say. Carry it mindfully but *loosely*. Don't be afraid to mix a metaphor now and then. To boldly split an infinitive.

I'd recently seen just a little too much of that other viewpoint. And it colored my reaction to the doctor's news.

## First, there was Dan.

Susan's husband, my replacement. Roughly my age—two years older. Over the years, once the kids were in college, she and I had communicated less frequently. We talked on the phone when there was some business to conduct—tuition payments here, consultation on the *angsts* and *faux pas* of youth there, bits of need-to-know news to relay from an excited conversation with a maturing Becca or Chris. Susan and I had lunch together a couple of times a year when she came up to the Bay Area to visit them or give a talk. She attended the labor and delivery of all three of our grandchildren; she called me immediately to bubble about how it had gone. Elisabeth and I had our choppy moments and in the bleak depth of those moments I was always tempted to call Susan for commiseration; I didn't, but as time passed we acquired a pretty good sense of the emotional weather, the satisfactions and the rubs, in each other's second marriages. "My new and improved marriage," she once remarked lightly.

"Fuck you," I responded.

I was stung—she hung up on me and we didn't talk for months until I apologized for my intemperate language—but she was right. We were both bettah off. (That was a joky tagline we'd shared for years, after an anecdote in a Herb Caen column: A colorful Chinese restaurant owner in San Francisco invariably gushed to a regular patron about the brains, class and beauty of the wife who always accompanied him. One day the man entered alone. "Where your beautiful wife?" the restaurateur inquired. Sadly the man allowed that she had left him. The restaurateur sniffed, "You bettah off.")

For me, Elisabeth's sense of herself as an artist made us more *simpático*. Or is it *empático?* She validated my writing as Susan never had. Elisabeth *encouraged* me to use my time to eke out fiction—novels that never got published, short stories that rarely did—instead of the journalism that brought checks in the mail. One year the assignments really rolled in and I earned what would have been a decent mid-management salary back when I was a corporate employee. I mentioned it to Susan because I knew she'd react, as she did, with approval for my industry and success; Elisabeth, on the other hand, admitted she thought I was wasting my talent. She actually liked it, or assured me she did, when I read her my morning's painstakingly crafted three or four hundred words as we sipped wine at the end of the day. I'd stopped doing that very early on with Susan, whose attention was so clearly strained and grudging, preoccupied as she was with her own day's exciting business. And although Elisabeth had plenty of vinegar in her temperament—she could be giddy, she could spit nails, she could wilt into brief melancholy—she wasn't given to the weepy, brooding depressions that had overcome Susan with regularity. (I'd tiptoe around, unsure whether to buck her up with solicitude and platitude or just shut up. Was I the cause, an inadequacy on my part? Was it the postpartum letdown after a frenetic project had been concluded? Was it hormonal? I never figured it out. The

415

mood did always swing within a day or two.)

Dan brought things to Susan's "new and improved marriage" I never could. He made good money. He had prestige—in a realm she thoroughly respected. He could appreciate her work at a nuanced level. How much he valued it was a separate question, a source of occasional unease for her. He could be acerbic in his criticisms, she confessed to me. A certain professional jealousy seemed to come out as she gained stature. In fact, she admitted, that was partly what had drawn her to him at the beginning: He was a father figure. His approval fulfilled some childhood lack, a perceived paternal indifference or maybe just a gap in understanding. Extramarital sex was a lagniappe, the currency of esteem. Dan became a father figure and a husband rolled into one. And a dessert topping and a floor wax. I assume he was an adequate, maybe even a superior, lover—not that she ever expressed any dissatisfaction with my attentions. Dan had had no children of his own, and he was happy to assume an uncomplicated backstop role in the parenthood of mine. I have to credit him with tact in that—although maybe a certain fatherly remove is a guy thing anyway. He wasn't as good looking as I am, but she couldn't have everything.

Then he got sick.

I don't know all the details, of course, just the outlines from Susan's group e-mailings and weary telephone accounts. Apparently Dan walked out of his La Jolla office one evening, got into his car and lapsed unconscious. He was found and roused by a security guard; exhaustion, he reasoned. He drove himself home despite a terrible headache—he'd been having them recently—fell into bed and arose next morning feeling slightly better. Still, at Susan's coaxing, he made an appointment to see a doctor. He was referred for tests, which led to more tests... X-rays, needle biopsies, CT scans, a PET scan, claustrophobic insertion into the borborygmic bowel of an MRI.... with increasingly calamitous findings.

Like everyone our age Dan had smoked. Pack of cigarettes a day from high school until about the time he met Susan. Then, like almost everyone our age, he'd tapered off. Like me to zero. Notwithstanding his decades of virtuous abstinence, the X-rays revealed a "mass" in his lungs. His chest was punctured; the sample was malignant. The pathologist classified the carcinoma as oat cell type—the most ravenous kind. And yes, the follow-ups confirmed, it had already spread. He had metastatic hot spots in several lymph nodes and a tumor in his brain.

Half of all patients who receive this diagnosis are dead within four months, he and Susan were told. But aggressive treatment could palliate the impending pain, and at least offer hope of postponing the final extinction. He might be in the lucky half and live another six months. Or eight, or... who knew? He might even be among the fifteen percent of patients with his specific disease profile who achieve long-term survival, Susan wrote.

Meaning, she acknowledged, "> 2 years."

I am in no way faulting Dan—I can understand the choices he was about to make. But I'm not sure, given those prospects and odds, I wouldn't have just tossed in my marbles right then and there. Gimme a sack of doobies and a script for a powerful opiate, doc, and send me home with a good thick book. *War and Peace,* say. Never did get around to reading that.

Sometime between bidding goodbye to Maartje and meeting Elisabeth I jumped high for a rebound on the basketball court and got undercut—presumably by accident. (The guy gushed apologies and he wasn't all that athletic; good players never take an opponent's legs out from under him unless they're retaliating for some egregious foul and are ready to trade punches, or are just mean-spirited assholes like George W. Bush on the intramural courts of

Yale.) The fall was messy. I twisted to land on my humped shoulders but caromed off surrounding hips and legs and struck on my tailbone. I did manage to keep the back of my head from clacking on the asphalt, but the pain that shot through my torso and down my left leg practically knocked me senseless anyway. I lay gawping like a piked fish until a couple of guys with hands extended responded to my nod and hoisted me to my feet. I crab-walked to the sidelines on pride and adrenaline and collapsed supine to recover for a return to action. I figured I'd just had the wind knocked out of me. But when I finally rolled over and tried to rise it was as if I'd been whacked in the small of the back with a baseball bat. (Remember "Peter Pain," by any chance? He was cartoon character in a green leprechaun costume—the little villain in an advertising strip in the Sunday comics of my childhood—who'd sneak up invisibly behind people and take a full two-handed swing with a shillelagh at their lumbar spine. Then some relative or friend would recommend Ben-Gay ointment to the suffering victim, the backache would be magically relieved and Peter Pain's malevolent glee would turn to misanthropic bile once again.)

That was the beginning of the iffy relationship I've endured with L-4 and L-5 ever since. I limped home clutching my bike as a walker— stabbed periodically by an almost paralyzing pain—popped an overdose of ibuprofen, slathered on reeking, peppery liniment, collected an icebag from the freezer, plugged an electric hotpad into the wall socket by my bed and fell onto the mattress with a moan.

I spent most of the next two weeks there. The World Cup had just started and I happened on a first-round match—they were being broadcast almost round-the-clock on the Spanish-language channel. That kept me engrossed and distracted from my swollen vertebrae until the final "*GOOOOOOOOOL! GOL-GOL-GOL! GOLASO! GOLASO! GOOOOOOL!*" I even tuned my ear to spoken Spanish and broadened my vocabulary. (*"Tiro de esquina," "saque de mano."*) So that's what I'd do if I had Dan's diagnosis, I believe: I'd make myself as comfortable as possible... baste shirtless in the warm sunlight at noon without fear of melanoma, snuggle in front of a crackling fire if it's rainy or wintry, read, find sports or old movies to absorb me from among the five thousand channels our basic satellite TV package brings into our receiver, sample a few $100 bottles of wine, smoke weed until I'd tapped into the great cosmic consciousness that ripples at the rim of perception when you're high... and pass gentle into that good night.

Well, it's a pleasant fantasy, isn't it? Leaves out the sordid details—the bone-pain, the nausea, the delirium, the incontinence... although maybe if I was lucky they'd shoot me up with enough morphine to keep me oblivious. Great parting gift, though, great last memories I'd be offering Elisabeth.

Dan took a different course. He wangled enrollment in an ultra-experimental clinical trial—being at Scripps he had access, of course, to medical care as sophisticated as any in the world. Despite forewarning that the effects would be debilitating physically and, quite possibly, mentally—and would improve his odds of survival (that two-year goal) only infinitesimally—he began high-dose chemotherapy with a combination of new, caustic drugs. He had his brain irradiated. He was adamant that he was "going to beat this thing," Susan wrote.

He was dead within seven weeks. And the treatments had immediately reduced him to a shambling, somnolent, burnt-out, semi-coherent shell.

Poor Susan. The cure had almost certainly been worse than the cancer. With no different result.

# So that was Dan.

At the funeral, Rebecca told me, he was extolled for his courage—he was a fighter to the end, everyone said. Elisabeth's father too fought to the end... or at least hung onto the ropes, alternately railing and whimpering, terrified of going down for the count.

Ben was his name—Benjamin. With an ingrained deference to elders (laughably—I was already middle-aged myself when I met him) I found it uncomfortably familiar to address him as "Ben." He was "Dad" to Elisabeth; I sometimes called him that too, although with an underlying sense of betrayal of my own father (who dropped dead of a heart attack, bim-bam, only a little older than I am now; way to go, Dad). Mostly I just cleared my throat loudly and stared at Ben pointedly whenever I was trying to get his attention.

Ben had his own heart problems. And over the years he'd received virtually every treatment on the cardiology menu, from simple nitroglycerin after the first angina attacks to a pace-maker, open-heart surgery, angioplasty and a couple of coronary artery bypass grafts, not to mention the doggy-bagfuls of potent pharmaceuticals he always took home after an operation—beta-blockers, calcium channel blockers, digoxin, diuretics, heparin, blood thinners, nitrates, ARBs and ACE inhibitors, antiarrhythmics... who knows what? As a generously health-insured faculty member at the Stanford Medical Center's parent institution, he, like Dan, enjoyed carte-blanche to browse the salad bar of advanced interventions. He might as well have had Velcro strips sewn to his chest. God knows how many hundreds of thousands of dollars—perhaps close to a million?—had been invested in sustaining this single upper-middle-class American until he could snatch the oxygen tube out of his nostrils long enough to wheeze obediently into the sixteen candle-flames on his last birthday cake, his eighty-eighth.

Elisabeth's mother had lived into her eighties too. Dorothy—known as Dot to intimates. She'd developed late-onset diabetes, which may have contributed, according to a recent hypothesis, to the Alzheimer's dementia that ultimately overwhelmed her. Ben took care of her at their Palo Alto home for as long as he could before she disappeared into the fog. He'd retired, an emeritus writing his sixth book—on John Jay and the anti-federalists. (Objections to a centralized government and early debate over the Constitution had been his specialty. Like most conservatives he had a love-hate relationship with the Bill of Rights.) When even live-in assistance became inadequate Dot was moved to a skilled nursing facility.

I visited her there with Elisabeth a couple of times. I'd been introduced to the couple, Ben and Dot, when they were not quite into their seventies. Both were still extraordinarily vital then: skiers, back-packers, adventure-travelers who made us envious with their perky postcards from Kenya, the Turquoise Coast, the Taj Mahal, the Galápagos.

The first time I saw Dot in her pleasant room in the Alzheimer's SNF she was lucid and bubbly; she had no idea who I was, of course, and there were moments when I wondered whether she really knew who Elisabeth was, but she was aware enough of her confusions to mask them adeptly under polite forms. The last time I saw her she lay huddled in her bed, knobby bones in a loose pouch of wizened skin, mumbling strange, random, hallucinatory phrases in response to the halting questions we posed out of duty to connect, or try to. It was pitiful. It was wrenching—to see a human life so reduced. All the more so for Elisabeth, needless to say. And it would get worse. Eventually Dot lost the ability to speak, to hold a spoon, to drink from a cup, finally to swallow. Yet still, intubated at Ben's insistence, she breathed and shat. Even for Elisabeth, I think, the call from her sobbing father telling us Dot had "passed away" the previous night was actually welcome, a relief. Other than as a kind of protoplasmic life-form she had drifted over the horizon long, long ago.

I attended her memorial service and dutifully stood up with the others to stammer an extemporaneous remembrance. Upbeat, of course: about how witty she'd been, a woman who liked to confide raunchy jokes with an air of refined innocence, as if she didn't quite understand the punch line—belied by the salty chuckle that followed after a pause, and the fact that she usually had a cigarette in one hand and a bourbon-on-the-rocks in the other. She always joked of anything unpleasant that it was "a dirty Communist plot." I found that amusing, charming. Ben would have meant it if he'd said it (I didn't mention that, of course); she was quietly having him and his ilk on.

Ben stumbled around the house alone in Palo Alto for a couple of years until the ambulance trips to the emergency room accumulated. Clearly he needed closer supervision. He'd burnt his hands badly when a pot he'd forgotten on the stove caught fire. He'd neglected to use his inhaler and had twice had panic attacks in the middle of the night—"I couldn't breathe! I thought I was dying!" he wailed. And to be sure he was. But we couldn't just tell him as much. He was in the tightening grip of congestive heart failure. He'd fallen twice, luckily with no worse damage than cuts and huge, garish bruises. He'd probably experienced adverse interactions among the confusing array of drugs he'd been prescribed by various specialists.

Elisabeth was an only child. She convinced her father to sell the big empty house in Palo Alto and move to a well regarded assisted living community for "seniors" near us in Mendocino. Getting him resettled was as much fun as you would imagine. Now I could watch him at near hand as he raged—or rather bellyached—against the dying of the light.

It wasn't pretty. He hated being weaned from the glistening high-tech medical amenities and "leading authorities" he'd grown used to having at his immediate disposal at Stanford. Medical care had become his reason for living. He'd joined listservs on the internet to commiserate with and pick the brains of fellow sufferers from conditions he was sure he had or might have, if only his doctors were more competent at diagnosis. He'd been in a couple of fender-benders—nothing serious but his own fault and embarrassing... enough to shake his confidence in his twilight- and peripheral vision. Although he refused to surrender his license he agreed to park the car more or less permanently. He constantly importuned Elisabeth to drive him to Santa Rosa to see some presumptively bigger shot than the humble listing of physicians in the local yellow pages offered, or to get himself admitted to a larger hospital for a more thorough workup than the little twenty-five-bed Coast District Hospital in Fort Bragg was equipped to lavish on his latest symptom.

Not that he wasn't perfectly well cared for the few times he did have to spend a night or two there as an inpatient. Even Ben conceded, grudgingly, that the nurses were far more attentive than at the big anonymous institutions he truly respected. But he devalued solicitude as merely compensation for lack of expertise. "Loving hands at home," he growled dismissively.

His primary care physician was a woman—an internist with a subspecialty in geriatrics who was Elisabeth's doctor too. It was Ben's first experience with a woman physician; initially he'd doubted her capabilities because of her sex, but her warm manner had soon won him over, giving him a new incentive to plead the necessity of a visit. He also liked his cardiologist, who divided his practice between Santa Rosa and the coast one day a week. The man was a Stanford alum, thus to Ben a respectable clinician *de facto*, and he shared his patient's disdain for "Democrat" policies. (It was a usage, the insultingly truncated noun-as-adjective, Ben enjoyed galling me with.) The problem, Ben complained, was that he needed to be seen much more often and spontaneously than once a week.

## He claimed still to be working on his book.

There was no evidence except a few scribbled notes on the top sheets of lined legal pads we sometimes found on the arm of his couch or fallen between the cushions a day or two after a pep-talk by Elisabeth. The source books piled next to his computer never changed position. His conversations seldom included references to anything intellectual; mostly they were just reports on the intimate workings of his own body—the color of his sputum or the phlegm he'd coughed up that morning, the consistency of his latest bowel movement... thanks for sharing—and repetition of the right-wing obsession of the moment that had infiltrated his brain through talk radio or Fox News. His reading had apparently narrowed to medical web sites and, from time to time, the op-ed pages of the *Wall Street Journal,* which he still got by mail. (Elisabeth brought it to him daily after one or the other of us visited the post office to check his box along with ours.) His eyesight had gotten so bad, he complained, that reading was difficult except in snatches.

By day the TV set in front of his couch flickered constantly, the Fox News stable of ranters his company, his pseudo-human contact. By night the radio muttered at his bedside. Doctor appointments were the events of his days—why not? They offered the spice of anticipation—a chance to dress up in something smarter than the track suit and laceless tennis shoes he shuffled around in during his waking hours at home; a venture into the outside world on an errand of significance; an opportunity to talk about his symptoms to someone who had invited the gush and would listen patiently. And the settings were pleasant. His primary care doctor's office was on Main Street, with a big window in the waiting room that looked out on the churning ocean, and examination rooms lit by sunlight splashing off an interior courtyard hung with flowering plants. Even the cardiologist's office and the hospital in treeless Fort Bragg were bright and sparkly in the salt-wind. He wasn't into gardening. Elisabeth had given up trying to take him on recreational outings she thought he might enjoy—he didn't. And he made no bones about it.

So here was this really bright man, an intellectual in his prime, a former college professor, scholar and author... whose interests had narrowed to the tawdry ephemera of party-line politics and, even more, the minutest signs of the degradation of his organs. Since medical science had kept him alive to this point he was convinced there was a treatment that would cure him of whatever ailed him—if they'd just get to the bottom of it. For a smart man he'd become remarkably childish in his inability to comprehend or unwillingness to accept that, rounding on the age of ninety, his component parts were approaching the limits of built-in obsolescence.

"I don't understand why I get so out-of-breath sometimes," he'd pant.

"Are you using your inhaler?" Elisabeth would inquire. "Are you using your oxygen?"

"I just don't have any energy," he'd parry. "I must not be getting enough iron. I couldn't sleep last night. My heartbeat was very irregular. And then it started pounding. I probably need a VAD. They need to put me on the transplant list."

Elizabeth would shake her head. "I'm not sure that at your age...."

"They can't do transplants *here*," he'd sneer, oblivious. "I'd have to go back to the Peninsula for that...."

"Dad...," Elisabeth would soothe him. "You're tired because you're... because you've lived a long time, you know? It's just natural you don't have the stamina you did when you were a twenty-year-old. You have to accept it. And when you get short of breath you're supposed to use your oxygen, remember?"

"No. This is different. There's something wrong with me."

"Well *of course* there is! You're eighty-seven years old! But you're doing amazingly well! Look at you! Mom would have told you to count your blessings."

Tears began to trickle down his rutted cheeks. "I don't want to go on like this. Sometimes I think I ought to just die."

It was a risible comment: He still regarded death as optional.

And when the telephone rang at our bedside at three in the morning—Ben whimpering that he needed to go to the emergency room immediately—it was obvious he had no intention of letting the inevitable take place anywhere but in an ICU. He had signed a do-not-resuscitate order—not without misgivings.

"Do you really want to be kept on life support no matter what, Dad?" Elisabeth had confronted him after he initially refused. "Do you really want to be hooked up to a bunch of machines at the end? If you're no longer conscious, and there's no hope you're ever going to come out of it with any kind of... 'quality of life?'" She'd done her reading.

"I don't want to be in pain," Ben said. "That's all. I've had my share and I can take it, but...."

"I know. Don't worry, you'll still get all the pain relief

you need," she assured him. "They'll do everything they can to keep you comfortable. You won't be giving up 'comfort care,' see?"

He slumped beside her, his oxygen clips in his nostrils, the tank clacking softly with each breath. She tapped the pertinent phrases on the form with her fingertip.

"All a DNR means is that if your heart finally stops beating, or if you stop breathing, they won't start pounding on your chest.... they won't zap you with a defibrillator... they won't shove a tube down your throat for a mechanical ventilator... they won't pump 'cardiotonic' drugs into you.... Wouldn't you rather go... wouldn't you rather be at peace, when you...?"

"Look," he said, voice firming. "I know perfectly well what's on a DNR. People have been shoving those things under my nose for years. I'm not completely senile."

"Sometimes you make me wonder."

"My heart's stopped and started up more times than you can count, don't you think? My chest's been whacked and zapped and sawn open... thank God! That's why I'm still around! I'm not sure I want to just sign away the possibility altogether now."

"So don't. It's your decision. We'll honor it."

"No. Here, I'll sign it. I don't want you to be stuck with me if I'm a vegetable."

He died in the Coast District hospital. Not in the ICU. Elisabeth and I were at his side listening to his last stentorian gasps. He'd been awake after lunch, talking about when he might go home. He'd murmured feebly about the possibility of a heart transplant. Then he'd dozed off. We went to Harvest Market to do some shopping and came back for a quick look-in. He hadn't roused. He was unresponsive. His breathing became more labored, a desperate sucking for air as if he were drowning. Which he was, in fact, his own fluids filling the last interstices of his lungs. Elisabeth worried that he was in pain. The doctor said no, but after a while agreed to give him a low-dose shot of morphine.

He quieted immediately. Forever.

## There's a lot to be said for construction work.

Except for swimming and walks on the headlands—and a little tennis, and the occasional ski trip, and every now and then a Sunday afternoon pickup basketball game in Comptche... well, building and repairing stuff is still the principal exercise I get these days. Alone it would be more than enough.

When Susan and I were first married I couldn't have told you what lay behind the surface of a wall. It hadn't occurred to me to wonder. My father had prided himself on avoiding manual labor—understandable, I guess, for a man with a profession, the first in his family line to have gone to college. Not that he was transcending blue-collar expectations; his father and uncle had run a small dry goods store they'd managed to buy when the owner my Dad's Dad had clerked for died. You'd have to go back another generation to find a Schubert who worked with his hands: my great-great-great grandfather, the first Schubert to leave Bavaria for America—according to the 1850 Cincinnati census, a shoemaker.

I don't know if my father, the pampered only son, had ever so much as pushed a lawnmower. (He'd been plenty physical when it came to sports, he just didn't seem to care for sweating non-recreationally.) I do know he never pushed one after I was tall enough to reach the handlebars. Cutting the grass in our front and side yards was my weekly summer chore, for which I was paid a quarter. I got another dime for scrubbing the little hexagonal bathroom floor tiles on

Saturdays after swimming or tennis lessons. I'm happy to say as an adult I've never lived in a house with a lawn or a bathroom.

Okay, the first is true.

If snow needed shoveling, if the car needed washing, if weeds needed pulling or fence slats needed painting, either I or Paul did it. (And Paul was a master at evading chores.) If a drain clogged, if something motorized sputtered or if an appliance went "on the fritz"—his technical assessment—my father called in a professional. Even flat tires were changed by Triple-A. I'd probably have followed the same pattern if I hadn't been infected by the countercultural values that inspired the Whole Earth Catalog. I remember as a reporter hearing Mario Savio urge effete students disillusioned with the system to learn self-reliance, to roll up their sleeves and gain the practical skills that would allow them to drop out of mass society and seize the levers of technology. Or something like that. The village of Mendocino owes its reincarnation in the nineteen-seventies to artists and communards who responded to that nascent back-to-the-land *zeitgeist*. And it had resonated with me. I was ashamed to acknowledge to myself, then, that I couldn't fix *anything*.

It was about that time that Susan and I bought our first little house, and before long she was pregnant with Matty. Matt-Matt Magoo. Matthew  Kirkpatrick Schubert, for long—MKS on the sterling silver baby cup Anne and my father gave us and that he barely got to slurp from... our monkey-faced, twinkly-eyed first-born with the fatally botched heart. Susan's mother once mused aloud that perhaps the defect could be traced to my having experimented with LSD. Experimented! But maybe once was enough to have cracked my chromosomes. Or perhaps it was Susan's fault for having sipped at a passed joint on rare social occasions while she was pregnant. But then, we'd both drunk martinis before dinner every night until the onset of labor. (At least

I hadn't blown any second-hand tobacco smoke at her; she didn't like the stench inside the house.)

I'm not aware of an increased incidence of congenital deformities for all the barbarous prenatal practices of that age. And postnatal. It's amazing any of our children survived the dangers and neglect my generation subjected them to. No car seats; no lap-belts on high-chairs; babies napping in the back seat of locked car parked in front of the restaurant where their parents were enjoying a meal unaccompanied by squalling. Becca and Chris chuckle tolerantly but you can tell they don't have a lot of sympathy for the *laissez faire* child-rearing practices I recount to them from the Pleistocene. Their kids were born healthy. They haven't yet had reason to doubt the ability of earnest parents to shield children from catastrophe.

To tell the truth, I don't think about Matty very often. His ten months on earth were too short and too fraught to compete in memory with the everyday in-your-faceness of two large-as-life, normal, maturing siblings. Not that I mean to relegate him to the abnormal, or the subnormal—the fact is, though, that Susan one day observed that taking care of infant Becca, for all the typical vicissitudes of her babyhood, was a piece of cake by comparison. None of that constant heaviness of heart, none of the low-level anxiety of trying to soothe Matty's fretfulness, no agonizing over his discomfort if not pain—what frame of reference do babies have?—no shuttling back and forth to stew in waiting rooms for news to come down from the surgical suite at Oakland Children's Hospital. The state, more generous back then, paid all the bills; we could have sent him anywhere—Johns Hopkins, Denton Cooley's Texas Heart Institute—but our pediatric cardiologist expressed confidence in local expertise if that's what we chose. We did. Wrongly? Who knows?

Periodically, as repairs allowed more oxygen to reach his lungs, Matty pinked up and suckled with vigor. But well meaning ICU nurses had habituated him to pacifiers dipped in honey, and bottles with soft preemie nipples were usually more suited to his nursing capability than Susan's swelling breasts. It wasn't all worry and gloom, though. He laughed, grabbed at rattles, gurgled, drooled as he teethed, wriggled on the floor... when he died I subsumed my sense of loss in a poem listing in free verse all the things I could think of that gave him pleasure: "Matt-Matt Magoo/knew what he liked/ and as far we know, he liked what he knew./He liked...."

I wish I could remember now what I wrote.

Susan gasped and erupted in wracking sobs when the surgeon, still in greens, booties and floppy cap, solemnly informed us that they'd been unable to bring Matty around after the last procedure. It caught me by surprise. But I couldn't say I was astonished. To tell the truth, again, I felt a certain relief. Maybe, terrible to say it, I'd even hoped for such an outcome. Although tetralogy of Fallot seems now to be largely correctible, it was a thoroughly dispiriting diagnosis for a parent in that decade. It meant, we were told, that Matty would always be physically frail, always smaller than other kids his age, he'd be unable to play vigorously or to participate in sports, and he'd have to undergo regular hospitalizations and surgeries... until he died at, on average, the age of about thirteen. How's that for a prognosis? Better all around, I—callously, selfishly—concluded, that Matty had slipped away before he could know and Susan and I endure such a bleak arc.

We reeled home to the little house where the empty crib would never again hold our burbling infant Matthew, and next day consigned his tiny remains to a funeral home that promised to scatter his ashes from a plane over the Pacific Ocean. Susan, who'd borne him, took months to emerge from mourning. Eventually, as a distraction, we spent two months traveling in Europe. She half-heartedly explored appointments to research facilities and I came up blank on writing jobs for expatriate Americans. In a fourth-floor walkup in a peeling hotel on the Rue du Sommerard, in Paris's Cinquième, we conceived Rebecca. We made friends with a few Americans our age (everyone we met was from New York or the Bay Area, drawn like moths to the flame of student revolt that still simmered in the streets around the Sorbonne). We wrapped our necks in scarves, popped roasted chestnuts and crèpes bought from curbside vendors, huddled in steamy basement restaurants touted in the dog-eared pages of our *Europe on Five Dollars a Day*, but the November chill of Paris was too much for my BelAir-bred bride. (Try saying that three times fast.) We rode a bus to Luxembourg and flew back to the States on Icelandic, open bar and one-stop through Reykjavik.

With a baby again on the way, we knew from experience we really ought to have another bedroom. As a birthday present Susan's father sent up a pair of carpenters from his company to get the project started and, over two long weekends, they tutored me in form-building and framing. I wasn't altogether enthusiastic about taking on this worrisomely ambitious chore, but I was a solicitous young husband and I liked the idea of doing a man's work. It's not rocket science. With the help of an illustrated carpentry textbook and my mentors' tips—flex your wrist and let the hammerhead do the work when you drive a sixteen-penny nail; if you misstrike and need to pull a bent nail, rock the hammer sideways and work the nail loose rather than straining to jerk it straight out by main force; here's how you use a framing square to pattern the bird's-mouth in a rafter or mark the tread and rise on a stair stringer; you can quickly notch a two-by-four by making a series of close parallel cuts to the desired depth with your power-saw, then knock and scrape the wafers out with the claw of your hammer—I got competent enough at wood butchery to satisfy the building inspectors.

Rather than the nemeses I expected them to be, they too became allies and advisors. In fact, they began swinging by periodically to cheer on our progress and volunteer suggestions. One even brought us odd materials, like a set of rough-hewn corbels from a demolition site: "I don't know," he shrugged, "I thought you might like these." For most of these crusty former-tradesmen-turned-minor-municipal-bureaucrats, we were their first experience with the new wave of hippie do-it-yourselfers. Between my eager-to-please naiveté and my pretty young wife's big eyes, flowing hair, micro-miniskirt and bulging stomach, we had them clucking over us like paternal roosters.

So that's what started it. Next thing I knew Susan was drawing up a more ambitious addition based on her collection of articles ripped from *Sunset* magazine. Eventually the plans included two stories with a sky-lit master bedroom and bath upstairs, a new bathroom with sunken tiled tub downstairs and a bedroom for the second baby we foresaw in our near future. We had no money, really, just Susan's modest salary and some income I'd bring in sporadically from free-lance gigs. It was enough to buy materials on a just-in-time basis—and the labor was free. The one thing I had to contribute in abundance was time. And an afternoon of physical work is a perfect complement to a morning at a desk stringing together sentences on a legal pad. (Mostly I wrote in longhand—scratching out, erasing, substituting *mots plus justes* for *mots moins justes,* inserting new clauses and paragraphs until the mess was illegible, then starting fresh and only typing up the final manuscript for rejection by editors and agents. It was easier than scrubbing and scribbling on a typewriter platen—a word for that roller-thingy I had to look up, it's been so long. Nowhere has the advent of the computer been more welcome and revolutionary than in the scrivener's trade.)

By the time Christopher was squalling in his

bassinette I could frame, roof, run electrical cable and galvanized pipe, wire outlets and switches, set toilets, sweat copper fittings, lay tongue-and-groove oak flooring, hang cabinets and tackle without fear just about any challenge building, renovating or maintaining a house throws at you. On weekends and vacations Susan pitched in too. We'd park tiny Becca safely in the deep tub surrounded by toys while I scampered on scaffolding or squirmed under sink-drains and Susan set tile, grouted, taped and textured sheetrock or painted.

These days you can find a schematic or an instructional video clip on practically anything you need to know or have forgotten—like how to connect the legs of a four-way switch—on the internet. Back then we had to consult the diagrams in one of the pulpy D-I-Y booklets we'd pick up from a rack at the hardware store or what I came to call my home away from home, Truitt & White, Berkeley's best lumberyard. I even bought the *Compleat Idiot's* guide to Volkswagen repair and for the first time in my life delved into the greasy innards of an engine compartment to adjust the valves on the used camper that had replaced my battered, tattered bug when it died. My father smiled thinly when I described my new virtuosity; it bemused him, like writing fiction without an advance. That was the zenith of my car repair experience, I might add. I remain baffled by anything more complicated than the simple VW engine. My brief faculty stood me in good stead, however, when I had to replace a broken fan belt in the Sonora desert on our first excursion after Christopher was born.

I maintained my calluses for most of the intervening years. Without the goad of a female companion I slacked off a bit during my interlude as a single homeowner. Still, by habit—because I could—I built a nice redwood deck at the rear of my cottage where I wrote *en plein air* when it wasn't rainy or cold. And a house, like a human body, is a structure in constant decay. (God damn entropy.) The former has the advantage of being a Newtonian collection of discrete parts that can be repaired or replaced indefinitely to preserve or expand the integrity of the whole. We've tried hard but we haven't gotten there yet with organisms, interlaced as they are by invisible feedback loops—even gene-splicing can have unforeseen and undesirable side effects. But I digress. The point is: I was never at a loss for fix-it jobs to keep my hand in.

When I moved in with Elisabeth I gradually resumed the role of architectural enabler. Hers to propose an improvement, mine to dispose. The house belonged to her. She still paid the mortgage, although we pooled our finances and informally split the bills. Sweat equity was the least I could contribute to the "shelter" column on the balance sheet. For a long time I was reluctant to suggest changes because they might imply criticism, dissatisfaction with a habitat she'd grown comfortable in and I had no problem adapting to. Also, did I really want to volunteer for a lot of gratuitous labor? But it turned out she was full of pent-up ideas. She'd always thought it would be nice to have a balcony cantilevered off the upstairs bedroom facing east, with double doors you could throw open on warm summer mornings—go outside in your bathrobe with a cup of coffee, she pictured, to inhale the warm, fragrant sunlight rising over the treetops of the Mendocino Woodlands. So I built one for her. A deck and French doors along the west side of the house would be a natural extension of the small dining room, she suggested—a place to sit on fine evenings and watch the disc of the setting sun redden and fade behind the high tendrils of offshore fog. Sounded good to me. I built it.

Then we put in a greenhouse. And a pergola. And a new chicken house to replace the one a bear ripped apart one night. (Three of the six chickens survived.) Lately I'd been busy resuscitating Elisabeth's ramshackle studio.

## But decks are probably my favorite.

You're working out in the fresh air, there's room to swing your arms, it's new construction so you don't have to improvise problematic tie-ins and workarounds. You're sawing and assembling aromatic redwood—sustainably harvested, of course, which means by a timber company that isn't out raping the old-growth forest. (Recycled's even better if you can find it and afford it. I approve in principle some of the alternative eco-friendly synthetic materials, but natural wood is my indulgence as long as it's available in reasonably good conscience.) And you can put together everything in a deck with screws and bolts, so if you have second thoughts or adjustments to make (okay, mistakes to correct) you can undo what needs redoing without destructive application of a pry-bar. It's kind of like writing on a computer versus a typewriter.

Deck-building gives you the opportunity to exercise creativity—in the design, the size, the structure's harmony with the architecture of the house and the terrain, and the amount of embellishment you put into railings, posts, built-in benches and the like. I take time to chamfer the bottoms of posts where they attach to the deck-beam. Same with the free-standing tops. I like to miter rail caps and use wide one-by-six planks as balusters, notched in Arts-and-Craftsy, Swiss chalet style—very Berkeley. I like to run a jig-saw blade set at a forty-five-degree angle along the edges of posts unevenly, so they look as if they'd been dressed by a hand-adze. I like to use big, malleable iron washers, like rosettes, that rust under exposed hex bolts. And I like a canopy overhead, a loggia of two-by-sixes with fluted ends set on edge like rafters to support the sky, all entwined after a few years by the gnarled runners of climbing plants like grapes or honeysuckle or hops. Rustic, to me, is the effect *nec plus ultra.*

Which is convenient, because it's an adjective you can use to counter other assessments like "clumsy" or "slapdash."

You can throw up a nice deck comparatively quickly. There's not much delay to gratification. And unlike plumbing, say—which I'm now in position to pay someone else to deal with—the frustration index is low. The closest I've ever come to true existential despair was the afternoon I sweated the last tee on the labyrinth of copper pipes that supplied the bathrooms in my first major project—eagerly anticipating Susan's pleasure when she came home from the lab and I turned on a tap to demonstrate my triumphal *fait accompli.*

I had shut off the water at the main so I could tie into the existing lines; I walked outside to open the valve and returned to admire my handiwork. I was confronted by dozens of tiny hissing sprays from pinholes in the joints I'd so painstakingly soldered. I spent the next several hours trekking back and forth to turn off the water, drain the lines, train the tip of the blue flame from my little propane canister-torch on the leaky fitting to melt loose the solder that had failed to take. I would work the pipe and connector apart, dry and wipe away the old solder coat (rasping skin off my knuckles as I fumbled in the cramped space between studs or ceiling rafters), then brush on flux, reassemble the joint and heat the copper on both sides until it darkened and shimmered and the flux sizzled—hot enough for the fitting to suddenly suck in the molten solder from the silver coil whose tail-end I dabbed gently around the socket. All the while trying not to set the house on fire.

Over and over I did this, waiting until the work

cooled and then turning on the water to test my repairs. Some of them took on the first try. Some on the second or third. A few never. At twilight I slumped exhausted, utterly disheartened, moaning, on the verge of tears. The back of my throat was raw from barking out thwarted rage and howling absurd repetitions of every obscenity the paltry American vocabulary has to offer. My shirt was soaked. My fingertips were blackened and blistered from impatiently grabbing hot copper too soon. My vision had tunneled. The job was impossible, beyond me. I had failed. Life had no meaning. All my previous work was for naught. The house might as well be demolished. I'd ruined it. There was no way out.

Well, of course there was. After a little rest and Susan's soothing commiseration—plus a martini—I remembered and reconciled myself to the expedient of calling a plumber. The guy came out a couple of days later with a more formidable torch and did, although not without difficulty, get the recalcitrant joints to seal.

There are important lessons in that experience.

The primary one, for me, was to let somebody else have the fun of plumbing.

And I suppose if that's the closest I've come to real despair in my lifetime I'm either a very fortunate or a very shallow man. Certainly the former is true. It's a lucky human being who gets to live seven decades without ever having endured hunger or serious illness, deadly violence, the ravages of war... never maimed, never imprisoned, never impoverished... one could say never tested, but I suspect the assertion that one's character is improved in the crucible of extreme misfortune is just a way of putting a good face on a lousy draw. Sure, I've pulled a couple of low cards, but— except for Matty—they've been like, what, eights? And I can't just say they were all dealt by fate, either. I look at my hand and mostly it's jacks or better.

And yes, I guess I am a shallow man. It's the

simple stuff that keeps me happy. Food, drink, female companionship, sex, reading, writing, physical exertion, whether at play or at labor. I'm more into process than accomplishment. Means over ends. To be sure I value skill—the ability to succeed at what one attempts. When I drop a ball, both figuratively and literally, I'm keenly disappointed in myself. Setbacks annoy me. To put it mildly—as Susan and Elizabeth... and my kids, indeed anybody who knows me...would emphasize. They've seen me throw tantrums, hurl tools, go momentarily berserk when I'm balked by an unexpected complication. It's not an attractive trait. I think I've managed to damp it somewhat as I've gotten older. Still, as both my wives have observed, I tend to work mad. Angry. What's that about?

Well, seems to me it's a combination of innate laziness and low-stakes fear. I resent the imposition on my leisure of the task I'm engaged in, and at some level I blame the person whose good regard I'm seeking when I undertake it at her bidding. Which is the underlying motivation in my mind, whether or not she actually did the bidding. And yes, almost invariably it's "she," "her." (Probably that's why I didn't do as much work on my own house when I lived alone as I might have.) Every snag that brings me up short or trips me in the course of a project proves that my dubiety going in, my suspicion that I'd be inadequate, was well founded. Who wouldn't be testy at that prospect?

Carpentry is similar to sport. It requires hand-eye coordination, strength, balance, nerve. I still find myself muscling four-by-eight plywood panels up ladders in a crosswind. Clean-and-jerking ten-foot four-by-twelve beams into place overhead. Tippy-toeing across open rafters twenty feet above the ground. There's that edge of danger, of risk, that makes all true sport exhilarating. (Is golf a true sport? I guess so, to the extent that you could get conked by an errant drive. Fishing? Curling? I suppose you could drown or slip and crack your head on the ice. But they're namby-pamby pastimes compared to construction work. Let your attention wander when you're ripping a board on a table saw and you can easily slice off a finger or get impaled by a kickback. Hold a hair-trigger nailgun carelessly and you might shoot a sinker into your brain.)

So how come I didn't approach sports with the same subliminal resentment I feel for plumbing, wiring or carpentry? Nowhere are the boundaries of one's ineptitude more regularly showcased than on a court or a playing field. Even the greatest stars have off nights. They score forty-two points but clank the last-second potential game-winner off the rim. They hit three homers and then whiff in the crucial bases-loaded, two-outs, bottom-of-the-ninth at-bat. That's why a lot of people play mad. Although maybe what we call "mad," or "angry," is just "intense." Focused to a hot pinpoint. I could be intense, to a degree, but when I actually did play mad I just fell apart. In my version it wasn't a constructive emotion. Maybe that's why I've never been a champion. In anything. Just adequate. Better than average, I flatter myself. Just good enough to feel good about myself. Which is enough, no?

So. I have this love-hate thing with construction work. On the negative side it's tiring, challenging and often frustrating. On the positive side it's tiring, challenging and usually rewarding. You're absorbed—mind and hands kept busy assembling or preserving something solid, something that, thanks to you, will live on in the material world. It's a little victory. It's like going into the record books. Of course, just as that record will soon enough be eclipsed and disappear from memory, what you build will eventually burn down, or collapse in an earthquake, or be eaten by termites, or rot with damp, or splinter under the demolition hammer to be used as kindling and replaced by somebody else's concept and labor. Just as the children you sire may die without offspring. Or their children, your grandchildren, may be barren and your line and all memory of you gutter out.

In fact, that fifty-year-old cottage and the soaring addition Susan and I lavished so much energy on, where both our children were born, was razed to the ground in the huge Oakland hills wildfire of 1991. We'd long since moved, of course, our lives taken their divergent courses. But I went to scuff through the ashes—other people's ashes by then—a few weeks later. Even the concrete foundation we'd poured and the tiles we'd lovingly lined the sunken tub with—baby Becca's playpen—had vanished, devoured by the raging heat.

*Sic transit gloria mundi.*

## I never did go in for that biopsy.

I mulled it for several weeks as I completed a writing assignment and installed the new sliding patio door in Elisabeth's studio. The possibility, the likelihood, even, that one has a clump of malignant cells festering in one's fundament is, to be sure, unsettling. But I always returned to the basic proposition that something inside you... *everything* inside you... is inexorably wearing out, going bad, curdling, clotting, liquefying, hardening, misfiring, mutating... slowly turning against you in some clandestine way that sooner or later, depending on how efficiently the subsystem decompensates, will be listed as your cause of death.

The human body is a masterpiece of organization and synergy. But it's only wetware, after all, Jell-O: within, say, a hundred and twenty years absolute max—fifty-two divisions is the limit our cells are allotted, according to Hayflick—the parts will have dissolved once again into the encompassing molecular soup.

Do you want to know which part is melting fastest? Which part has already become infested with slavering zombie cells juiced on the telomerase that will allow them to divide and conquer forever until they've suicidally consumed the host and every other part within reach? Well, *sure*, if the doctors can fix it! Sure, if they can saturate the ailing part with poisonous chemicals or riddle it with radioactive particles that will pick off *only* the cannibal zombie cells... no, realistically, at best *mostly* the cannibal zombie cells.

Sure, you want to know which part is infested with pathogens if the docs can neatly slice away the rotten spots or cleanly pluck out the whole sick organ without severing vital lines of communication among its functional partners. All that wondrous synergy that's your human glory means the bullets they fire into you had better be magic. But there are damn few of those in the medical bandolier, unfortunately. If any. None that I'm aware of for prostate cancer.

"What did he say?" Elizabeth asked after I'd hung up the phone. I hadn't kept it secret that I'd gone in for a second PSA test.

I acknowledged the news.

"*How* high?"

"Would it mean anything to you if I said a number?" I was feeling self-protective, a little prickly. I wanted to keep her concern at arm's length. I didn't want it to infect me. This was *my* problem. To own on *my* terms.

At the same time I now had a victim card to play. There's always a temptation to bid for sympathy.

"I've done some reading," she said.

"You care about me, huh?"

"I do. Was it over ten?"

"Nope."

She waited a beat for more precision.

"Okay, so you don't want to tell me."

"Eight," I said. The sympathy impetus.

"Well. That's not... terrible. Is it? I mean, it's still well within the gray zone. Right? What's he say you ought to do?"

"He suggested a biopsy."

"Hm. So when would you do it?"

"I don't know. You heard what I told him. I said I'd have to think about it."

We were lucky in that we had good health insurance. So that wasn't a concern. We were both on Medicare, and Elisabeth's inheritance from her father had allowed us to buy a generous Medi-gap policy.

"When are you going in for your biopsy?" she kept pestering me throughout the week.

"Couple of days or so, probably," I temporized.

"You need to get it done right away!" she insisted finally. "They can *treat* prostate cancer. Especially if they catch it early."

"So they say," I nodded. "You've read up on it. Did you pay attention to the treatments? What they are and what the side effects are? How do you feel about impotence?"

"Oh...."

"No, that's a huge one!"

"Well, I'd rather have you alive...."

"Than fucking? I appreciate the sentiment, but I've grown quite fond of our bimonthly slap-and-tickle."

"Bimonthly...," she bristled.

"Kidding," I said. The fact was we made love more or less weekly. Not quite a metronomic beat, but close. And we both got what we wanted. For my part I might have preferred to sidle closer, to send the signals, a little more frequently. But rebuff's a downer for both parties. I was content to follow her rhythm—and when I wasn't I could always wait till she went to bed, then flip on one of the soft-porn programs that loop through the early night on the premium channels. Self-reliance is an Emersonian, a quintessentially American virtue. Pull yourself up by

443

your own.... True, my erections were no longer as sturdy as they'd once been. But that didn't make me any readier to consign sex to history. A few months before, I'd even gotten a prescription from Jacobs for a booster pill, a mere quarter of which popped a few minutes before an assignation made me reliably "strrrong like bool." (That's a piece of dialogue that has stuck with me from a television series about the Roman Empire, spoken by a winsome young prostitute, a slave from Dalmatia, dissembling after the fact on behalf of the profoundly uninterested teenaged Octavius, who'd been sent to her to have his cherry broken.... I guess you had to have been there.)

"There are lots of ways besides intercourse to make love," Elizabeth declared.

"Intercourse," I scoffed. Stilted word in conversation.

"Penetration?" she challenged, an eyebrow lifted in amusement. She understood my reaction.

"Penile vaginal insertion," I proposed.

"Isn't that backwards?"

"You don't care for backwards," I deadpanned. "Whatever. Sure, it's easy to make a woman happy. Not so much the guy."

"That isn't true," she said. "You don't have to have an erection to have an orgasm. At least that's what I've read."

"Okay," I said. "You're right. But it's not as much fun."

"Have you experienced that?"

"I've experienced a lot of stuff."

"Well, anyway, that's just one *possible* side-effect," she observed. "It's not guaranteed."

"I think it almost is," I countered. "I've read it's, like, eighty percent. Of men. Seventy-eight percent or something. Of men who have a prostatectomy, or radiation treatment, end up... can't get it up any more."

"But is that so important to you that you'd risk your life over it?"

444

"Yeah, I kind of think it is," I said. "Part of my image of myself is that I'm a stud. Stud muffin."

"Uh-huh. You take a pill as it is. Although I'm not sure why you need it."

"Puts my mind at rest," I said. "You're right, I don't absolutely *have* to have it. But you know, I mean, even besides the erectile thing there's incontinence... loss of bladder control, leaking urine... uugh! Bowel problems. Chronic diarrhea. Yich! Go around in an adult diaper. Like your father. You gotta really *hate* having a cancer inside you to risk all *that* downside. And it's everything they can do about it that messes you up that way... you know, whether they put in little radioactive seeds, or do external radiation, or just cut it out, even laparoscopic surgery... you still get the same package. Same potential side effects. *Side* effects! Hell, those are fucking *forefront* effects, as far as I'm concerned!"

"But unless you have a biopsy...."

"...I won't *know! Exactly!* That's the *point,* isn't it? In fact, I won't have a *disease!* Not until someone tells me I'm diseased. I don't have any of the symptoms. How do I know the lump in my prostate... the *alleged* lump... isn't perfectly benign? A lot are, supposedly. And even if it's a cancer, they grow very, very slowly. Very slowly, usually, apparently."

"Head in the sand. That's your approach then?"

"Darn right. My first big mistake was letting that guy stick his finger up my butt. Never should have agreed to that. Never should have gone down this road at all. If you're going to be sick you ought to feel like you're sick. Until then, never mind."

"That's crazy. Juvenile. What if I decided not to have mammograms?"

I shrugged. "That's up to you entirely, Elisabeth. I make no recommendations to anyone else. Do what makes you comfortable. Although I will say there's a school of thought that most of the lumps they find with mammograms are never going to kill you. And the ones they find that *are* gonna kill you are so aggressive you're probably a goner no matter how radically they treat it. So all this constant screening does is put women through a lot of useless mental turmoil and unnecessary surgical procedures."

"Easy for you to say."

"Men get breast cancer," I noted.

"They don't get mammograms. Breast cancer rates are falling!"

"That's supposedly because fewer women are using hormone replacement therapy."

"Well. I don't know. I started up again, because.... Low-dose, though. I just decided...."

"You *decided!* There you go! You weighed the risks and benefits and made your own decision."

"And that's a good reason for getting a mammogram every year. My doctor does."

"And I'm not gainsaying that. I'm just pointing something out. Sensitivity versus specificity. Mammograms and those whole-body CT scans are great at finding stuff that requires more specific testing to determine whether they're false positives. Which is great for the medical industry."

"Yeah, yeah. We've been all over that ground."

"Well, it's the same with my PSA tests. That's why Jacobs wants to ream me out, to see if he can come up with any cancer cells. So far it's not even a false positive... it's *no* kind of positive. Two months ago I was happy, healthy as a clam. They're notoriously healthy, you know. Who ever heard of a sick clam? How could you tell? But anyway, nothing's changed."

"Ignorance is bliss."

"You might say. Some would call it magical thinking. I can live with that."

"How about die with that?"

"I'm going to die *somehow*. Sorry to break the news

to you, darling."

"Have the biopsy, damn it! Richard? At least we'll know what we're dealing with."

"You know what? If I have the biopsy one of two things will happen. Either I'll find out I don't have cancer and nothing will have changed, I won't do anything different. Except I'll have gone though a lot of... okay, *some* totally needless discomfort. Or I'll find out I *do* have cancer and I'll opt for 'watchful waiting.' Because that's what's going to be my choice. I've already made that decision. No limp dick for me. So, consider me watchfully waiting already."

I bowed my head pointedly and stared at my fly.

"That's how you're watching?"

"You could help me. I invite you to." I leered at her. "There are signs. If I start not being able to piss, or pissing blood, or... there are signs. I'll know if something's going wrong. Believe me."

"But by then it'll be much later. The cancer'll be way more advanced."

"If there is a cancer. And if it's a fast-moving one. Then instead of dying at a hundred and six I'll die at seventy-something. Or eighty-something. Or ninety-something. Probably shot in the back by a jealous husband before the cancer has a chance to do me in."

"You know, that's less amusing to me than you appear to find it."

"Because you don't have as well developed a sense of humor. Sense of the ridiculous."

"Perhaps not. Watching my Dad die was no joke. I'm not looking forward to doing it with you. I want you around, mister. We can think up a lot of ways to keep ourselves occupied. In all areas."

"I don't want you occupied with changing my diapers."

"Yeah, I know. Me either. But you deal with what

you have to deal with."

"'It is what it is.' Huh?"

"Mm. All that 'better or worse' crap, you know?"

"Here's what I think," I said. "When you're in your late sixties or early seventies and you spend a lot of time hanging out with people who're in their late eighties or nineties, people who're frail and querulous, demented, people who're clearly on their last legs, people who're *old* old, whose bodies are failing, minds failing, all the joy and hopes tapering... *tapered* off, they're just hanging in there, for no good reason except they're hanging in there... you start to identify. If you're forty you feel sorry for them. You patronize them a little, maybe. You can sort of dismiss the ugly parts and focus on the glimmers of... what's the word? *Vivacity* or something. The way we did with your mother for a long time. You don't really see yourself in them because your own life is so full and distracting, even if a lot of the filling is bad stuff... you've got a long horizon. Things will turn around. But if you're over sixty you look at those old-olds and you *do* see yourself. Just a slightly worse-off self. You're all too aware of your own wrinkles, your own age spots, your aches and pains, all the things you used to be able to do that you can't do any more, like dunk a basketball. Or seduce the milkman...."

"As if," Elisabeth snickered. "When's the last time you saw a milkman?"

"Yeah! We're old enough to *remember* milkmen! Which makes us feel older *still!* And then you look at the old-old and you're already so aware of your own oldness that pretty soon you think you're in exactly the same place they are. Your life's behind you. It's all pain and woe from here on out. You're practically dead. But you know, I don't think that's the case. Frankly, I've never felt better in my life! Really! I mean, it's *ridiculous!* I swim, I ski, I climb up and down ladders, I play tennis now and then. I even went down to Comptche and ran in a couple of pickup games last summer, right? If you can call it 'running.' I've still got my shot, though. Still got plenty of energy. Still loose and limber, comparatively. My back hardly ever gives me any trouble any more. I'm a lover...."

"You do not look your age," Elisabeth allowed. "Or, for that matter, act it."

"I'll take even the last one as a compliment. And you don't either, I might add," I assured her. "We're both freaking marvels of nature."

"Bite your tongue," she said. *"Hubris."*

"I know. I sound like one of those smug personals ads in the *New York Review of Books.* 'Tall, slender, handsome, rich, athletic M, septuagenarian...' When at any moment I could end up like one of those ads in the *London Review.* 'Sad, halitotic, craven husk of a man in the terminal stages of a loathesome disease....' It could all go...." I snapped my fingers. "...like that! *Will* go. But at this moment we're still lucky as hell. We've still both got lots of life left in us. Plenty of piss and vinegar."

"Yuck."

"Could be a third again of all the years we've lived already, still ahead of us."

"How do you figure that?"

"Well, twenty-five is a third of seventy-five, and neither of us is seventy-five! Actuarially we could both live well into our nineties. Or beyond, God help us."

"That's another argument for why I want you to get that biopsy."

"That's my argument for not. It's like the first step down the path to medicalization. Of the whole last quarter of my life, maybe. Pretty soon it's like your Dad, in and out of hospitals, in and out of doctors' offices, recuperating from this or that massive insult to your system that leaves you progressively weaker and weaker. Somebody tells you you have cancer, or whatever, and that's how you come to think of yourself from there on out. It becomes your definition. You're a 'cancer victim.' Or a 'cancer *survivor*.' Ugh! You're a 'heart patient.' Is that any way to spend the last significant chunk of your life? If it isn't forced upon you? For me, at this point, it would be voluntary. Maybe if it was a different kind of cancer I'd be singing a different tune. Right now, though, I don't think I'd be doing you any favors."

"I'm not asking for favors. So I won't ask you to do it for my sake. You know what's best for you. But give it some more thought."

"I've been giving it thought," I said. "Rest assured."

I stood, walked over to her, put my hand on her shoulder and bent down.

She lifted her lips to my kiss.

**4**

**The water temperature in the pool where I swim at least an hour every couple of mornings rarely falls below eighty degrees Fahrenheit.**

Even that feels pretty brisk when you first hop in to clock your laps.

The water temperature in the Pacific Ocean off Point Reyes "rarely exceeds fifty degrees Fahrenheit," the National Park Service advises.

That's cold as a motherfucker (a technical measurement) the instant your bare skin encounters it.

The biggest shock, of course, is when your head goes under. But the tumult of the surf crashing over you and the output of energy required to fight through it—blind, heart hammering, holding your breath, the water thick with swirling sand and shell—offers immediate distraction. I plowed forward with my arms and used a dolphin kick I'd recently mastered to burrow through the icy vichyssoise. When I felt the forces churning around me ease a bit I flexed my joined legs twice more and arced for the surface.

Salt stung my eyes when I flapped open my lids. I filled my lungs with sweet, nourishing air. The incoming crest was bearing toward me fast—Gaby was not in my fleeting view. I put my face down in the cold seawater again and stretched for the horizon, arms stroking hard, feet fluttering in counterpoint at full throttle. She was in front of me somewhere; once beyond the shallows and free of breaks I could tread water and orient myself.

I was in the rip now too. I opened my eyes to the acrid, salt-shimmery glare of sky each time I twisted my neck to suck in a breath, but there were no visible markers, just the rise and passage of the waves. I swam through two of them—upslope, downslope, rise again, then fall away—before halting to see how far out I was and how close by now to Gaby.

Riding over the crest of the swell I spotted her—a little to my left and still maybe forty yards further to sea. I looked over my shoulder and was astonished to see the distance I'd covered in so brief an effort. The figures clustered on the beach goggling at me, at us, were already miniatures. Their mouths were working—I had a sense some were hailing, yelling... advice, remonstrance, encouragement? Who knows? As I'd judged correctly from windward, their voices were utterly lost in the busy hubbub of wind and ocean.

I bicycled my legs, paddled my open hands to stay afloat, blinked my eyes hard to clear the prickly film, gulped air and spat out the trickles of saline water that ran down my face and filtered between my lips when my chin dipped under the surface. The crest of the wave surged past me, blotting out the beach. I kicked myself around and lifted my arm to wave at Gaby.

She raised her hand and fluttered it at me.

I slid toward the bottom of the trough. She was eclipsed by the intervening swell.

I buried my face and resumed my crawl. My body had adjusted to the water temperature; I was no longer aware of discomfort. I breathed over my left shoulder now and cocked my head slightly on each breath to get a better forward view when I opened my eyes. A little water always seeps into your nostrils—I was conscious of the bite of the brine outlining the hollows of my nasal passages. I find nose clips uncomfortable. Although I protect my eyes with goggles, I never wear nostril-pinchers in a pool—a few CCs of pungent chlorine squeaking in your sinuses at the end of a workout seems like part of the experience. But maybe, I mused, I'd rethink that if I ever took up ocean swimming. I wondered if Becca used nose clips when she was threshing her way across the Bay toward Alcatraz. I knew she wore a wetsuit.

It was true, I had to acknowledge: She'd have been much better suited to this rescue mission than I was. But the arguments against letting her undertake it still held water. As it were.

When I caught my next glimpse of Gaby— corroborating that my course was accurate—it was of milling arms. She was swimming to meet me. I kept up my pace for another couple of strokes, then halted and trod water to make sure we didn't actually collide. She'd appeared to be perfectly self-possessed, but I didn't want her to suddenly swarm all over me in desperate, hysterical gratitude for my arrival, clutching for a solid perch in the insubstantial liquid. That's the first tenet of life-saving, I recalled. A panicky victim can take you down with her. Even if Gaby *was* so much smaller and slighter... biting and clawing, superhuman strength fueled by the meth of fear... I wouldn't want to have to try to punch her unconscious. Break the poor kid's jaw or something. Then have to tow her in, cumbersome as a sandbag, and apologize profusely to Noelle.

What the textbook says to do, I remembered, is not to struggle but to fill your lungs and then submerge, exhale hard, go down, resolutely descend as fast and deep as you can until your terror-stricken cargo releases her death-grip and scrambles for the surface. Put that dread of drowning to work for you.

She was still swimming more or less directly into the rip so she was barely closing the gap between us. Even though I was drifting toward her she was working to overcome the same offset. She'd shown good form when I'd watched her initially from shore, but now she was keeping her head up, eyes on me. It made her crawl jerky and reduced her aquadynamic efficiency. I didn't want her to tire herself out any more than she already had—there was still plenty of distance to cover to circle back safely to dry land. I held up my palm, fingers splayed, and waggled it at her.

"Stop!" I called. "Gaby! Stop! Stop swimming! *Cessez! De nager! Attendez! Attends-moi! Je viens. Plus proche à toi!*"

I hadn't spoken French for a long time and my command was rusty—only vaguely stirred out of hibernation by the few moments of playful *franglais* I'd attempted in conversation with Noelle over the oysters. I realized I should be using *tu* forms to address a child... a young person... still a child, really. On the other hand, she'd claimed to be conversant in English.

"*Stop!*" I gave it a French pronunciation. "I'm coming there! To you! *Stop! Arrêt! Arrêt! M'attends là! Un moment, je viens!*"

Between my gestures and my shouts—even though she was still upwind I thought she was probably close enough to hear me, at least faintly—my message came across. She hesitated in her stroke, pulled up, gaped at me uncertainly. Her eyes were immense in her small oval face—even bigger and more dramatic because they glittered out of dark, ragged hollows. Her makeup—eye shadow, mascara, eye liner, who knows what-all—had not proved impermeable to saltwater.

Gaby looked more like her mother than I'd registered at first glance: same prominent nose, same small, slightly receding chin, same elegant neck. I'd been distracted on the beach by the fresh ripeness of Gaby's body, and it was that youth rather than any classic perfection of features that made her face "pretty." Not that she wouldn't always, as a Frenchwoman, know how to maintain a soignée beauty. Like her mother. But meanwhile her winsomeness was only enhanced by the smudge of cosmetics and the skinny tendrils of unraveling side-braids that had washed loose from the bun at the back of her head to trail down her cheeks—just a little girl now, masquerading under adult face-paint and a *chic* coiffeur.

I resumed my crawl. But now I held my head above water too, eyes front. The rip was pushing me along and I could use a more measured stroke to cover the interval quickly. Once again I halted warily when I was ten or fifteen feet away.

"*Bon jour,*" I greeted her with a sarcastic lilt in my voice. I used a hard bicycle-kick and a kind of underwater pushup to hike my chin higher and display my grin. "*Fait beau aujourd'hui, non?*"

She replied with a snort—neither incredulity nor amusement, simply expulsion of water and breath. She gasped, snorted again, dribbled water between her lips as she bobbed.

"*Il n'y a pas d' problem,*" I hastily assured her. "*Tout va bien. Maintenant... nous pouvons re... tourner à la... plage... ensemble. N'est-ce pas? Compris?* You are okay?"

"*Ouais, merde! Je m'efforce, mais... Maman va m... m... me tuer! Merci qu' tu... es... ve... venu!*"

"*De rien,*" I replied. I was thoroughly conscious of the banality of these textbook phrases under the circumstances. I was trying to play the whole scene in the lowest key, as if there were absolutely no cause for worry. As if we had both just come out for a routine paddle in the ocean on a summery beach day.

"*Tu nages... très fort,*" I complimented her. I wanted to encourage her. And maintaining the tone of platitudinous chitchat would be calming, I hoped.

"*Ah, merde, non! Putain de... bordel!*" she hissed. "*Ça caille, la mer! Non?*"

I wasn't sure what the verb meant, what she was saying about the sea. I flared my eyebrows in ambiguous reply.

"*Et ce putain de c... courant!*" she added. "*C'est em... merdant. J'ai essayé... mais... c'est vachement trop... tu sais... trop fort! Je je commence... à me me... fatiguer... un peu.*"

I wasn't completely up to speed on French slang either. Expressions that once qualified as profanity have a way of transitioning into commonplace usage over time. (No bull, which sucks.) Both of us were breathing with effort, our sentences broken gasps, sputtered as we buoyed ourselves unsteadily in the choppy sea. But I was pretty sure she'd used some unexpectedly salty language for a fourteen-year-old. I was actually a bit shocked—not that I hadn't overheard plenty of foul effusions from Becca and Christopher when they were of otherwise tender age. Mostly picked up, can't deny it, from their father. And Gaby was certainly under exculpatory stress. Gutter speech was a good sign, I decided. It suggested she still had a reserve of angry spirit to draw on.

"No, no. You're... looking good," I said. "You're not... too tired... yet. Come on. What we've... got to.... *Ce que... nous... devons... faire... est de... nager là bas.*" I lifted my left hand out of the water and flipped drops off my fingers in a southerly direction. "We're... *nous sommes... dans un... mauvais courant!* Rip current, called. *Courant de...* reep? *Très mauvais. C'est pas... possible... retourner... à la plage... directement. C'est beaucoup trop fort... contre nous... la force. Faut nager... au dehors. Là bas, au sud. Allons. Suivez... suis-moi.* Okay?"

She was frowning at me with great concentration.

"*Me comprends?*"

"*Ouais,*" she nodded, although I thought a bit uncertainly. I noticed the whole knot of braids at the back of

456

her head was beginning to unfurl and sag toward her nape.

"English? Can you... under... stand me better... *anglais?*"

"*C'est égal,*" she muttered. "*Anhh,* is cold!"

"Yeah, little bit," I sympathized. Women, with their voluptuous pads of flesh, survive longer than men in cold seas. But for all her precocious curves, Gaby didn't yet have that much body fat for insulation. Slip of a girl.

"Okay. Follow me," I said. I cocked my head toward the south. "*Viens avec....* We'll swim together. *Allons ensemble. This* way."

I scissored my feet and, carefully watching to make sure she was along for the ride, set out with steady, leisurely strokes for the hazy hump from whose base shines the famous Point Reyes Light.

## We didn't have to swim there, of course—not that we could have.

It was probably ten miles away. All we had to do was work our way out of the backwash that was setting us toward Tokyo Bay. I hoped that wouldn't prove easier said than done.

People used to—and a lot still do—talk about "undertow." But the term has been discredited. It's a myth: The action of the water doesn't suck you *down,* it sweeps you *out.*

To sea.

Except, actually, somewhere beyond the line of breakers where the invisible bed beneath you has deepened sufficiently, out beyond whatever protean conformation in the sandy bottom has temporarily created a drainage channel for the surf to swirl through as it recedes, the force dissipates. The official National Weather Service explanation is that "when waves break strongly in some locations and weakly in others, this can cause circulation cells which are seen as rip currents: narrow, fast-moving belts of water traveling offshore."

So one piece of advice for swimmers who find themselves caught in a rip current is to relax—"remain calm to conserve energy and think clearly"—float or tread water, and let the thalassic conveyor belt shunt you out as far as it wants to. Which won't be all that far, supposedly. Within a couple of hundred yards at worst—supposedly—it'll wane and you'll be freed to make your merry way back to shore.

How would you know, though, I'd always wondered… what would reveal to you that you were no longer in the current's grip?

It was obvious Gaby and I had been carried well out from the beach. We were now at least a football field's length from the spirit squad cheering us on from the water's edge. That's my standard unit of distance-measurement. But it was hard to judge from eye-level. (I'd never lain in one end zone peering downfield at a figure in the other—a cornerback, say, celebrating his interception of a pass meant for you and his hundred-and-two-yard return in the opposite direction after you'd missed the tackle.) So I had no baseline for accurate size-distance comparison from this perspective. It was apparent we'd been whisked out damn far, whatever—scary-far when you're struggling to stay afloat in an inhospitable ocean and you're hopped up on anxiety-juice. I couldn't really sense whether we were becalmed or still outbound.

But it didn't matter. All the diagrams I'd seen on beach-safety placards showed arrows labeled "escape" pointing ninety degrees from the band of dangerous flow.

"Swim out of the current in a direction following the shoreline," I remembered the captions' counsel.

Squinting at Gaby earlier from the beach, maybe because I was right handed, I'd tried to signal her to head north. Now, gazing back at our destination and perhaps from the same handedness bias, I'd opted for south. I couldn't see anything in the qualities of the swells rolling toward and over us that might indicate the margin of the rip channel. I had to draw comfort from that vague adjective "narrow" in the literature. The main thing was to take a perpendicular tack. And the set of the waves did appear to be very slightly southerly. Seemed best to go with the flow.

Gaby had already expended energy trying to buck the rip. She had to take two strokes for my every one to stay abreast, even though I'd throttled down to a lazy beat that I sometimes use in the pool as I'm closing in on my seventy-second lap. (Seventy-point-four add up to a mile, so I swim a round number to get back to the end of the pool where I started. And the little extra tacked on *gratis* builds character, after all... which maybe I'll have acquired by the time I pop off.)

I was gliding with one arm extended until I'd stretched the other one out completely, parallel to it. Only then would I roll on my side to complete the first stroke's underwater pull. I'd retarded the rhythm of my kick, too, only scissoring my feet together with each snatch of my hand. While I was desperately eager to bring this outing to a quick and happy conclusion, we weren't in a race. Our paramount need was to conserve strength.

I only hoped Gaby had as much physical endurance left in her as she seemed to have moxie. She'd never cried for help. She'd never signaled frantically. She wasn't whining or complaining now, and she wasn't fighting the ocean. Thank God for that. She could have eased her effort by not keeping her head up most of the time—it's the antithesis of streamlining and it's hard on the neck and shoulders. She was swimming the way water polo players swim, so they can watch the ball—my head being the ball for her. She was swimming the way Esther Williams swam in her movies, the way Johnny Weissmuller swam as Tarzan... nineteen-forties movie stars, I guess, being expected to show their highly paid faces at all times when on camera. But it certainly made them look amateurish. Williams' daintily shortened arm strokes, elegantly cocked wrists and primly joined fingers were the natatory equivalent of drinking tea with an extended pinkie. Weissmuller just pounded the water and rubbernecked, as if in search of a crocodile to wrestle. It was hard to credit the Olympic prowess that had earned them both their film contracts. But who was I to talk? Gaby had my example to emulate: My neck too was cranked back and my chin lifted as I swam. I couldn't risk losing sight of *her* either.

Decades of reading the news had taught me that people can go under suddenly. You only have seconds to feel for them in the murk of a roiling ocean. Even if they pop up again you may never spot them. You learn that lesson from man-overboard drills in the Navy. As soon as the shout rings out—and a lookout heaves a life-ring into the water as a place-marker—whoever first descries the bobbing head locks his eyes on it and points at it fixedly. You might never locate so small an object again in the foam and chop if you let your gaze or your fingertip waver.

Susan and I briefly owned a sailboat. Every so often I'd instruct her in the rescue of a rubber fender lobbed into the Bay... practice in case of emergency, in case she or I or little Becca or baby Christopher, muffled in their orange kapok life jackets, were ever toppled out of the heeling cockpit. (We kept the kids roped to a cleat against just such a frightening contingency.) There's always a risk you'll be caught unawares by a swinging boom or tripped by a toe rail when you're between handholds on a shroud. We practiced the recovery: Whoever's at the helm luffs instantly—points the bow into the wind until the breeze spills from the sail, slamming on the air-brake, so to speak—then tosses a cushion into the water and circles about to position the boat upwind of the person overboard. That way you'll be blown down onto the victim rather than drifting quickly apart—since hull and sails in profile offer much greater wind resistance than a human head. And the water's calmer in the lee of the hull, making it easier when you reach over the side to haul the waterlogged unfortunate, who's now pinned by the wind to the boat's side, up over the gunwale and back aboard.

Which, admittedly, would have been a Herculean task for Susan if I were the one who'd pitched into the Bay.

I'd considered those factors when deciding whether to convoy Gaby on the shoreward or seaward side. It didn't make much difference, I'd concluded... except that if I should need to get to her fast it would be better not to have to fight the rip. And since I present a bigger mass I'd presumably be washed *toward* her faster than, positions reversed, she'd be washed to me.  So I swam on the  beach side.

### "You're doing fine!" I encouraged her.

She flared her eyebrows.

"Just take it... easy. Don't... try too hard. Don't wear... yourself out."

She ducked her head in apparent affirmation.

*"Comprends?"*

Another putative nod.

"Let me know... tell me... if you need... to stop and rest."

Her expression was blank.

*"Dis-moi...,"* I said, then corrected myself, remembering the lover's refrain from *South Pacific*: "*Dites-moi.... S'il faut... rester.*"

461

But that, I realized, was a *faux ami*. *Rester* means "stay." I tried to think of a synonym for "rest." There's "relax," but that wasn't quite the advice I wanted to give her. Take it... *doucement*. "Gently." Same objection. They connote lassitude.

"*Si tu... deviens... trop fatiguée*," I corrected myself... then the verb *reposer* popped to mind. "*...Nous pouvons*," I added, "*nous reposer... un peu.*"

"I am... okay," she gasped.

"Great!" I exclaimed.

We'd covered, what? Maybe three, four pool lengths in our southerly swim? A hundred yards? That proverbial football field?

The water was still a uniform pale jade. Immersed in it I could see no difference in color between the humps of the swells ahead of us and those behind. How narrow is "narrow?" I was obviously anxious to veer for shore but I was afraid if we tried prematurely and were frustrated it would be demoralizing. For her, anyway. Me, I was good.

"Let's keep going... this way... a little further," I urged Gaby.

"*Maman...,*" she gulped, "...has tell me... is... *requin ici.*"

"Ah," I replied. "*Requin.*"

It was not a word I could have plumbed out of dormant vocabulary on my own initiative, but I understood it when I heard it. Definitely abetted by context.

"Shark!" I translated.

"Shark, *ouais.*" It was not an easy word for a francophone to pronounce. "Shairque," she repeated, more or less. "You think yes?"

"No," I lied.

"Don't worry," I added. "Sharks... eat seals. *Les requins... mangent... des phoques.*" For some reason the word for that sea creature came instantly to tongue. "*Nous... ne sommes pas... des phoques."*

*"Je l'espère bien. Mais... j'en ai... vu... au ciné. Ils mangent... des humains. Ça craint, non? Ils me foutent... les jetons... ces putains... de requins.* I am... shit scare, *non?* Of fucking... shairque. And... *calmars. Géants."*

"Giant... octopus," I translated. Or, I realized, maybe giant... *squid!* I snorted, amused. "Don't worry. None of those... around here... pretty sure."

I was glad for the comic relief—distraction from a specter that, to be honest, had been nagging at my subconscious ever since I'd plunged into water that was over my head.

Even now I bristled with foreboding that somewhere below us, or cruising just a few yards to seaward, was a hulking, slavering albino shark. Great saber-toothed maw agape, balefully reconnoitering our bare toes and exposed bellies.

I too am shit-scared of sharks, I confess. Not long ago a recreational abalone diver, a guy in his sixties, if I recall, or anyway fifties, a grizzled warrior I could identify with, was happily prying the big mollusks (they're outsize snails really, delicious when pounded tender and sautéed in butter) off the rocks near Kibesillah. That's maybe half an hour from our house, north of Ten Mile River. Suddenly his diving buddy only a few feet away felt a massive change in water pressure. Something immense and indistinct swooped past, he recalled. He turned to glimpse a dorsal fin. Then the water around them erupted in froth and blood. His diving companion vanished. Two days later the body washed ashore—*sans* head.

You read about attacks like this up and down the California coast. Surfers dragged screaming off boards bitten in two, scuba divers, snorkelers, kayakers, off-shore swimmers.... A common characteristic is they're wearing wetsuits. The glistening black neoprene hide, and perhaps the torpedo-like silhouette of the board or the kayak and the stubby projecting appendages—hands, feet or paddle blades—give them a shark's-eye-view resemblance to a seal. Especially near shore, where the water is cloudy.

Like here.

At least we weren't wearing wetsuits.

That seems to be current conventional wisdom. About why sharks are lured to chomp into victims they invariably spit out. A nice succulent pinniped is a premier repast for a hungry great white—which everyone agrees is the menacing species around here. Humans don't contain enough omega-three fatty acid or something; we leave a bad taste on the shark palate. You never hear about anybody being *devoured* by a shark—at least not close to land. Death always results from massive hemorrhage after a leg or an arm—or a head—has been wrenched off. Or a major artery severed. That was the cause of death of the only swimmer I could remember being killed by a shark. Not only had she been wearing a wetsuit, she'd been using flippers. And she was frolicking with a pod of feeding seals. And it was early morning. Sharks supposedly fill up for the day at breakfast.

Sounds like an agonizing way to die, dissected alive by a shark. Out of the blue, literally, an enormous weight slams into you and simultaneously a buzzsaw of pyramidal teeth ravens through your flesh, cracks bone, shreds muscle and punctures vital organs.... But, in fact, they say death comes fast when the feedstock for your brain is hosing out of a severed artery. And there's shock. Sudden numbing shock... the opiate that lets a gazelle stand there calmly while the lions gnaw out its intestines.

As violent death goes, maybe shark-bite is not so awful.

The thing to keep in mind, I told myself as those absorbed news accounts and images and fancied sensations licked amorphously through my brain—the connotative subtext evoked by the word *shark* in this setting, where the possibility of a deadly encounter was real—is that attacks are rare. Very rare. You could count all the deaths by shark-bite in Northern California in the past half century on the fingers of one hand, I was pretty sure. That's probably why the notion is so terrifying. When a risk is remote, and grisly, it haunts us... while a similar risk that is commonplace loses its power to appall. Airline crashes are headlined nationally; fatal automobile accidents, unless they're particularly gory, earn a couple of ho-hum column inches in the local news. Someone pointed out that hundreds of people are bitten by dogs every year, yet few people harbor an instinctive dread of dogs. (For some reason ailurophobia, terror of cats, seems to be more common.)

Not that human maulings by dogs don't get page-one coverage, but that's because they too are comparatively few and far between. When you get right down to it, I consoled myself, the likelihood of our drawing the interest of a shark was only slightly greater than that of our suddenly feeling the tentacular caress of a giant squid.

I could be grateful to Gaby for the perspective.

## But if one of us *were* to be targeted by a great white shark, it would probably be her.

She.

Right now she was the one swimming to seaward—closer to the carnivores' cruising lanes. So I supposed *noblesse* obliged, or anyway strongly hinted, that I, as a gentleman, the elder, the protector, ought to veer to the right to put the vulnerable maiden to my inside.

"...Sudden as a shark...."

That phrase abruptly murmured in my inner ear. A

465

line from a poem. By a guy I'd never heard of until I'd read a review of his collected works a little while back: Seidel. I'd liked the excerpts and would have bought the book except the list price was forty bucks. Probably discounted if I'd bought it online. But that's an awful lot of poetry to slog through for a desultory poetry consumer. Still, his stuff, on the examples cited, engaged me: muscular, pithy, provocative, colloquial... not opaque but not popcorn. "Transgressive," I believe was the reviewer's faintly disapproving praise.

"Sudden as a shark."

Frederick Seidel. Another guy about my own age. Lived through the same things I have. One of about five contemporary poets I could name... several of them dead, in fact. And all I knew of Seidel was a couple of lines, not even one whole poem. Maybe I ought to rectify that, I thought, when I got home to my laptop again. Pop for the damn book. Honor a guy who wrote a line, a metaphor so terrifyingly perfect.

"Sudden as a shark."

He was describing a Ducati motorcycle, I remembered. But it's not a comforting trope to have looping in one's brain as one lowers one's face into the opaque sea and angles out toward the ominously teeming vasty.

I shuddered, literally.

...*If* I got home to my laptop again....

Saltwater or no, I flapped my eyelids open between breaths and tried to peer through the stinging gray-green murk beneath me. Us. Scout for the loom of danger.

Maybe if I saw it coming I could wrench myself around and get my feet in front of me, I thought. Jam a heel as hard as I could into the in-rocketing snout. That's how you're supposed to fend off a shark, I'd read. Fight off a shark. Whack it, kick it, punch it in the rubbery nose—a sensitive spot. That's almost always the best advice for victims of predators, it seems. Don't turn and run, don't flop and cover up—don't play possum. You'll just get savaged. End up dead. Like the opossum whose limp corpse, full of puncture wounds on close inspection, I found in our yard in Berkeley back when Susan and I had a Siberian husky on overnight patrol. (Till a pizza delivery guy left the gate unlatched and Amaruq moseyed off to San Leandro, where she darted between parked cars and met the tires of an AC Transit bus.)

Lot of good their instinctive passivity did for those weird little marsupials when they'd trespassed on Amaruq's territory. She cornered a raccoon once, not much bigger than a possum, and the little masked marauder put up a hell of a battle. I heard the snarling and screeching and jumped out of bed. Amaruq was distracted by my bare-ass appearance and the raccoon scuttled into a tree—slightly lamed and obviously the worse for wear. But then so was Amaruq, her muzzle striped with bloody gashes. I pinioned her and daubed the wounds with astringent alcohol, taking satisfaction in the therapeutic punishment and hoping it would reinforce the lesson not to engage feisty raccoons. The lesson for me was that resistance pays. Which, I believe, is the current wisdom for humans. Offense is the best defense, whether the assailant is a mountain lion or a grizzly bear or a rapist... or a shark.

At worst you'll have the satisfaction of going down lumpy, not smooth.

Some satisfaction.

Exposing my tender eyeballs to the sea-brine was painful. As noted, when I'm grinding out my laps in the pool I wear goggles. I watch the lane markers and the T where the line breaks to warn that the wall is coming up in two meters. Gauge when to arch my shoulders and tuck, let the water pressure from my momentum drive me down onto my back, somersaulting into the flip-turn. Flatten soles and heels against the vertical tiles invisible behind me, unbend crouched knees with a sudden propulsive shove, roll belly-down and level out. One or two underwater dolphin kicks, a respite for the arms. Then breakout onto the surface, suck air and resume the stroke.

It's a neat maneuver and I'm pleased with myself for having mastered it finally, belatedly. Or at least for having adopted it into my freestyle repertoire, even if I have plenty of polishing still to do on it if I want to be competitive.

Which I don't. I have to keep reminding myself of that. Even though a couple of people I see at workouts and the coach of the club's youth program—whom I politely ply for tips on technique when I encounter her on the pool deck—have suggested I might consider entering a master's race.

I started swimming laps in college to boil off energy in winter when the tennis courts were muffled in snow or steeped in rain. Good alternative if the gym was too crowded to hone my jump shot. I once volunteered as a timer for an intramural swim meet and got dragooned into entering the last event, a half-mile, because no one else on my fraternity's team had the energy left for it and we could win the meet if somebody simply completed the distance. It didn't even matter where I came in, just that I finished.

As it happened, only one other guy stood beside me with his toes crooked over the lip of the pool when the starter raised his pistol. I knew him, a Beta—our main rival. His team was in second-place and they stood to win if I gave up in mid-race or drowned.

I did neither. In fact, I went out at my accustomed pace and opened a very comfortable lead. But by about the twelfth lap my opponent had overcome the lost ground, and for the next couple of laps we swam neck and neck. Then, to my astonishment, he broke his crawl and began to sidestroke.

That was illegal, I thought for an instant. Disqualifying. Then I remembered that the race is, after all, called the "freestyle." Nevertheless, his behavior seemed to me unsporting somehow.

Especially sine he was actually *keeping pace.*

My arms by then were weary and my thighs burned. My kick had become labored, sporadic—my feet more drag that propellant. It was late fall; I hadn't worked out in a pool for months. I'd never swum for time anyway. I tried to pick it up. But there he was, still alongside me two lanes over... starting to fall off a little bit, yet maintaining that leisurely, gliding motion, watching me. It was humbling. I couldn't outswim a guy who was doing the *sidestroke!*

And he did beat me. On the last lap he resumed the crawl and with the strength he'd preserved he slowly pulled away. We still won the meet, my fraternity—thanks to me, in fact. Big consolation. Anyway, that—hey, a second-place in an eight-hundred meter free, I could always boast—marked the extent of my competitive natation career.

**For a while after Maartje returned to Holland I'd eat a sandwich, read a book, sunbathe and then swim a few laps during lunch hours at the Strawberry Canyon upper pool.**

I was drawn there as much by the fact that comely coeds often lolled topless *à la française* as by any interest in staying fit. (Funny how that moment in American history passed.)

But I wasn't so fixated on cocoa-buttered nipples that I failed to note the serious Aquatic Masters pushing their kickboards and ticking off intervals in their dedicated lanes. Someday, I mused, I might go that route. If I could hang on long enough, I reasoned, infirmities would winnow and handicap my field of rivals. With physical luck, a little stylistic tuning and some aerobic toughening, I could finally ascend into the natatorial elite—the diminished elite, whose primary qualification had been reduced to survival.

Something of that mentality led me to experiment with intervals and strokes when, about a year earlier, I got bored with the routine of simply chugging up and down the pool for three-quarters of an hour. Not that boredom isn't part of the appeal of distance swimming. Gradually your brain powers down, your thoughts shred. You lose yourself in the rhythmic stresses and twinges of your muscles, the steady flexion of your joints, the pumping of your heart between the bellows of your lungs. Periodically you're conscious of form and you think about your line in the water, the position of your head, the extension of your fingers and toes, the rotation of your hips and torso. Then habit and muscle memory take over again. Consciousness fuzzes. You count off the laps—I consider one length of the pool up and one back a lap, fifty meters together. To help me keep track I alternate breathing over my right shoulder and my left, switching each lap. And I check the big round clock above the deck. Soon enough all I had to do was glance at the time, consider which leg I was on—heading for the far wall or returning to home base—and which side I was breathing on, odd or even, to calculate how many laps I'd clicked off. Which was convenient, since my lazing mind often lost track. Suddenly I'd realize I was on the thirtieth lap and the last lap I could recall counting was the tenth. It's a bit like transcendental meditation. Instead of intoning a silent mantra to suppress or override skittery thought, you let the metronomic labor of your body do the lulling.

For all that it's refreshing, this prospect can come to seem a little dull, though. The internet, where I spend half my mornings researching articles and avoiding actual writing, is a great resource for improving the mechanics of one's swimming stroke. You can watch instructional online videos narrated by Olympic coaches. You can pick up helpful pointers from the comment threads on swimmers' message boards. Periodically I'd dip into web sites where I'd skim posts touting the benefits of interval training. Pretty much irrelevant, I thought, until I began to toy with the idea of trying my mettle at a masters' event. It was obvious I'd have to work on my speed. And the best way to get faster, according to the consensus I gleaned, is to chop up your pool sessions into a lot of segments of varied lengths and varied strokes, all swum at sprint tempo. I decided to give it a whirl.

I'm not disciplined enough to maintain an inflexible routine. So I'd mix and match. A typical workout would consist of some combination of a slow freestyle warmup of maybe ten laps, then a kick set of maybe a dozen lengths— gliding on my side, alternately left and right, with one arm extended in front and the opposite hand trailing at my hip, which is supposed to improve your balance in the water and habituate you to rotating your body as you swim, which in turn increases efficiency and speed. Then I'd swim a pyramid of distances in twenty-five-yard increments, twenty-five to a hundred and back, each going as fast as I could, using a different stroke and taking only a short rest to catch my breath between. Then another kick set, a few cool-down backstroke lengths and a final all-out freestyle sprint to impress the sensation of maximum effort on my muscles as their default setting in the pool.

I can do the butterfly but I don't like it. It's fast, but too frenzied and too exhausting for the payoff, it seems to me. And way too much strain on my well-used shoulder joints. I can do its antecedent, the classic breaststroke, sort of, but I don't much like that either. Too slow, too mannered somehow, too basic an amphibian adaptation with its weird frog-kick and tortoise-like side-sweep of the arms. Really, it's just one step up the evolutionary scale from the dogpaddle.

(Don't repeat my opinion to any breaststrokers, though—to ratchet the pace of their métier to racing level they have to be very tough; they'd kick my ass.) So although every so often I'd thrash through a fly lap or undulate jerkily up and down the pool in my clunky version of the breaststroke, I mostly truncated my own individual medley to the free and the back.

I always figured my only shot at medaling in my age group would be in something long, like the sixteen-fifty. An event where grit counts more than fast-twitch muscle fiber. But when I looked up the times being recorded for that distance by the graybeards in my category, I realized I was kidding myself. The top guys were clocking in at under thirty minutes. One seventy-two-year-old feenom posted a finish in twenty-three-twenty-five. My best time was thirty-six minutes and change, and I was woozy when I finally touched. Had a pain between my shoulder blades that took a month to wear off. Pushing up my training schedule to five or six days a week, even if I had the stomach for it, wasn't going to pare down that big a differential, I could be pretty certain.

Then I had my visit with the good Doctor Jacobs, of the fiery digit. In my ensuing prowl through the internet to educate myself on pathologies of the prostate I encountered the story of a dedicated masters swimmer who was diagnosed with prostate cancer, decided to have radical laparoscopic surgery and within just ten days was back in the pool for gingerly workouts. Three months later he knocked a second and a half off the world record for the two-hundred-meter breaststroke in his age group. He was seventy. He'd been a top pool racer all his life. There were guys like him out there in every event, I could be sure. Healthy longevity is a demographic wave, not my private spa, unfortunately. Or I guess, from a more altruistic standpoint, fortunately.

My momentary enthusiasm for grooming to pit myself against rivals waned. I went back to workmanlike up-and-down-the-pool hauls that at least have kept my stomach fairly flat and regularly flushed some oxygen through my ropy muscles. I still occasionally wonder how I'd stack up in a race against contemporaries. Probably very well, I can continue to flatter myself—as long as I never test the proposition.

Is that a form of denial? I guess so. I deny I can be bested at something by avoiding the occasion of being bested. I deny I have a disease by spurning a definitive test for it. I deny I'm in my old age by refusing to acknowledge that I've acquired any of its distinguishing characteristics. Not yet, anyway. I'm rational enough to recognize there may come a time.... *May.* Meanwhile, I'm on reasonably solid ground. I'm pretty sure I don't smell funky. My mind hasn't closed. I'm not cranky—it would be okay by me if kids played on my grass, if I had any. I don't dodder. I'm no more forgetful than I remember *ever* having been.... Bottom line, I deny whatever's negative by refusing to let consideration of it sully my pristine brain. (Still barely used.) What's wrong with that? *Vive* denial!

And so, I reminded myself to keep denying that there were sharks in these waters. At least right then. At least right there. And if there were... I didn't want to see them coming.

I want whatever's coming to get me to surprise me.

Well, up to a point.

I rolled on my back, blinked my eyes clear and took heart in the soothing sight of the crystal-dry empyrean swathing this aqueous planet. I swung my right arm over my head as far as I could reach and sliced my cupped fingers down through the gelid fluid in a lazy backstroke.

Gaby's slim arms were doggedly chopping the surface ten yards behind me, to my right.

The cold was beginning to seep into my bones. Were we out of the rip by now?

### "Maintenant, Gaby," I called, "allons-y... à la plage!"

I stopped swimming and trod water to make sure I had her eye. "*Ça suffit. Je crois. J'espère. Voyons,*" I said, "*si ça... va... mieux içi... pour retourner.*"

She seemed to be looking directly at me, eyes wide. Her smudged face ticked back and forth with her strokes as she continued to plow toward me.

I pointed my finger at the beach. There were people clustered at the tideline—Elisabeth distinctive in her white shift, Susan in shorts clutching Olivier's hand, Becca in her lavender sports bra, broad-shouldered Chris shirtless with Patrick in his arms, Joel flanked by Molly and Élodie... Noelle, Deirdre.... I recognized each of them instantly without conscious effort or inventory. Around and behind them clustered anonymous extras. They'd all trailed along, mirroring our progress as we'd swum south. We were further out than I'd have hoped—but maybe no further than it had seemed when I'd glanced toward them blurry-eyed and preoccupied between facial immersions for shark surveillance.

"Come on! Follow me," I urged Gaby.

Perhaps English would help focus her attention, I thought. "Let's try... now...t' get back. 'Kay? Here! We! Go!" I semaphored my arm at the shore. "*Comprends?*"

I thought she bobbed her head affirmatively. But she was still swimming straight ahead. She was only a few yards away from me now and almost abreast.

I burrowed my right shoulder and ear, lay on my hip

and scissored my legs hard to scoot across her path. Set the course for home.

"*Aprés moi!*" I barked.

("...*Le deluge,*" my brain silently appended.)

I took a couple of slow sidestrokes. I didn't want to get too far ahead of her. At the same time I wanted to test whether we were finally free of the offshore set.

I couldn't judge my progress so casually. We'd have to swim into it a little bit more to really find out. But Gaby hadn't veered.

"*Viens,* Gaby!" I shouted at her. "*Suis moi. Compris?*"

She was still plying her course like an automaton—crook arm, dig... crook arm, dig... crook arm, dig... crook arm, dig.... She looked like a puppy tossed off a dock, chin up, nose high, eyes glazed in desperate concentration on the physical effort to stay afloat and paddle back to dry land. Except she'd apparently lost her compass. Maybe she was in the hypnotic grip of the repetitions the way I sometimes zoned out while notching lap after lap.

"Hey! Gaby!" I shouted again. "Gaby!"

She crossed my wake, relentlessly headed south.

"Gaby!"

I hesitated, trod water, spun and splashed after her.

I pulled alongside a couple of arm's-lengths to her left. I resumed the sidestroke and studied her oscillating profile. I could tell she was aware of my presence because her left pupil flicked into the corner of her eye, at me, every time she swung her right arm forward. I couldn't read her expression. Her face was blank. Dazed, determined, scared... her eyes were as wide as adrenaline could dilate them.

"Gaby! Answer me!" I said. "*Réponds. Tu m'entends?*"

"*Ouais. Ouais. Ouais,*" she spluttered.

"*Cessez un moment,*" I said. "*Il faut rester... reposer... un peu. Tu vas.... Nous allons... nous fatiguer... trop.*"

I wanted to instruct her to tread water but I couldn't

think how to say it.

"*Suis... fatiguée... peu,*" she gasped. She was still swimming but she'd relaxed her pace. It occurred to me that she might not even have heard me calling to her.

"*Il faut... tourner maintenant,*" I told her. "*Enfin.* We're almost there. *Voyons... si le mauvais... courant... a fini... est fini.* "

"*F... f... fatiguée. Vachement....*"

"*Arrêt, Gaby. Je t'en pris.*"

"*J... je me... gele... ge... gele... les c... couilles!*"

She was freezing... her *balls* off! My God, I thought, do young girls say that now too? Hilarious.

As for my own balls, I'd long since lost touch with them. If I looked I'd probably find a vagina now, not external genitalia. We'd been in the water for, I don't know... five minutes? No, no... more than that. Ten? Probably less, but it's hard to keep track when you're having fun. Whatever, you don't want to spend too much time in water this temperature. Fifty's refreshing—briefly, and maybe up to your knees. But immersed in it you have only about an hour before it'll sap you of consciousness. And although you'd presume otherwise, swimming—vigorous activity—only cools the body faster, they say.

Gaby's features were pinched. Except for the faint grey runnels of mascara her cheeks were colorless, her skin almost milk-blue. Her lipstick—a light rose, a natural shade skillfully applied—had proved more water resistant than her eye makeup, so her lips still had an artificially healthy glow. But they were rimmed with purple. They quavered when she spoke, spat, dribbled seawater. She half-treadmilled, half-dogpaddled—her sleek young deltoids and the tendons in her long thin neck pulsing with faint tremors.

Shit, I thought, we really *did* have to get back to the beach quickly. She was shivering. She was getting hypothermic.

"*Vamos!*" I instructed her. "*À la....*" I realized I'd just spoken Spanish. But my brain locked. Suddenly I couldn't remember how to construct a phrase as basic as "let's go" in French. Some form of *ir*... no, that was the Spanish verb too. Never mind.

"*À la plage,*" I managed. "*Là bas.*"

I lifted my finger out of the water to point. I didn't want there to be any confusion about the direction, obvious as it seemed. I wasn't sure how clearly she was thinking.

"*Ou... ouais,*" she acknowledged.

She hung in place, breathing hard, as if waiting for my lead. But I didn't want to swim out in front of her again. At the same time I was wary of getting too close unless it became absolutely necessary. She appeared to be adequately self-possessed. She was keeping herself afloat without much difficulty. I doubted she'd suddenly lunge and snag me in deadly anaconda coils.

I drifted closer. I stretched out my right arm. I brushed the flesh of her upper arm with my fingertips and let them linger: human contact, the moral support of physicality.

"*Tu vas bien,*" I assured her. "You're... doing great. You understand... my English?"

"Understand. Yes," she replied.

"Okay. *Allons, enfin. 'Allons, enfants....'*" I couldn't resist the pun. "'*...De la patrie....,*'"

I repeated the syllables to the tune, but broke off after the first four notes. I felt a flash of remorse, the wincing recognition that one has just said or done something silly, something childish and inappropriate to the circumstances.

Maybe I was starting to lose it too.

I backpedaled quickly. It was the crazy lameness of the invocation of the *Marseillaise* that had given me pause, but I was also disturbed by the fact that I'd touched her. It verged on the overly intimate. In this day and age old men don't caress teenage girls' arms. They don't lay a finger on them without acknowledging an undercurrent of lust.... without feeling a tingle of resistance to the potential sexual charge.

My impulse was fatherly... but what did that mean in mitigation? All fathers are attracted to their nubile daughters at some unspeakable Freudian level. Hasn't that been ingrained in us in Psych 101? How perverse would it look, I thought with dread, if I actually did end up having to tow Gaby ashore, or ferry her on my back, her precocious breasts flattened against my trapezius, her chin in the crook of my neck, her bare female skin pasted to my bare male skin...? Fewer red flags would be hoisted all around if she were eight years old... or thirty-five... or a boy.

I looked at her with a conscious effort to see her as a child. Shed any sense of Gaby as tempting naiad. It wasn't hard. She was pretty wrung out.

"Don't worry," I told her. *"Je serai... toujours... avec toi. À ton...."* I thought for a second to come up with the word. *"Coté."*

She nodded. Teeth chattering she resumed her dogpaddle. I frog-kicked to stay abreast. Finally we were both facing the shore.

"Doing good," I encouraged her. "Doing well."

Keep those brain cells of hers firing by constantly prodding them with English, I told myself. Preferably grammatical English.

I squinted at the beach. Indeed, the human figures seemed to be a little bigger than before. Were we actually getting closer? Or was it just wishful thinking? At least they didn't appear smaller. In theory, if we had broken out of the anomalous rip we were going to be washed ashore eventually whether we helped ourselves along or not. Two limp bulbs of human kelp swept in by the waves curling up the slope of the continental shelf.

We'd be about the same drab, sodden, semitransparent color as kelp by then too, our dead bodies. Unless we'd nourished the sharks.

"I see... your mother," I told her. *"Tu la vois? Tú ma... ta maman? Elle est... là. Elle t'attends. Tu la vois?"*

*"Ouais,"* she grunted.

*"Tous les gens... nous attendent,"* I encouraged her. *"Nos amis.* 'Friends and family.'" I recited the cliché phrase with the stilted inflection of an English teacher.

*"Koko,"* she murmured.

I didn't know what that meant. *"Nageons... plus fort,"* I suggested. *"Si tu peux."*

*"...Vois pas,"* she said. *"Oú...?"*

*"Quoi?"* I asked.

*"P'tit chien.... Ko... k...ko.."*

*"Comprends pas,"* I said.

*"Ah... non, non... non, je... c... commence... à rêver."*

"Gaby? Can you swim... harder now? *Faut nager plus... fort...! Somos... nous sommes... p... presque là.* Almost h... home. *Chez nous."*

Our home element. Hard ground.

Jesus the water was cold! Really getting to me now too, this fucking frigid Western Ocean!

*"Plus fort!"* I urged. *"Comme... ceçi!"*

I lowered my face into the icewater to set an example and risked batting out three strong overhand strokes without breathing. Then I rolled onto my back, blinked and tucked my chin to look over my knees to see if....

Gaby was nowhere in sight.

**I jack-knifed, flapped my arms, veed and unveed my legs beneath me in a desperate effort to boost myself higher in the water.**

I swiveled my neck to orient myself. My throat had seized, my stomach lurched with dread.

Oh, God, no! No! To lose her *now!*

In a pool there are the lane markers below you, ropes on floats at each elbow, to guide your course. Ranging free in the ocean you've got to pick out some reference point to keep on a steady bearing every time you roll your head and open your eyes as you breathe. Otherwise you're pretty sure to yaw. I know *I* have a tendency to drift right as I swim in open water unless I check and correct my heading frequently. I think that partly explained why Gaby wasn't where I thought she'd be at first glance. In just those three long strokes I'd veered enough...

...But even as I spun about and yo-yoed in panic I still couldn't locate her.

"*Gaby!*" I shrieked. "Where are you? *Gaby!*"

Sucking air to yell, I inhaled the bitter dregs of saltwater trickling around the heel of my tongue. I strangled, hacked reflexively to clear my larynx. The spasm made me snort more seawater. For an instant, until I regained control, tears blinded me and I coughed helplessly. Dilute snot oozed down my upper lip. I coughed and spat.

Where, where had she gone under? I'd last seen her... a few yards back, obviously, a little to the left in the heaving sea....

All I could do was take a wild guess. Swim to the arbitrary spot, fill my lungs and dive. Kick down, probe with salt-bleared eyes and outstretched fingers for some dim solidity.... I already knew I couldn't see far at all under these boiling onshore waters. Even if I had a goggle or mask....

The swells had begun to steepen as they surged across the rising bottom. Their period was fairly short and about halfway between me and the beach they built to their peak, then curled and caved in on themselves with a ceaseless background rumble like an artillery barrage. The wind seemed to have picked up. The heaving surface around me was flecked with spume and chop. When I eased my struggle to raise my torso—like a water-polo player after rearing to fire a shot at the net—my shoulders sloshed under and a riffle slapped me in the face. I blinked, snorted to clear my nostrils again, spat salt. I glanced quickly back at the beach with the sudden idea, hope—and instant recognition of its futility—that those who were watching could intuit my confusion, somehow signal me, direct me to where they'd last spotted her....

But even if it were possible, the audience too had disappeared momentarily below the crest of the breaker.

My inner ears registered the elevator rise of the running swell that was carrying me up its hump. I paddled against the momentum sweeping me further from where I'd left Gaby....

...And just as I was about to kick into a serious crawl down the backside... there she was again!

Oh, my God! *There she was!* Little disheveled blond head, arms cranking away, still swimming across the trough toward me.

I *hadn't* lost her!

*Jesus!* The lump of despair in my craw instantly dissolved. I could only guess she'd been masked behind the intervening swell. Or I'd just focused beyond or in front of her somehow. That can happen in so busy a visual field. That's why rescue planes fly blithely over lifeboats filled with frantically waving shipwreck survivors. Why I once turned onto the left leg of a familiar Y in the road driving home to Susan and felt a jarring thud. The afternoon was sunny, the street empty. I was puzzled—*something* had happened. Then a helmeted head rose into view above my right front fender. I'd turned directly in front of a motorcyclist who'd had the time and the presence of mind to lay his machine down before slamming into my front tire. I was appalled. But he was unhurt and actually drove off without the fuss I deserved. Even refused my offer of my telephone number. Broad daylight and I'd never seen him coming! A man on a motorcycle! Invisible, apparently, because my brain was programmed to look for the approaching bulk of an automobile at that intersection, not the pencil-thin one-eyed silhouette of a motorcycle head-on....

I struck out toward Gaby. Never again, I resolved, would I let her get more than an arm's length away.

"Ah, m... mon... Dieu... Gaby!" I exclaimed when I slid alongside. "Pour... un moment...." Then I bit off the phrase I was about to blurt. It would not boost her morale, I decided, to voice my apprehension. Raise that specter.

"Ça va... bien... maintenant," I declared. "Je crois... suis... j'en suis... sûr... que nou...zavons... échappé... le courant. Pouvons... regagner... la p... pl... pl...plage maintenant. Faut s... seulement... nager. Là bas. Non? Courage! Nage fort. T' es... brave... et forte... non?"

Her head, I thought, twitched in the affirmative.

And yes! Yes, you could feel it now. You could—*we* could—we could *see* the progress. We were finally riding an onshore set. Getting closer to the people on the beach with each stroke. Nearing safety, an end to the ordeal.

Gaby must have sensed it too. She was swimming harder at my side. Beginning almost to flail....

No, she *was* flailing, I realized... or at least she'd lost the self-possessed cadence she'd maintained up until now. Her hands and forearms were slapping the water in syncopated bursts of effort, but she was no longer really pulling through the stroke. Her head gyrated loosely. This was how a drowning person swims, a desperate person, punching at the enemy water rather than using it to advantage.

"*Calme toi toi, Gaby!*" I sputtered at her. "*Faut pas... n... nager trop.* Easy. Ea... easy d... does it. Relax. Mostly... let ... waves... c... carry us. *Les nuages... vont... vont... nous emporter... soi même.*"

She relented. She turned her milk-blue face to me. I noticed a tiny pucker of uncertainty between her eyebrows.

"*M... m... merde... que ça... c... c... caille,*" she gasped through chattering teeth. She switched momentarily to a kind of dogpaddle.

I broke my own lazy stroke to straighten my arm above my head, wave acknowledgement to the onlookers. Signal that we were okay and headed home at last. Encouragement for my poor, plucky little companion too.

The waves were humping more sharply. We were beginning to....

There was an itch at the back of my mind. What had I called them? What was the word for "waves?" *Nuages.* No, no. That wasn't right, I realized. That was the word for... "clouds." I'd told her the clouds would carry us in. Well, not so far off, I guess. Poetic. Probably added to her confusion a little bit, though. I liked it. The clouds would waft us in. But I searched my vocabulary for the *traduction juste.* I drew a blank.

"*Comment... dit-on... w... w....w... wave?*" I asked her. "*Ollas.* No... *olas? Ondas! Microondas....*"

She rolled her eyes at me. Even if I'd been making sense she was near the point of exhaustion.

"*En anglais,*" I persisted. "W... wave. Wave. *Vague!*" I remembered. "*Les vagues!*"

"*Ouais, vagues. Putains,*" she echoed faintly, "*bordel... de vagues....*"

"We can... ride them... now!" I exclaimed. "Body surf!

483

*Le... surfing....*" I gave it a French pronunciation: "sewer-fing. *Au c... corps....* Or something. Huh? *Avez vous...? Avez tu...? As tu...s... surfé? Fait de la surf? As tu... fait du... b...* body surfing?"

We were almost to the break. The *vagues* were still outpacing us... lifting and whisking us with them briefly before pulling ahead. Because of my size and weight the current wanted to drag me along faster than Gaby. I turned my shoulders and hips, feathered my hands and braked with frog-kicks on the backsides to try to let her catch up. But it was getting more difficult to slosh to a halt against the sea's manic urge to dash me ashore.

Mustn't lose contact with her, I rallied myself.

"*Da me... t... tu... m... m... mano... Gaby!*" I panted. I fought the water and stretched my arm toward her. "*Da... de....*" I knew there was something wrong with what I was saying but I couldn't figure out what or how to correct it. "Hold! My... hand," I pleaded.

She was swimming the crawl once more. "*Non! Non!*" she cried, angling away from me and altering her stroke evasively as I stabbed my claw at her, trying to snare her thin wrist. She looked terrified. "*Non! Veux pas! G... gare...!*" She twisted and kicked her feet hard, at me... as if fending off a shark.

She was right. Bad idea. We would have been wrenched apart in the surf. But probably not before being slammed together bone on flailing bone beneath its cascading mass.

And suddenly there it was. The last wave.

I was snatched up before I had a chance to orient myself... to deploy my wings, my ailerons, and plane on the face of the wave as I'd envisioned—the classic body-surfer's brief, exhilarating, spread-armed horizontal flight... which I'd experienced once, one exhilarating afternoon of it, at Makapu'u, during a stopover at Pearl when we'd been given the week off after escorting the *Ranger* out from San Diego for carrier quals. It was just before Christmas and our magnanimous captain turned everybody off-watch loose each morning after officers call. The palm-fringed sands, once you got beyond Waikiki, were virtually deserted in those days. I remember garlands of twinkling holiday lights all over Honolulu, carols and pop tunes evocative of snow and hot chocolate tinkling paradoxically in hotel lobbies as we foraged for tropical cocktails and *puupuus*. Four of us met a trio of bubbly Navy nurses one night and they suggested we go skinny-dipping on the beach after the bar closed. Disappointingly, they meant with their bras and panties on. We guys dutifully waded into the moonlit shallows in our white Navy-issue boxer skivvies—which was actually more daring for us because of the gaping pee-slits in the front. (Out of potential embarrasment Tim Denison crouched behind a trash barrel and turned his around backwards before revealing himself.) We flirted and played porpoise and splashed one another, tipsily titillated by the shadings and contours of imaginary nakedness under soaked underwear. Then we dressed and said goodnight, bound respectively for shipboard bunks and hospital nurses' quarters. As I said, it was a different time. A time of putative virginity, a time before the pill, when one-night stands were all but off the table. That week, too, I learned to push myself upright and carve a tentative *wedeln* on a long board. But when Tim and I tried to refine our newly acquired skills back in our homeport of Long Beach, in January, without wet suits (I mean, who knew? It was Southern California, and we were two Midwestern boys; did anyone in *Gidget* wear a wetsuit? It was almost forty years ago and they'd barely been invented), the fun wore off very quickly. And the surf dribbling in through the oil platforms was lousy to boot.

But these curls, pummeling the Great Beach at Point Reyes, were worse. Even colder, more jumbled, snub-nosed, building to one sudden, convulsive collapse. Instead of accelerating me smoothly forward, the climactic swell plucked me up and immediately flung me over its brink—crumpled on itself and buried me in the aqueous avalanche. I was driven upside down beneath it, hammered head-first like a slack pile into the sandy bottom, where I was wrenched and tumbled and bounced—elbows, shoulders, hips, knees rasped by the grit as I wrestled to escape the surf's pin, struggled to clamber free.

I scrabbled to my feet, faltered forward a step and pitched on my face in the surging run-out. My legs were weak as a baby's. But people—Chris and Becca and Elizabeth and Susan—had run out bravely to grab me, to drag me up the beach. And when I twisted my lolling head to make sure Gaby had been disgorged along with me, I saw her too somersault out from under the cataract and sluice ashore, floppy as a ragdoll, spinning into the clutching hands of her mother and Deirdre and some guys who'd splashed out to seize her, to help her to safety.

We'd made it.

*She'd* made it!

We'd *both* made it!

No tragedy would end up poisoning *this* carefree picnic afternoon.

# 5

**I'd never been so cold in my life.**

I was wracked by shivers that were practically convulsions. Every single muscle, it seemed, no matter how deep or minor, was vibrating to its own uncontrollable arrhythmia. Even though I strained to keep my molars clamped—I was afraid for the margins of my tongue—my teeth were in constant percussion. Here I'd been worrying about the water's chill getting to little Gaby. Obviously I was well into hypothermia myself.

With Chris and Becca's support I'd risen and managed to stagger upslope past the tide line. There I sank to one knee and braced myself unsteadily, forearms across my upthrust thigh, head bowed, regaining my breath, draining my sinuses, waiting for the vertigo—rapture of ground-level solidity—to wane. It seemed like a more dignified posture, more manly—the classic shot of the injured football warrior gathering himself on the sidelines for a return to combat—than sprawling prone to embrace the heat of the sand. Which I probably would have done immediately, like a cat flattening its belly against sunny pavement, if image weren't involved. After all, I'd just done a kind of a squirrelly thing, going out into that water. I didn't want to look as if I'd almost drowned for my folly.

"That was pretty impressive, Daddy," Becca

murmured. She and Elisabeth were bent over me on either side scrubbing at my back and ribcage and hair with wonderfully tepid, slightly gritty beach towels they'd scrounged. "You almost gave us heart attacks, but somebody had to do it."

I nodded my accord.

"Good on ya, Pops," Chris echoed.

"Always got to be the center of attention," Elisabeth teased, "don't you?"

"'S me... m... me, all right," I agreed.

Others I didn't know circled in to offer gruff approbation. I acknowledged with exhausted, self-deprecatory flicks of my hand. Somebody had fetched a striped cotton tablecloth or something, which Becca threw over my head and draped around my shoulders. At least it cut the wind. She and Elisabeth bustled to tent me in its folds more thoroughly, which I appreciated. I was still shivering like a motherfucker. Any second I was going to shake myself off balance and topple on my side ignominiously.

"Really. That was quite a wonderful thing you did," Susan threw in. "Maybe not the smartest thing, but Gaby's here with us. She might not be... she probably wouldn't be... otherwise."

"D... didn't d... d... do much," I demurred. "Just s... showed her wh... which way t... t' swim. She okay?"

"They've got her all wrapped up in blankets. She's cool as a cucumber," Susan said. "Literally. Shivering to beat the band... like you... but no damage. Noelle's fussing over her. Keeps calling her *idiote*. She's a tough little number."

"Great. Excellent," I said. "Sh... she is th... that."

"You should lie down, Daddy," Becca advised. "Lie flat. Let us tuck you in real tight, ball you up like a cocoon. You're freezing."

"Am, g...gotta admit," I admitted. "Water's fuck... fucking f... fr... freezing once you've b... been in it a while!

P... pardon my Fr... French."

"Go for it," Elisabeth murmured.

"I was sp... *speaking* French to her," I chuckled. "All g... garbled up. And... Spanish and God kn... kn... knows what else there. I was g... goin' off my rock... rocker a bit, I think think. T... toward the end."

"Here's another one. Little thicker," Chris said, returning with a light woolen Army blanket he'd borrowed from among the picnickers. Most of them seemed to have drifted back to the vicinity of the barbecue grill now that the excitement was concluded.

I eased myself into a sitting position while Elisabeth and Becca bundled me into the second layer of swaddling. The first was already clammy with the seawater absorbed from my lower body and wet underpants. I thought of dragging them off undercover but decided it would be too much trouble.

"Really was a bad rip, huh?" Chris said. "Seems like you got carried out pretty far."

"Yeah. Jus... just h... had to g... get... out of it," I said. "Like... I... s... said. Sorry my tee... teeth are ch... chattering so much. I'll w... w... warm up in a m... minute."

"Thank you, thank you, oh, thank you, Rick!" I heard Noelle's voice calling from behind my shoulder. She floundered closer through the loose sand and leaped at me. I staggered backwards against her weight. She clasped me in a long hug. "Oh, that was *so* brave of you. You have saved her life, my Gabrielle, I think."

If so, I thought, it required very little of me. I didn't know how to respond—acknowledgement would be taking too lavish credit, denial would sound like false modesty or at least be ungracious. Maybe I *had* saved Gaby's life. Might as well think so. I took refuge in a weak smile and indulgence in a spate of shivers. She released me. "G... G... Gaby is ver... very strong," I offered. "Is sh... is she all r... right?"

"Oh, yes," Noelle said. "She is so sorry...."

"No!" I exclaimed. "*Ce... ce n... n... n'était pas sa faute! C'était... la mer que l'a ap... appris. Une v... vague que la p... pris... p... par surprise. Et un courant m... mal... mal... méchant.* Rip current. We call it. Don't... don't be angry with her. *Ce... ce n'était pas... pas... pas sa faute.*"

"Oh, I am not, I am not," Noelle assured me.

"*Elle était tr... très brave. Toujours. Une b... bonne fille. Très s... sage.*"

"*Elle te remercie de tout son coeur,*" Noelle assured me.

"*N'y a p... pas de quoi,*" I smiled. "Just g... glad she's okay. Tell... tell her that for me. We... we'll t... talk in a minute."

"I will," Noelle said.

The kids went off to tend to their kids. Élodie had rushed over to pay me her compliments after helping see to Gaby. I lay back and hugged myself—a slab of ice cream, sandwiched between the warm sand and the radiant sun, desperate to melt. The two of us, Gaby and I, lay a few yards apart, mummified in blankets. Noelle was stretched out alongside her daughter.

"You're s... supposed to take... off all your c... clothes and lie inside the b... blankets on top of me," I suggested to Elisabeth.

"Dream on," she said.

"No, really," I persisted in a mock-serious tone. "Isn't that wh... what they s... say to do to someone who's hype... hypothermic? So... so the body heat g... gets transferred?"

"You're going to survive without that," she said. "I have every confidence."

"Maybe," I conceded. "W'... would help, though. Up t... t' you."

"I'll keep you company," she said, settling beside me. "I'll be your windbreak." She wriggled close, her weight snug against me and her arm thrown across my chest. I turned my face towards hers.

"Gotta keep a close eye on you, so you don't get into any more trouble," she smiled.

I roused myself enough to lean into her and give her a peck on the lips.

She shuddered. "Brr!" she said. "You *are* a block of ice."

"I actually f... feel a little warmer," I told her.

After a few moments she asked, "Were you afraid at all?"

"I was fri... frightened of sharks," I allowed. "But mostly I was too busy busy s... swimming and thinking about how far we had to go to get out of the rip. Worrying whether Gaby would h... hold up."

"You had me terrified," she said. "I thought I was about to end this day a widow."

"Like Su... Susan," I noted. "Deirdre."

"Mm," she agreed.

"You'll be one some day."

"That's a lovely thought," she chided. "Thanks for the reminder. Which I hardly need right now. Anyway, who knows? Maybe I'll be the one who goes first. You seem to lead a pretty charmed life."

"Hope so," I said. "Not, I mean, that y... you'll die first, but...."

"I know what you mean," she said. "So. Are you going to go and get that biopsy now?"

"Oh, my *God...!*" I yelped.

"Make sure it *stays* charmed! Set my mind at rest...?"

"...You pick this moment to harp on *that?*"

"Whatever," she muttered sulkily. I felt her shrug. "You made me think of it."

"God, I'm just thankful that everything turned out all right *today!*" I said. "Let me at least enjoy *that* for a few minutes."

"Certainly," she allowed.

I pushed myself up on my elbows and looked over at Gaby. "Hey, Gaby!" I trumpeted. *"Comment ça va?* Feeling better now? I am!"

She wiggled inside her swaddling. "Yes, yes," she answered in a thin, high voice. "V... very good. I too now. *Je je m... m'en sors b... bien. Grâce à vous, m... monsieur."*

*M'sieu.* The formality startled me. It was wounding in a way, distancing after the intimacy of the episode we'd shared. I'd been calling her Gaby all along, using the familiar *tu* with which adults patronize children and pets. Friends and family and inferiors. I think in fact Noelle may have introduced me as Rick or Richard, but I'm not sure. But what else except *monsieur* was a polite young girl to call an older man who wasn't related to her?

*"Tu... t... tu peux me t... tutoyer maintenant, Gaby. Ap... p... près notre... notr' aventure ensemble? Ça me pleurait. Non.* Plair*ait. Ça me plairait. Je suis... suis ton... je suis ton... Oncle Richard."* I pronounced it *Ree-shar.* "Will you call me that? *M'appeller cela? Oncle Richard?* Is that okay with you, Noelle? I'm *Oncle Richard* now?"

"Of course! It's perfect for her!" she beamed.

"I just acquired a niece," I said to Elisabeth.

"I'm happy for you," she replied, sitting up. "I suppose that makes me *Tante Elissabet.*"

"Ipso f... facto," I said.

"Our dishy new niece."

"Whoa, do I detect a note of jealousy? Of a fourteen-year-old?"

"Don't be silly," she objected.

"She's a pretty bedraggled little dish at the moment. And I didn't swim out there after her because of my hormones."

"I know. I didn't say you did."

"That's the implication."

"Well, don't imply it. Don't...."

"Infer it," I beat her to the correction. "Is what *I* do."

"Thank you," Elisabeth scowled. "That wasn't what I meant. I was just making an observation. She's very... cute. That's all I was saying. I like her."

"Good. I'm glad. Where are my c... clothes? I guess they're still back where I left them."

"I'll go find them for you," Elisabeth offered. "I'll bring them to you." She rolled onto her knees and, with a grunt, got to her feet.

"I guess I could walk down the beach now myself with these blankets around me," I said. "Not too indecent."

"Stay where you are. You're still shivering. I'm going to see if I can find you something hot to drink."

"Bring one for Gaby too, if you do," I reminded her.

"Of course!" she snapped, with that frown of remonstrance we give each other when a nag has preempted intention.

"Okay," I muttered. "Oh! And my sunglasses? If you can find 'em? It's really bright!"

"Where are they?" she asked.

"I don't know. I threw 'em down somewhere over there, before I went in the water. Maybe Becca has 'em."

"Okay. I'll be back in a minute," she said. "You just concentrate on thawing out."

"Yes, ma'am," I said. "Thanks."

## I lay back, head on the hard sand, and listened to the unrelenting boom of the ocean.

The bedrock beneath me seemed to quiver at the pounding. It was amazing to think I'd gone out into that turbulence voluntarily. But I had. And I was alive to tell the tale.

Gaby was recovering. Perhaps she would eventually have figured out for herself what to do to get back to the beach. Or finally understood instructions waved at her. Or the rip current would have dwindled or shifted—as it may have anyway. Who could say whether I'd been smart or we'd been lucky? And what difference did it make, given the outcome?

Elisabeth returned after a few minutes with my rounded-up pants, shirt, flipflops and sombrero. She also brought my sunglasses, a thermos of coffee and two nested styrofoam cups. She poured me one while I squirmed into a sitting position and freed an arm. A brief shiver still coursed through me every so often, but I was definitely regaining my lost core heat. The harsh glare of the sun off the ocean immediately softened when I interposed the Polarized gray lenses. I lifted the cup to my lips, tested the steaming brown liquid and swallowed a gulp. Thin, bitter dishwater. But this was no time for coffee connoisseurship. And it did burn a heartening track alongside my spine going down.

Elisabeth went over and filled the other cup for Gaby, who wormed a glistening bare shoulder out of her blankets like an emerging chrysalis and sipped eagerly. I guess fourteen-year-olds in France are used to coffee—the breakfast *bol de café et tartine*. Except I think it tends to be *chocolat* for *les gosses*. Still, even teenyboppers here in the United States now flock to the ubiquitous coffee franchises, which obviously aren't required to card their customers. I'm always surprised and mildly, reflexively disapproving when I see adolescents caffeinating themselves... at that age I'd been sternly warned it would stunt my growth. Like inhaling nicotine into your lungs. Neither of which had held any appeal for me until I'd belatedly waded into the welter of vices during my postgraduate merchant-seaman sailabout.

Already into my twenties.

Susan had come back with the clothes Gaby had peeled off to soak in the sun and play at the water's edge with Molly. I heard them all agreeing it was probably time to call it an afternoon. Apparently Susan had chauffeured Noelle and Gaby out here from San Francisco. She and Noelle helped Gaby to her feet and the four women—diminutive Gaby shuffling along cowled and entrained in her blanketing as if wearing some kind of outsize *abaya*—circled around me to exchange goodbyes.

I beckoned to Elisabeth to relieve me of my coffee cup and she gave me an arm while I disentangled myself enough to rise. Every joint ached when I cracked the brittle stalactites and stalagmites that were my tendons and ligaments. Nor was the effort to unfold made any easier by my determination not to allow any glimpses of my sodden underpants and the no doubt wizened penis cupped within. Not that there hadn't been full disclosure already. Still.

"We need to get Gaby out of the weather and into dry clothes again," Susan said. "I think we've all had enough excitement for one day, wouldn't you say?"

"Mm," I concurred.

Susan leaned forward and brushed my cheek with her lips. "You were great," she murmured. "To do that. Actually," she added in a confidential whisper, "it's no less than I would have expected of you."

"Hm!" I exclaimed, flaring my eyebrows. "I'm flattered." I was. "Unless you mean, 'do something really, really idiotic.'"

"No, no," she replied earnestly. "Something... something that needed to be done. Where others might hesitate. You did your duty as you saw it."

"Yep," I said. "That's how I saw it."

"You always were a hothead," she said. "I'm sorry we didn't get a chance to talk more," she added, pulling away from me and once again using her social voice.

"I'll call you," I told her. I couldn't help glancing at Elisabeth, whose face was, of course, blank except for the little convivial smile we all wore.

"Well, don't do it tomorrow," Susan said. "I'm driving home. I'll be on the road most of the day."

"You don't like to natter away on your cellphone?" I teased. "To pass the time while you're driving? That's the only time I hear from Chris or Becca. When they're ferrying kids to a soccer practice or something."

"I don't, really," Susan said. "I've started listening to audiobooks, actually."

"Well, good for you," I said. "Uplifting."

"I'll be back in the lab Monday. But I'm usually free in the evenings. Call me then. If you want."

"Sure," I said. I had a flash sensation that this was like dating, and that I was very likely to renege. Once again I glanced at Elisabeth. She was well aware, of course, that my first wife and I still had occasion to talk.

Noelle gave me another octopoidal embrace. I leaned into it and we touched cheeks as I air-kissed her over both shoulders. I couldn't reciprocate the hug because my arms were folded tightly against my ribs, clasping the coverings around me.

"Great s... seeing you again, Noelle," I said. "I'll get your e-mail address from Susan."

"Yes, do," Noelle said. "And I yours. We must all keep in contact again more now."

"Gaby?" I said. "It was a pleasure swimming with you."

She gave me a quizzical grin.

"*C'était mon plaisir de nager... d'avoir nagé avec toi.*"

She giggled. "*Et moi aussi,*" she replied. "*C' était vachement effrayant, la mer.*" She glanced to her mother. "*À vous je dois ma vie, je crois...Oncle Richard.*"

I laughed with pleasure. *"Merci,"* I said.

*"Mais, non! C'est* vous *que je dois remercier.* You have save my life, I am sure, I believe," she repeated, gracing me with English and a fleeting, radiant smile.

*"Mais, j'ai cru que nous allions nous tutoyer de maintenant."*

*"Ah, ouais,"* she agreed, looking down shyly at her invisible toes. She didn't offer her own parting embrace. Just as well. I was kind of apprehensive about that.

"Okay. *À la prochaine,"* I told them all. To Noelle I added, "Elisabeth and I may turn up in Paris one of these days. Be forewarned."

"Oh, but you must!" she exclaimed. "We would love it, of course. We would enjoy to take you around to see many interesting places. I have a book that tells much about Paris that even I didn't know. Yes, Gaby?"

Gaby nodded and smiled.

"I'll walk over there with you," Elisabeth said to them. Gaby, I realized, was naturally going to change out of her wet bikini in the cavernous restroom at the end of the parking lot. The image flashed unbidden across my mind—little risen pink nipples, tan lines, trimly waxed pubic patch. The lurid detail made me angry at myself. I thought I'd gotten *past* that! She was *fourteen!*

"You want to come with us, Rick? Get dressed there too?"

"Nah," I muttered. "I want to de-ice for a couple minutes more. I'll just put my clothes on here. I've got a blanket to shield me. Nobody's gonna be outraged when I'm this far away. You could give me a coffee refill, though. If there's any left in there that's still hot."

She turned the cup over and shook its dregs into the breeze, refilled it from the thermos. I poked a hand through my wraps to take the cup, then folded it back inside against my breastbone and savored the warmth on my palm. The halo of steam misted my skin.

"We should probably go ourselves pretty soon too," Elisabeth said to me, "don't you think? We have a drive ahead of us."

"Yeah, I'll be ready when you get back," I nodded.

I watched them walk away toward the other guests clumped loosely around the barbecue grill. Their progress, what with bidding goodbyes to Deirdre and others, exchanging well wishes and post-morteming Gaby's *contretemps,* would be slow.

I turned to face the clamorous surf. After a moment I sank into a creaky crouch and plopped onto my butt. Coffee sloshed from the cup and dribbled down my chest. It was hot enough to make me wince, but not scalding.

I deserved scalding. Burn out that rank, hairy-haunched, goat-hoofed homunculus I harbored.


## On the other hand, I was still around to feel lust, wasn't I?

No one would have rated *that* a slam dunk a few minutes ago.

And it wasn't really *lust,* I keep insisting. That's defined by a desire for consummation. The notion of actually lying with Gaby, a child, was abhorrent at every level. Except the unconscious, or the subconscious, or however the Freudian terminology would have it—the id. I was simply responding instinctively to the musk of the female, the primal pull of reproductive chemistry. It was like waking out of hazily lubricious dreams as a fourteen-year-old boy with a hard-on and a gluey sheet—no need, the Jesuits assured us, to confess that confusing semi-pleasure. It wasn't sin. Just Nature priming the pump, as it were.

Had I become more lecherous with age? I couldn't recall ever having fantasized sex with Noelle when she was our *au pair*. But again, I wasn't fantasizing sex *per se* with her daughter either. Perhaps Noelle's glasses and gangly earnestness at seventeen had defended her from my predacious fortyish surmise. Or perhaps familiarity does breed, if not contempt, indifference. That was when Susan was losing interest in *me* after sixteen years. She transferred her affections to a nerdy father figure, not some adolescent Adonis. I went for Maartje. But I suppose the existence of male strippers who gyrate in jock-straps for whooping middle-aged women does demonstrate that the allure of a toned young body is a two-way street.

I could still imagine sleeping with Susan. Every so often a memory of her naked, her legs curled around my back, would creep for some reason into my mind. An idle mind, as they say... although "idle" might not be an accurate descriptive in those circumstances. Dirty mental pictures of a younger Susan no longer had much oomph, in fact. Elisabeth, whose ample flesh was at hand and whose image splayed *à l'odalisque* freshly on file, had assumed prurient dominance. Which is as it should be, certainly. I chafed at no bit, I had no desire to complicate my life with another woman. Thank God I could still get it up for anybody; Elisabeth more than filled the bill. Meets or exceeds expectations. I *loved* her, moreover, which spices the sex. And yet, now that Susan was a widow and our bad bygones mostly bygones... who knows? The embers of our sensual life had never died completely. Probably it was a good thing we lived so far apart.

What a fortunate man I was. To repeat myself. Never, I exhorted myself, lose sight of that. The only thing worse than letting death catch you unprepared is letting life dribble by unappreciated. Taking the grace notes for granted. Everything's luck. No one fails to notice and lament the bad luck; it's the good that tends to sneak under the radar.

Short of winning the lottery, you get lulled into discounting daily good luck as the default. It's not. I learned that when my mother died. So when a rich, fat, hale, emotionally fulfilled North American, or any other similarly endowed world citizen, forgets his or her tenuous fortuity—or worse, confuses it with merit—it's like spitting on everybody who's on the downside of the bell curve.

A responsive wife. A friendly ex-wife. Two self-sufficient adult children. Two ditto step-children. Four smart, vivacious, hale grandchildren. A roof over my head. A little money in the bank. A few writing assignments to keep the cerebral gears engaged. Even against the latest odds, brain and body still functioning. What more could a man of my age ask? Although how healthy those last two might be, I suppose, lay open to question.

The brain was obviously riddled with evil thoughts. Or so they would have been characterized by my childhood mentors. To my credit of some sort, I'd accumulated a modest harem of past lovers to summon *en deshabille* when my mind wandered in search of titillation. More good fortune. And no blots on the ethical escutcheon—never an adultery, except in the Jimmy Carter sense. Well, or in reverse, as correspondent, just that once. With the troubling... Victoria. Victoria... Cashman.

As to my physical body, it too might be riddled, to use the hackneyed verb for cancer's effect... although I'd staunchly chosen to believe my prostate was simply puffed up with manly vigor. Doesn't recent research suggest that frequent orgasm protects against cancer of the prostate? And counting all the instances in which I'd taken matters into my own hands, I'd bet I'd averaged... nah, not worth the effort at calculation. But on those grounds, at least, my little gland should be aglow with health, I reckoned.

According to the cliché, your whole life passes before your eyes when you're drowning. One of those speeded-up montage reversals of time... but hell, my whole life passes before my eyes all the time. Okay, maybe not my "whole life..." rather, selected short subjects. And maybe not "my eyes" but the cerebral screening room inside my skull, and maybe not "all the time" but rather pretty randomly often.

At night, say. On my back in the dark with the pillow over my eyesockets and Elisabeth snoring softly beside me... I suddenly flop on my belly on my new Flexible Flyer and take off on a disastrous descent of Deadman's Hill at Henke's Woods—every snow-covered rock and lacerating snag still vividly envisioned....

...In the crisp early morning grinding up and down the Ft. Bragg pool... I'm back doing the same thing at a downtown Cincinnati athletic club whose name I've forgotten—on my lunch break from my awful summer job as a filing clerk for a friend's Dad's company, naked as was the custom then at male-only pools, newly confident in my nakedness because over the winter I'd sprouted pubic hair....

...In a hot shower with the droplets drumming on my nape and the steam seeping into my tingly joints like WD-40... a tiny Japanese masseuse starts trampling a path across my back at a ryokan below a ski-hill at Chuzenjiko....

...At my desk staring over my laptop through the fog of word-clouds swirling in my brain... I sidle up to the sole, lonely looking black guy at an executive conference I'm covering and try to make conversation ("Most of the guys I play basketball with are black"), deservedly earning his disdain and betraying the racism I'd so naively meant to belie....

...Lulled by the gnarr of the sander as I round off a ripped edge... I cut for the basket, snatch the pass, take off with the ball in my right hand, see the defender nimbly flying at me to block the shot, switch the ball to my left hand and, twisting to fend him off, flip it in off the backboard before my feet hit the ground—to onlookers' whoops, probably my favorite shot of all time.....

...Cradling a martini before the hypnotic gyre of the log fire... it's the semifinals, I'm down two sets to five, I've been broken twice, I'm second-serving at love-forty and my American twist has been consistently arcing long; nevertheless....

But you get the idea. Who needs drowning as catalyst?

Anyway, survivor accounts don't seem to corroborate the "life-passing-before-your-eyes" convention. I can, however, testify that *not* drowning is a great way to start the pages of the mental flip-book riffling.

So there I sat, bare as a baby in a diaper under swaddling cloths, nearly three-quarters of a century of experiences embodied in the sack of wrinkled gooseflesh uncomfortably enclosed—the long passage from chubby infant to desiccated old man, full arc, mewling and puking to puling and... well, doesn't work out as cleverly as I'd hoped, *mewking* not being a word. Although it ought to be. There I sat, an old man puling and mewking—postnasal trickles of caustic seawater still drained from my sinuses—conscious despite all the recent opportunity I'd handed fate to extinguish this particular nexus of axons and dendrites... reviewing the table of contents for my *Apologia Pro Vita Sua*. My *Scenes from the Seven Ages of Man*... or rather, of *A* man....

Only why seven? Far be it from me to question Shakespeare or his source, apparently Ecclesiastes. But that seems an odd divisor, doesn't it? In more than the numerical sense. You could just as easily use three, say, like the periods in ice hockey and lacrosse. Childhood, vigorous adulthood, senility. Or five, like the sets in men's tennis. Or nine, for that matter, like the innings in baseball... even fifteen, the rounds in a championship boxing match, if you're into really fine-grained detail. Granted, the World Series can go to seven games. But four strikes me as the most *à propos* segmentation of a human life—like the quarters in football and basketball. Childhood, young adulthood, middle age, old age. *My Life in Four Quarters.* Obvious sports metaphor. I like that title.

Of course, not all lives are played into the fourth quarter. Not if normal game time these days is, let's say, four-score. And there's often substantial injury time. But at least as many lives get rained out early. The whistle that stops play shrills at the Referee's discretion. (And, yes, I'm egregiously mixing sports metaphors here. And no, I don't believe there is a Referee.)

Whatever, all lives are ultimately called on account of darkness.

Ha. One thing I can be proud of: I have taken banal to a whole new level.

## That's the only reason I would even consider asking for a Mulligan if the option were available.

Sure, there are lots of little and not-so-little instances—demeaning, embarrassing, hurtful, stupid moments—when everyone involved would benefit if I could have a do-over. But the big question, when I assess my life, is: Have I really used it to its capacity?

Unfortunately, or probably fortunately, that's an unanswerable question. Some lives are like eggplant slices, able to soak up as much oil as they're immersed in. Others are like baby lettuce leaves that have to be dressed delicately or they'll wilt. Napoleon Bonaparte v. Emily Dickinson. Which one didn't meet his/her potential?

One of my best friends in the Navy, a fellow junior officer on the *Busby* for a year before he was reassigned, gradually revealed himself to be the scion of a major Rust Belt dynasty. (I'd never heard of it, and only learned the extent of the family's wealth and stature in retrospect.) Mason had gone to Groton, and to Harvard College, where he was a Porcellian—the most rarefied of nob credentials, but an utterly down-to-earth guy. He was an ice hockey player. He had an adequate tennis game, and when the *Busby* was ordered to Hunter's Point Naval Shipyard for a four-month refit, he signed me up as an honorary member of the posh California Tennis Club. There he introduced me to squash, to wreak his revenge for the defeats I'd eked out on the unwalled court upstairs. He also knew all the socially connected girls in the City, which got me into a lot of big houses in Pacific Heights. At one of them I met Tess Barton, a lanky, auburn-haired beauty with a hearty laugh, the daughter of a big Central Valley rice grower. She'd just graduated from Berkeley with a degree in art history and was working as a junior buyer at I. Magnin's while, par for the course in those days, looking for a suitable husband.

Tess and I went out maybe half a dozen times. She took me (I paid the tabs) to good little offbeat restaurants, a play at the Geary, the Buena Vista for Irish coffee nightcaps, a picnic at Stinson Beach, her family's cabin at Squaw Valley for a weekend of skiing. We made out in the guest bedroom there at her initiative, but she pushed away before things got serious, which was only to be expected. I liked her company and found the eclectic group of arty friends she kept around her—several clearly gay—amusing. But the chemistry between us was inert. When the *Busby* returned from a couple of weeks of sea trials and instrument calibrations at Dabob Bay—my first glimpse of Seattle, in weather so dreary I never knew there were mountains on the Olympic Peninsula—the relationship had sputtered out.

But here's the thing. A couple of years later Tess married one of the richest men in America. I began to read about her soirées, receptions, travels: hostess to visiting royalty, patron of the opera and the symphony, museum donor, backer of films and stage productions, jet-setting friend and supporter of noted politicians, producers, directors, actors, writers, scientists. Eventually she even acquired one of America's leading avant-garde publishing houses. (Her reclusive husband was apparently content simply to fund her enthusiasms.)

Mason, meanwhile, was diagnosed with a congenital disease that ended his naval service but obviously didn't affect his business acumen. With seed money from his inheritance he founded a successful brokerage chain that flowered as an early adapter to the internet. He sits on the board of several Fortune Fifty conglomerates, chairs the family charitable foundation and has a building at Harvard named after him. What's more—I learned all this when, to my astonishment, I recognized him in an interview on ESPN—he'd bought both the National Hockey League franchise and the major league baseball team in his native city!

I think about Mason and Tess and the contrast between their lives and mine when I encounter their names in the media. They're living larger, no question. Sometimes I consider getting in touch. Recall old times. But why? What do we have in common? Only old acquaintance. Not forgot, at least on my end, but hardly a basis for rekindled relations. Those had their moment. Now I'm afraid they'd just think I was trying to reingratiate myself because of their prominence. And maybe that would be true.

It's the parable of the talents. Since we're all wired differently, talents vary. I really don't regret that I haven't met some of the conventional benchmarks of success. I wasn't wired to covet superfluous wealth, or celebrity, or power over others. My failure to achieve them, and not to have strived for them, is a function of my personality. Maybe it's just rationalization, sour grapes. But I feel quite sure I would not be happy as a famous guy... although, yes, I'd probably enjoy fifteen minutes of the world's admiration, as long as no one knew what I really looked like. I would not be happy commanding minions, unless, perhaps, I could do it as an *éminence grise*. With plausible deniability. And a four-week annual vacation.

Sitting at the very foot of the boiling surf your horizon is foreshortened. Sometimes in Mendocino, sipping wine on the patio of a friend's house above Caspar Cove or following Main Street as it curves away from the village to skirt the barren headlands, I see the tiny, distant silhouette of a tanker or a containership *en* lonely *route* between the Golden Gate and the Columbia River or Puget Sound. Those sightings have become even rarer and fainter since the maritime traffic lane was offset further from shore, but you know they're out there, all the time: huge vessels crisscrossing the seas, laden with the essential cargo that keeps modern industrial/commercial society functioning as we've become dependent on it.

When Becca was a baby strapped to one or the other of us in a sling when she wasn't free to crawl, Susan and I traveled with her to the island of Roatán, off the coast of Honduras. She took her first steps there, a milestone by which I date the trip. I also remember the kind of defiant pride with which I swaggered through Latin American airports and city streets—a tall, bearded *gringo,* stunning *novia* at the hip... with an infant in a wrap-around carrier clinging to my chest. My updated bandolier. The new *macho. Norteamericano*-style.

We were visiting Susan's mother and her new husband, "Cap'n Gary" Schaeffer, the owner of a tiny bone-fishing resort. The mood was sour in the United States, or in Berkeley, anyway—Nixon was President, Reagan governor, the Vietnam War had expanded into Cambodia and Laos, National Guard troops had actually gunned down callow student protesters at Kent State... it seemed a good time to find respite from daily bad news in a sunny, remote and in those days virtually undeveloped speck of jungle ringed by coral reefs in a backwater of the Caribbean.

We flew in serially smaller planes to Miami, Guatemala City, Tegucigalpa, San Pedro Sula and finally La Ceiba, where we boarded a stripped-down DC-3 for the hop to Roatán. We landed on the beach outside Coxens Hole, the shabby, one-street capital of the *Islas de la Bahía*. From there we coasted down the roadless island in a whaleboat piloted by Susan's handsomely grizzled new (although not for long, another story) step-father. For the next two weeks we bunked in one of the two tin-roofed cabins he'd built next to a palm-shaded main guest-house overlooking the narrow beach he'd dynamited out of the reef. While Becca toddled or napped under the cooing supervision of Nelly the cook, or one or another of the Caracol women who lived in stilt-houses along the dirt path to Oak Ridge Harbour, Susan and I would step into long rubber flippers, duckwalk a few steps out into the tepid, waist-deep water, adjust our masks and breathing tubes and launch ourselves for a leisurely snorkel among the coral heads.

The water was crystalline. The waves broke on the crest of the reef a few hundred yards out. Inside the sheltered lagoon the surface was placid. Below us, pockets of sand and eel grass, thrusting coral knobs and the winding, jagged aisles between them teemed with fantastic marine life. We didn't have to dive to enjoy the color-show: spiny black urchins, pink anemones, yellow starfish pliant as soft-pretzels, scuttling lobsters that the young island men would wade ashore waving in each hand at sunset to sell to Nelly for a few *lempira*... shy, translucent octopi, troglodytic eels, a ray cruising the surface as silvery young barracudas shot beneath it like a salvo of misfired torpedos... and, of course, everywhere the *pièces de résistance*: flitting shoals of

fluorescent angelfish, blue chromis, banded butterflyfish—
an aquarium of brilliantly hued, striped, spotted and/or
whimsically shaped tropical species whose particularities I
can't remember if they were ever identified to me.

At its deepest the bottom of the reef-flat was probably
no more than ten or fifteen feet down. But if you swam out
through the surf over the algal ridge to the fore-reef, there
were greater depths and new types of coral formations to
explore. Here you found bigger fish like groupers, grunts,
beaked parrotfish and chevroned sergeant majors. Steroidal
turtles with mournful faces loomed like aquatic UFOs,
drifting lazily in to nibble at the reef wall's barrel sponges.
Here we often made little descents to nose among limber sea
fans and the intricate limestone skeletons of their staghorn
and lettuce-coral cousins—always wary of the needle-
toothed morays that might be lurking in crevices.

You'd exhale into your mouthpiece, gulp a
replenishing lungful of air through the snorkel tube, hump
your back and kick down. I've always been a wuss about
pressure on my eardrums, so I never ventured very deep.
Only once did we ever do any real diving in snorkel gear.
That was when Gary took us for a picnic—down-island
past the mangrove-clotted channel that wound across the
island to the north shore, past the crumbled stones of the
old pirate fortress of Port Royal, past the forested hump of
Roatán's trailing satellite island, Morat, to tiny Pigeon Cay—a
few palm trees on a mound of white sand. Along the way
we pulled into a cove where, looking down through water
translucent as glass, we could see the shadows cast by fat
amber conch shells scattered across the sandy bed. Gary
gave us string bags and Susan and I stroked down repeatedly,
maybe twenty feet down, to harvest enough for a hearty
conch chowder, which Nelly served us at lunch next day.

Susan could hold her breath underwater longer than
I could, at least comfortably. My head felt as if it were in a

vise that was slowly squeezing my brains into my sinuses and ear canals. No sooner did I touch the bottom, upside down, than I began to fear that I wouldn't be able to make it back to the surface before desperation triggered an involuntary, fatal gasp—or that I wouldn't have enough stale residual air left in my lungs to blow my tube clear when I finally did break into the blessed atmosphere. I'd dutifully snatch at the two or three conchs nearest to hand and scuttle skyward while Susan continued womanfully foraging.

I didn't go very far down or linger the only other times I dove deep, either. (Pardon my grammar, but *dove* is a much more satisfactory past tense than the clumsy *dived.*) Another few hundred yards to seaward of the barrier crest the reef floor suddenly fell away. Beyond lay open ocean. From this empty, murky, fathomless, ultramarine abyss there seemed to rise a synesthetic moan: a warning—this way lies peril—coupled with a lament for the corpses of the sunk ships and drowned souls strewn across the bottom of the Earth's seas from here to the poles. Roatán is only thirty-five miles from the mainland, but this offshore trench is what gave Honduras—"depths," in Spanish—its name, after all.

I made a couple of hasty reconnoiters of the reef-wall, edgy tests of how far down I dared descend without a SCUBA tank. But the sea-life was sparser, the coral darker and I was always nervous that something was sneaking up on me from behind. We'd been warned that hammerheads and massive whale sharks forage along the reef-wall, but assured neither is routinely dangerous to man. I never saw any. But I wasn't keen to put their docility to the test.

There's a point to this reminiscence—no doubt prompted by the setting and my recent immersion. It came to me that you could find in it an analogy to the way I'd led my life.

Some people—like Mason and Tess, I suppose—aspire to be captains of those great ships out plying the main:

giving orders, setting course, supervising crews, shmoozing up important passengers, peering through fogs, weighing the reports of lookouts and navigators, shepherding weighty cargoes through wind and storm... exercising authority and responsibility, rising in rank. That's all very well. I admire them, with reservations. I've walked in that direction myself for short periods. It's what, in your megalomaniac twenties, you expect of yourself if you've always been labeled a "high achiever." It didn't suit me.

Instead I'm among those who prefer to loll in the shallows of a quiet lagoon observing through a face mask the reef life pulsing close around them.

On the bridge of a ship, whether you're the captain or a junior officer entrusted with the conn, your attention is constantly absorbed by external demands. You're scanning the darkness for hazards, pinpricks of light, icebergs, shoals, eyeing the compass, checking the chart, listening and speaking to others along the chain of responsibility. When you're snorkeling you have only your own sensations to monitor. Your body is always on your mind. Consciousness narrows and intensifies: the hollow suck of your breath, the crackle of your Eustachian tubes adapting to pressure, the complexly coordinated zero-gravity dance to maneuver underwater, the increasingly shrill argument between brain and lungs as the seconds tick off without a new infusion of oxygen.... Your vision is channeled by the glass oval whose rubber gasket blocks peripheral distractions, its field magnified by the seawater lens. A strange world of hidden beauty flickers before you, a microcosm within reach of your outstretched fingers, as rewarding to contemplate in its immediate intricacy as human history or metaphysics.

Anyway, that's how, musing on the pitch of my life on the Great Beach at Point Reyes one fraught afternoon, I put a spin on it.

**I wasn't allowed the luxury of brooding for long.**

My solitude stirred solicitude. People drifted over to check on me.

First came Joel with Molly, who was brandishing a Frisbee. She asked me if I wanted to throw it with her.

"Don't worry, even if you can't catch it and it goes in the water the waves always bring it right back, Pop-pop," she assured me.

"I've noticed that," I said. "Although it doesn't happen *always*. Maybe I will in a bit."

"I don't think Pop-pop wants to play anywhere near the water," Joel told her, "not any more today. You shouldn't either. Remember what happened to Gaby. It's dangerous."

She nodded in grudging obedience. "But you," she said to me impishly, "got to go swimming."

"It wasn't any fun," I told her. "That ocean's very cold and rough. You know how cold it is. The only reason I did it was because I had to, because Gaby needed a little help. That was when you got knocked over too. Believe me, Molly, Gaby didn't enjoy it at all. She was scared. So was I. It's very scary, very dangerous! You be careful."

"I will," Molly said. "Come on, Daddy. *You* throw it with me, okay?"

As Joel turned to go he reached out a hand and wordlessly squeezed my shoulder. It was an intimate male gesture of solidarity and encouragement, so unexpected from a son-in-law it almost moved me to tears.

Deirdre brought over another blanket. "This one's dry," she said. "It's one of those microfibers. It'll feel a lot better than what you've got over you... I'm sure they're all wet through now."

"Okay, thanks," I said. I hesitated for a moment, then decided the hell with it, floundered upright and bared myself to her to make the substitution. My skin had dried, so exposure to the air wasn't nearly as chilly as I'd anticipated except under my dripping underpants. Deirdre stretched to drape the new blanket around my back. It was a Black Watch plaid with a fringe—amazingly light, feather-soft and instantly warming. "Wow, this is great!" I said with a shiver of relief.

We exchanged some perfunctory chitchat. We'd gotten the obsequies for Jack and what *she* was up to now out of the way in earlier conversations.

"You know, there were a couple of people who were about to drive down to park headquarters and try to get a rescue helicopter out here," Deirdre noted. "It was Susan who argued against it. She said she was sure you'd get back with little Gaby okay."

"Really."

"It was too far, she thought. By the time they could scramble a helicopter it would be too late, she said. If there was any chance anybody was going to get that little French girl back to the beach safely it was gonna be you, she said."

"I wish I'd shared her confidence at the time," I said. "What did Elisabeth say?"

"I don't know. I know she was pretty worried."

"Well, I'm glad it didn't go that far, in retrospect," I said. "There'd be all kinds of questions and lectures about beach safety and official reports and maybe even citations, I don't know. There could even be some expense involved. When you call out a rescue team and it's a false alarm. Sure would have made what turned out to be just an unfortunate moment into a major deal. Sure would've spoiled the rest of the occasion."

"Well, we have you to thank that it didn't. I'm sure somewhere Jack's looking down on all of this as relieved as we are that everything turned out okay."

"Yeah," I agreed.

Right.

"I'll take these back for you," she said. She gathered up the damp, sandy tablecloth and frayed wool Army blanket I'd discarded.

I remained on my feet staring out at the ocean. The churn of the waves seemed to generate a subtle gravitational force. Despite having just fought free of it, my body tingled to an irrational appeal to wade back in.

I thought of the summer of my nineteenth year, when I was climbing in the Tetons. More than once, edging across a narrow shelf or teetering triumphantly erect on a knife-edge summit and gazing past my boot-toes at the scree a thousand feet below me, I was tempted to jump. For no good reason—although a couple of years earlier I had decided it would make more sense to end one's life at a moment of ecstasy than of despair. I've since felt that same fleeting urge to jump from the upper floors of skyscrapers looking at the street below. At twenty I found myself off-watch lounging at the stern-rail of the MV *Peer Gynt* as we steamed through the Strait of Malacca. The purl of the wake trailing behind us was hypnotic, and the storybook gleam of the tropical beach sliding past so close to starboard seemed to beg me to swim for it. I was on the very verge of trying. Kick off my shoes, dive overboard, stagger out of the surf with only the clothes on my back, follow the beach to one of those thatch-and-stick-hut villages that peeked here and there from the seaside jungle, make my way down the peninsula to Singapore and then maybe, oh, Australia, New Zealand... throw my future to a completely new and unfathomable fate. Assuming I made it.

Only a belated awareness that the sea was carpeted

by tiny, writhing green snakes stanched the impulse. I was ready to brave death by drowning but not by snakebite.

What is it with that? What is the siren allure of a void—and class the ocean as a void too, a boundless, bottomless soup of elemental matter—that you're drawn to hurl yourself into it? Or at least you *sense* the pull. It's the rare experience of ultimate confrontation with finality, perhaps. The vertiginous knowledge that it would take only one tiny synaptic act of will to exit consciousness. Like sitting on the edge of a bed with the muzzle of a pistol jammed against your temple and your finger on the cold metal trigger. Riding a motorcycle on the freeway at three a.m. with the speedometer needle at a hundred-and-ten. To be or not to be. All the quotidian in-between wriggle-room compressed to a split-second whim.

Becca approached. She had an oyster on the half-shell in each hand.

"I thought you could use these," she said. "Help regain your strength."

"Oyster-man," I nodded. "Don't have the mental energy to try to figure out what my special powers are...."

"An armored shell? You repel bullets," she suggested.

"But don't move very fast. Hardly move at all."

"You shit pearls," she offered with a giggle.

"Yech," I said, the corners of my mouth turned down. "That's a power?"

"Like firing bullets out of your ass. Pearl bullets, at the bad guys. It's your signature. Like the Lone Ranger's silver bullets."

"I'm shocked. Nice young ladies don't talk that way," I chided her. "Especially in front of their fathers. Where did we go wrong?"

"You, um, got divorced?"

I slurped the first oyster. It was raw, doctored with lemon juice and red cocktail sauce. She knows how I like them—which is how she likes them too. The horseradish felt like a little pilot flame being dropped into a cold furnace. I downed the second. "Mm!" I declared. "I have to say those hit the spot."

Chris and Élodie joined us. I didn't have much to say. The talk among them forked on tangents whose references I didn't share except, perhaps, for some vague memory of a TV commercial or an internet allusion. It pleased me, though, to witness brother and sister and sister-in-law relating so chummily. At the rare holiday big-family gatherings with Scott and Jeremy and Scott's wife Ilana and Jeremy's girlfriend-of-the-moment in attendance, along with Chris and Becca and Élodie and Joel—the decibel-level cranked up against an undertone (undertow) of sniffly, shrieking, bawling grandkids—the young-adult camaraderie can get really opaquely uproarious. Elisabeth has a tendency to feel left out and turn sulky, but I love watching the interplay for itself. Jeremy and Becca are the silliest and the loudest, Joel and Ilana (who's Czech) the quietest and most level-headed, Élodie and Scott the slyest and quickest wits—but there isn't a true introvert among them. Once in a while a nasty little argument might ignite tempers, usually over some political nuance... ironic, since there isn't a conservative in the room either.

"Come on, get dressed. Get your own oysters," Becca urged me.

"I will," I said.

"Don't be a mope. You're a hero!"

"Yeah."

"A Superhero! Oyster-man!"

"That's me. Go away and leave me to my secretions."

"Ha-ha!" Becca chortled. I guess you could see where she got her sense of humor.

**It always amazed me, the deft aplomb with which women could slip out of their dresses and into bathing suits to sunbathe during lunch hour in Frogner Park.**

The American girls I knew back then would never have been so daring. Certainly not in a public place. What's more, they would have blushed or tittered at the shamelessly nude surrounding statuary: Gustav Vigeland's chunky, anatomically correct children, parents, lovers, wizened grandparents... wrestling, snuggling, canoodling, group-groping, drop-kicking babies in antic illustration of his "cradle-to-grave" theme.

Despite all that sculptural celebration of the unclad human body, Oslo's comely secretaries, students and shop workers scrupulously managed to shuck their underclothing without revealing a sliver of private skin. They'd lay out a towel on the grass, sit demurely cross-legged, hike the waist of their dress or skirt up over their shoulders, reach into their bag and after a few quick, tented shrugs and shimmies emerge in impeccable beach attire. Which was, in Norway in those days, already usually a two-piece suit. That was another welcome contrast to the stiffly constructed one-piece pool-corsets the girls in Cincinnati still favored. It made a bicycle ride through Frogner Park on a summery day worth the effort. Too bad I could never muster the nerve to risk annoying one of those luscious, luxuriating blondes. Even if my Norwegian was rudimentary, they all spoke English.

I recalled that intriguing Scandinavian skill as I hunched under my blanket and labored to squirm out of my underpants, finally. More sensible to go commando than to harbor a clammy fifth column inside the Wranglers I'd have to sit in for the next five hours, I decided. I fingered apart my damp penis and scrotum so air could circulate—a comfort-reflex whenever I free myself from the pouch of snug briefs. Grunting at the effort, I wriggled my sandy feet into the rolled-up legs of my pants until my gnarled toes emerged. I lurched upright—turning as I rose to keep the dangling blanket between me and the nearest audience, as if anyone were looking, or even cared whether I flashed. I dusted my butt, gave my pants a final shake, pulled the wadded bottoms up over my calves and wiggled the waistband into place. I tucked in my equipment and, very careful not to snag a pubic hair, zipped the fly. Stomach still sucked in, belt ends dangling, I shrugged out of my drapery.

Even though I do it three or four times a week at the pool, I'm still slightly bashful about baring my chest. My withered dugs. To be sure, there are times when I look at myself in the full-length mirror in the half-light of our bedroom and think my physique is still passably youthful. Swimming and carpentry have kept my pecs, lats, triceps and biceps, even the abs (a faint four-pack rather than a six-pack, I've got to admit) reasonably toned. It's the flesh they're bagged in that has sagged and puckered.

It can only get worse. Every so often Elisabeth hesitates at the mirror to pinch a jowl or slap a jiggly, vein-shot saddlebag in disgust. In a weary tone of despair, tears welling, she murmurs, "I... look... so... *old!*"

All I can do is assure her she doesn't, really. But, of course, she does. That is, she no longer looks twenty-five. When she was ravishing. Or forty-five. When she was stunning. (All those clichéd adjectives to describe movie stars come to mind when old family photos float up from the detritus in a drawer; I stare gob-smacked at her image from a Golden Age and think how incredibly lucky I was to have been with such a woman. Or perhaps I wasn't yet... but the pictures of Susan in the kids' houses can trigger the same pang of recognition, nostalgia, awe at having been married to so blooming a beauty *d'antan.)*

No, Elisabeth looks her age. Less, actually, she'd be happy to hear. Despite her bravely undyed salt-and-pepper hair, a choice I vigorously encourage because it dramatically suits her, people always express surprise when she reveals her true age. What's the expression? She's got great bone structure. That's a compliment almost always dropped *faute de mieux*, but it's what—combined with sparkle, enthusiasm, *élan vital*—still has a woman of a very, very *certain âge* turning men's heads. Besides mine. Oh, yeah, it happens. When she goes into her *coquette* mode....

Nevertheless... sometimes her face is noticeably seamed, blotchy, crinkly, puffy. Sometimes the wattles appear more than incipient. Sometimes the limp flesh of her upper arms, the cleavage between her slackening breasts... but I'll spare her the catalog. I try not to notice and I usually don't. I'm seeing her through rose-colored lenses—coke-bottle thick with mutual history and Vaselined with affection. So what if the elastin or whatever it is that gives human skin pith and resilience has lost its oomph. It's okay. Hey, it better be! Considering the alternative.

Which is *not* to try to disguise it. Then you just look weird and pitiful. Like, I'm sorry to say, my old girlfriend (if you can call her that) Tess, whose picture at some gala appeared in the *Chronicle* recently: grinning hideously into the camera like the Masque of Death, rouged face flayed and microstitched to pin the flesh taut across the front of her skull, lips puffed by Botox and collagen injections, eyes permanently saucered by serial lid-lifts, her hair a teased mane of eerily wine-dark curls... a woman *my* age! Anyway, older than Elisabeth. You think her hair hasn't gone grey? White! You think that face hasn't been ironed on? Who could

Tess possibly think she's fooling?

Herself, sadly.

Élodie recently sent me a picture in which Patrick is in my arms smiling winsomely into the camera as I grin fondly at him in profile. It's a close-up, sharply focused, unforgivingly sunlit. It's horrifying. With my liver-spotted cheeks, scraggly white whiskers, yellow fangs and keratotic dome I could be *ninety*-five. His *great*-grandfather! Dug up from the crypt! It's a wonder the kid isn't howling in revulsion.

But it's okay. I can live with that. What scares me is not that you lose something as trivial—I keep reminding myself—as your looks. It's that at some point everything really important goes to hell. Judgment, memory, eyesight, digestion, strength, posture, balance, sphincter control... have I missed anything?

Dignity. Yeah. Dignity. And purpose. Purpose beyond mere survival. You become a dead-weight... a living weight. A drag on society. A drag on your wife—who may be just about as ga-ga as you are by then, maybe mercifully—and on your children. Who, if not actively nursing you through your awful dissolution, your pre-mortem putrefaction, have to bear witness to it. *That's* what I dread. That's what I'm dead-set... yeah, what I'm really, really, *really* keen on avoiding.

Oh, is that so? I hear the snicker. Needless to say, that gambit may prove impossible to pull off. Debility sneaks up on you. Suddenly it's too late to circumvent the mortifications. You're too weak to rise from bed or chair, too depressed to envision alternatives, too stricken and frightened to think beyond your pain, stupefied by medication, maybe paralyzed, maybe semi-comatose.... If your brain has decayed into dementia it's all moot, of course. At least for you. Not for those in anguished attendance.

You could argue—as religionists certainly do—that

dignity actually *requires* you to suffer through those terminal humiliations. The Jesus example. Redemption depends on dragging yourself down the whole *Via Dolorosa*.

It occurs to me, too, that if life is like a game, honor requires you to play it out honestly. You don't say, "Fuck it!" and quit, slink off the court in a sullen snit. Even though you're absorbing a terrible beating, overmatched and down four touchdowns or a dozen buckets with two hopeless minutes to go—every pass you complete, every tackle you make or jumper you drain a meaningless effort (except as empty padding to your statistics, bitter comfort)—you stay in there between the lines and you do your best. If life is about mindfully savoring physical sensation—the only point as far as I can see, the mindful part what distinguishes us humans from ant or trout or hummingbird, for whom physical sensation is life *in* and *per se*—then you owe it to... yourself? humankind?... to take your beating, to *savor* it, as long as destiny rains the blows.

That's one, not very encouraging, even masochistic, way of looking at it.

I poked my arms into my shirtsleeves. I shrugged the yoke snug around my shoulders, fastened the snaps one by one down the front, folded the cuffs back two turns... and for the first time missed my watch. Becca must still have it, I recalled. I unbuttoned my pants and zipped open my fly. I stuffed the shirttails inside the waistband, redid the package and buckled my belt.

In life as in sports it's all about timing. Hadn't I just proved by my rescue—yeah, hell, let's just go with that, my *rescue* of Gaby... *daring* rescue, in *shark-infested waters*—that I was still within hailing distance of the peak of my game? Like one of those grizzled quarterbacks, battered and older than anybody else on the field, who still has the touch: Brett Favre, Joe Montana... or for that matter a receiver, Jerry Rice... Barry Bonds, bam, over the right field wall like a rope into McCovey Cove... Pelé in soccer... Michael Jordan in basketball... my old Cincinnati classmate Oscar Robertson... gifted athletes who never really lost the ability to perform at a world-class level, only the ability to perform at the level they'd come to measure themselves by in their prime. Even when they finally decided it was time to hang up the uniform they still had game.

Not that I'm fatuous enough to compare myself to such superstars in anything but superannuated vigor. On the evidence of the afternoon's swim, I had plenty of that left in me.

But there was that unknown something going on in the little gland tucked in the lee of my pubis... for that matter, unknown somethings going on all through my wetworks. The trick was going to be figuring out what I wanted to know and when I wanted to know it. And what I wanted to do about it when I knew about it. And at what precise moment on the inevitable downward trajectory I'd reached the threshold of no return.

Watchful waiting.

The secret of life.


## "How're you doing?"

Somehow she'd snuck up on me.

"Agh!" I flinched. "Jesus! You caught me lost in thought."

"Sorry."

"I'm doing okay."

"Ready to go?"

"Ready as I'll ever be."

Her hair was disheveled, tousled by the wind—and not in a flattering way. She had on a pair of outsize round sunglasses I'd never much liked even when they were in fashion. Plus she must have sat on them or something: a temple was bent; they rode skewed on her nose. The Guatemalan dress was rumpled—a slightly glorified flour sack that refused to define breasts or waist, only amplified bulk and butt.

"Your glasses are all crooked," I said. "Here, lemme fix 'em."

I took a couple of steps toward her and plucked the glasses off her nose. I compared the angles of the tortoiseshell ear-pieces and carefully pushed the one that was low back into apparent adjustment. I slid them on her face and tilted my head to judge my handiwork.

"There," I said. "Now you're beautiful again."

"I thank you, presumably."

"My pleasure."

I leaned forward and pecked her lips. "I love you," I said. "I'm glad I'm still around to say that."

I could see I'd pleased her. "No less I," she responded brightly.

"That's a very erudite construction," I observed.

"I *am* very erudite. And don't you forget it, buster."

"I won't. I've always suspected as much. Despite the paucity of evidence."

Her lips compressed. Maybe that was a little over the line.

"Kidding, kidding," I assured her unnecessarily.

"Paw City is where you'll be living if you keep up the nasty remarks."

"Ooh, nice! The dog house, huh? We're in fine fettle this afternoon, aren't we?"

I could see her mind working for a split second on "fettle"—fine fettle of kish, or something.

"Should be a wildly entertaining ride home," I grinned.

"I'm looking forward to it," she replied. "Especially since I'm driving."

"No, you're not."

"Yes, I am. I was biting my lip all the way down here. Now it's your turn to have the blue knuckles."

"I hate being a passenger. You drive crazier than I do anyway."

"No, I don't."

"Who passes on the right on gravel turnouts?"

"Okay, I did that once. When the guy absolutely refused to use the turnouts."

"I'm just sayin'. I enjoyed it, actually."

"So you can enjoy it again. You've got to be tired. And I want to drive. Turnabout is fair play."

"Whatever," I conceded. "Maybe you're right. I am kind of beat."

"I would *think* so!"

I retraced my steps to grab the blanket, my sombrero and my flipflops. When I bent and reached down, pain nipped the small of my back—one of those treacherous lumbar vertebrae. I froze.

Leaning forward with a slight twist is always dangerous. But you get careless, you forget. I straightened slowly, hoping it was nothing serious. I got another nip. Just a nibble, though. I hadn't had a full-on, immobilizing back spasm for years, knock wood. I stretched to full height, lifted my chin, rolled my shoulders, pinched my shoulder blades and rocked my pelvis to unkink muscles and spine. The levator scapulae ached dully on either side of my neck. Both hips were sore. Nothing particularly special about any of that after significant exercise. Pain, someone once said and I've often repeated, is nature's way of assuring you you're alive.

"Maybe I'll take a nap if you're driving," I said.

"Sure. Go for it. You've earned it."

"Beer... sun... oysters... no wonder I'm feeling sleepy.

But, you know, as for the swimming... I do much more of that every time I go to the pool for a workout than I did today."

"Yeah, but... even so, there isn't the same tension."

"Mm-hm. Got that right."

"And the ocean's rougher. You had to fight against the current and all."

"Absolutely."

"And the water's colder."

"Sure is. All of the above. Wasn't Gaby great? When you look back on it?"

"She was. Kept her poise, didn't panic or anything, apparently."

"She didn't. Good kid."

"Yes, she seems to be," Elisabeth agreed. "Spunky."

"Strong," I said. I screwed the sombrero down over my brow and grasped her hand.

The picnic party had dwindled. Those who remained greeted us as we hove near. We zigzagged among the clusters, speaking our exit lines. I got clapped on the back a couple of times. Elisabeth collected her salad bowl and the cooler. We said goodbye to all the kids, who agreed that they were about to leave too. I asked Becca if she still had my watch; she dug into the pocket of her shorts. I slid it on my wrist and clicked the clasps. I was surprised to note the time: a quarter to six. We waved to the grandkids, who waved back. They were still distracted by play and too much trouble to round up individually for kisses.

No one was tending the grill, I noticed. The charcoal had burned to white ashes. I considered downing a few raw oysters *en passant* as fortification for the ride home, but decided prying open the shells would take too much time and effort. When I thanked Deirdre for the last time she hugged me effusively. She insisted that I take home a plastic bagful of oysters—a tradition, she reminded me. I declined out of politeness. Then I yielded out of politeness.

Not unhappy at the prospect of a Hangtown fry—or six—for Sunday morning breakfast.

## At the parking lot Elisabeth and I veered toward the handicap-ramped restroom and split at our separate doors.

When I'd finished I walked down to wait for her at the railing above the beach.

The sun was midway between zenith and horizon. I bowed my head slightly so the brim of the sombrero would shade my eyes. The sand was more sparsely populated than when we'd arrived. Sunset was close to four hours away, but there'd still be some people around then, I was sure: jogging, exercising dogs on long leashes, blinking at the tiny oblate blob of life-sustaining orange brilliance deflating into the horizon—hoping to catch the last green flash. Unless the fog rolled back in, this would be a promising evening for it.

There might be a beach party or two after dark. Driftwood fires softly glowing, sparks erupting when a new log's been tossed on, mutters of conversation, muted peals of laughter, singing, a guitar.... That's the cozy ambience on Big River Beach when Elisabeth and I take walks there on rare warm nights—celebrating, although by now it's only a vague association, the morning stroll there after our first tryst. What we're really celebrating is the opportunity to enjoy the local oceanfront after sundown without muffling ourselves in down jackets. Only the hardiest souls brave Northern California's usual summer climate for nocturnal beach-strolls or clambakes.

So by ten or eleven, I imagined, the Great Beach

would be deserted. Overnight camping isn't permitted at the National Seashore. This parking lot would be empty. I could picture a full moon hovering where the sun was now—silver disk with its faint, lugubrious face contemplating the watery mother planet, silver tracks across the ocean's swells... the eleven-mile break a phosphorescent scrawl embellishing the length of blanched shore. I envisioned a calm night. Even so the salt-breeze would prickle the cheeks, the manic surf clog the ears with its grumble. I'd look around to make sure I was alone. Then I'd descend to the sand. I'd trudge out through the loose ruck until I reached the scatter of kelp that demarcates the hardpack. As I approached the rearing break its din would grow louder, scarier. I'd put a hand down— feel the residual warmth in the clumpy granules between my fingers—and settle. Sit. Cross-legged, I pictured. But my joints might no longer be pliable enough for that yogic position, I realized. I'd had a foretaste this afternoon. Already I was having trouble pulling my socks on after a swim—the struggle to dress and undress sometimes seemed like more of a workout than the workout.

Whatever, tailor-style or splay-legged, spine tense and erect—torso attentively angled toward the sea—or reclining on my elbow at uneasy ease, I'd definitely need some time to just sit. Compose myself. Examine my conscience, as the nuns and priests used to instruct us. Make a perfect act of contrition. Say three Our Fathers and three Hail Marys. Penance enough for the piddling sins of a pre-teen but hardly sufficient—what *would* be sufficient?—for a man who'd bungled his way through seven or eight decades of normal adult life.

No, I wouldn't be praying. I'd be trying to attune myself to the music of the spheres.

It's not all that hard with a moon, a few fat planets and a billion stars blazing overhead. Plus the occasional pinprick trail of a satellite or the pulsing running lights of a transpacific jet at high altitude. Military or civilian? I always wonder about that for an instant. Then settle into awed contemplation of the slow, silent, stratospheric progress. Human overlay on the jeweled mechanism of the universe, yes, but somehow only further corroboration of the grand scheme—demonstration of the wondrous, immutable laws of physics. Gravity, orbits, trajectories. An ant heap of my species swarming the Earth around me (yet not another one, no worker, soldier, nurse or queen, in sight); tiny aluminum tubules of them far above, redistributing themselves among the rotating continents; a near-infinitude of glistering suns and planetary systems exploding beyond, bound for infinity: blue stars, yellow stars, orange stars, red stars, brown dwarfs, white stars... all ringed by captive clods of rock and gas... black holes inexorably hoovering up everything that drifts into their deadly field, to be spat out into some inverse, mirror cosmos... galaxies, clusters, nebulae, quasars, filigreed by asteroids, meteors, comets—the "shooting stars" whose sightings my mother taught me to prize, along with the mnemonic human overlay of mythic constellations....

Stare at all of that for a few quiet minutes and your body slows naturally to the rhythm of eternity.

Smoking a joint would probably help. Ought to be easy enough to score some. Weed, grass, shit, whatever the current jargon might style it. Maybe my own kids—Elisabeth's son Jeremy, surely—could supply me. Medical marijuana of a sort. Maybe I'd even have a legitimate prescription for it by then. All the more convenient for cultivating the requisite mode of oceanic bliss.

But, in fact, I wouldn't want to be fuzzy-headed in any way. Or hacking through the scratchy throat and singed nasal passages that now accompany inhalation of smoke. Until a few years ago I'd occasionally get a yen for a cigarette, but whenever I indulged it the pleasure turned out to be false memory. Tobacco only left a bad taste on the tongue and an irritated respiratory system. And a sour odor on the fingers. How did I ever acquire the habit? How does anybody? And yet, my father smoked hungrily until the day his heart went kablooie. According to my stepmother, his lungs were as pink as a baby's—so the pathologist reported. It was his coronary vasculature that was wrecked.

He'd been on his way to his office, I was told. Still actively practicing law, albeit at a stately pace: outside counsel to a regional health insurance company, on comfortable retainer with license to accommodate Anne's urge to travel several times a year. Mild adventures he had come, against a lifetime's disinclination and to his own surprise, to enjoy. Seventy-five years old. No more infirm than I am, probably, although less physically active. A walker, however—striding down Fifth Street from the parking lot on a rainy morning, overcoat collar turned up, snap-brim fedora jauntily atilt, briefcase in hand. He appeared to slip on the wet sidewalk and fall. Bystanders bent over him when he didn't rise, EMTs arrived quickly, no use. What a *clean* exit!

And who knows? Maybe with luck the same quick excision is in store for me. Like Cashman, in Burma, I recalled. Way too young, though, that guy was. What made it sad. My stepmother, brother and stepsister mourned my father, who from my perspective was far too young too. But, really, there's nothing tragic about a person his age, my age, abruptly completing the cycle. The only way it could have been any neater was if he'd simply failed to wake up one morning in his own bed. Although that still would have left Anne with a corpse to dispose.

No, my father had been granted the perfect death. For all concerned. It would have been nice, sure, if he could have tacked on another eight or ten healthy years. Even more. But how much better is it to have the game called when you're a run ahead in the seventh inning than to have to keep on playing for another inning or two under worsening weather—with nothing in it for you but downside?

There comes a time when it behooves a person to get out of the way. Indians wandered off into the canyons or the mountains. Eskimos hopped an ice-floe. We Anglos lack that tradition.

Nevertheless.

Take a few deep breaths. Cleansing breaths. Inspiration. *S'encourager*. Inhale the tang, the wrack and seasalt... amniotic fluid. Tug off boots, peel off socks... everything, including underpants. Loosely fold and pile them aside under the weight of the boots, so the wind won't immediately scatter them. A clue, the clothes, whether purposefully stacked or strewn, but not definitional. Why not an innocent if misguided solitary midnight swim?

Rise and walk out naked through the race and ebb, into the swirling surf. Frigid, momentarily, but familiar now. You've been there before; the adaptation's rapid. Keep your footing when the icy surge engulfs your tender privates. Follow the blinking silver path, the pixelated moonglow. Feet apart as you wade deeper. Arms cruciform for balance. Ocean now navel high, now washing up over your nipples....

With a gasp of determination crouch into it.

Go under.

Push forward.

Stroke. Kick. Hard.

Like being born.

The good thing about swimming is that you can always turn around. Change your mind, come back.

Or mean to.